Spook: specter, ghost, revenant. Slang for "intelligence agent."

Country: in the mind or in reality. The World. The United States of America, New Improved Edition. What lies before you. What lies behind.

Spook Country: the place where we all have landed, few by choice. The place we are learning to live.

Hollis Henry is a journalist, on investigative assignment for a magazine called Node, which doesn't exist yet. Bobby Chombo is a producer, working on cutting-edge art installations. In his day job, Bobby is a troubleshooter for military navigation equipment. He refuses to sleep in the same place twice. He meets no one.

Hollis Henry has been told to find him.

"Arguably the first example of the post-post-9/11 novel, whose characters are tired of being pushed around by forces larger than they are—bureaucracy, history and, always, technology—and are at long last ready to start pushing back . . . When they breathe a sigh of relief for the invitingly uncertain world that awaits them, Gibson can, too: The future is a clean slate for all of them, and whether his characters realize it or not, the author surely understands that this is a symbol of ultimate freedom." —*The New York Times Book Review*

"Sentence for sentence, few authors equal Gibson's gift for the terse yet poetic description, the quotable simile—people and products are nailed down with a beautiful precision approximating the platonic ideal of the catalog . . . the phrasing is itself a delirious surge of pleasure-center prose."
—*Los Angeles Times*

"A fitful, fast-forward spy tale . . . It's to Gibson's credit that he weaves his strands of disparate narrators, protagonists and foils, and his panoply of far-forward technology, into a vivid, suspenseful and ultimately coherent tale. He has managed to convert his cybernetic future into present tense." —*USA Today*

continued . . .

TITLES BY WILLIAM GIBSON

spook country

WILLIAM GIBSON

BERKLEY BOOKS, NEW YORK

THE BERKLEY PUBLISHING GROUP
Published by the Penguin Group
Penguin Group (USA) Inc.
375 Hudson Street, New York, New York 10014, USA
Penguin Group (Canada), 90 Eglinton Avenue East, Suite 700, Toronto, Ontario M4P 2Y3, Canada
(a division of Pearson Penguin Canada Inc.)
Penguin Books Ltd., 80 Strand, London WC2R 0RL, England
Penguin Group Ireland, 25 St. Stephen's Green, Dublin 2, Ireland (a division of Penguin Books Ltd.)
Penguin Group (Australia), 250 Camberwell Road, Camberwell, Victoria 3124, Australia
(a division of Pearson Australia Group Pty. Ltd.)
Penguin Books India Pvt. Ltd., 11 Community Centre, Panchsheel Park, New Delhi—110 017, India
Penguin Group (NZ), 67 Apollo Drive, Rosedale, North Shore 0632, New Zealand
(a division of Pearson New Zealand Ltd.)
Penguin Books (South Africa) (Pty.) Ltd., 24 Sturdee Avenue, Rosebank, Johannesburg 2196,
South Africa

Penguin Books Ltd., Registered Offices: 80 Strand, London WC2R 0RL, England

SPOOK COUNTRY

A Berkley Book / published by arrangement with the author

PRINTING HISTORY
G. P. Putnam's Sons hardcover edition / August 2007
Berkley trade edition / June 2008
Berkley premium edition / March 2009

ISBN: 978-0-425-22671-1

BERKLEY®
Berkley Books are published by The Berkley Publishing Group,
a division of Penguin Group (USA) Inc.,
375 Hudson Street, New York, New York 10014.
BERKLEY® is a registered trademark of Penguin Group (USA) Inc.
The "B" design is a trademark of Penguin Group (USA) Inc.

PRINTED IN THE UNITED STATES OF AMERICA

10 9 8 7 6 5 4 3 2 1

For Deborah

February 2006

1. WHITE LEGO

Rausch," said the voice in Hollis Henry's cell. "*Node,*" it said.

She turned on the bedside lamp, illuminating the previous evening's empty can of Asahi Draft, from the Pink Dot, and her sticker-encrusted PowerBook, closed and sleeping. She envied it.

"Hello, Philip." *Node* was her present employer, to the extent that she had one, and Philip Rausch her editor. They'd had one previous conversation, the one which had resulted in her flying to L.A. and checking into the Mondrian, but that had had much more to do with her financial situation than with any powers of persuasion on his part. Something in his intonation of the magazine's name, just now, those audible italics, suggested something she knew she'd quickly tire of.

She heard Odile Richard's robot bump lightly against something, from the direction of the bathroom.

"It's three there," he said. "Did I wake you?"

"No," she lied.

Odile's robot was made of Lego, white Lego exclusively, with some odd number of black-tired white plastic wheels underneath, and what she assumed were solar power cells screwed across its back. She could hear it moving patiently, however randomly, across the carpet of her room. Could you buy white-only Lego? It looked right at home here, where lots of things were white. Nice contrast with the Aegean-blue table legs.

"They're ready to show you his best piece," Rausch said.

"When?"

"Now. She's waiting for you at her hotel. The Standard."

Hollis knew the Standard. It was carpeted in royal-blue Astroturf. Whenever she went there she felt as though she were the oldest living thing in the building. There was a sort of giant terrarium, behind the registration desk, in which ethnically ambiguous bikini-girls sometimes lay as if sunning themselves, or studying large, profusely illustrated textbooks.

"Have you taken care of the billing here, Philip? When I checked in, they still had it on my card."

"It's been taken care of."

She didn't believe him. "Do we have a deadline on this story yet?"

"No." Rausch sucked his teeth, somewhere in a London she couldn't be bothered imagining. "The launch has been rolled back. August."

Hollis had yet to meet anyone from *Node*, or anyone else who was writing for them. A European version of *Wired*, it seemed, though of course they never put it that way. Belgian money, via Dublin, offices in London—or, if not offices, then at least this Philip. Who sounded to her as though he were seventeen. Seventeen and with his sense of humor surgically excised.

"Plenty of time," she said, not certain what she meant, but thinking, however obliquely, of her bank balance.

"She's waiting for you."

"Okay." She closed her eyes and clamshelled her phone.

Could you, she wondered, be staying in this hotel and technically still be considered homeless? It felt like you could, she decided.

She lay there under a single white sheet, listening to the French girl's robot bumping and clicking and reversing. It was programmed, she supposed, like one of those Japanese vacuum cleaners, to keep bumping until the job was done. Odile had said it would be collecting data with an onboard GPS unit; Hollis guessed it was.

She sat up, a very high thread count sliding to her thighs. Outside, wind found her windows from a new angle. They thrummed scarily. Any very pronounced weather, here, worried her. It got written up, she knew, in the next day's papers, like some lesser species of earthquake. Fifteen minutes of rain and the lower reaches of the Beverly Center pancaked; house-sized boulders coasted majestically down hillsides, into busy intersections. She'd been here for that, once.

She got out of bed and crossed to the window, hoping she wouldn't step on the robot. She fumbled for the cord that opened the heavy white drapes. Six floors below, she saw the palms along Sunset thrashing, like dancers miming the final throes of some sci-fi plague. Three-ten on a Wednesday morning and this wind seemed to have the Strip utterly deserted.

Don't think, she advised herself. Don't check your e-mail. Get up and go into the bathroom.

Fifteen minutes later, having done the best she could with all that had never been quite right, she descended to the lobby in a Philippe Starck elevator, determined to pay its particulars as little attention as possible. She'd once read an article about Starck that said the designer owned an oyster farm where only perfectly square oysters were grown, in specially fabricated steel frames.

The doors slid open on an expanse of pale wood. The Platonic ideal of a small oriental carpet was projected across part of this from somewhere overhead, stylized squiggles of light recalling slightly less stylized squiggles of dyed wool. Originally intended, she remembered having been told, to avoid offending Allah. She crossed this quickly, heading for the entrance doors.

As she opened one of these, into the weird moving warmth of the wind, a Mondrian security man was looking at her, one ear Bluetoothed beneath the shaven cliff of a military haircut. He asked her something, but it was swallowed by a sudden down-drafting gust. "No," she said, assuming he'd asked if she wanted her car brought up, not that she had one, or if she wanted a cab. There was a cab, she saw, the driver reclining behind the wheel, possibly asleep, dreaming perhaps of the fields of Azerbaijan. She passed it, a weird exuberance rising in her as the wind, so wild and strangely random, surged along Sunset, from the direction of Tower Records, like the back draft from something straining for takeoff.

She thought she heard the security man call to her, but then her Adidas found actual unstyled Sunset sidewalk, a pointillist abstract in blackened chewing gum. The monster open-doors statuary of the Mondrian was behind her now, and she was zipping up her hoodie. Heading, it felt, not so much in the direction of the Standard as simply outward bound.

The air was full of the dry and stinging detritus of the palms.

You are, she told herself, crazy. But that seemed for the moment abundantly okay, even though she knew that this was not a salubrious stretch for any woman, particularly alone. Nor for any pedestrian, this time of the morning. Yet this weather, this moment of anomalous L.A. climate, seemed to have swept any usual sense of threat aside. The street was as empty as that moment in the film just prior to Godzilla's first footfall. Palms straining, the very air shuddering, and Hollis, now hooded blackly, striding determinedly on. Sheets of newspaper and handouts from clubs tumbled past her ankles.

A police car whizzed past, headed in the direction of Tower. Its driver, slumped resolutely behind the wheel, paid her no attention. To serve, she remembered, and protect. The wind reversed giddily, whipping her hood back and performing an instant redo on her hair. Which was in need of one anyway, she reminded herself.

She found Odile Richard waiting under the Standard's white porte cochere and the hotel's sign—displayed, for reasons known only to its designers, upside down. Odile was still on Paris time, but Hollis had offered to accommodate her with this small-hours meeting. Also, evidently, it was optimal for viewing this kind of art.

Beside her stood a broad young Latino with shaven head and retro-ethnic burgundy Pendleton, sleeves scissored away above the elbows. The shirt's untucked tails reached nearly to the knees of his baggy chinos. "Vote for Santa," he said, beaming, as she walked up to them, raising a silver can of Tecate. There was something tattooed in very bold and ultra-elaborated Olde English lettering down the length of his forearm.

"Excuse me?"

"À votre santé," corrected Odile, dabbing at her nose with a frayed wad of tissue. Odile was the least chic Frenchwoman Hollis could recall having met, though in a kind of haute-nerd Euro way that only made her more annoyingly adorable. She wore a black XXXL sweatshirt from some long-dead start-up, men's brown ribbed-nylon socks of a peculiarly nasty sheen, and see-through plastic sandals the color of cherry cough syrup.

"Alberto Corrales," he said.

"Alberto," she said, allowing her hand to be engulfed in his other, empty hand, dry as wood. "Hollis Henry."

"The Curfew," Alberto said, his smile widening.

The fan thing, she thought, amazed as ever, and just as suddenly ill at ease.

"This dirt, in the air," Odile protested, "it is disgusting. Please let us go now, to view the piece."

"Right," said Hollis, grateful for the distraction.

"This way," Alberto said, neatly lobbing his empty can into a white Standard waste container with Milanese pretensions. The wind, she noticed, had died as if on cue.

She glanced into the lobby. The reception desk was deserted, the bikini-girl terrarium empty and unlit. Then she followed Alberto and the irritably snuffling Odile to Alberto's car, a classic Volks Beetle gleaming under multiple coats of low-rider lacquer. She saw a volcano flowing with incandescent lava, big-busted Latinas in mini-loincloths and feathered Aztec headdresses, the polychrome coils of a winged serpent. Alberto was into some kind of ethnic culture jamming, she decided, unless VWs had entered the pantheon since she'd last looked at this stuff.

He opened the passenger-side door and held the seat up while Odile slid into the back. Where there seemed already to be equipment of some kind. Then he gestured for Hollis to take the passenger seat, almost a bow.

She blinked at the sublimely matter-of-fact semiotics of the old VW's dashboard. The car smelled of some ethnic air-freshener. That too was part of a language, she guessed, like the paintjob, but someone like Alberto might deliberately be using exactly the wrong freshener.

He pulled out onto Sunset and executed a tidy U-turn.

They headed back in the direction of the Mondrian, over asphalt thinly littered with the desiccated biomass of palms.

"I've been a fan for years," Alberto said.

"Alberto is concerned with history as internalized space," contributed Odile, from a little too close behind Hollis's head. "He sees this internalized space emerge from trauma. Always, from trauma."

"Trauma," Hollis repeated involuntarily, as they passed the Pink Dot. "Stop at the Dot, please, Alberto. I need cigarettes."

"Ollis," said Odile, accusingly, "you tell me you are not smoke."

"I just started," Hollis said.

"But we are here," said Alberto, taking a left at Larrabee and parking.

"Where's here?" Hollis asked, cracking the door and preparing, perhaps, to run.

Alberto looked grave, but not particularly crazy. "I'll get my equipment. I'd like you to experience the piece, first. Then, if you like, we can discuss it."

He got out. Hollis did too. Larrabee sloped steeply down, toward the illuminated flats of the city, so steeply that she found it uncomfortable to stand. Alberto helped Odile from the backseat. She propped herself against the Volks and screwed her hands into the front of her sweatshirt. "I am cold," she complained.

And it was cooler now, Hollis noticed, without the warm blast of the wind. She looked up at a graceless pink hotel that loomed over them, while Alberto, draped in his Pendleton, rummaged in the back of the car. He came up with a battered aluminum camera case, criss-crossed with black gaffer tape.

A long silver car glided silently past on Sunset, as they followed Alberto up the steep sidewalk.

"What's here, Alberto? What are we here to see?" Hollis demanded, as they reached the corner. He knelt and opened the case. The interior was padded with blocks of foam. He extracted something that she at first mistook for a welder's protective mask. "Put this on." He handed it to her.

A padded headband, with a sort of visor. "Virtual reality?" She hadn't heard the term spoken aloud in years, she thought, as she pronounced it.

"The hardware lags behind," he said. "At least the kind I can afford." He took a laptop from the case and opened it, powering it up.

Hollis put the visor on. She could see through it, though only dimly. She looked toward the corner of Clark and Sunset, making out the marquee of the Whiskey. Alberto reached out and gently fumbled with a cable, at the side of the visor.

"This way," he said, leading her along the sidewalk to a low, windowless, black-painted façade. She squinted up at the sign. The Viper Room.

"Now," he said, and she heard him tap the laptop's keyboard. Something shivered, in her field of vision. "Look. Look here."

She turned, following his gesture, and saw a slender, dark-haired body, facedown on the sidewalk.

"Alloween night, 1993," said Odile.

Hollis approached the body. That wasn't there. But was. Alberto was following her with the laptop, careful of the cable. She felt as if he were holding his breath. She was holding hers.

The boy seemed birdlike in death, the arch of his cheekbone, as she bent forward, casting its own small shadow. His hair was very dark. He wore dark, pin-striped trousers and a dark shirt. "Who?" she asked, finding her breath.

"River Phoenix," said Alberto, quietly.

She looked up, toward the marquee of the Whiskey, then down again, struck by the fragility of the white neck. "River Phoenix was blond," she said.

"He'd dyed it," Alberto said. "Dyed it for a role."

2. ANTS IN THE WATER

The old man reminded Tito of those ghost signs, fading high on the windowless sides of blackened buildings, spelling out the names of products made meaningless by time.

If Tito were to see one of those announcing the very latest, the most recent and terrible news, yet could know that it had always been there, fading, through every kind of weather, unnoticed until today, that might feel something like meeting the old man in Washington Square, beside the concrete chess tables, and carefully passing him an iPod, beneath a folded newspaper.

Each time the old man, expressionless and looking elsewhere, pocketed another iPod, Tito noticed the dull gold of his wristwatch, its dial and hands almost lost behind the worn plastic crystal. A dead man's watch, like the ones jumbled in battered cigar boxes at the flea market.

His clothes were like a dead man's as well, cut from fabrics Tito imagined exuding their own chill, a cold distinct from the end of this uneven New York winter. The cold of unclaimed luggage, of institutional corridors, of steel lockers scoured to bare metal.

But surely this was costume, the protocol of appearance. The old man could not be genuinely poor and do business with Tito's uncles. Sensing an immense patience, and power, Tito imagined that this old man, for reasons of his own, disguised himself as a revenant from lower Manhattan's past.

Each time the old man received another iPod, accepting it the way an ancient and sagacious ape might accept a piece of some not particularly interesting fruit, Tito half expected him to crack its virginal white case like a nut, and then to draw forth something utterly peculiar, utterly dire, and somehow terrible in its contemporaneity.

And now, across a steaming tureen of duck soup, in this second-floor restaurant overlooking Canal Street, Tito found himself unable to explain this to Alejandro, his cousin. In his room, earlier, he had been layering sounds, attempting to express in music these feelings the old man woke in him. He doubted he would ever play that file for Alejandro.

Alejandro, who had never been interested in Tito's music, looked at him now, his brow smooth between shoulder-length, center-parted hair, said nothing, and carefully ladled soup, first into Tito's bowl, then into his own. The world outside the restaurant's windows, beyond words in a red plastic Cantonese neither of them could read, was the color of a silver coin, misplaced for decades in a drawer.

Alejandro was a literalist, highly talented but supremely practical. This was why he had been chosen to apprentice under gray Juana, their aunt, the family's master forger. Tito had lugged ancient mechanical typewriters through the downtown streets for Alejandro, impossibly heavy machines purchased in dusty warehouses beyond the river. He had run errands for their inked-cloth ribbons and the turpentine Alejandro used to wash out most of their ink. Their native Cuba, Juana taught, had been a kingdom of paper, a bureaucratic maze of forms, of carbon copies in triplicate—a realm the initiate might navigate with confidence and precision. Always precision, in the case of Juana, who had herself been trained in the white painted subbasements of a building whose upper stories afforded narrow views of the Kremlin.

"He frightens you, this old man," Alejandro said.

Alejandro had learned Juana's thousand tricks with papers and adhesives, watermarks and stamps, her magic in improvised darkrooms, and darker mysteries involving the names of children who had died in infancy. Tito had sometimes carried, for months on end, decaying wallets bulging with fragments of the identities Alejandro's apprenticeship had generated, prolonged proximity to his body removing every trace of the new. He had never touched the cards and folded papers the heat and movement of his body sueded so convincingly. Alejandro, removing them from their stained envelopes of dead man's leather, had worn surgical gloves.

"No," Tito said, "he doesn't frighten me." Though really he wasn't sure; fear was a part of it, but he didn't seem to fear the old man himself.

"Perhaps he should, cousin."

The strength of Juana's magic had faded, Tito knew, amid new technologies and an increasing governmental stress on "security," by which was meant control. The family relied less now on Juana's skills, obtaining most of their documents (Tito guessed) from others, ones more attuned to present needs. Alejandro, Tito knew, was not sorry about this. At thirty, eight years older than Tito, he had come to regard life in the family as at best a mixed blessing. The drawings Tito had seen, taped to fade in sunlight against the windows of Alejandro's apartment, were a part of this. Alejandro drew beautifully, seemingly in any style, and there was an understanding between them, unspoken, that Alejandro had begun to carry the subtleties of Juana's magic uptown, into a world of galleries and collectors.

"Carlito." Alejandro named an uncle now, carefully, passing Tito a small white china bowl of greasy, scented warmth. "What has Carlito told you about him?"

"That he speaks Russian." They were speaking Spanish. "That if he addresses me in Russian, I may reply in Russian."

Alejandro raised an eyebrow.

"And that he knew our grandfather, in Havana."

Alejandro frowned, his white china spoon poised above his soup. "An American?"

Tito nodded.

"The only Americans our grandfather knew in Havana were CIA," Alejandro said, more softly now, though there was no one else in the restaurant other than the waiter, who was reading a Chinese weekly on his stool behind the till.

Tito remembered going with his mother to the Chinese cemetery behind Calle 23, shortly before he had come to New York. Something had been retrieved from an ossuary there, one of the small houses of bones, and Tito had delivered this elsewhere, proud of his tradecraft. And in the reeking toilet behind a Malecon restaurant he had flicked through the papers, in their mildewed envelope of rubberized fabric. He had no idea what they might have been, now, but he knew they had been typed in an English he'd scarcely known how to read.

He had never told this to anyone, and now did not tell Alejandro.

His feet, in black Red Wing boots, were very cold. He imagined himself slipping luxuriously into a deep Japanese bath of this same duck soup. "He looks like the men who used to stand in the hardware stores along this street," he said to Alejandro. "Old men in old coats, with nothing else to do." The hardware stores of Canal were gone now, replaced by cellular shops and counterfeit Prada.

"If you were to tell Carlito that you had seen the same van twice, or even the same woman," Alejandro told the steaming surface of his soup, "he would send someone else. The protocol demands it."

Their grandfather too was gone, the author of that protocol, like those old men along Canal Street. His complexly illegal ashes had been flung, one chilly April morning, from a Staten Island Ferry, the uncles shielding ritual cigars against the wind, while the vessel's resident pickpockets hung well back, away from what they rightly perceived to be a most private activity.

"There has been nothing," Tito said. "Nothing to indicate any interest."

"If someone pays us to pass this man contraband— and by the nature of our business we pass nothing else— then someone else is surely interested."

Tito tested the joints of his cousin's logic, finding them sound. He nodded.

"You know the expression 'get a life,' cousin?" Alejandro had switched to English. "We all need lives, Tito, eventually, if we're to stay here."

Tito said nothing.

"How many deliveries, so far?"

"Four."

"Too many."

They ate their soup in silence then, hearing trucks rumble over metal, along Canal.

LATER TITO STOOD before the deep sink in his single tall room in Chinatown, washing winter socks with Woolite. Socks were no longer quite so foreign in themselves, but the weight of these, wet, still amazed him. And still his feet were sometimes cold, in spite of a variety of insulated insoles from the surplus store on Broadway.

He remembered the sink in his mother's apartment in Havana. The plastic bottle filled with the henequen sap she used as a detergent, the pad of coarse fibers from the interior of the same plant, and a small can of charcoal. He remembered the tiny ants, speeding along the edge of his mother's sink. In New York, Alejandro had once pointed out, ants moved much more slowly.

Another cousin, relocated from New Orleans in the wake of the flood, had spoken of seeing a swarming, glittering ball of red ants in the water. This was how ants avoided drowning, it seemed, and Tito, hearing the story, had thought that his family was like that as well, afloat in America, less numerous but supported by one another on their invisible raft of tradecraft, the protocol.

Sometimes he watched the news in Russian, on the Russian Network of America, on his Sony plasma screen. The voices of the presenters had begun to acquire a dreamlike, submarine quality. He wondered if this was what it felt like, to begin to lose a language.

He rolled his socks, squeezed water and suds from them, emptied and refilled the sink, put them back in to rinse, and dried his hands on an old T-shirt he used as a towel.

The room was square, windowless, with a single steel door and white-painted plasterboard walls. The high ceiling was raw concrete. He sometimes lay on his mattress, staring up, and traced the edges of vanished sheets of plywood there, fossil impressions dating from the pouring of the floor above. There were no other live-in residents. His floor-neighbors were a factory where Korean women sewed children's clothing, and another, smaller firm, something to do with the Internet. His uncles held the lease here. When they required a place to do certain kinds of business, Tito sometimes slept at Alejandro's, on his cousin's Ikea couch.

His own room had a sink and toilet, a hotplate, a mattress, his computer, amp, speakers, keyboards, the Sony television, an iron, an ironing board. His clothing hung on an ancient wheeled iron rack, rescued from the sidewalk on Crosby Street. Beside one of his speakers stood a small blue vase from a Chinese department store on Canal, a fragile thing he had secretly dedicated to the goddess Ochun, she whom Cuban Catholics knew as Our Lady of Charity, at Cobre.

He cabled his Casio keyboard, added warmer water to the rinsing socks, pulled a long-legged folding director's chair close to the sink, and climbed up into it. Perched in the tall, unsteady chair, from that same Canal Street department store, he settled into the sling of black canvas and lowered his feet into the water. With the Casio across his thighs, he closed his eyes and touched the keys, searching for a tone like tarnished silver.

If he played well, he would fill Ochun's emptiness.

3. VOLAPUK

Milgrim, wearing the Paul Stuart overcoat he'd stolen the month before from a Fifth Avenue deli, watched Brown unlock the oversized steel-sheathed door with a pair of keys taken from a small transparent Ziploc bag, exactly the sort of bag that Dennis Birdwell, Milgrim's East Village dealer, used to package crystal.

Brown straightened up, fixing Milgrim with his habitual look of alert contempt. "Open it," he ordered, shifting slightly on his feet. Milgrim did, keeping a fold of overcoat between his hand and the knob. The door swung open on darkness and the red power indicator of what Milgrim assumed was a computer. He stepped in before Brown had a chance to shove him.

He was concentrating on the tiny tablet of Ativan melting beneath his tongue. It had reached that stage where it was there but not there, merely a focal point of grittiness, reminding him of the microscopic scales on the wings of a butterfly.

"Why do they call it that?" Brown asked, absently, as the uncomfortably bright beam of his flashlight began a methodical interrogation of the room's contents.

Milgrim heard the door click shut behind them.

It was uncharacteristic of Brown to ask anything absently, and Milgrim took it to indicate tension. "Call it what?" Milgrim resented having to speak. He wanted to concentrate fully on that instant when the sublingual tablet phase-shifted from being to not-being.

The beam came to rest on one of those director's-chair barstools, standing beside some kind of janitorial sink.

The place smelled of someone living there, but not unpleasantly.

"Why do they call it that?" Brown repeated, with a deliberate and ominous calm. Brown was not the sort of man to willingly voice words or names he found beneath him, either for reasons of their insufficient gravitas or because they were foreign.

"Volapuk," said Milgrim, feeling the Ativan finally do its not-there trick. "When they text, they're keying in a visual approximation of Cyrillic, the Russian alphabet. They use our alphabet, and some numerals, but only according to the Cyrillic letters they most closely resemble."

"I asked you why they call it that."

"Esperanto," Milgrim said. "That was an artificial language, a scheme for universal communication. Volapuk was another. When the Russians got themselves computers, the keyboards and screen displays were Roman, not Cyrillic. They faked up something that looked like Cyrillic, out of our characters. They called it Volapuk. I guess you could say it was a joke."

But Brown was not that sort of man. "Fuck that," he said flatly, his definitive judgment on Volapuk, on Milgrim, on these IFs he was so interested in. IF was Brownspeak, Milgrim had learned, for Illegal Facilitator, a criminal whose crimes facilitated the crimes of others.

"Hold this." Brown passed Milgrim the flashlight, which was made of knurled metal, professionally nonreflective. The pistol Brown wore beneath his parka, largely made of composite resin, was equally nonreflective. It was like shoes and accessories, Milgrim thought; someone does alligator, the next week they're all doing it. It was the season of this nonreflective noncolor, in Browntown. But a very long season, Milgrim guessed.

Brown was snapping on a pair of green latex surgical gloves he'd taken from a pocket.

Milgrim held the flashlight where Brown wanted it, savoring the perspective being afforded by the Ativan. He'd once dated a woman who liked to say that the windows of army surplus stores constituted hymns to male powerlessness. Where was Brown's powerlessness? Milgrim didn't know, but now he could admire Brown's surgically gloved hands, like undersea creatures in some fairyland aquatic theater, trained to mimic the hands of a conjurer.

From a pocket, these had produced a small transparent plastic case, and from this they were cleverly extracting a tiny thing, palest blue and silver, colors that Milgrim thought of somehow as Korean. A battery.

Everything needs batteries, Milgrim thought. Even whatever spooky little unit Brown's cohort was using to grab the IF's texting, what little there was of it, both incoming and outgoing, out of the air in this room. Milgrim was curious about that, because as far as he knew it shouldn't be possible, not without actually having a bug in the IF's phone. And this IF, Brown had said, seldom used the same phone, or account, twice. He bought them and tossed them on a regular basis—which was no more than Birdwell did, now he thought about it.

Milgrim watched as Brown knelt beside a rack of clothing, feeling with gloved hands beneath the wheeled, cast-iron base at one end. Milgrim wanted to check the labels in the IF's clothes, some shirts and a black jacket, but he had to keep the light on Brown's hands. APC, maybe, he judged, squinting. He had seen the IF once, when he and Brown had been sitting in a magazine-and-sandwich place on Broadway. The IF had walked past, beyond the steamed window, and had actually looked in. Brown, taken by surprise, had lost it, hissing codes into his headset, and Milgrim hadn't understood, at first, that this mild-looking little guy with the black leather porkpie turned up at the front was Brown's IF. He'd looked, Milgrim thought, like an ethnic version of a younger Johnny Depp. Brown had once referred to the IF and his family as Cuban-Chinese, but Milgrim would have been unable to make an ethnic identification. Filipino, in a pinch, but that wasn't it either. And they spoke Russian. Or texted in an approximation of it. As far as Milgrim knew, Brown's people had never intercepted any voice.

These people of Brown's, they worried Milgrim. Many things worried Milgrim, not the least of them Brown, but he had a special mental folder for Brown's unseen people. There seemed to be too many of them, for one thing. Was Brown a cop? Were whoever did this text-tapping thing for him cops? Milgrim doubted it. Brown's people had fed written all over their MO, it seemed to Milgrim, but if that were the case, what did that make Brown?

Brown, as if in answer to this unvoiced query, made a soft, worryingly satisfied grunting sound, from where he knelt on the floor. Milgrim watched the green-gloved hand-creatures reemerge, into their limelight, bearing something matte, black, and partially covered in equally matte and black tape. It had a six-inch rattail of matte black wire, with its own bit of tape, and Milgrim guessed that it might be using this old Garment District rack as an additional antenna.

He watched Brown swap in the fresh battery, careful to keep the beam on what Brown was doing, and out of his eyes.

Was Brown a fed of some kind? FBI? DEA? Milgrim had encountered examples of both, enough to know them as very different (and mutually antagonistic) species. He couldn't imagine Brown as either. These days, though, there must be feds in flavors Milgrim had never even heard of. But something about Brown's apparent IQ, not terribly high, as Milgrim judged it, and the degree of autonomy he seemed to be manifesting in this operation, whatever it might be, kept niggling at him, right through the hard-bought perspective of the Ativan he needed just to keep standing here without screaming.

He watched Brown replace the bug beneath the rusty base of the old rack, head down, intent on his task.

When Brown stood up, Milgrim saw him knock something dark from the crossbar of the rack. It made no sound when it hit the floor. As Brown took the flashlight and turned, playing it once more over the IF's belongings, Milgrim reached out and touched a second dark thing that still hung there. Cold wet wool.

Brown's flashlight's uncomfortable brilliance found a cheap-looking little vase, made of something nacreous and blue, that stood beside one of the speakers for the IF's sound system. The amped-up blue-white diode light lent the vessel's lacquered surface an unreal translucence, as though some process akin to fusion were beginning within it. When the light went out, it was as though Milgrim could still see the vase.

"Out of here," Brown announced.

On the sidewalk outside, walking briskly toward Lafayette, Milgrim decided that Stockholm syndrome was a myth. Going on a few weeks now, and he still wasn't empathizing with Brown.

Not even a little bit.

4 . INTO THE LOCATIVE

The Standard had an all-night restaurant off its lobby—
a long, glass-fronted operation with wide booths upholstered in matte-black tuck-and-roll, punctuated by the
gnarled phalli of a half dozen large San Pedro cacti.

Hollis watched Alberto slide his Pendelton-ed mass
along the bench opposite hers. Odile was between Alberto and the window.

"See-bare-espace," Odile pronounced, gnomically, "it
is everting."

"'Everything'? What is?"

"See-bare-espace," Odile reaffirmed, "everts." She
made a gesture with her hands that reminded Hollis, in
some dimly unsettling way, of the crocheted model
uterus her Family Life Education teacher had used as an
instructional aid.

"Turns itself inside out," offered Alberto, by way of clarification. "'Cyberspace.' Fruit salad and a coffee." This last, Hollis realized after an instant's confusion, addressed to their waitress. Odile ordered café au lait, Hollis a bagel and coffee. The waitress left them.

"I guess you could say it started on the first of May, 2000," Alberto said.

"What did?"

"Geohacking. Or the potential thereof. The government announced then that Selective Availability would be turned off, on what had been, until then, strictly a military system. Civilians could access the GPS geocoordinates for the first time."

Hollis had only vaguely understood from Philip Rausch that what she would be writing about would be various things artists were finding to do with longitude, latitude, and the Internet, so Alberto's virtual rendition of the death of River Phoenix had taken her by surprise. Now she had, she was hoping, the opening to her piece. "How many of those have you done, Alberto?" And were they all posthumous, though she didn't ask that.

"Nine," Alberto said. "At the Chateau Marmont"— he gestured across Sunset—"I've most recently completed a virtual shrine to Helmut Newton. On the site of his fatal crash, at the foot of the driveway. I'll show you that after breakfast."

The waitress returned with their coffees. Hollis watched as a very young, very pale Englishman bought a yellow pack of American Spirit from the man at the till. The boy's thin beard reminded her of moss around a marble drain. "So the people staying at the Marmont," she asked, "they have no idea, no way of knowing what you've done there?" Just as pedestrians had no way of knowing they stepped through the sleeping River, on his Sunset sidewalk.

"No," said Alberto, "none. Not yet." He was digging through a canvas carryall on his lap. He produced a cell phone, married with silver tape to some other species of smallish consumer electronics. "With these, though . . ." He clicked something on one of the conjoined units, opened the phone, and began deftly thumbing its keypad. "When this is available as a package . . ." He passed it to her. A phone, and something she recognized as a GPS unit, but the latter's casing had been partially cut away, with what felt like more electronics growing out of it, sealed under the silver tape.

"What does it do?"

"Look," he said.

She squinted at the small screen. Brought it closer. She saw Alberto's woolen chest, but confused somehow with ghostly verticals, horizontals, a semitransparent Cubist overlay. Pale crosses? She looked up at him.

"This isn't a locative piece," he said. "It's not spatially tagged. Try it on the street."

She swung the duct-taped hybrid toward Sunset, seeing a crisply defined, perfectly level plane of white cruciforms, spaced as on an invisible grid, receding across the boulevard and into virtual distance. Their square white uprights, approximately level with the pavement, seemed to continue, in increasingly faint and somehow subterranean perspective, back under the rise of the Holly-wood Hills.

"American fatalities in Iraq," Alberto said. "I had it connected to a site, originally, that added crosses as deaths were reported. You can take it anywhere. I have a slide show of grabs from selected locations. I thought about sending it to Baghdad, but people would assume real grabs on the ground in Baghdad were Photoshopped." She looked up at him as a black Range Rover drove through the field of crosses, in time to see him shrug.

Odile squinted over the rim of her white breakfast bowl of café au lait. "Cartographic attributes of the invisible," she said, lowering the bowl. "Spatially tagged hypermedia." This terminology seemed to increase her fluency by a factor of ten; she scarcely had an accent now. "The artist annotating every centimeter of a place, of every physical thing. Visible to all, on devices such as these." She indicated Alberto's phone, as if its swollen belly of silver tape were gravid with an entire future.

Hollis nodded, and passed the thing back to Alberto.

Fruit salad and toasted bagel arrived. "And you've been curating this kind of art, Odile, in Paris?"

"Everywhere."

Rausch was right, she decided. There was something to write about here, though she was still a long way from knowing what it was.

"May I ask you something?" Alberto had gotten through half of his fruit salad already. A methodical eater. He paused, fork in midair, looking at her.

"Yes?"

"How did you know the Curfew was over?"

She looked him in the eye and saw deep otaku focus. Of course that tended to be the case, if anyone recognized her as the singer in an early-nineties cult unit. The Curfew's fans were virtually the only people who knew the band had existed, today, aside from radio programmers, pop historians, critics, and collectors. With the increasingly atemporal nature of music, though, the band had continued to acquire new fans. Those it did acquire, like Alberto, were often formidably serious. She didn't know how old he might have been, when the Curfew had broken up, but that might as well have been yesterday, as far as his fanboy module was concerned. Still having her own fangirl module quite centrally in place, for a wide variety of performers, she understood, and thus felt a responsibility to provide him with an honest answer, however unsatisfying.

"We didn't know, really. It just ended. It stopped happening, at some essential level, though I never knew exactly when that happened. It became painfully apparent. So we packed it in."

He looked about as satisfied with that as she'd expected him to be, but it was the truth, as far as she knew, and the best she could do for him. She'd never been able to come up with any clearer reason herself, though it certainly wasn't anything she continued to give much thought. "We'd just released that four-song CD, and that was it. We knew. It only took a little while to sink in." Hoping that would be that, she began to spread cream cheese on one half of her bagel.

"That was in New York?"

"Yes."

"Was there a particular moment, some particular place, where you'd say the Curfew broke up? Where the band made the decision to stop being a band?"

"I'd have to think about it," she said, knowing that was really not what she should be saying.

"I'd like to do a piece," he said. "You, Inchmale, Heidi, Jimmy. Wherever you were. Breaking up."

Odile had started shifting on the tuck-and-roll, evidently in the dark as to what they were talking about, and not liking it. "Eenchmale?" She frowned.

"What are we going to see while I'm in town, Odile?" She smiled at Alberto, hoping she signaled Interview Over. "I need your suggestions. I need to arrange time to interview you," she said to Odile. "And you too, Alberto. Right now, though, I'm exhausted. I need sleep."

Odile knit her fingers, as well as she could, around the white china bowl. Her nails looked like something with very small teeth had been at them. "This evening, we will pick you up. We can visit a dozen pieces, easily."

"Scott Fitzgerald's heart attack," suggested Alberto. "It's down the street."

She looked at the crowded, oversized, frantically ornate letters inked in jailhouse indigo down both his arms, and wondered what they spelled. "But he didn't die then, did he?"

"It's in Virgin," he said. "By the world music."

*　*　*

AFTER THEY'D HAD a look at Alberto's memorial to Helmut Newton, which involved a lot of vaguely Deco-styled monochrome nudity in honor of its subject's body of work, she walked back to the Mondrian through that weird, evanescent moment that belongs to every sunny morning in West Hollywood, when some strange perpetual promise of chlorophyll and hidden, warming fruit graces the air, just before the hydrocarbon blanket settles in. That sense of some peripheral and prelapsarian beauty, of something a little more than a hundred years past, but in that moment achingly present, as though the city were something you could wipe from your glasses and forget.

Sunglasses. She'd forgotten to bring any.

She looked down at the sidewalk's freckling of blackened gum. At the brown, beige, and fibrous debris of the storm. And felt that luminous instant pass, as it always must.

5. TWO KINDS OF EMPTY

Coming back from the Sunrise Market on Broome, just before they closed, Tito stopped to look in the windows of Yohji Yamamoto, on Grand Street.

A few minutes after ten. Grand was completely deserted. Tito looked each way. Not even the yellow of a cab moving in either distance. Then he looked back at the asymmetrical lapels of a sort of cape or buttoned wrap. He saw his own reflection there, dark eyes and dark clothing. In one hand a plastic Sunrise bag, with its nearly weightless burden of instant Japanese noodles in white foam bowls. Alejandro teased him about these, saying he might as well be eating the white bowls, but Tito liked them. Japan was a planet of benign mystery, source of games and anime and plasma TV.

Yohji Yamamoto's asymmetrical lapels, though, were

not a mystery. This was fashion, and he thought he understood it.

What he sometimes struggled with was some understanding that might begin to hold both the costly austerity of the window he stared into now and the equally but differently austere storefronts he remembered from Havana.

There had been no glass in those windows. Behind each crudely articulated metal grating, at night, a single fluorescent tube had cast a submarine light. And nothing on offer, regardless of daytime function: only carefully swept floors and blotched plaster.

He watched his reflection shrug softly, in Yamamoto's window. He walked on, glad of his thick dry socks.

Where would Alejandro be now? he wondered. Perhaps in the nameless Eighth Avenue bar he favored, below Times Square, its neon announcing TAVERN and nothing more. Alejandro made his gallery contacts meet him there; he enjoyed taking curators and dealers into that reddish twilight, amid sleepy Puerto Rican transvestites and a few hustlers taking their breaks from Port Authority. Tito disliked the place. It seemed to occupy its own reptilian delta of time, a dead-end continuum of watered drinks and low-level anxiety.

COMING INTO HIS ROOM, he saw that one of the socks he'd washed earlier had fallen from where he'd left it to dry, on the wheeled rack. He replaced it.

6. RIZE

Milgrim was enjoying the superior brightness of the nitrogen-filled optics in Brown's Austrian-made monocular well enough, but not the smell of Brown's chewing gum or his proximity in the back of the chilly surveillance van.

The van had been parked on Lafayette, where one of Brown's people had left it for them. Brown had run a red light to get up here and into position, after his earphone had told him that the IF was headed this way, but now the IF was staring into the window of Yohji Yamamoto, unmoving.

"What's he doing?" Brown took the monocular back. It matched his gun and his flashlight, that same not-color of grayish green.

Milgrim leaned forward, to get a better unassisted

view through his spy-hole. The Econoline had a half dozen of these sawn through its sides, each one covered by a screwed-on, moveable scrap of black-painted plastic. These coincided, on the graffiti-tagged exterior, with solid black areas of the various tags. Assuming those were all genuine tags, Milgrim wondered, collected by leaving the van on the street, would the van's disguise still fool a tagger? How old were those tags? Were they the urban equivalent of using out-of-season vegetation for camouflage? "He's looking in a window," Milgrim said, pointlessly and knowing it. "Are you going to follow him home now?"

"No," said Brown. "He could notice the truck."

Milgrim had no idea how many people Brown had had watching the IF stock up on Japanese groceries, while they'd entered his place and changed the bug's battery. This world of people following and watching other people was new to Milgrim, though he supposed he'd always assumed that it was there, somewhere. You saw it in movies and read about it, but you didn't think about having to breathe someone else's condensed breath in the back of a cold van.

Now it was Brown's turn to lean forward, pressing the monocular's resilient lip against the van's cold, sweating skin, for a closer view of the IF. Milgrim wondered idly, almost luxuriously, what it might be like to pick something up, just then, and hit Brown in the head with it. He actually glanced around the back of the van, to see what might be available, but there was nothing but the upended plastic milk crates they both squatted on, and a folded tarp.

Brown, as if reading Milgrim's thoughts, turned suddenly from the eyepiece of the monocular, glaring.

Milgrim blinked, hoping to convey mildness and harmlessness. Which shouldn't be that hard, as he hadn't hit anyone in the head since elementary school, and wasn't likely to now. Though he'd never been held captive before, he reminded himself.

"Eventually he'll send or receive something from that room," Brown said, "and when he does, you'll translate it."

Milgrim nodded dutifully.

THEY CHECKED INTO the New Yorker, on Eighth Avenue. Adjoining rooms, fourteenth floor. The New Yorker seemed to be on Brown's list. This was their fifth or sixth time here. Most of Milgrim's room was taken up by its double bed, which faced a television mounted in a particleboard cabinet. The pixels in the cabinet's wood-grain veneer were too large, Milgrim thought, as he took off his stolen overcoat and sat on the edge of the bed. That was something he'd started to notice, how you only got the high-resolution stuff in your better places.

Brown came in and did his trick with the two little boxes, one on the door, one on the doorframe. They were that same shade of gray, like the gun and the flashlight and the monocular. He'd do the same with his own door, and all of this, as far as Milgrim knew, so that he, Milgrim, wouldn't decide to leave while Brown was sleeping. Milgrim had no idea what the boxes did, but Brown had said not to touch the doors when they were up. Milgrim hadn't.

Brown tossed what Milgrim took to be a four-pack bubble-card of Ativan down on Milgrim's flowered bedspread and returned to his own room. Milgrim heard Brown's television come on. He knew that music, now: FOX News.

He glanced toward the bubble-pack. It wasn't the boxes on the doors that would keep him here.

He picked it up. "RIZE," it said, there, and "5MG," and what looked like, yes, Japanese writing. Or the way Japanese looks when they dress it up for packaging.

"Hello?" The connecting door was still open, between their rooms. The sound of Brown's fingers, on his armored laptop, stopped.

"What?"

"What is this stuff?"

"Your medication," said Brown.

"It says 'Rize,' and there's Japanese writing on it. It's not Ativan."

"It's the same fucking thing," Brown said, his delivery slowing threateningly. "Same DEA Schedule fucking Four narcotic."

Milgrim looked at the bubble-card.

"Now shut the fuck up."

He heard Brown begin to type again.

He sat back down on the bed. Rize? His first impulse

was to phone his man in the East Village. He looked at the phone, knowing that that wasn't on. His second was to ask Brown if he could borrow his laptop, so that he could Google this stuff. The DEA had a page with all the Schedule Four products, foreign brands too. But then, he thought, if Brown was really a fed, he might even be getting this stuff from the DEA. And borrowing Brown's laptop, he knew, was no more on than using the phone to call Dennis Birdwell.

And he owed Birdwell money, under awkward circumstances. There was that.

He put the bubble-pack on the corner of the nearest bedside table, aligning its sides with the edges, both of which had black arcs where previous guests had let cigarettes burn down. The shape of the burns reminded him of McDonald's arches. He wondered if Brown was going to order sandwiches soon.

Rize.

7. **BUENOS AIRES**

Hollis dreamed she was in London with Philip Rausch, walking fast down Monmouth Street, toward the needle of Seven Dials. She'd never met Rausch, but now, in the way of dreams, he was also Reg Inchmale. It was daytime, but deep in winter, the sky a directionless gray, and suddenly she was cringing beneath a lurid carnival glow, as above them descended all the vast Wurlitzer bulk of the mothership from *Close Encounters*—a film released when she was seven, and a great favorite of her mother's—but here now, hugely and somehow able to fit down into the narrowness of Monmouth Street, like some electric element meant to warm reptiles in their cages, as she and Inchmale cowered, mouths agape.

But then this Rausch-Inchmale said, brusquely releasing her hand, that it was after all only a Christmas ornament, however grand, suspended there between hotel to their right and coffee shop to their left. And yes, now she plainly saw the wires supporting it, but a phone was ringing, through the window of a shop nearby, and she saw that this was some sort of field telephone from the Great War, its canvas case smeared with pale clay, as were the rough wool cuffs of Rausch-Inchmale's trousers—

"Hello?"

"Rausch."

Rausch yourself, she thought, her open cell to her ear. Los Angeles sunlight gnawed at the edges of the Mondrian's layering of drapes. "I was sleeping."

"I need to speak with you. The researchers have turned up someone you need to meet. We doubt Odile knows him yet, but Corrales certainly does."

"Who is it, that Alberto knows?"

"Bobby Chombo."

"Chombo?"

"He's their king of tech assist, these locative artists. Their geohacker. GPS signals can't penetrate buildings. He does work-arounds. Triangulates off cellular towers, other systems. Very clever."

"You want me to meet him?"

"If you can't arrange it through Corrales, phone me. We'll work something from this end."

He wasn't asking. She raised her eyebrows in the dark, nodded silently: Yes, boss. "Will do."

There was a pause. "Hollis?"

She sat up in the dark, assuming a loosely defensive lotus position. "Yes?"

"When you're with him, be specially alert to anything that might reference shipping."

"Shipping?"

"Patterns of global shipping. Particularly in light of the sort of geospatial tagging Odile and Corrales are about." Another pause. "Or iPods."

"iPods?"

"As a means of data transfer."

"How some people use them as drives?"

"Exactly."

There was something about this, suddenly, that she really didn't like, and in some entirely new way. She imagined the bed a desert of white sand. Something circling, hidden, beneath its surface. Perhaps the Mongolian Death Worm that had been one of Inchmale's imaginary pets.

There are times when saying the least you can is the best thing to do, she decided. "I'll ask Alberto."

"Good."

"Have you taken care of the billing here, yet?"

"Of course."

"Hold on," she told him, "I'm phoning the desk on the other line."

"Give it ten minutes. I'll just double-check."

"Thanks."

"We've been talking about you, Hollis." That vaguest of managerial "we's."

"Yes?"

"We're very happy with you. How would you feel about a salaried position?"

She sensed the Mongolian Death Worm draw closer, amid the cotton dunes. "That's a big one, Philip. I'll need to think about it."

"Do."

She closed her phone.

Exactly ten minutes later, she used the room phone to call the desk, receiving confirmation that her bill, all incidentals included, was now on an AMEX card in the name of Philip M. Rausch. She had herself switched to the hotel's salon, found there was an opening within the hour, and booked an appointment for a cut.

It was just after two, which made it just after five in New York, with Buenos Aires two hours later. She pulled up Inchmale's number on the screen of her cell, but dialed on the room phone. He answered immediately. "Reg? Hollis. I'm in Los Angeles. Are you in the middle of dinner?"

"Angelina's feeding Willy. How are you?" Their one-year-old. Angelina was Reg Inchmale's Argentinian wife, whose maiden name had been Ryan, and whose grandfather had been a ship's pilot on the Río Paraná. She'd met Inchmale while employed by either *Dazed & Confused* or another magazine. Hollis had never been able to keep them straight. Angelina knew as much about magazine publishing in London as anyone Hollis could think of.

"Complicated," she admitted. "How are you?"

"Steadily less so. On good days, anyway. I think fatherhood agrees with me. And it's so, I don't know, deeply old-school here. They haven't sandblasted anything yet. It looks the way London used to look. Black with grime. Or New York, come to think."

"Can you ask Angelina something for me?"

"Would you like to speak to her yourself?"

"No, she's feeding Willy. Just ask her what, if anything, she knows about a magazine start-up called *Node*."

"*Node*?"

"It wants to be like *Wired*, but they aren't supposed to say that. I think the money's Belgian."

"They want to interview you?"

"They've offered me a job. I'm on assignment for them, freelancing. I wondered if Angelina would have heard anything."

"Hold on," he said. "Have to put this down. Wired into the wall on a curly-cord . . ." She heard him rest the handset on a surface. She lowered her own phone and listened to afternoon traffic on Sunset. She had no idea where Odile's robot had gotten to, but it was quiet.

She heard Inchmale pick up the phone in Buenos Aires.

"Bigend," he said.

From Sunset, she heard brakes, impact, breaking glass. "What was that?"

"Bigend. Like 'big' and 'end.' Advertising magnate."

The wobble of a car alarm.

"The one who married Nigelia?"

"That's Saatchi. Hubertus Bigend. Belgian. Firm's called Blue Ant."

"And?"

"Ange says your *Node*'s a Bigend project, if indeed it's a magazine. *Node*'s one of several small firms he has in London. She had some dealings with his agency, when she was on the magazine, now I think about it. Some run-in with them." She heard the alarm cut out, and then the wail of an approaching siren. "What's that?" Inchmale asked.

"Accident on Sunset. I'm at the Mondrian."

"Do they still use a casting director to hire the bellmen?"

"Looks like it."

"Is Bigend paying?"

"Absolutely," she said. Very close, she heard another squeal of brakes, and then the siren, which had gotten very loud, died.

"Can't be all bad," he said.

"No," she said, "it can't." Could it?

"We miss you. You should stay in touch."

"I will, Reg. Thanks. And thank Angelina."

"Goodbye."

"'Bye, then."

Another siren was approaching, as she hung up. An ambulance this time, she guessed. She decided that she wasn't going to look. It hadn't sounded too bad, but she really didn't want any bad at all, right then.

With a perfectly sharpened Mondrian pencil she wrote BIGEND in block caps in the dark, on a square block of embossed white Mondrian notepaper.

She'd Google him later.

8. CREEPING HER OUT

She watched Alberto trying to explain the helmet and the laptop to Virgin security. These two blandly uniformed functionaries didn't look like they were much into the locative. At this point, she had to admit, neither was she.

Alberto had some kind of Jim Morrison piece he wanted to show her, up on Wonderland Avenue, and that just wasn't going to work for her. Even if it somehow managed to bypass the Lizard King's iconic churlishness, and focus on, say, Ray Manzarek's calliope pieces, she still didn't want to have to write about invisible virtual monuments to the Doors, any of them. Though as Inchmale had several times pointed out, back when they themselves had been in a band, Manzarek and Krieger had worked wonders, neutralizing the big guy's sodden crankiness.

Standing out here in the evening hydrocarbon, in this retail complex on the corner of Crescent Heights and Sunset, watching Alberto Corrales argue that she, Hollis Henry, really should be allowed to view his virtual rendition of Scott Fitzgerald's heart attack, she felt a sort of detachment descend, some extra slack-cutting—due, quite possibly, to her new haircut, executed to her complete satisfaction by a charming and talented young man in the Mondrian's salon.

It hadn't been fatal, Fitzgerald's heart attack. Missing Alberto's depiction of it wouldn't be fatal for her article, either. Or missing most of it, as she had in fact been afforded a brief glimpse: a man in a tweed jacket, clutching his chest at a chromed Moderne counter, a pack of Chesterfields in his right hand. The Chesterfields, she decided, had been in slightly higher resolution than the rest of the place, which had seemed interestingly detailed, down to the unfamiliar shapes of the vehicles out on Sunset, but Virgin security's unhappiness with anyone donning a mask or masklike visor in the world music aisle had put a stop to that, with Hollis quickly handing the visor-rig to Alberto and hustling straight on out of there.

Odile might have been cute enough to charm these guards, but she'd succumbed to an attack of asthma, she'd said, brought on either by the airborne biomass of the previous night's storm or by the near critical mass of aromatherapy product to be variously encountered in the Standard.

And still this calm descended on Hollis, oddly; this unexpected clarity, this moment perhaps of what the late Jimmy Carlyle, the Curfew's Iowan bass player, prior to departing this vale of heroin, had called serenity. Wherein (this calm) she knew herself to be that woman of the age and the history that were hers, here, tonight, and was more or less okay with it, all of it, at least up till *Node* had come calling, the week before, with an offer she could neither refuse nor, really, understand.

If *Node* was, as the youthful but metallic Rausch had described it, a technology magazine with a cultural twist (a technology magazine, as she thought of it, with interesting trousers), did it really follow that she, former vocalist for the Curfew and sometime obscure journalist, would be hired for seriously good money to write about this witheringly geeky art trend?

But no, said something at the still heart of her moment's calm. No indeed. And the core anomaly here was embodied, revealed almost certainly, in Rausch having injected that apparent order to meet Bobby Chombo, whoever or whatever he might be, and having met him, to watch for something to do with shipping, "patterns of global shipping." That, she saw, was it, whatever "it" in this case might be, and likely had nothing to do with Odile Richard and the rest of these people.

And then, her gaze on the passing stream of Sunset, she saw the Curfew's drummer, Laura "Heidi" Hyde, driving what Hollis, never really a car person, took to be a smallish SUV of German extraction. If further confirmation had been needed, she knew that Heidi, with whom she hadn't spoken in almost three years, lived in Beverly Hills now, and worked in Century City, and had almost certainly been glimpsed, just now, heading home at day's end.

"Fascist dipshits," Alberto protested, flustered, stepping up beside her with his laptop under one arm, the visor under the other. Somehow he seemed too serious-looking to say something like that, and for an instant she imagined him as a character in some graphically simplified animation.

"It's okay," she assured him. "Really, it's okay. I got a look. I saw it. Got the general idea."

He blinked at her. Was he on the verge of tears?

"BOBBY CHOMBO," she said, when they were settled in Hamburger Hamlet, to which she had had Alberto drive them from Crescent Heights.

Concern creased Alberto's brow.

"Bobby Chombo," she repeated.

He nodded, grimly. "I use him for all my pieces. Brilliant."

She was looking at the crazily elaborated black-letter work down the outside of both his forearms. She could make absolutely no sense of it. "Alberto, what does that actually say, on your arms?"

"Nothing."

"Nothing?"

"It was designed by an artist in Tokyo. He does these

alphabets, abstracts them till they're completely unreadable. The actual sequence was generated randomly."

"Alberto, what do you know about *Node*, the magazine I'm writing for?"

"European? New?"

"Did you know Odile, before she turned up to do this?"

"No."

"Had you ever heard of her, before?"

"Yes. She curates."

"And she got in touch with you, about getting together with me, for *Node*?"

"Yes." Their server arrived with two Coronas. She picked hers up, clinked the neck of his, and drank from the bottle. After a pause he did the same. "Why are you asking me this?"

"I haven't worked for *Node* before. I'm trying to get a feel for what they're doing, how they do things."

"Why did you ask about Bobby?"

"I'm writing about your art. Why wouldn't I ask about the tech end?"

Alberto looked uncomfortable. "Bobby," he began, stopped. "He's a very private person."

"He is?"

Alberto looked unhappy. "The vision's mine, and I build the work, but Bobby hacks it for me. Gets it to work, even indoors. And he gets the routers installed."

"Routers?"

"At this point, each piece needs its own wireless."

"Where's the one for River?"

"I don't know. The one for the Newton's in a flower bed. The Fitzgerald's really complicated, not always there."

"He wouldn't want to talk to me?"

"I don't think he'd like it that you've even heard of him." He frowned. "How did you?"

"My editor at *Node*, in London, the one supervising the piece? His name is Philip Rausch. He said he thought you'd know him, but probably Odile wouldn't."

"She doesn't."

"Can you get Bobby to talk with me, Alberto?"

"It's not . . ."

"He's not a Curfew fan?" Something inside her cringed at playing the card.

Alberto giggled. It came bubbling out of his big frame like carbon dioxide. He grinned at her, happily starstruck again. He took another drink. "Actually," he said, "he does listen to you. The Curfew's music is something we were able to bond around."

"Alberto, I like your work. I like what I've seen. I look forward to seeing more. Your River Phoenix piece was my first experience of the medium, a powerful one." His face went very still, expectant. "I need your help, Alberto. I haven't done a piece like this before. I'm trying to get a feel for how things work at *Node*, and *Node* is asking me to talk with Bobby. There's no reason I should expect you to trust me—"

"I do," he said, with a remarkably groomly cadence.

Then: "I do trust you, Hollis, it's just . . ." He winced. "You don't know Bobby."

"Tell me. About Bobby."

He put a forefinger on the white cloth, tracing a line. Crossed it with another, at a right angle. "The GPS grid," he said.

She felt minute hairs shift, on the small of her back, just above the waistband.

Alberto leaned forward. "Bobby divides his place up into smaller squares, within the grid. He sees everything in terms of GPS gridlines, the world divided up that way. It is, of course, but . . ." He frowned. "He won't sleep in the same square twice. He crosses them off, never goes back to one where he's slept before."

"You find that strange?" She did, certainly, but had no idea what passed for eccentric, for Alberto.

"Bobby is, well, Bobby. Strange? Definitely. Difficult."

This wasn't going where she wanted it to. "I also need to know more about how you make your pieces." That should do it, she thought. He brightened immediately.

Their burgers arrived. He looked as though he wanted to brush his aside, now.

"I start with a sense of place," he began. "With event, place. Then I research. I compile photographs. For the Fitzgerald, of course, there were no images of the event, precious little in the way of accounts. But there were pictures of him taken in roughly the same period. Wardrobe notes, haircut. Other photographs. And everything I could find on Schwab's. And there was a lot on Schwab's, because it was the most famous drugstore in America. Partly because Leon Schwab, the owner, kept claiming that Lana Turner was discovered there, sitting on a stool at his soda fountain. She used to deny that there was any truth to the story, and it seems like Schwab made it up to get customers into the store. But it got the place photographed for magazines. Lots of detail."

"And you make the photographs . . . 3-D?" She wasn't sure how to put it.

"Are you kidding? I model everything."

"How?"

"I build virtual models, then cover them with skins, textures I've sampled, or created myself, usually for that specific piece. Each model has a virtual skeleton, so I can pose and position the figure in its environment. I use digital lights to add shadows and reflections." He squinted at her, as if trying to decide whether she was really listening. "The modeling is like pushing and pulling clay. I do that over an inner structure of joints—the skeleton, with a spine, shoulders, elbows, fingers. It's not that different from designing figures for a game. Then I model multiple heads, with slightly different expressions, and combine them."

"Why?"

"It's more subtle. The expressions don't look made up, if you do that. I color them, then each surface in the model is wrapped with a texture. I collect textures. Some of my textures are real skin, scanned in. The River piece, I couldn't get the skin right. Finally I sampled a very young Vietnamese girl. It worked. People who knew him, they said so."

She put her burger down, swallowed. "I didn't imagine you doing all that. Somehow I thought it would all just . . . happen? With . . . technology?"

He nodded. "Yeah. I get that a lot. All the work I have to do, it seems sort of old-fashioned, archaic. I have to position virtual lights, so shadows will be cast correctly. Then there's a certain amount of 'fill,' atmosphere, for the environment." He shrugged. "The original only exists on the server, when I'm done, in virtual dimensions of depth, width, height. Sometimes I think that even if the server went down, and took my model with it, that that space would still exist, at least as a mathematical possibility, and that the space we live in . . ." He frowned.

"Yes?"

"Might work the same way." He shrugged again, and picked up his burger.

You, she thought, are seriously creeping me out.

But she only nodded gravely and picked up her own burger.

9 . A COLD CIVIL WAR

The message tone woke him. He reached for his phone in the dark, watched Volapuk scroll briefly past. Alejandro was outside, wanting in. It was ten after two in the morning. He sat up, pulled on his jeans, socks, sweater. Then his boots, whose laces he tied carefully: This was protocol.

It was cold in the hallway, as he locked his door behind him, less cold in the elevator. In the narrow, fluorescent-lit foyer below, he rapped once on the street door, heard his cousin's three raps in reply, then one. When he opened the door, Alejandro stepped in, surrounded by a nimbus of colder air and the smell of whiskey. Tito closed and locked the door behind him.

"You were sleeping?"

"Yes," Tito said, starting for the elevator.

SPOOK COUNTRY 59

"I went to Carlito," Alejandro said, following Tito into the elevator. Tito pushed the button; the door closed. "Carlito and I have our own business." Meaning separate from family business. "I asked him about your old man." The door opened.

"Why did you do that?" Tito unlocked his door.

"Because I didn't think you had taken me seriously."

They entered the darkness of Tito's room. He turned on the small shaded lamp attached to his MIDI keyboard. "Shall I make coffee? Tea?"

"Zavarka?"

"Bags." Tito no longer made tea in the Russian way, though he did steep his tea bags in a cheap Chinese tchainik.

Alejandro seated himself on the foot of Tito's mattress, knees drawn up before his face. "Carlito brews the zavarka. He takes it with a spoon of jam." His teeth shone in the light from the MIDI lamp.

"What did he tell you?"

"Our grandfather was the understudy of Semenov," Alejandro said. Tito turned on his hotplate and filled the kettle.

"Who was that?"

"Semenov was Castro's first KGB advisor."

Tito looked back at his cousin. This was something like hearing a fairy tale, though not an entirely unfamiliar one. And then the children met a flying horse, his mother would tell him. And then Grandfather met Castro's KGB advisor. He turned back to the hotplate.

"Grandfather was one of the less obvious participants in the formation of the Dirección General de Inteligencia."

"Carlito told you that?"

"I knew it already. From Juana."

Tito thought about this as he put the kettle to boil on the element. Their grandfather's secrets could not have gone with him entirely. Legends grew like vines, through a family like theirs, and the midden of their shared history, however deep, was narrow, constrained by the need for secrecy. Juana, so long in charge of the production of required documents, would have enjoyed a certain overview. And Juana, Tito knew, was the deepest of them all, the calmest, most patient. He often visited her, here. She took him to El Siglo XX Supermarket to buy malanga and boniato. The sauces she prepared for these were of a potency he already found alien, but her empanadas made him feel as if he were blessed. She had never told him about this Semenov, but she had taught him other things. He glanced toward the vessel holding Ochun. "What did Carlito say, about the old man?"

Alejandro looked over his knees. "Carlito said there is a war in America."

"A war?"

"A civil war."

"There is no war in America."

"When Grandfather helped found the DGI, in Havana, were the Americans at war with the Russians?"

"That was the 'cold war.' "

Alejandro nodded, his hands coming up to grip his knees. "A cold civil war."

Tito heard a sharp click from the direction of Ochun's vase, but thought instead of Elleggua, He Who Opens And Closes The Roads. He looked back at Alejandro.

"You don't follow politics, Tito."

Tito thought of the voices on the Russian Network of America, drowning somehow, taking his Russian with them. "A little," he said.

The kettle began to whistle. Tito took it off the element and dashed some boiling water into the tchainik. Then he added the two tea bags and poured the water with a habitual fast flourish. He put the lid on.

The way that Alejandro sat on his bed reminded Tito of crouching with his schoolmates, at dawn, to whip a wooden top from one cobble to the next, the day's heat gathering in the street around them. They had worn pressed white shorts and red scarves. Did anyone spin tops, in America?

Leaving the tchainik to steep, he sat beside Alejandro on the mattress.

"Do you understand how our family came to be what it is, Tito?"

"It began with Grandfather, and the DGI."

"He wasn't there long. The KGB needed its own network in Havana."

Tito nodded. "On Grandmother's side, we had always been in Barrio de Colón. Juana says before Batista."

"Carlito says that people in the government are looking for your old man."

"What people?"

"Carlito says that it reminds him of Havana here now, of the years before the Russians left. Nothing now is business as usual. He tells me that this old man was instrumental in bringing us here. That was a big magic, cousin. Bigger than our grandfather could have worked alone."

Tito suddenly remembered the smell of the English-language papers, in their mildewed case. "You told Carlito you thought it was dangerous?"

"Yes."

Tito got up to pour two glasses of tea from the tchainik. "And he told you that our family is under an obligation?" He was guessing. He looked back at Alejandro.

"And that you were specifically requested."

"Why?"

"You remind him of your grandfather. And of your father, who was working for this same old man when he died."

Tito passed Alejandro a glass of tea.

"Gracias," said Alejandro.

"De nada," said Tito.

10. NEW DEVONIAN

Milgrim was dreaming of the Flagellant Messiah, of the Pseudo Baldwin and the Master of Hungary, when Brown reached down into the hot shallows of his sleep, dug his thumbs into his shoulders, and shook him, hard.

"What is this?" Brown kept asking, a question Milgrim had taken to be purely existential, until Brown had wedged those same thumbs into the junctures of Milgrim's jaw and skull, hard, producing a degree of discomfort so severe that Milgrim was initially unable to recognize it as pain. Milgrim seemed to levitate through no will of his own, mouth opening to scream, but Brown, green-gloved as ever for these more intimate moments, clapped a hand over it.

He smelled the fresh latex covering Brown's index finger.

The other hand presented the screen of a BlackBerry. "What is this?"

A personal digital assistant, Milgrim was on the brink of answering, but then squinted through tears, recognizing, on the BlackBerry's screen, a very short specimen of the IF's family Volapuk.

The smell of Brown's glove retreated as Milgrim's mouth was uncovered. " 'I'm outside,' " Milgrim promptly translated. " 'Are you there?' Signed A—L—E. 'Ale.' "

"That's all?"

"Nothing. Else. There." Milgrim's own fingertips massaged the hinges of his jaw. There were big nodes of nerve there. Paramedics used that on overdose victims. It got your attention.

"Ten after two," Brown said, looking at the screen of the BlackBerry.

"You know your bug works now," Milgrim offered. "You changed the batteries; now there's proof it works."

Brown straightened and returned to his own room, without bothering to close the door.

You're welcome, thought Milgrim, as he lay back on the bed, eyes open, perhaps to reimagine the Flagellant Messiah.

The stolen Paul Stuart overcoat had contained, in its slash-flapped side pocket, a chunky 1961 paperback history of revolutionary messianism in medieval Europe. Owing to copious underlining in black fountain pen, this copy had most recently sold for $3.50, perhaps to the man from whom Milgrim had stolen the coat.

The Flagellant Messiah, as Milgrim imagined him,

was a sort of brightly colored Hieronymus Bosch action figure molded from some very superior grade of Japanese vinyl. Tightly hooded in yellow, the Flagellant Messiah moved about a dun-colored landscape inhabited by other figures as well, all of them rendered in this same vinyl. Some of them were Bosch-influenced: say, an enormous and ambulatory pair of bare buttocks, from between which protruded the wooden shaft of a large arrow. Others, like the Flagellant Messiah, sprang from the stolen history, which he read every night, but after a rather circular fashion. He had never had any interest in this sort of thing before, that he could recall, but now he found it somehow comforting, to have his dreams colored this way.

He saw the IF, for whatever reason, as a bird-headed Bosch creature, pursued by Brown and Brown's people, a brown-hooded posse astride heraldic beasts that weren't quite horses, their swirling banners inscribed with slogans in the IF's Volapuk. Sometimes they journeyed for days into the stylized groves bordering that landscape, glimpsing strange creatures in wooded shadow. At times Brown and the Flagellant Messiah would merge, so that Milgrim sometimes woke from dreams in which Brown tore his own flesh with whips whose barbs were coated with the same grayish green that covered his pistol, flashlight, and monocular.

But this new Devonian sea, the blood-warm shallows in which these visions swam, belonged not to Ativan but to Rize, a Japanese product for which Milgrim had immediately formed a firm respect. There were possibilities inherent in Rize, he sensed, that might only be revealed with further application. There was a sense of mobility that had been lacking recently—though he wondered if that had anything to do with the fact that he was being held captive.

The advent of Rize, though, made it easier to get his head around that concept, captivity, and he was finding that it rankled. He hadn't been in a very good state at all, when Brown had turned up, and someone with Ativan and orders had seemed like not such a bad idea. Indeed, Milgrim reminded himself, he might be dead now, were it not for Brown. Such were the possibilities of seizures, he knew, should he be withdrawn too quickly from medication. And sources, when one had no money, were problematic at best.

But still. How long was one expected to live one's life in the tautly strung fug of Brown's curdled testosterone? "I could be disappeared," said a version of Milgrim's own voice, somewhere within some remaining citadel of self. He might never have used the verb before, in that peculiarly Argentine sense, but now it applied. Or could apply, easily enough. As far as his previous life went, such as it had gotten to be, he'd already been disappeared. Nobody knew where he was, other than his captor. Brown had taken his identification. Milgrim had no cash, no credit card, and he slept in rooms with grayish-green boxes on their doors, to alert Brown should he attempt to leave.

Most crucially, though, there was the matter of medication. Brown provided. Even if Milgrim were to manage to escape, he could only leave with at most a day's supply of functionality. Brown never provided more than that.

He sighed, settling through the warmly rippling amniotic soup of his state.

This was good. This was very good. If only he could take it with him.

11. BOBBYLAND

East on Santa Monica, Alberto steered the Aztec-lacquered VW, Hollis beside him. "Bobby's agoraphobic," he told her, waiting at a light behind a black Jeep Grand Cherokee Laredo with heavily tinted glass. "He doesn't like going out. But he doesn't like sleeping in the same spot twice, so that's hard."

"Was he always like that?" The Cherokee pulled away, ahead, and Alberto followed. She wanted to keep him talking.

"I've known him for the past two years, and I couldn't tell you."

"Does he have a reputation, in the community, for what he does?" Leaving "community" unlabeled, in hope he'd fill a blank or two for her.

"He's the best. He was the chief troubleshooter for a

company in Oregon that designed professional navigation gear, some military stuff. Says they were very innovative."

"But he's down here now helping you put your art
together?"

"Enabling. If it weren't for Bobby, I couldn't get my
stuff up on the grid. Same for the rest of the artists I
know here."

"What about the people who're doing this in New
York, or Tulsa? It's not just an L.A. thing, is it?"

"Global. It's global."

"So who does it for them, what Bobby does?"

"Some of the New York work, Bobby's involved with
that. Linda Morse, she does the bison in Nolita? Bobby.
There are people doing it in New York, London, wherever. But Bobby's ours, here . . ."

"Is he like . . . a producer?" Trusting that he'd know
she meant music, not film.

He glanced over at her. "Exactly, although I'm not
sure I'd want to be quoted."

"Off the record."

"He's like a producer. If someone else were doing what
Bobby's doing for me, my work would be different. Would
reach the audience differently."

"Then would you say that an artist, working in your
medium, who had Bobby's full skill set, would be . . ."

"A better artist?"

"Yeah."

"Not necessarily. The analogy with recording music
holds true. How much of it is the strength of the material,

of the artist, and how much the skill and sensibility of the producer?"

"Tell me about his sensibility."

"Bobby's a tech guy, and a kind of mimetic literalist, without knowing it."

Bobby, she gathered, wasn't going to be afforded too much aesthetic influence here, however enabling he might be.

"He wants it to look 'real,' and he doesn't have to tie himself in knots over what 'real' means. So he gets a kind of punch into the work . . ."

"Like your River?"

"The main thing is, if I didn't have Bobby, I couldn't do any interior pieces. Even some of the exterior installations work better if he triangulates off cell towers. The Fitzgerald piece, he's actually using Virgin's RFID system." He looked worried. "He won't like it, if I bring you."

"If you'd asked him, he would've said no."

"That's right."

She checked a street sign as they crossed an intersection; they were on Romaine now, in a long stretch of low, nondescript, mostly solder-looking industrial buildings. There was very little signage, the rule here seeming to be a tidy anonymity. There would be film vault companies, she guessed, effects houses, even the odd recording studio. The textures were homely, nostalgic: brick, white-washed concrete blocks, painted-over steel-mullioned windows and skylights, wooden power poles supporting massive arrays of transformers. It looked like the world of

American light industry as depicted in a 1950s civics text. Apparently deserted now, though she doubted it would be much busier by day.

Alberto turned off Romaine, pulled over, parked, reached back to get his laptop-and-helmet outfit. "With any luck we'll be able to view some new work," he said.

Out of the car, her PowerBook slung over her shoulder in its bag, she followed him toward a featureless, largely windowless structure of white-painted concrete. He stopped beside a green-painted sheet-metal door, handed her the interface device, and pressed a button, set into concrete, that looked like a design-apport from the Standard.

"Look up there," he said, pointing at nothing in particular, above and to the right of the door. She did, assuming there was a camera, though she couldn't see it. "Bobby," he said, "I know you don't like visitors, let alone uninvited ones, but I think you'll want to make an exception for Hollis Henry." He paused, like a showman. "Check it out. It's her."

Hollis was about to smile in the direction of the invisible camera, then pretended instead that she was being photographed for a Curfew rerelease. She'd had a trademark semi-frown, in those days. If she invoked the era and sort of relaxed into it, that expression might emerge by default.

"Alberto . . . Shit . . . What are you doing?" The voice was tiny, directionless, devoid of gender.

"I've got Hollis Henry from the Curfew out here, Bobby."

"Alberto . . ."

The tiny voice seemed at a loss for words. "I'm sorry," she protested, handing the visor rig back to Alberto. "I don't want to intrude on you. But Alberto's been showing me his art, explaining how important you are to what he's doing, and I—"

The green door rattled, opening inward a few inches. A blond forelock and one blue eye edged past it. This should've looked ridiculous, childish, but she found it frightening. "Hollis Henry," he said, his voice no longer tiny, gender restored. The rest of Bobby's head appeared. He had, as indeed had Inchmale, the true and archaic rock nose. The full-on Townshend-Moon hooter. She only ever found this problematic in males who hadn't become pop musicians; it seemed, then, in some weirdly inverted way, affected. It looked, to her, as though they'd grown large noses in order to look like rock musicians. More weirdly, perhaps, they all tended—certified accountants, radiologists, or whatever—to the flopping forelock that had traditionally gone with it, back in Muswell Hill or Denmark Street. This, she'd once reasoned, must be due in one of two ways to hairdressers. Either they saw the rock mega-nose and dressed the hair above it out of a call to historical tradition, or they weighed the issue in some instinctive, deeply hairdresserly way, arriving at that massive slash and heft of eye-obscuring forelock through some simple sense of balance.

Bobby Chombo hadn't much in the way of a chin, though, so perhaps it all was balance for that.

"Bobby," she said, thrusting out her hand for his. She shook a cool soft hand that felt as though it wanted, though quietly, to be anywhere else at all.

"I wasn't expecting this," he said, opening the door a few more inches. She stepped around it, around his unease, and past him.

And found herself at the edge of an unexpectedly large space. She thought of Olympic pools and indoor tennis courts. The lighting, at least in one central area, was swimming-pool bright: hemispheres of faceted industrial glass and suspended from girders overhead. The floor was concrete, under a coat of some pleasantly gray paint. It was the sort of space she associated with the building of sets and props, or with second-unit photography.

But what was being built here, while possibly very large, was not available to the naked eye. The gray floor had been marked out in what she guessed were two-meter grid squares, loosely drawn in some white powder delivered by one of those spreaders they use on athletic fields. She could see one of these, in fact, a forest-green uniwheeled hopper, propped against the far wall. This grid didn't seem to be perfectly aligned with whatever grid system the city and this building were aligned with, and she made a note to ask about that. In the illuminated area stood two twenty-foot folding tables, gray, attended by a scattering of Aeron chairs and by carts loaded with PCs. It looked to her like workspace for two dozen people, though there didn't seem to be anyone here but this big-nosed Bobby.

She turned back to him. He was wearing an electrically green Lacoste golf shirt, narrow white jeans, and a pair of rubber-soled black canvas sneakers with peculiarly long, sharply pointed toes. He might be thirty, she decided, but not much older. She thought he looked as though his clothes were cleaner than he was; there was still a vertical crease down either side of the front of the knit cotton shirt, the white jeans were spotless, but Bobby himself looked in need of a shower. "Sorry to turn up unannounced," she said, "but I wanted to meet you."

"Hollis Henry." He had his hands in the front pockets of the white jeans. It looked as though it took work, getting hands into those pockets.

"Yes, I am," she said.

"Why'd you bring her here, Alberto?" Bobby wasn't happy.

"I knew you'd want to meet her." Alberto walked over to one of the gray tables and put down his laptop and visor rig.

Beyond the table, something like the shape a child draws to represent a rocket ship had been roughly outlined on the floor in Safety Orange gaffer tape. If she was guessing the size of the grid squares correctly, the pointed shape was a good fifteen meters long. Within it, the white gridlines had been rubbed out.

"Have you got Archie up?" Alberto was looking in the direction of the orange tape outline. "They animate the new skins yet?"

Bobby pulled his hands from the pockets of his jeans and rubbed his face. "I can't believe you did this. Turned up here with her."

"It's Hollis Henry. How cool is that?"

"I'll leave," she said.

Bobby lowered his hands, tossed his forelock, and rolled his eyes to heaven. "Archie's up. Maps are on."

"Hollis," said Alberto, "check it." He was holding what she took to be a VR visor of Bobby's, one that looked nothing like anything you'd find at a garage sale. "Wireless." She walked over to him, took it from him, and put it on. "You're going to love this," he assured her. "Bobby?"

"On my one. Three . . . Two . . ."

"Meet Archie," said Alberto.

Ten feet above the orange tape outline, the glossy, grayish-white form of a giant squid appeared, about ninety feet in total length, its tentacles undulating gracefully. *"Architeuthis,"* Bobby said. Its one visible eye was the size of an SUV tire. "Skins," Bobby said.

The squid's every surface flooded with light, subcutaneous pixels sliding past in distorted video imagery, stylized kanji, wide eyes of anime characters. It was gorgeous, ridiculous. She laughed, delighted.

"It's for a Tokyo department store," Alberto said. "Over a street, in Shinjuku. In the middle of all that neon."

"They're already using this, for advertising?" She walked toward Archie, then under him. The wireless visor made a difference in the experience.

"I have a show there, in November," said Alberto.

Yeah, she thought, looking up at the endless rush of imagery along Archie's distal surface, River would fly, in Tokyo.

12. THE SOURCE

Milgrim dreamed he was naked in Brown's room, while Brown lay sleeping.

It wasn't ordinary nakedness, because it involved an occult aura of preternaturally intense awareness, as though the wearer were a vampire in an Anne Rice novel, or a novice cocaine user.

Brown lay beneath New Yorker sheets and one of those beige hotel blankets that sandwich a sheet of plastic foam between layers of polyester moleskin. Milgrim regarded him with something he recognized as akin to pity. Brown's lips were parted slightly, the upper one quivering slightly with each exhalation.

There was no light at all, in Brown's room, save for the red standby-indicator on the television, but Milgrim's aural dream-self saw, in some other frequency entirely, the furniture and objects in Brown's room presented like screens of carry-on baggage. He saw Brown's pistol and flashlight, beneath Brown's pillow, and a rounded rectangle, beside them, that he took to be a large folding knife (no doubt in that same greenish gray). There was something vaguely touching about Brown sleeping with these favorite things so close to hand, something child-like.

He found that he was imagining himself as Tom Sawyer, Brown as Huckleberry Finn, and these rooms in the New Yorker, and in the other hotels they kept returning to, as their raft, with Manhattan as their chilly Mississippi, down which they floated—when he suddenly noticed that there, on the particleboard cabinet, identical to his own, that housed Brown's television, was a bag. A paper bag. A crumpled paper bag. Within it, revealed by the potent aural vision that was his in his nakedness, and which perhaps made all other things naked, were the unmistakable oblongs of pharmaceutical bubble-packs.

Lots of them. Really quite a number of them. Quite a supply, really. Perhaps a week's worth, if one were frugal.

He craned forward, as if drawn by magnets embedded in the bones of his face—and found himself, having experienced no transition whatever, back in his own airless, overheated room, no longer supernaturally naked but clad in a pair of black cotton briefs that could have done with changing, and with his nose and forehead pressed against the cold glass of his window. Fourteen floors below, Eighth Avenue was virtually empty, save for the yellow rectangle of a passing cab.

His cheeks were wet with tears. He touched them, shivering.

13. BOXES

She stood beneath Archie's tail, enjoying the flood of images rushing from the arrowhead fluke toward the tips of the two long hunting tentacles. Something about Victorian girls in their underwear had just passed, and she wondered if that was part of *Picnic at Hanging Rock*, a film which Inchmale had been fond of sampling on DVD for preshow inspiration. Someone had cooked a beautifully lumpy porridge of imagery for Bobby, and she hadn't noticed it loop yet. It just kept coming.

And standing under it, head conveniently stuck in the wireless helmet, let her pretend she wasn't hearing Bobby hissing irritably at Alberto for having brought her here.

It seemed almost to jump, now, with a flowering rush of silent explosions, bombs blasting against black night. She reached up to steady the helmet, tipping her head back at a particularly bright burst of flame, and accidentally encountered a control surface mounted to the left of the visor, over her cheekbone. The Shinjuku squid and its swarming skin vanished.

Beyond where it had been, as if its tail had been a directional arrow, hung a translucent rectangular solid of silvery wireframe, crisp yet insubstantial. It was large, long enough to park a car or two in, and easily tall enough to walk into, and something about these dimensions seemed familiar and banal. Within it, too, there seemed to be another form, or forms, but because everything was wireframed it all ran together visually, becoming difficult to read.

She was turning, to ask Bobby what this work in progress might become, when he tore the helmet from her head so roughly that she nearly fell over.

This left them frozen there, the helmet between them. Bobby's blue eyes loomed owl-wide behind diagonal blondness, reminding her powerfully of one particular photograph of Kurt Cobain. Then Alberto took the helmet from them both. "Bobby," he said, "you've really got to calm down. This is important. She's writing an article about locative art. For *Node*."

"*Node*?"

"*Node*."

"The fuck is *Node*?"

"Magazine. Like *Wired*. Except it's English."

"Or Belgian," she offered. "Or something."

Bobby looked at them as though they, not he, were crazy.

Alberto tapped the control surface she'd touched accidentally. She saw an LED go out. He carried the unit to the nearer of the two tables and set it down.

"The squid's wonderful, Bobby," she told him. "I'm glad I saw it. I'll go now. Sorry to have disturbed you."

"Fuck it," Bobby said, heaving a sigh of resignation. He crossed to the other table, rummaged through a scattering of small loose objects, and came up with a pack of Marlboro and a pale-blue Bic. They watched as he lit up, then closed his eyes and inhaled deeply. Opening his eyes, he threw his head back and exhaled, the blue smoke rising toward the faceted fixtures. After another hit on the cigarette, he looked at them over it, frowning. "Fucks with me," he said. "I cannot believe how seriously it fucks with me. That was nine hours. Nine. Fucking. Hours."

"You should try the patch," Alberto suggested. He turned to Hollis. "You used to smoke," he said to her, "when you were in the Curfew."

"I quit," she said.

"Did you use the patch?" Bobby drew on his Marlboro again.

"Sort of."

"Sort of how?"

"Inchmale read the original accounts of the English discovering tobacco in Virginia. The tribes they ran into weren't smoking it, not the way we do."

"What were they doing?" Bobby's eyes looked considerably less crazy now, from beneath the thatch.

"Part of it was what we'd call passive smoking, but deliberate. They'd go into a tent and burn a lot of tobacco leaves. But the other thing they were doing was poultices."

"Polt—?" He lowered what was left of the Marlboro.

"Nicotine's absorbed very quickly through the skin. Inchmale would stick a bunch of damp, pulverized tobacco leaf on you, under duct tape—"

"And you quit, that way?" Alberto's eyes were wide.

"Not exactly. It's dangerous. We found out later that you could just drop dead, doing that. Like if you could absorb all the nicotine from a single cigarette, that would be more than a lethal dose. But it was so unpleasant, after a time or two it seemed to work like some kind of aversion therapy." She smiled at Bobby.

"Maybe I'll try that," he said, and flicked ash on the floor. "Where is he?"

"Argentina," she said.

"Is he playing?"

"Gigging a little."

"Recording?"

"Not that I know of."

"And you're doing journalism now?"

"I've always written a little," she said. "Where's your toilet?"

"Far corner." Bobby pointed, away from where she'd seen Archie and the other thing.

As she crossed the floor in the direction indicated, she eyed the grid drawn in what looked like flour. The lines weren't perfectly straight, but close enough. She was careful not to step on or scuff any.

The toilet was a three-staller with a stainless-steel

urinal, newer than the building. She locked the door, hung her bag from the hook inside the first stall, and hauled out her PowerBook. While it booted up, she got settled. There was, as she'd been fairly certain there would be, wifi. Would she like to join the wireless network 72fof-H00av? She would, and did, wondering why an agoraphobic isolationist techie like Bobby wouldn't bother to WEP his wifi, but then she was always surprised at how many people left them open.

She had mail, from Inchmale. She opened it.

Angelina reiterates her concern about your being, however indirectly or only potentially, employed by le Bigend, which she points out is more correctly pronounced "bay-jend," sort of, but seldom is, she says, even by him. More urgently, perhaps, she emailed her good friend Mari at Dazed, and has it back, on very good authority, that your Node must be closely held indeed, as nobody there has ever heard of it. Keeping a magazine moderately secret until you publish would be fairly odd, but your Node no-shows where any mag should show, even if it were being kept under relative wraps.

XOX "male

Another layer added to her general cognitive dissonance, she thought, as she washed her hands. In the mirror, her Mondrian haircut still worked. She put the PowerBook to sleep, and back into her bag.

Having recrossed the wonky grid of flour, she found Alberto and Bobby sitting at one of the tables in Aeron chairs. These had the down-at-heels look that came of having been purchased for some subsequently failed start-up, seized by deputies, auctioned, resold. There were holes in the carbon-gray see-through mesh, where lit cigarettes had touched the taut material.

Strata of blue smoke drifted under the bright lights, reminding her of stadium shows.

Bobby's knees were drawn up to his chin, the nonexistent heels of his Keds-clone winkle-pickers caught in the gray mesh of the Aeron's seat. In the litter on the table he'd turned the chair away from, she made out Red Bull cans, oversized waterproof marking pens, and a candy-like scattering of what she rather reluctantly recognized as white Lego bricks.

"Why white?" She picked one up as she took her own Aeron, twirling on it to face Bobby. "Are these the brown M&Ms of locative computer art?"

"Was it the brown ones they wanted," asked Alberto from behind her, "or was it the brown ones they didn't want?"

Bobby ignored him. "More like duct tape. They're handy if you need to patch electronics together and don't want to scratch-build a chassis. If you stick to one color, it's less confusing visually, and the white's easiest on the eye, and easiest to photograph components against."

She let the Lego roll back into the palm of her hand. "But you can buy them that way, a bag of just white ones?"

"Special order."

"Alberto says you're like a producer. You agree?"

Bobby studied her from behind the forelock. "In some very vague, overgeneralized way? Sort of."

"How did you get into this?"

"I was working on commercial GPS technology. I'd gotten into that because I'd thought I wanted to be an astronomer, and I'd gotten fascinated with satellites. The most interesting ways of looking at the GPS grid, what it is, what we do with it, what we might be able to do with it, all seemed to be being put forward by artists. Artists or the military. That's something that tends to happen with new technologies generally: The most interesting applications turn up on the battlefield, or in a gallery."

"But this one's military to begin with."

"Sure," he said, "but maybe maps were, too. The grid's that basic. Too basic for most people to get a handle on."

"Someone told me that cyberspace was 'everting.' That was how she put it."

"Sure. And once it everts, then there isn't any cyberspace, is there? There never was, if you want to look at it that way. It was a way we had of looking where we were headed, a direction. With the grid, we're here. This is the other side of the screen. Right here." He pushed his hair aside and let both blue eyes drill into her.

"Archie, over there"—she gestured in the direction of empty space—"you're going to hang him over a street in Tokyo."

He nodded.

"But you could do that and still leave him here, couldn't you? You could assign him to two physical locations. You could assign him to any number of locations, couldn't you?"

He smiled.

"And who'd know he was here, then?"

"Right now, if you hadn't been told it was here, there'd be no way for you to find it, unless you had its URL and its GPS coordinates, and if you have those, you know it's here. You know something's here, anyway. That's changing, though, because there are an increasing number of sites to post this sort of work on. If you're logged in to one of those, have an interface device"—he pointed to the helmet—"a laptop and wifi, you're cruising."

She thought about it. "But each one of those sites, or servers, or . . . portals . . . ?"

He nodded. "Each one shows you a different world. Alberto's shows me River Phoenix dead on a sidewalk. Somebody else's shows me, I don't know, only good things. Only kittens, say. The world we walk around in would be channels."

She cocked her head at him. "Channels?"

"Yes. And given what broadcast television wound up being, that doesn't sound so good. But think about blogs, how each one is actually trying to describe reality."

"They are?"

"In theory."

"Okay."

"But when you look at blogs, where you're most likely

to find the real info is in the links. It's contextual, and not only who the blog's linked to, but who's linked to the blog."

She looked at him. "Thanks." She put the piece of white Lego down on the table, beside the origami-beautiful packaging from someone's new iPod. There were the instructions and warranty papers, still heat-sealed in their vinyl bag. A thin white cable, factory-coiled, in another, smaller bag. A bright-yellow rectangle, larger than the Lego. She picked this up, letting her fingers do the thinking. "Then why aren't more people doing it? How's it different from virtual reality? Remember when we were all going to be doing that?" The yellow rectangle was made of die-cast hollow metal, covered with glossy paint. Part of a toy.

"We're all doing VR, every time we look at a screen. We have been for decades now. We just do it. We didn't need the goggles, the gloves. It just happened. VR was an even more specific way we had of telling us where we were going. Without scaring us too much, right? The locative, though, lots of us are already doing it. But you can't just do the locative with your nervous system. One day, you will. We'll have internalized the interface. It'll have evolved to the point where we forget about it. Then you'll just walk down the street . . ." He spread his arms, and grinned at her.

"In Bobbyland," she said.

"You got it."

She turned the yellow thing over, saw MADE IN CHINA

in tiny bas-relief capitals. Part of a toy truck. The box on the trailer. Container. It was a toy shipping container.

And that was what the rectangular volume of wireframe had represented, full scale. A shipping container.

She put the miniature down beside the white Lego, without looking at either.

14. JUANA

He remembered her apartment in San Isidro, near the big train station. Exposed wires crossed the high walls like vines, bare bulbs suspended, pots and pans on sturdy hooks. Her altar there was a maze of objects, charged with meaning. Vials of foul water, the half-assembled plastic kit of a Soviet bomber, a soldier's felt shoulder patch in purple and yellow, old bottles with bubbles trapped within their glass, air from days gone a hundred years or more. These things comprised a mesh, Juana said, about which the deities were more easily manifest. Our Lady of Guadalupe had looked down upon it all, from her painting on the wall.

That altar, like the one here in her Spanish Harlem apartment, had been dedicated primarily to He Who

Opens The Way, and to Ochun, their paired energies never quite in balance, never entirely resting.

The slaves had been forbidden the worship of their home gods, so they had joined the Catholic Church and celebrated them as saints. Each deity had a second, a Catholic face, like the god Babalaye, who was Lazarus, raised by Christ from the dead. Babalaye's dance was the Dance of the Walking Dead. In San Isidro, deep in the long evenings, he had seen Juana smoke cigars, and dance, possessed.

Now he was here with her, these years later, early in the morning, seated before her New York altar, as tidily dusted as the rest of her apartment. Those who didn't know would only think it a shelf, but Tito saw that her oldest bottles were there, the ones with ancient weather trapped in their cores.

He had just finished describing the old man.

Juana no longer smoked cigars. Nor danced, he supposed, though he wouldn't bet on it. She reached forward and from a small plate on her altar took four pieces of coconut meat. She passed the fingers of her other hand across the floor, before kissing the fingertips and their wholly symbolic dust. She closed her eyes, praying briefly in the language that Tito could not understand. She asked a question in that language, her tone firm, shook the coconut pieces in her cupped hands, and tossed them down. She sat, elbows on her knees, considering them.

"All have fallen meat to heaven. It speaks of justice."

She collected them and threw them again. Two up, two down. She nodded. "Confirmation."

"Of what?"

"I asked what comes with this man who troubles you. He troubles me as well." She tossed the four shards of coconut into a tin Dodgers wastebasket. "The orishas may sometimes serve us as oracles," she said, "but that doesn't mean they'll tell us much, or even that they'll know what will happen."

He moved to assist her, when she rose, but she brushed his hands away. She wore a dull-gray dress with a zippered front, like a uniform, and a matching kerchief, or babushka, beneath which she was largely bald. Her eyes were dark amber, their whites yellowed like ivory. "I will make your breakfast now."

"Thank you." It would have been useless to decline, though he had no desire to do that. She shuffled slowly toward her kitchen in gray slippers that seemed to match her institutional dress.

"Do you remember your father's place at Alamar?" Over her shoulder from the kitchen.

"The buildings looked like plastic bricks."

"Yes," she said, "they wanted it as much like Smolensk as possible. I thought it perverse of your father, to live there. He had his choice, after all, and so few did."

He stood, the better to watch her old hands patiently slice and butter the bread for the toaster oven, fill the tiny stovetop aluminum espresso maker with water and coffee, put milk in a steel jug.

"He had choices, your father. More perhaps than had your grandfather." She looked back, meeting his eyes.

"Why was that?"

"Your grandfather was very powerful, in Cuba, though secretly, while the Russians stood to remain. Your father was a powerful man's first son, his favorite. But your grandfather had known, of course, that the Russians would be going, that things would change. When they left, in 1991, he anticipated the 'special period,' the shortages and deprivation, anticipated Castro reaching for the very symbol of his archenemies, the American's dollar, and of course he anticipated his own subsequent loss of power. I will tell you a secret, though, about your grandfather."

"Yes?"

"He was a Communist." She laughed, a startlingly girlish sound in the tiny kitchen, as though someone else might be there. "More a Communist than a santero. He believed. All the ways things failed, and in the ways we knew, that the ordinary people could not know, and still, in his way, he believed. He, like myself, had been to Russia. He, like myself, had had eyes to see. Still, he believed." She shrugged, smiling. "I think that it allowed him some extra degree of leverage, some special grasp, on those to whom we, through him, had become fastened. They had always sensed that about him, that he might believe. Not in the tragic, clownish fashion of the East Germans, but with something like innocence." The smell of toasting bread filled the kitchen. She used a small bamboo whisk to froth the milk, as it neared boiling. "Of course, they had no way to prove it. And everyone purported to believe, at least publicly."

"Why do you say that he had fewer choices?"

"The head of a large family has duties. And we had already become a different sort of family, a firma, as we are today. He put his family before his desire for a more perfect state. If it had been him, alone, I believe he would have stayed. Perhaps he would be alive today. Your father's death, of course, strongly affected his decision to bring us here. Sit." She brought a yellow tray to the small table, with the tostada on a white saucer, and a large white cup of café con leche.

"This man, he enabled Grandfather to bring us here?"

"In a sense."

"What does that mean?"

"Too many questions."

He smiled up at her. "Is he CIA?"

She glowered at him from beneath the gray kerchief. The pale tip of her tongue appeared at the corner of her mouth, then vanished. "Was your grandfather DGI?"

Tito dunked and chewed a piece of his tostada, considering. "Yes."

"There you are," said Juana. "Of course he was." She brushed her wrinkled hands together, as if wishing to be free of the traces of something. "But who did he work for? Think of our saints, Tito. Two faces. Always, two."

15. SPIV

Inchmale had always been balding and intense, and Inchmale had always been middle-aged—even when she first met him, when they were both nineteen. People who really liked the Curfew tended to like Inchmale or to like her, but seldom both. Bobby Chombo, she thought, as Alberto drove her back to the Mondrian, was one of the former. But that had been a good thing, really, because it had meant that she'd been able to lay out her best public pieces of Inchmale without revealing herself, then shuffle them, palm them, rearrange them, withdraw them, to help keep him talking. She'd never asked Inchmale, but she took it for granted he did the same with her.

And it hadn't hurt that Bobby was himself a musician,

though not in the old plays-a-physical-instrument-and/
or-sings modality. He took things apart, sampled them,
mashed them up. This was fine with her, though like
General Bosquet watching the charge of the Light Bri-
gade, she was inclined to think it wasn't war. Inchmale
understood it, though, and indeed had championed it,
as soon as it was digitally possible, pulling guitar lines
out of obscure garage chestnuts and stretching them,
like a mad jeweler elongating sturdy Victorian tableware
into something insectile, post-functionally fragile, and
neurologically dangerous.

She'd also assumed that she had Bobby's Marlboro
binge on her side, though she'd noticed that she was starting to count his smokes, and to worry, as he neared the
bottom of his pack, about having one herself. She'd tried
distracting herself with sips of room-temperature Red
Bull from a previously unopened can she'd excavated from
the table clutter, but it had only made her bug-eyed with
caffeine, or perhaps with taurine, the drink's other famous ingredient, extracted supposedly from the testicles
of bulls. Bulls generally looked more placid than she now
felt, or perhaps those were cows. She didn't know cattle.

Bobby Chombo's sampling talk had helped her make
a kind of sense of him, of his annoying shoes and his
tight white pants. He was, basically, a DJ. Or DJ-like, in
any case, which was what counted. His day job, trouble-
shooting navigational systems or whatever it was, made a
sort of sense too. It was, often as not, the wonk side of
being DJ-like, and often as not the side that paid the
rent. Either it was his wonk-hipster thing that had so

strongly evoked Inchmale for her, or that he was the sort of jerk that Inchmale had always been able to handle so efficiently. Because, she supposed, Inchmale had been more or less that sort of jerk himself.

"It went better than I expected it to," said Alberto, interrupting her thoughts. "He's a difficult person to get to know."

"I went to a gig in Silverlake, a couple of years ago, what they call reggaeton. Sort of reggae-salsa fusion."

"Yeah?"

"Chombo. The DJ was a big deal in that scene: El Chombo."

"That's not Bobby."

"I'll say. But why's our Bobby white-guy a Chombo too?"

Alberto grinned. "He likes people to wonder about that. But his Chombo's a kind of software."

"Software?"

"Yes."

She decided there wasn't much to be thought about that, at this point. "He sleeps there?"

"He doesn't go out, unless he has to."

"You said he won't sleep twice in the same square of that grid."

"Never mention that to him, no matter what, okay?"

"And he does gigs? DJs?"

"He podcasts," Alberto said.

Her cell rang.

"Hello?"

"Reg."

"I was just thinking about you."

"Why was that?"

"Another time."

"Get my e-mail?"

"I did."

"Angelina asked me to call, re-reiterate. Ree-ree."

"I get the message, thanks. I don't think there's much I can do about it, though, except do what I'm doing and see what happens."

"Are you taking some sort of seminar?" he asked.

"Why?"

"You sounded uncharacteristically philosophical, just then."

"I saw Heidi, earlier."

"Christ," said Inchmale. "Was she walking on her hind legs?"

"She drove past me in a very nice-looking car. Headed in the direction of Beverly Hills."

"She's been headed in that direction since the birth canal."

"I'm with someone, Reg. Have to go."

"Toodles." He was gone.

"Was that Reg Inchmale?" Alberto asked.

"Yes, it was."

"You saw Heidi Hyde tonight?"

"Yes, while you were getting rousted in Virgin. She drove past on Sunset."

"Wow," said Alberto. "How likely is that?"

"Statistically, who knows? Subjectively, feels to me,

not so weird. She lives in Beverly Hills, works in Century City."

"Doing what?"

"Something in her husband's company. He's a tax lawyer. With his own production company."

"Eek," said Alberto, after a pause, "there really is a life after rock."

"You'd better believe it," she assured him.

ODILE'S ROBOT appeared to have died, or to be hibernating. It sat there by the drapes, inert and unfinished-looking. Hollis nudged it with the toe of her Adidas.

There were no messages on the hotel voice mail.

She got her PowerBook out of the bag, woke it, and tried holding the back of the open screen against the window. Did she want to rejoin trusted wireless network SpaDeLites47? Yes, please. SpaDeLites47 had treated her right, before. She assumed SpaDeLites47 was in the period apartment building across the street.

No mail. One-handed, supporting the laptop with her other, she Googled "bigend."

First up was a Japanese site for "BIGEND," but this seemed to be a brand of performance motor oil for dragsters.

She tried the link for his Wikipedia entry.

Hubertus Hendrik Bigend, born June 7, 1967, in Antwerp, is the founder of the innovative global advertising agency Blue Ant. He is the only child of Belgian industrialist Benoît Bigend and Belgian sculptor Phaedra Seynhaev. Much has been made, by Bigend's admirers and detractors alike, of his mother's early links with the Situationist International (Charles Saatchi was famously but falsely reported to have described him as "a jumped-up Situationist spiv") but Bigend himself has declared that the success of Blue Ant has entirely to do with his own gifts, one of which, he claims, is the ability to find precisely the right person for a given project. He is very much a hands-on micromanager, in spite of the firm's remarkable growth in the past five years.

Her cell began to ring, in her bag, back on the table. If she moved the PowerBook, she'd lose the wifi from across the street, though this page would still be cached. She crossed to the table, put the laptop down on it, and dug her phone out of her bag. "Hello?"

"Hubertus Bigend, for Hollis Henry."

It sounded as though her phone had received some sort of corporate upgrade. She froze, out of primeval fear that he'd caught her Googling him, peering into his Wiki.

"Mr. Bigend," she said, giving up on the idea of any attempt at the Franco-Belgian pronunciation.

"Miss Henry. Consider us introduced, shall we? You may have no idea why I'm calling. The *Node* start-up, you see, is a project of mine."

"I've only just Googled you." She opened her mouth wide, wider, in the silent scream that Inchmale had taught her reduces tension.

"Ahead of the game, then. What we want in a journalist. I've just spoken myself with Rausch, in London."

If Rausch is in London, she wondered, then where are you? "Where are you?"

"I'm in the lobby of your hotel. I was wondering if you might like a drink."

16. KNOWN EXITS

Milgrim was reading the *New York Times*, finishing his breakfast coffee in a bakery on Bleecker, while Brown conducted a series of quiet, tense, and extremely pissed-off conversations with whoever was supposed to be in charge of watching the IF's known exits, when the IF was home sleeping—or whatever the IF did, when he was home. "Known exits" seemed to Milgrim to imply that the IF's neighborhood might be riddled with gaslit opium tunnels and the odd subterranean divan, a possibility Milgrim found appealing, however unlikely.

Whoever was on the other end of this particular call was not having a good morning. The IF and another male had left the IF's building, walked to the Canal Street subway, entered, and vanished. Milgrim knew, from having also overheard Brown's half of other conversations, that the IF and his family tended to do that, and particularly around subways. Milgrim imagined that the IF and his family had the keys to some special kind of subway-based porosity, a way into the cracks and holes and spaces between things.

Milgrim himself was having a better morning than he recalled having had in some time, and this in spite of Brown's having shaken him awake to translate Volapuk. Then he'd fallen back into some dream he could no longer remember, not a pleasant one, something about blue light coming from his skin, or beneath it. But all in all very pleasant to be here in the Village this early in the day, having coffee and a pastry and enjoying the *Times* someone had left.

Brown didn't like the *New York Times*. Brown actually didn't like news media of any kind, Milgrim had come to understand, because the news conveyed did not issue from any reliable, that was to say, governmental, source. Nor could it, really, under present conditions of war, as any genuine news, news of any strategic import whatever, was by definition precious, and not to be wasted on the nation's mere citizenry.

Milgrim certainly wasn't going to argue with any of that. If Brown had declared the Queen of England to be a shape-shifting alien reptile, craving the warm flesh of human infants, Milgrim would not have argued.

But midway through a third-page piece on the NSA and data mining, something occurred to Milgrim. "Say," he said to Brown, who'd just ended a call and was looking at his phone as if he wished he knew a way to torture it, "this NSA data-mining thing . . ."

It hung there, between them, somewhere above the table. He wasn't in the habit of initiating conversations with Brown, and for good reason. Brown looked from the phone to Milgrim, his expression unchanged.

"I was thinking," Milgrim heard himself say, "about your IF. About the Volapuk. If the NSA can do what it says they can, here, then it should be pretty easy to fold an algorithm into the mix that would grab your Volapuk and nothing else. You wouldn't even need much of a sample of their family dialect. You could just find half a dozen dialectal examples of the form and shoot for a kind of average. Anything that went through the phone system, after that, that had that tag, bingo. You wouldn't need to be changing any more batteries on the IF's coat-rack."

Milgrim was genuinely pleased with having thought of this. But Brown, he saw, was not happy with Milgrim for having thought of it. "That's only good for overseas calls," Brown said, and seemed to be considering whether or not to hit him.

"Ah," Milgrim said. He put his head down and pretended to read, until Brown got back on the phone, quietly chewing someone else out for losing the IF and the other male.

Milgrim couldn't get back into his article, but continued to pretend to read the paper. Something was working its way up, inside him, from some new and peculiarly discomfiting angle. So far he'd taken it for granted that Brown, and by extension his people, were government agents of some kind, presumably federal. And yet, if the NSA had been doing what this *Times* article said they had been doing, and he, Milgrim, was reading about it, why should he suppose that what Brown had said was true? The reason Americans weren't freaking out over this NSA thing, Milgrim assumed, was that they'd already been taking it for granted, since at least the 1960s, that the CIA was tapping everybody's phone. It was the stuff of bad episodic television. It was something little kids knew to be true.

But if there were Volapuk being texted in Manhattan, and the real government really needed it as badly as Brown seemed to need it, wouldn't they get it? Milgrim folded his paper.

But what if, asked the upwardly burrowing voice, Brown was not really a government agent? There had until now been some part of Milgrim willing to suppose that being held captive by federal agents was in a sense the same as being under their protection. While the majority of him had suspected this was a dubious formulation, it had taken something, perhaps the new calm and perspective afforded by his change of medication, to bring him to this moment of unified awareness: What if Brown was just an asshole with a gun?

It was something to think about, and to his surprise he found that he could. "I need to use the washroom," he said.

Brown muted his phone. "There's a back door," he

said, "out the kitchen. Someone's out there, in case you think you're leaving. If they thought you might get away, they'd shoot you."

Milgrim nodded. Got up. He wasn't going to run, but for the first time, he thought Brown might be bluffing.

In the washroom he ran cool water over his wrists, then looked at his hands. They were still his. He wiggled his fingers. Amazing, really.

17. PIRATES AND TEAMS

The front of her Mondrian haircut had started to remind her of Bobby Chombo's elephantiasis-of-the-forelock, the result of an ongoing interaction of product with particulates. Whatever the stylist had applied had by now sucked in every molecule of the brew that was the air of the L.A. basin, plus however many cigarettes Bobby Chombo had recently smoked in her immediate vicinity.

None of this looks very good, she thought, meaning not so much the generally poor appearance she felt she was able to muster, to meet her new employer, but the overall arc and apparent direction of her life so far. Everything, right that minute, down to Chombo and his gridded floor. Chombo afraid to sleep in the same grid square twice . . .

But still. Lip gloss. Earrings. Top and skirt and hose from the worse-for-wear Barneys bag she was using to separate dress-up from workaday.

For a purse, she chose one of her black makeup bags, dumped it, refilled it minimally. The shoes from the dress-up bag were mutant black ballet slippers, by a Catalan designer long since gone into some other field.

"Out of here," she told the woman in the mirror.

Once again ignoring the video art in the elevator.

The door opened on the buzz and tinkle of Starck's lobby in late-evening bar mode. A brown-haired bellman, in trademark pale suit, stood centered in the projected faux-Islamic squiggles of the carpet-of-light device, smiling mightily in her direction.

This functionary's teeth, illuminated by the accidental fall of a single sunny squiggle, were presented with billboard clarity. As she approached him, scanning for her Belgian advertising magnate, the smile increased in both width and magnitude, till, as she was about to pass, the luxurious tones last heard on her cell emerged, startling her: "Miss Henry? Hubertus Bigend."

Instead of screaming, she took his hand, finding it firm, dry, and of a neutral temperature. He squeezed hers lightly in return, his smile expanding still further.

"Pleased to meet you, Mr. Bigend."

"Hubertus," he insisted, "please. Are you finding the hotel satisfactory?"

"Yes, thanks." What she'd taken for a Mondrian doorman's suit was crisp beige wool. His sky-blue shirt was open at the collar.

"Shall we try Skybar?" he asked, consulting a watch the size of a small ashtray. "Unless you'd prefer something here." He indicated the high, narrow, surrealistically long alabaster table, atop some number of tall, biomorphic Starck legs, that was the lobby bar.

There's safety in numbers, said an inner voice that wanted to stay right here, have the required drink and the absolute polite minimum of talk.

"Skybar," she opted, not certain why, but recalling that it might well be impossible to get in, let alone get a table. As he led her toward the pool and the shed-sized flowerpots, each with its ficus tree, she recalled fragments from the last few times she'd been here, at the end of and just after the Curfew's official cessation. People who didn't know the music industry, Inchmale said, believed that the movie business was the ne plus ultra of vicious, asshole-chewing, hyena-like behavior.

They passed a Brobdingnagian futon, in whose squishy depths a covey of vicious, asshole-chewing, hyena-like, and exceptionally pretty young people reclined with their drinks. But you don't know that about them, she reminded herself; it was just that they looked like A&R people. But then almost everyone here did.

He led her past the bouncer as though the bouncer weren't there. Indeed, the Bluetoothed bouncer was hard pressed to get out of Bigend's way in time, so thoroughly did it seem that Bigend was unaccustomed to anyone being in his way.

The bar was packed, as she remembered it having always been, but he had no trouble getting them a table.

Looking broad, bright-eyed, and, she supposed, Belgian, he held her heavy, library-style oak chair for her. "I was quite a fan of the Curfew," he said to her ear.

And a huge Goth altogether, I'll bet, she resisted replying. The idea of a baby Belgian advertising magnate raising his Bic in some darkened Curfew concert was best left unexamined. These days, according to Inchmale, they raised their cell phones, and the screens gave out quite a startling amount of light. "Thank you," she said, leaving it ambiguous as to whether she was thanking him for having told her he'd liked the Curfew, or for having held her chair.

Seated opposite her now, beige elbows on the table, manicured fingers steepled in front of him, he was managing a good approximation of the look she was given by male Hollis Henry aficionados who were actually seeing some private inner version of Anton Corbijn's portrait of her, the one in the deconstructed tweed miniskirt.

"My mother," he began on an unexpected note, "enjoyed the Curfew immensely. She was a sculptor. Phaedra Seynhaev. When I visited her Paris studio for the last time, she was playing you. Loudly." He smiled.

"Thank you." She decided not to go with the dead mother. "But I'm a journalist now. No credentials to coast on, there."

"Rausch is very pleased with you as a journalist," he said. "He wants you on staff." Their waiter arrived, and went away for Hollis's gin-tonic and Bigend's piso mojado, a new one on Hollis.

"Tell me about *Node*," she suggested. "It doesn't seem to be generating much in the way of industry gossip."

"No?"

"No."

He lowered his finger-steeple. "Anti-buzz," he said. "Definition by absence."

She waited to see if he'd indicate that he was joking. He didn't. "That's ridiculous."

The smile unshuttered, gleamed, shuttered, and then their drinks arrived, in disposable plastic that protected the hotel against barefoot poolside litigations. She afforded herself a quick scan of the rest of the clientele. Were a cruise missile just then to impact the corrugated roof of Skybar, she decided, there would be no great need for *People* to change its next cover. The fancy, as Inchmale had called them, seemed to have moved on. Just as well, for present purposes. "Tell me," she said, leaning slightly forward over her gin.

"Yes?"

"Chombo. Bobby Chombo. Why did Rausch make such a point of my meeting him?"

"Rausch is the story's editor," he said, mildly. "Perhaps you should ask him."

"Something else is going on," she pressed. She felt as though she were marching out to confront the Mongolian Death Worm on its own ground; probably not that good an idea, but somehow she knew she must. "His urgency didn't feel to me like part of the story."

Bigend studied her. "Ah. Well. Part of another story,

then. A much bigger one. Your second *Node* story, we hope. And you've just come from meeting him— Chombo?"

"Yes."

"And what did you think?"

"He knows he knows something nobody else does. Or thinks he does."

"And what do you think that might be, Hollis? May I call you Hollis?"

"Please do. I don't think Bobby's all that keen on his position in any locative avant-garde. He likes being on top of any breaking phenomenon, I'd guess, but is basically bored with the grunt work. When he was helping to invent the context of the locative thing, to whatever extent he did, he probably wasn't bored."

Bigend's smile opened again. It reminded her of the lights in another train when trains pass at night, going in opposite directions. Then it closed. It was like she'd entered a tunnel. "Go on." He sipped his piso, which looked a lot like NyQuil.

"And it's not DJ-ing," she said, "or making mash-ups, or whatever else he does publicly. It's whatever makes him mark the floor of that factory according to the GPS grid. He won't sleep in the same square twice. Whatever makes him confident he's important is also what's making him crazy."

"And that might be?"

She thought of the wireframed cargo container, how Chombo had so abruptly tried to yank the helmet off her head, almost pulling her over. She hesitated.

"Pirates," he said.

"Pirates?"

"The Straits of Malacca and the South China Sea. Small, fast boats, preying on cargo vessels. They operate from lagoons, coves, islets. The Malay Peninsula. Java, Borneo, Sumatra . . ."

She looked from Bigend to the crowd around them, feeling like she'd fallen into someone else's pitch meeting. A ghostly studio log line, left to hover near the bar's massively timbered, corrugated ceiling, had fallen on her, the first likely victim to sit at this table. A pirate movie. "Arrrr," she said, meeting his gaze again and downing the last of her gin-tonic, "matey."

"Real pirates," Hubertus Bigend said, unsmiling. "Most of them, anyway."

"Most?"

"Some of them were part of a covert CIA maritime program." He put his empty plastic glass down as though it were something he was considering bidding on at Sotheby's. He framed it with his fingers, a director considering a shot. "Stopping suspect cargo vessels to search for weapons of mass destruction." He looked up at her, unsmiling.

"Irony-free?"

He nodded, a tiny movement, very precise.

Thus perhaps did diamond factors nod in Antwerp, she thought. "This isn't bullshit, Mr. Bigend?"

"It's as expensively quasi-factual as I can afford it to be. Material like this tends to squirm a bit, as you can well imagine. One rather deep irony, I suppose, is that this program, which had apparently been fairly effective, fell victim to blowback from your domestic political struggles here. Prior to certain revelations, though, and to the name of a cover company being made public, CIA teams, disguised as pirates, accompanied real pirates boarding merchant vessels suspected of smuggling weapons of mass destruction. Using radiation detectors, and other things, they inspected cargo holds and containers, while the real pirates took whatever more mundane cargo they chose to acquire. That was the payoff for the pirates, that they could have their pick of cargo, provided the teams were given a first look at all of the holds and containers."

"Containers."

"Yes. Pirates and teams provided one another with mutual backup. The teams would have amply bribed any local authorities, and of course the U.S. Navy would stay well away when one of these operations was under way. The ships' crews were never the wiser, whether contraband was discovered or not. If something were found, the interdiction came later, nothing to do with our pirates." He gestured to a waiter for another piso. "Another drink?"

"Mineral water," she said. "Joseph Conrad. Kipling. Or a movie."

"The pirates who proved best at this were out of Aceh, in northern Sumatra. Prime Conrad territory, I believe."

"Were they finding much, the faux pirates?"

The diamond factor's nod again.

"Why are you telling me this?"

"In August 2003, one of these joint CIA-pirate operations boarded a freighter with Panamanian registry,
bound from Iran to Macau. The team's interest centered
on one particular container. They'd broken its seals,
opened it, when orders came by radio to leave it."

"Leave it?"

"Leave the container. Leave the vessel. Those orders
were followed, of course."

"Who told you that story?"

"Someone who claims to have been a member of the
boarding team."

"And you think that Chombo, somehow, has something to do with that?"

"I suspect," Bigend said, leaning closer and lowering
his voice, "that Bobby periodically knows where that
container is."

"Periodically?"

"Apparently it's still out there, somewhere," Bigend
said, "Like the Flying Dutchman." His second piso arrived, along with her water. "To your next story," he
toasted, touching the rims of their fresh plastic glasses.

"The pirates."

"Yes?"

"Did they see what was in it?"

"No."

"MOST PEOPLE don't self-drive these," Bigend said, pulling
out onto Sunset, headed east.

"Most people don't drive them at all," Hollis corrected, from the passenger seat beside him. She craned her neck for a glimpse back into what she supposed could be called the passenger cabin. There seemed to be a sort of frosted skylight, as opposed to any mere moonroof. And a lot of very glossy wood, the rest in carbon-colored lambskin.

"A Brabus Maybach," he said, as she turned her head in time to see him give the wheel a little pat. "The firm of Brabus extensively tweaks the product of Maybach, to produce one of these."

" 'Darth my ride'?"

"If you were riding in back, you could watch for locative art on the monitors in each front seatback. There's MWAN and a fourplex GPRS router."

"No thanks." The seats back there, upholstered in that gunmetal lamb, obviously reclined, becoming beds, or possibly chairs for high-end elective surgery. Through the smoked glass at her side, she saw pedestrians at the intersection, staring at the Maybach. The light changed and Bigend pulled away. The vehicle's interior was still as a museum at midnight. "Do you always drive this?" she asked.

"The agency has Phaetons," he said. "Good stealth cars. Mistake them for Jettas, at a distance."

"I'm not a car person." She ran her thumb along a lambskin seat seam. Like touching the butt of a supermodel, probably.

"Why have you decided to interest yourself in journalism, if you don't mind my asking?"

"Looking for a way to make a living. Curfew royalties don't amount to much. I haven't been that talented an investor."

"Few people are," he said. "If they're successful at it, of course, then they imagine they are. Talented. But they're all doing the same things, really."

"I wish someone had told me what they're doing, in that case."

"If you need to earn money, there are more lucrative fields than journalism."

"Are you discouraging me?"

"Not at all. I'm simply encouraging you in a broader way. I'm interested in what motivates you, and how you understand the world." He glanced sideways at her. "Rausch tells me you've written about music."

"Sixties garage bands. I started writing about them when I was still in the Curfew."

"Were they an inspiration?"

She was watching a fourteen-inch display on the Maybach's dash, the red cursor that was the car proceeding along the green line that was Sunset. She looked up at him. "Not in any linear way, musically. They were my favorite bands. Are," she corrected herself.

He nodded.

She glanced back down at the dash display and found the street map gone, replaced by wireframe diagrams of a helicopter, its bulbous profile unfamiliar. Now it appeared above the wireframe profile of a ship. Either a small ship or quite a large helicopter. Cut to video of the actual aircraft in flight. "What's this?"

"The Hook, so-called. It's an older, Soviet-made helicopter, one with tremendous lifting capacity. Syria owns at least one of them."

The Hook, or another just like it, was lifting a Soviet tank now, as if in demonstration. "Drive," she ordered. "Don't be watching your own PowerPoint."

Cut to a colorful, simplified animation, illustrating how a helicopter (not looking very Hook-like) could shuffle cargo containers on the deck and in the holds of a freighter. "The container in your story," she began.

"Yes?"

"Did they say whether it was very heavy?"

"It's not, that we know of," said Bigend, "but it's sometimes at the center of a stack of much heavier containers. That's a very secure position, as there's ordinarily no way at all, at sea, to access a container in that position. The Hook, though, would allow you to do that. Plus you could have arrived from somewhere else, another ship say, with your container Hooked. Decent cruising range, reasonably fast."

He got on the 101 Freeway, southbound. The Maybach's suspension turned the pockmarked pavement into something silken, smooth as warm fudge. She could sense the car's power now, held effortlessly in check. On the dash display, lines symbolizing signals were being emitted by a shipping container. They rose at a sharp angle, to be intercepted by a satellite, which bounced them back down, past the curve of the earth. "Where are we going, Mr. Bigend?"

"Hubertus. To the agency. It's a better place to discuss things."

"Agency?"

"Blue Ant."

And here on the display, now, unmoving and crisply hieroglyphic, was that insect itself. Blue. She looked back up at him.

His profile vaguely reminded her of someone.

18. ELLEGGUA'S WINDOW

Tia Juana sent him walking, crosstown along 110th, to Amsterdam and the Cathedral of St. John the Divine, the better to consult Elleggua. The owner, she said, of the roads and doors in this world. Lord of the crossroads, intersection of the human and the divine. For this reason, Juana maintained, there had secretly been raised a window to him and a place of devotion, in this great church in Morningside Heights.

"Nothing can be done in either world," she said, "without his permission."

It had begun to snow, as he walked uphill, past chicken wire and poster-crusted plywood, where the retaining wall of the cathedral's grounds had been brought down, long ago, by rain. He turned up his collar, settled his hat, and walked on, no stranger now to snow. Though he was grateful, finally, to reach Amsterdam. He saw the unlit neon of V&T Pizza, like something pointing to the avenue's ordinary human past, and then he was passing the priest's house, and the garden that surrounded the perpetually dry fountain, with its delirious sculpture, where the decapitated head of Satan dangled from the great bronze claw of the Holy Crab of God. It was this sculpture that had most interested him, when Juana first brought him here, that and the cathedral's four peacocks, one of them albino and, Juana said, sacred to Orunmila.

There were no guards at the cathedral's doors, but he found them within, waiting, with their suggestion of five dollars' donation. Juana had shown him how to remove his hat, and cross himself, and, ignoring them, pretending he spoke no English, to light a candle and pretend to pray.

So large a space, within this church; Juana said the largest cathedral in the world. And this morning of snow he found it deserted, or seemingly so, and somehow colder than the street. There was a fog here, a cloud, of sound; the tiniest echoes, set moving by any movement, seemed to stir ceaselessly among the columns and across the stone floor.

Leaving his candle burning beside four others, he went in the direction of the main altar, watching his own breath, and pausing once to look back at the dim glow of the giant rose window, above the doors through which he'd come.

One of the bays of stone that lined the sides of this

tremendous space was Elleggua's, and this was made
clear by images in colored glass. A santero consulting a
sheet of signs, among which would be found the numbers three and twenty-one, whereby the orisha recog-
nizes himself and is recognized; a man climbing a pole to
install a wiretap; another man studying the monitor of a
computer. All images of ways in which the world and
worlds are linked, and all these ways under the orisha.

Silently, within himself, as Juana had taught him,
Tito made respectful greeting.

There was a disturbance in the fog of sound, then,
louder than the rest, its source lost immediately in the
turning and stirring of echo. Tito glanced back, down the
length of the nave, and saw a single figure, approaching.

He looked up, to Elleggua's window, where one man
used something like a mouse, another a keyboard,
though the shapes of these familiar things were archaic,
unfamiliar. He asked to be protected.

The old man, when Tito looked back, was like some
illustration of perspective and the inevitability of the
given moment's arrival. Snow dusted the shoulders of
the man's tweed coat, and the brim of a dark hat held
against his chest. His head seemed bowed, slightly, as he
walked. His gray hair shone like steel, against the dull
putty tones of the cathedral's stone.

And then he was there, unmoving, directly in front of
Tito. He looked very directly into Tito's eyes, then up,
at the window. "Gutenberg," he said, raising his hat to
indicate the santero. "Samuel Morse sending the first

message," indicating the man using the mouse. "A line-man. A television set." This last was what Tito had taken for a monitor. He lowered the hat. His gaze returned to Tito. "You resemble both your father and grandfather, strongly," he said in Russian.

"Did she tell you I would be here?" Tito asked, in Spanish.

"No," the old man replied, his accent that of an older Cuba, "it was not to be my pleasure. A formidable woman, your aunt. I had you followed here." He switched to English: "It has been some time, since you and I have seen one another."

"Verdad."

"But we will be seeing one another again, and soon," the old man said. "You will be given another, identical item. You will bring it to me, as before. As before, you will be observed, followed."

"Alejandro was correct, then?"

"No fault of yours. Your protocol is highly correct, your systema adroit," injecting the Russian term into his English sentence. "It was made quite certain that you would be followed. We require it."

Tito waited.

"They will attempt to seize us," the man said, "as you make the delivery. They will fail, but you will have lost the item to them. That is essential, as essential as your escape, and my own. And you have a systema for exactly that, do you not?"

Tito nodded, moving his head only slightly.

"But then," said the old man, "you will be going away, as you've been prepared for. The city will no longer be safe for you. Do you understand?"

Tito thought of his windowless room. His computer. His keyboard. The vase for Ochun. He remembered the protocol established for his departure, carefully maintained. He had absolutely no idea what place would have been chosen for him, beyond that protocol. He only knew that it would not be New York. "I understand," he said, in Russian.

"There is an arch, here," the old man said, in English, "called the Pearl Harbor Arch." He looked up, and back along the nave. "It was pointed out to me, once, but I can no longer recall where it is. The masons laid down their tools, the day of the attack. The construction of the cathedral lapsed for decades."

Tito turned and looked up, uncertain as to what he was supposed to be looking for. The arches were so high overhead. He and Alejandro had once played with a helium-filled Mylar blimp, in Battery Park. A small radio-controlled airship. With such a thing, here, one could explore the nave's forest of arches, the shadows of its inverted deep-sea canyon. He wanted to ask this man about his father, ask him how and why his father had died.

When he turned back, the man was gone.

19. FISH

Brown took Milgrim back to the Korean-owned laundry on Lafayette Street, for parking. From what Milgrim had heard of Brown's end of the morning's cellular traffic, Brown felt that his team needed more talking-to about having lost the IF.

This time, Brown didn't bother to remind Milgrim that there were watchers outside, or that attempting to escape would be both futile and painful. Brown was starting to assume, Milgrim decided, that he, Milgrim, had internalized the watchers (whether they existed or not, and Milgrim now doubted they ever had). This was interesting, Milgrim thought.

Brown didn't say goodbye. Just turned and headed down the west side of Lafayette.

Milgrim and the Korean owner, a man in his seventies,

with an ageless and curiously nonreflective simulacrum of Kim Jong Il's jet-black haircut, eyed each other neutrally. Milgrim supposed Brown had some arrangement here, as the Korean never asked where Milgrim's laundry was, or why it was, otherwise, that Milgrim would sit for hours at the westernmost end of a red vinyl settee, either reading his medieval messianism book, thumbing through the Korean's dead gossip magazines, or just staring into space.

Milgrim unbuttoned the Paul Stuart, but seated himself without removing it. He looked at the thick compost of celebrity features on the coffee table in front of him (did navels count as features?) and noted the issue of *Time* with the president dressed up like a pilot, on the flight deck of that aircraft carrier. That issue was nearly three years old now, he decided, after some calculation, older than the majority of these gossip mags—which Milgrim did sometimes resort to, if twelfth-century messianism proved inconveniently soporific, as it certainly could. If he nodded out here, he'd learned, the Korean would come over and prod him in the ribs with a rolled-up *Us*.

At the moment, however, he was ready for William the Goldsmith and the Amaurian "Spirituals," who were the run-up, so to speak, to his favorite, the heresy of the Free Spirit. He was sliding his hand into his pocket, to retrieve the comfortingly worn volume, when a dark-haired girl in high brown boots and a short white jacket entered. He watched a transaction take place, the Korean giving her a receipt in exchange for two pairs of dark pants. Then, rather than leaving, she took out a phone, started carrying on a conversation in animated Spanish, crossed to the settee, and sat while talking, raking periodically and without much interest through the gossip magazines on the Korean's plywood coffee table. President Bush in his flight suit went under almost immediately, but she didn't manage to turn up anything Milgrim hadn't seen before. Still, it was pleasant to share this vinyl bench with her, and to enjoy the sound of a language he didn't understand. His seemingly innate fluency in Russian, he'd always assumed, had somehow been paid for with the loss of any ability in the Romance languages.

The girl dropped her phone back into her large purse, stood, smiled absently in his general direction, and walked out.

He was pulling his book from his pocket when he saw her phone lying there on the red vinyl.

He looked over at the Korean, who was reading the *Wall Street Journal.* Those weird little stipple portraits, at this distance, reminded Milgrim of fingerprints. He looked back at the phone.

His captivity had changed him. Prior to Brown, he would have pocketed the phone automatically. Now that he lived in the woodwork of Brown's world of surveillance, seemingly random encounters had become suspect. Had that been a real Spanish-speaking beauty, dropping off her office trousers for cleaning, or was she part of Brown's team? Was it really an accident, that she'd left her phone?

But what if it wasn't?

With an eye on the Korean, he palmed the phone. It was still warm, a small but vaguely shocking intimacy.

He stood. "I need to use the bathroom."

The Korean looked at him, over his *Wall Street Journal*.

"I need to pee."

Folding his paper, the Korean stood, held aside a curtain made of flowered fabric, and gestured Milgrim through. Milgrim walked quickly past a clutter of industrial ironing equipment and through a narrow beige-painted door with a silk-screened EMPLOYEES ONLY sign.

The walls of the cubicle, inside, were white-painted plywood, reminding Milgrim of the cabins at a summer camp he'd attended in Wisconsin. It smelled powerfully but not unpleasantly of disinfectant. On general principle, Milgrim secured the door with a fragile-looking piece of gold-tone Taiwanese hardware. He put the lid down on the toilet, seated himself, and had a look at the girl's phone.

It was a Motorola, with call display and camera. A model from a few years before, though as far as he knew they were still selling them. If he'd stolen it for resale, he would have been disappointed. As it was, it had an almost full battery charge and was roaming.

He looked up at a 1992 calendar, level with his eyes, and about ten inches away. Someone had quit pulling the months off, in August. It advertised a commercial real estate firm, and was decorated with a drastically color-saturated daytime photograph of the New York skyline, complete with the black towers of the World Trade Center. These were so intensely peculiar-looking, in retrospect, so monolithically sci-fi blank, unreal, that they now seemed to Milgrim to have been Photoshopped into every image he encountered them in.

Below the calendar, on a four-inch-wide ledge formed by a horizontal in the cubicle's framing, stood a bare tin can, its sides lightly freckled with rust. Milgrim leaned forward and studied its contents: a thin strata of nuts, bolts, two bottle caps, paper clips and thumbtacks, several unidentifiable metal components, corpses of small insects. Everything there that could oxidize was lightly, evenly rusted.

He settled back against the toilet tank and opened the phone. Hispanic full names in the phone book, interspersed with girls' names that mostly weren't.

He entered Fish's number from memory, closed his eyes, and thumbed Send.

Fish, short for Fisher, his surname, answered before a third ring. "Hello?"

"Fish. Hi."

"Who's this?"

"Milgrim."

"Hey." Fish sounded surprised to hear from him, but then Milgrim supposed he would be.

Fish was a fellow benzo user. Aside from that, what they most had in common was Dennis Birdwell, Milgrim's dealer. Former dealer, Milgrim corrected himself. Both Milgrim and Fish were long past doctor shopping, and neither was going to get anywhere with New York's triple-form prescription system. Fish had resources in New Jersey (a writing doctor, Milgrim assumed) but they both depended primarily on Birdwell. Or rather they both had, as Milgrim no longer could. "How are you doing, Milgrim?"

Meaning, Do you have any to spare? "Just getting by," Milgrim said.

"Oh," Fish said. He was always short. He did something in computer animation and had a girlfriend and a baby.

"Have you seen Dennis, Fish?"

"Uh, yeah. I have."

"How is he?"

"Well, ah, he's angry with you. That was what he said."

"Did he say why?"

"He said he'd given you money for something, and it didn't happen."

Milgrim sighed. "That's true, but it wasn't me letting him down. The guy I was going through, you know?"

A baby began to cry, behind Fish's voice. "Yeah. But, you know, I don't think you want to mess with Dennis, these days. Not that way." Fish sounded uncomfortable, and not just because of the crying baby.

"How do you mean?"

"Well," said Fish, "you know. It's his other stuff." Dennis's other stuff was crystal meth, increasingly his main stock-in-trade, and something neither Milgrim nor Fish had the least use for. It did, however, create in Dennis's other clients a need for powerfully soothing peripheral substances, hence Dennis's interest in the benzos they both relied on for peace and clarity. "I think he's dipping," Fish said. "You know. More."

Milgrim raised his eyebrows to the image of the twin towers. "Sorry to hear that."

"You know how they get."

"How do you mean?"

"Paranoid," Fish said. "Violent."

Dennis had once been a student at NYU. Milgrim could certainly imagine him angry, but imagining him violent was a stretch. "He collects *Star Wars* memorabilia," Milgrim said. "He sits there all night, looking for it on eBay."

There was a pause. Fish's baby fell silent too, in eerie-seeming synchrony. "He said he'd hire black guys from Brooklyn." The baby began to scream again, even harder.

"Shit," said Milgrim, as much to the rusty tin can as to Fish. "Do me a favor."

"Yeah?"

"Don't tell him you heard from me."

"Easy," said Fish.

"If I get extra," Milgrim lied, "I'll call you." He pressed End.

Back out front, he helped the unhappy Puerto Rican girl move the red settee so she could look under it. While she did that, he slid her phone under a hangnailed copy of *In Touch*, with Jennifer Aniston on the cover.

He was leaning against a dryer, reading about William the Goldsmith, when she found it.

20. TULPA

Had that woman in the wheelchair had an IV drip-stand in tow, one-handing her way across the intersection, the other hand keeping the chrome-plated upright of the stand erect?

Had she been legless? Hollis couldn't say, but after the skateboarder with no lower jaw it didn't seem like that big a deal.

"Your company's down here?" she asked Bigend, as he turned the Maybach into an alleyway that looked as though a Bradley fighting vehicle would be the wise man's ride of choice.

Past a delirious frozen surge of graffiti, a sort of street-fractal Hokusai wave, and under a lowering lip of coiled razor wire topping chain-link gates.

"Yes," he said, steering onto a concrete ramp rising fifteen feet as it hugged a wall that seemed to her as though it must belong to some city infinitely older than Los Angeles. Babylon, perhaps, its only graffiti cuneiform and discreet, furtive clerkish hen-scratchings applied to the odd brick.

The Maybach came to a temporary halt on a flat, truck-length platform, facing an articulated metal door. There were bulbous growths of smoked black plastic above this, pods housing cameras and perhaps other things as well. The door, decorated with a black pointillist portrait of Andre the Giant, Orwellian in scale, rose slowly, Andre's somber, thyroidal gaze giving way to halogen brilliance. Bigend drove forward into a hangarlike space, smaller than Bobby Chombo's empty factory but still impressive. A half dozen identical silver sedans were parked there in a row, beside a brand-new yellow forklift and tall, tidy stacks of new gypsum wallboard.

Bigend stopped the car. A ball-capped guard in black uniform shorts and matching short-sleeved shirt regarded them from behind mirrored glasses. A laden, multicompartmented black holster was strapped to his right thigh.

She felt a sudden intense desire to get out of the Maybach, and acted on it.

The door opened like some disturbing hybrid of bank vault and Armani evening purse, perfectly balanced bombproof solidity meeting sheer cosmetic slickness. The gritty concrete floor, blotched with crumbs of gypsum, felt comforting in contrast. The guard gestured with a remote. She heard segmented steel start to rattle down behind them.

"This way, please," said Bigend, over the clatter of the closing door. He stepped away from the Maybach without bothering to close his door, so she left hers open as well and followed him. She looked back, just as she was catching up with him, and saw it sitting open, its interior a soft, mouthlike cavern of gray lambskin under the high-resolution brilliance of the garage's lighting.

"We're losing the better part of the neighborhood's edge, as the reclamation continues," he said, guiding her around a ten-foot stack of drywall.

" 'Better part'?"

"Majority of. I'll miss it, myself. It unsettles visitors. Unsettled is good. Last week we opened a new suite of offices in Beijing. I'm not satisfied, not at all. Three floors in a new building, really nothing we could do with them. But it's Beijing." He shrugged. "What choice do we have?"

She didn't know, so said nothing. He led her up a wide flight of stairs and into what was obviously in the process of becoming a foyer. Another guard, studying CCTV windows on a panel display, ignored them.

They stepped into an elevator, its every surface taped over with white-dusted layers of corrugated cardboard. Bigend lifted a flap of the stuff and touched the controls. They rose two floors and the door opened. He gestured for her to go ahead.

She stepped out onto a scuffed runway of more of the

same cardboard, taped across a floor of some smooth gray product. The cardboard ran to a conference table, six chairs on a side. Above this, on the wall beyond, hung Anton Corbijn's portrait of her, in perfect resolution on a screen perhaps thirty feet on the diagonal.

"A wonderful image," he said, as she looked from it back to him.

"I've never been entirely comfortable with it."

"Because the celebrity self is a sort of tulpa," he said.

"A what?"

"A projected thought-form. A term from Tibetan mysticism. The celebrity self has a life of its own. It can, under the right circumstances, indefinitely survive the death of its subject. That's what every Elvis sighting is about, literally."

All of which reminded her very much of how Inchmale looked at these things, though really she believed it too.

"What happens," she asked him, "if the celebrity self dies first?"

"Very little," he said. "That's usually the problem. But images of this caliber serve as a hedge against that. And music is the most purely atemporal of media."

"'The past isn't dead. It's not even past,'" quoting Inchmale quoting Faulkner. "Would you mind changing channels?"

He gestured toward the screen. The Hook appeared in her place, the Soviet cargo helicopter, photographed from below. "What do you make of all this?" The smile flashed like a lighthouse. There were no apparent windows in this room, and at the moment this screen was the sole source of light.

"You like unsettled?"

"Yes?"

"Then you like me."

"I do like you. And something would be very wrong if you weren't. Unsettled."

She went to the conference table and ran a finger along its black surface, leaving a faint trace in gypsum dust. "Is there really a magazine?"

"Everything," said Bigend, "is potential."

"Everything," she said, "is potential bullshit."

"Think of me as a patron. Please."

"I don't like the sound of that, thanks."

"In the early 1920s," Bigend said, "there were still some people in this country who hadn't yet heard recorded music. Not many, but a few. That's less than a hundred years ago. Your career as a 'recording artist'"—making the quotes with his hands—"took place toward the end of a technological window that lasted less than a hundred years, a window during which consumers of recorded music lacked the means of producing that which they consumed. They could buy recordings, but they couldn't reproduce them. The Curfew came in as that monopoly on the means of production was starting to erode. Prior to that monopoly, musicians were paid for performing, published and sold sheet music, or had patrons. The pop star, as we knew her"—and here he bowed slightly, in her direction—"was actually an artifact of preubiquitous media."

"Of—?"

"Of a state in which 'mass' media existed, if you will, within the world."

"As opposed to?"

"Comprising it."

The light in the room changed, as he said this. She raised her eyes to the screen, where a metallic blue ant-glyph had taken over the screen.

"What's in Chombo's container?" she asked.

"It's not Chombo's container."

"Your container."

"It's not our container."

"'Our' being you and who?"

"You."

"It's not my container."

"Just as I said," said Bigend. And smiled.

"Whose is it, then?"

"I don't know. But I believe you might be able to find out."

"What's in it?"

"We don't know that either."

"What does Chombo have to do with it?"

"Chombo, evidently, has found a way to know where it is, at least periodically."

"Why don't you just ask him?"

"Because it's a secret. He's being paid handsomely to keep it a secret, and his personality is such, as you've noted, that he likes having a secret."

"Who's paying him, then?"

"That seems to be even more of a secret."

"Do you think it might be the container's owner?"

"Or its ultimate addressee, should it ever acquire one? I don't know. But you, Hollis, are the person I've found whom Bobby is most likely to talk to."

"You weren't there. He wasn't that glad to have Alberto bring me around. There were no suggestions of further invitations."

"That's where I'm convinced you're wrong," he said. "When he's gotten used to the idea that you're available for more face time, you may well hear from him."

"What have iPods got to do with it?"

He raised an eyebrow.

"Rausch told me to look for iPods being used for data storage. Do people still do that?"

"Chombo periodically loads an iPod with data and sends it out of the United States."

"What kind of data?"

"Music, ostensibly. We've had no way of finding out."

"Do you know where he sends them?"

"San José, Costa Rica, so far. We have no idea where else it might go, from there."

"Who receives it?"

"Someone whose job is to run an expensive post office box, essentially. There's a lot of that, evidently, in San José. We're working on it. Have you been there?"

"No."

"There's quite a community of retired CIA people there. DEA as well. We have someone there now, trying to have a quiet look into things, though so far it doesn't seem to be going anywhere."

"Why are you so interested in the contents of Chombo's container?"

Bigend removed a pale-blue microfiber dust cloth from his jacket pocket, pulled a chair out on its casters, and gave it a good dusting. "Seat?" He offered her the chair.

"No thanks. Go ahead."

He seated himself. He looked up at her. "I've learned to value anomalous phenomena. Very peculiar things that people do, often secretly, have come to interest me in a certain way. I spend a lot of money, often, trying to understand those things. From them, sometimes, emerge Blue Ant's most successful efforts. Trope Slope, for instance, our viral pitchman platform, was based on pieces of anonymous footage being posted on the Net."

"You did that? Put that thing in the background of all those old movies? That's fucking horrible. Pardon my French."

"It sells shoes." He smiled.

"So what do you expect to get out of this, if you can find out what's in Chombo's container?"

"No idea. None whatever. That's exactly what makes it so interesting."

"I don't get it."

"Intelligence, Hollis, is advertising turned inside out."

"Which means?"

"Secrets," said Bigend, gesturing toward the screen, "are cool." On the screen appeared their images, standing beside the table, Bigend not yet seated, captured by a camera somewhere above. The Bigend on the screen took a pale blue cloth from his pocket, pulled out a chair, and began to dust its arms and back and seat. "Secrets," said the Bigend beside her, "are the very root of cool."

21. SALT OF SOFIA

Tito crossed Amsterdam, passing the gray, snow-dusted stalks of a makeshift public garden, then walked quickly along 111th, toward Broadway.

The snow had stopped falling.

He recognized his cousin Vianca in the distance, by the Banco Popular, dressed like a teenager. Who else would be out, he wondered, for his ride back to Chinatown?

By the time he'd reached the Broadway median, Vianca was no longer visible. Attaining the western sidewalk, he turned south, heading for the 110th Street stop, hands in his pockets. Passing a framing shop, he picked her up in the depths of a mirror, crossing diagonally, a few yards behind his left shoulder.

Descending into the tiled trench of the subway, thinly roofed with iron and asphalt, he saw his breath rising.

The number 1 local arrived, like a sign, just as he reached the platform. He would return slowly, on the 1 to Canal, then walk east. He boarded the train, certain that Vianca and at least two others were doing the same. Protocol, for the detection and identification of followers, required a minimum of three.

AS THEY LEFT Sixty-sixth Street, Carlito entered from the car behind. Tito's car was almost empty. Vianca sat near the front end, apparently engrossed in a small video game.

Carlito wore a dark-gray topcoat, a scarf a shade lighter, black leather gloves that made it look to Tito as though his hands might be carved from wood, and black rubbers over the polished calfskin of his Italian shoes. He looked conservative, foreign, unassimilated, and somehow religious.

He seated himself to Tito's left. "Juana," he asked in Spanish, "she is well?"

"Yes," Tito said, "she seems well."

"You have met him." It was not a question.

"Yes," Tito said.

"You have your instructions."

"Yes."

Tito felt Carlito slip something into his pocket.

"*Búlgaro,*" Carlito said, identifying the object for him.

"Charged?"

"Yes. A new valve."

The Bulgarian's guns were close to a half century old now, but still functioned with great efficiency. It was sometimes necessary to replace the Schrader valve set into the flat steel reservoir that also served as a grip, but there were remarkably few moving parts. "Loaded?"

"Salt," Carlito said.

Tito remembered the salt cartridges, with their yellowed glassine membranes sealing either end of an inch-long, strangely scented cardboard tube.

"You must prepare now, to go away."

"For how long?" Tito knew that this was not an entirely acceptable question to ask, but it was the sort of question that Alejandro had taught him to at least consider asking.

Carlito didn't answer.

Tito was on the verge of asking what his father had been doing for the old man when he had died.

"He must not be captured." Carlito touched the knot in his scarf with his stiff, gloved hands. "You must not be captured. Only the item you are delivering must be captured, and they must not suspect you of having given it to them."

"What do we owe him, Uncle?"

"He saw our way here. He honored his word."

Carlito rose as the train pulled into Fifty-ninth Street. One gloved hand rested for an instant on Tito's shoulder. "Do well, nephew." He turned and was gone.

Tito glanced past boarding passengers, hoping to see Vianca still there, but she too was gone.

He reached into his jacket's side pocket, finding the

Bulgarian's singular, meticulously made weapon. It was folded loosely, within a fresh white cotton handkerchief from China, still stiff with sizing.

On drawing it from your pocket, those around you might think you were about to blow your nose. Without looking, Tito knew that the cardboard cylinder of carefully milled salt filled the entirety of the very short barrel. He left it where it was. Now that the Bulgarian's rubber gaskets had been replaced with silicone, an effective charge could be maintained for up to forty-eight hours.

The salt, he wondered, was it Bulgarian? Where had those cartridges been made? In Sofia? In Moscow, perhaps? In London, where the Bulgarian was said to have worked before Tito's grandfather had brought him to Cuba? Or in Havana, where he'd lived out his days?

The train pulled away from Columbus Circle.

22. DRUM AND BASS

Pamela Mainwaring, English, with blond bangs entirely concealing her forehead, drove Hollis back to the Mondrian in one of the big silver Volkswagen sedans. She'd worked for Blue Ant previously in London, she volunteered, before leaving to do something else, but then had been invited here to help oversee the expansion of the firm's local operation. "You hadn't met Hubertus before," she suggested, as they headed up the 101.

"Was it that obvious?"

"He told me, as he was leaving to meet you. Hubertus loves the opportunity to work with new talent."

Hollis looked up at the passing, shaggy heads of palms, black against a grayish-pink luminosity. "Having met him, I'm amazed that I hadn't heard of him before."

"He doesn't want you to have heard of him. He doesn't want people to have heard of Blue Ant, either. We're often described as the first viral agency. Hubertus doesn't like the term, and for good reason. Foregrounding the agency, or its founder, is counterproductive. He says he wishes we could operate as a black hole, an absence, but there's no viable way to get there from here." They left the freeway. "Do you need anything?"

"Pardon me?"

"Hubertus wants you to have anything you might need. That's rather literally anything, by the way, since you're working on one of his special projects."

"'Special'?"

"No explanations, no goals cited, no budgetary cap, absolute priority in whatever queue. He describes it as a species of dreaming, the company's equivalent of REM sleep. He believes it's essential." She took a card from a pocket in the VW's sun visor and passed it to Hollis. "Anything. Just call. Do you have a car?"

"No."

"Would you like this one? I can leave it for you."

"No thanks."

"Cash?"

"I'll submit receipts."

Pamela Mainwaring shrugged.

They rolled in, past the door sculptures. Hollis had her door unlatched before the car had come completely to a halt. "Thank you for driving me, Pamela. Nice meeting you. Good night."

"Good night."

Hollis closed the door. The silver sedan swung back out, onto Sunset, the lights of the Mondrian's entrance diminishing in its bodywork.

A night security man opened the door for her, a sort of decorative grommet clamped through the lobe of his ear. "Miss Henry?"

"Yes?"

"Message for you at the desk," he said, indicating the direction. She headed for the desk, passing a weird cruciform settee upholstered in virginal white leather.

"Here you are," said the shirt model at the desk, when she'd identified herself. She wanted to ask him what he used for his eyebrows, but didn't. He produced a square brown carton, twenty inches on a side, and had her sign the multicopy form attached to it.

"Thank you," she said, picking it up. It wasn't very heavy. She turned, heading back toward the elevators.

And saw Laura Hyde, aka Heidi, once the Curfew's drummer, waiting beside the cross-shaped settee. If nothing else, some quietly methodical part of her noted, this proved that that really had been who she'd thought she'd seen driving past Virgin Records, so much earlier in the evening. "Heidi?" Though there could be no doubt.

"Laura," Hyde corrected. She wore what Hollis took to be Girbaud, a sort of *Bladerunner* soccer-mom look, probably less out of place in this lobby than many things would be. Her dark hair seemed to have been cut to suit that, though Hollis would've been at a loss to explain how.

"How are you, Laura?"

"Bagged. Inchmale got my cell number from a friend in New York. Former friend." As if that number for Inchmale had put paid to that. "He called to tell me you were here."

"I'm sorry . . ."

"Oh, it isn't you. Really. Laurence is screening dailies two blocks from here. If I weren't here, I'd be there."

"He's producing?"

"Directing."

"Congratulations. I didn't know."

"Neither did I."

Hollis hesitated.

"Not what I signed on for." Her wide, full-lipped mouth went perfectly straight, never a good sign with her. "On the other hand, it may not last long."

Did she mean her husband's directing, or her marriage? Hollis had never been able to read the drummer very well. Neither had anyone else, according to Inchmale, who maintained that that was why the drumming was necessary, one species of primate signal that could always be seen to work.

"Would you like a drink, or . . ." Hollis turned, with the carton pressed against her chest, clutching her improvised purse in her left hand, and saw that the lobby bar had been transformed, stripped of its votive candles and candelabra and reset for a Japanese breakfast, or in any case a breakfast with black chopsticks, one not yet being served. Profoundly disinclined to invite Heidi up to her room, she allowed herself to keep moving in the direction of the endlessly elongated marble table.

"No drink," Heidi said, settling that. "What the fuck's that about?" Pointing toward the rear of the space, past the closed and locked bar, its exterior modeled after an enormous rubber-wheeled road case.

Hollis had noticed the instruments before, when she'd checked in. A single conga drum, a set of bongos, and an acoustic guitar and electric bass, these last two hung on cheap chrome stands. These were used instruments, even well used, but she doubted they ever were used, now, or certainly not very often.

Heidi kept walking, her drummer's shoulders rolling smoothly beneath the matte indigo of her Girbaud blazer. Hollis remembered her biceps in a sleeveless shirt, as the Curfew had taken a stage. She followed her.

"What is this bullshit?" Glaring first at the instruments, then at Hollis. "We're supposed to think Clapton'll drop by? We're supposed to think they want us to jam after we've had our sushi?"

Heidi's distaste for trickiness in decor, Hollis knew, was actually an extension of her dislike of art in general. The daughter of an Air Force technician, she was the only woman Hollis had ever known who enjoyed welding, but only for the purpose of repairing something essential that was actually broken.

Hollis looked at the no-name wooden guitar. "Hootenanny time. I think they're referencing pre-Beatles Venice. Beach."

"'Referencing.' Laurence says he's referencing Hitchcock." She made it sound sexually transmissible.

Hollis hadn't met Laurence yet, and neither expected nor wanted to, and hadn't seen Heidi since shortly after the Curfew's cessation. Heidi's unexpected appearance here, and now this close-up look at Starck's Boy Scouts of America beatnik jazz tableau, were bringing up all the pain of Jimmy for her. It was as if she expected him to be there, as if he should be there, as if he actually were there, just out of focus, or around some corner. Hadn't spiritualists arranged instruments this way, in their séance parlors? Though of these four, the electric bass, Jimmy's instrument, was the only one you couldn't just pick up and play, were you determined to. No cord, no amp, no speaker. What had happened to Jimmy's Pignose, she wondered.

"He came to see me, a week before he died," Heidi said, causing Hollis to start. "He'd been to that place outside of Tucson, done the twenty-eight days. Said he was going to meetings."

"That was here?"

"Yeah. Laurence and I were just hooking up. I didn't introduce them. He didn't feel right, Jimmy. To me, I mean." That aspect of Heidi that Hollis was always surprised to remember she was fond of looked out for an instant, from behind her brusqueness, something childlike and startled, then vanished. "You were in New York, when he died?"

"Yes. But not upstate. I was in the city, but I had no idea he'd come back. I hadn't seen him for almost a year."

"He owed you money."

Hollis looked at her. "Yes. He did. I'd almost forgotten that."

"He told me about it, borrowing that five thousand from you, in Paris, at the end of the tour."

"He always told me he intended to pay it back, but I didn't see how that was likely to happen."

"I haven't known how to get in touch with you," Heidi said, hands in the pockets of her blazer. "I supposed you'd turn up eventually. Now here you are. I'm sorry I didn't get it to you sooner."

"Get what?"

Heidi drew a frayed white letter-sized envelope from her blazer pocket and handed it to her. "Fifty hundreds. Just the way he gave them to me."

Hollis saw her own initials in faint red ballpoint, upper-left corner. Her breath caught. She forced herself to sigh. Not knowing what else to do with it, she put the envelope atop the carton and looked over it at Heidi. "Thanks. Thanks for keeping it for me."

"It was important to him. I didn't feel like anything else he was talking about really was. The place in Arizona, the recovery program, some offer he'd had to produce, in Japan . . . But he wanted to be sure you got your money back, and I guess that giving it to me was one way to do that. For one thing"—she narrowed her eyes—"once he'd told me he owed you, he knew I wouldn't give it back to him to spend on smack."

Inchmale said that the Curfew had been built on the literal sonic foundation of Heidi's stubbornness and militant lack of imagination, but that knowing that had never made it any easier to get along with her, and that that had been true from the very start. Hollis had always thought she'd agreed with that, but just now it seemed more viscerally true than she'd ever felt it to be, before.

"I'm out of here," Heidi said, giving Hollis's shoulder a quick squeeze, a really exceptional display of warmth, for her.

"Goodbye . . . Laura."

Watching her march back across the lobby, past the cruciform settee and out of sight.

23. TWO MOORS

Brown left Milgrim in the Korean's laundry for a very long time. Eventually a younger Korean, perhaps the proprietor's son, arrived with a brown-bagged Chinese meal, which he presented to Milgrim with no comment. Milgrim cleared a space among the magazines on the plywood coffee table and unpacked his lunch. Plain rice, boneless chicken nuggets in red dye no. 3, fluorescent-green vegetable segments, finely sliced brown mystery meat. Milgrim preferred the plastic fork to the chopsticks. If you were in prison, he encouraged himself, you'd find this food a treat. Unless you were in a Chinese prison, some less-cooperative part of himself suggested, but he worked his way through it all, methodically. With Brown, it was best to eat what you could when the opportunity presented itself.

As he ate, he thought about the twelfth-century heresy of the Free Spirit. Either God was everything, believed the brethren of the Free Spirit, or God was nothing. And God, to them, was very definitely everything. There was nothing that wasn't God, and indeed how could there be? Milgrim had never been one for metaphysics, but now the combination of his captivity, medication on demand, and this text was starting to reveal the pleasure to be had from metaphysical contemplation. Particularly if you were contemplating these Free Spirit guys, who seemed to have been a combination of Charlie Manson and Hannibal Lecter.

And insofar as everything was equally of God, they taught, those who were most in touch with the Godness in every last thing would make it a point to do anything at all, particularly anything still forbidden by those who hadn't yet gotten the Free Spirit message. To which end they went around having sex with anybody they could get to hold still for it, or not, as the case might be—rape being viewed as particularly righteous, and murder equally so. It was like a secret religion of mutually empowered sociopaths, and Milgrim thought it was probably the gnarliest single example of human behavior he'd ever heard of. Someone like Manson, for instance, simply wouldn't have been able to get any traction, had he landed among the brothers and sisters of the Free Spirit. Probably, Milgrim guessed, Manson would've hated it. What good would it be to be Charlie Manson in a whole society of serial killers and rapists, each one convinced that he or she was directly manifesting the Holy Spirit?

But the other aspect of the Free Spirit that fascinated him, and this applied to the whole text, was how these heresies would get started, often spontaneously generating around some single medieval equivalent of your more outspoken homeless mumbler. Organized religion, he saw, back in the day, had been purely a signal-to-noise proposition, at once the medium and the message, a one-channel universe. For Europe, that channel was Christian, and broadcasting from Rome, but nothing could be broadcast faster than a man could travel on horseback. There was a hierarchy in place, and a highly organized methodology of top-down signal dissemination, but the time lag enforced by tech-lack imposed a near-disastrous ratio, the noise of heresy constantly threatening to overwhelm the signal.

The rattle of the door distracted him from these thoughts. He looked up from the remains of his lunch and witnessed the entrance of an extremely large black man, very tall and very wide, who wore a stout thigh length black leather coat, double-breasted and belted, and a black wool watch cap, pulled low around his ears. The watch cap put Milgrim in mind of the knitted woolen headgear Crusaders wore beneath their helmets, and that in turn made the leather barnstormer resemble a sort of elongated cuirass. A black knight stepping into the laundry from the early evening cold.

Milgrim wasn't sure that there had actually been black knights, but couldn't a Moor have converted, some African giant, and been made a knight in the service of Christ? Compared to that Free Spirit, it seemed the likeliest of scenarios.

Now the black knight had stepped up to the Korean's counter, and was asking him if he could clean furs. The Korean couldn't, he said, and the knight nodded, accepting that. The knight looked over and met Milgrim's gaze. Milgrim nodded too, unsure why.

The knight left. Through the window, Milgrim saw him join a second and remarkably similar black man, in yet another black, double-breasted, belted leather coat. They turned south, down Lafayette, in their matching black wool skullcaps, and instantly were gone.

As Milgrim tidied away his empty foam bowl and his foil dishes, he experienced a nagging sensation of having failed to pay adequate attention to something. Try as he might, he couldn't remember what that might have been.

It had been a very long day.

24. POPPIES

Votive candles had been lit in her darkened room. Beside the luminous cottons of the all-white bed, the water pitcher had been filled. She put the carton, dead Jimmy Carlyle's envelope of hundred-dollar bills, and her makeshift evening purse on the long-legged marble-topped table in the kitchenette.

She used the small unsharpened blade in the handle of the kitchenette's corkscrew to slit the transparent tape sealing the carton.

There was a note, in an oddly Sumerian-looking script, on a rectangle of plain gray card, resting on a fold of Bubble Wrap. "You need your own. Press On. H."

She set that aside and lifted the fold of Bubble Wrap. Something black and matte silver. She drew out what she took to be a more aggressively styled version of the

wireless helmet she'd used to view the squid at Bobby
Chombo's. Through the cutaway shell, she saw the same
few simple touch pads. She turned the thing over, looking for a manufacturer's logo, but found none. She did
find MADE IN CHINA in minute bas-relief, but then most
things were.

She tried it on, intending to do no more than glance
at herself in a candlelit mirror, but she must have touched
one of the control surfaces. "A locative installation, in
your room," Odile said, sounding as if she were inches
from Hollis's ear. She found herself atop the turned-down
bed, clutching Bigend's headgear, so unexpected had
this been. "Monet's poppies. Rotch." Rotch? "The poppies and whatever background, they are equiluminant."

And there they were, quivering slightly, reddish orange, arrayed as a field that filled her room, level with
the height of the bed.

She moved her head from side to side, scanning the
effect. "This becomes part of a series. The artist's Argen-
teuil series. Rotch." There it was again. "She fill spaces
everywhere with Monet's poppies. Call me when you
have received this. We must talk, also about Chombo."
She pronounced it "Shombo."

"Odile?" But it had been a recording. Still crouching
on the bed, she sat down and ran her left hand through
the poppies she knew weren't there. She almost thought
she could feel them. She swung her legs over the side
and found the floor, poppies around her knees. Wading
through them, toward the layered drapes, she felt mo-
mentarily as though they floated atop captive, unmoving

water. The artist might not have intended that, she thought.

Reaching the window, she held the drapes aside with her forearm and peered down at Sunset, half expecting to discover that Alberto had littered the street with dead celebrities, more tableaux of fame and misadventure, but there was nothing evident.

She took it off, returned to the table through the sudden absence of poppies, and touched various surfaces inside until a green LED went off. As she was putting it back in the carton, she noticed something else, amid the Bubble Wrap.

She pulled out a molded vinyl figurine of the Blue Ant ant. She stood it on the marble tabletop, picked up the evening's purse, and took that into the bathroom. While she ran a tub of hot on top of the day's allotment of shower gel, she emptied the purse and transferred its usual contents back into it.

She tested the water, undressed, and got into the tub, settling herself on her back.

She was no longer certain why Jimmy had needed to borrow that much money in Paris, why she'd been willing to part with it, or how it was that she'd been able to lay her hands on cash.

She'd given it to him in francs. It had been that long ago.

The water was deep enough that it rose along the sides of her face as she settled the back of her head against the bottom of the tub. A child-sized island of face above water. Isla de Hollis.

Odile's poppies. She remembered Alberto's description of how he sculpted and skinned-up a new celebrity misadventure. She guessed Odile's poppies were another, simpler kind of skin. They could be anything, really.

She raised her sunken head partially out of the water and began to work shampoo into her hair. "Jimmy," she said, "you really piss me off. The world is already weirder and stupider than you could ever have guessed." She lowered her shampooed hair back into the water. The bathroom kept on filling with the absence of her dead friend, and she'd started to cry before she could start to rinse.

25. SUNSET PARK

Vianca sat cross-legged on Tito's floor with his Sony plasma screen across her knees. Wearing a disposable hairnet and white knit cotton gloves, she was going over the Sony with an Armor All wipe. When she'd wiped it completely down, it would go back into its factory packaging, which in turn would be wiped.

Tito, in his own hairnet and gloves, sat opposite her, wiping the keys of his Casio. A carton of cleaning supplies had been waiting for them in the hall, beside a new and expensive-looking vacuum cleaner Vianca said was German. Nothing came out of this vacuum but air, she said, so there would be no stray hairs or other traces left behind. Tito had helped his cousin Eusebio with exactly this procedure, though Eusebio had mainly had books, each of which had needed, according to protocol, to be flipped through for forgotten insertions, then wiped. The reasons for Eusebio's departure had never been made clear to him. That too was protocol.

He looked up at the symmetrically spaced holes in the wall, where the Sony had been mounted. "Do you know where Eusebio is?"

Vianca raised her eyes from her wiping, eyes narrowing beneath the white paper band of the hairnet. "Doctores," she said.

"Pardon?"

"Doctores. In the Federal District. A neighborhood. Or maybe not." She shrugged, and went back to wiping.

Tito hoped he wouldn't have to go to Mexico, to Mexico City. He had not left the United States since being brought here, and he had no desire to. These days, returning here might be more difficult still. There were family members in Los Angeles. That would be his choice, not that he would have one. "We used to practice systema, Eusebio and I," he said, turning the Casio over and continuing to wipe.

"He was my first boyfriend," Vianca said, which seemed impossible until he remembered that she wasn't really a teenager.

"You don't know where he is?"

She shrugged. "Guessing, Doctores. But better not to be sure."

"How do they decide, where you go?"

She put her wipe down, on top of the Armor All container, and picked up a foam packing segment. It fit perfectly over one end of the Sony. "It depends on who they think might be looking for you." She picked up the segment for the other end.

Tito looked over at the blue vase. He'd forgotten about that. He'd have to find a place for it. He thought he knew where.

"Where did you go, after 9/11," she asked, "before you moved here?"

He had been living below Canal, with his mother. "We went to Sunset Park. With Antulio. We rented a house, redbrick, with very small rooms. Smaller than this. We ate Dominican food. We walked in the old cemetery. Antulio showed us Joey Gallo's grave." He put the Casio aside and stood, removing the hairnet. "I'm going up to the roof," he said. "I have something to do there."

Vianca nodded, sliding his foam-braced Sony into its carton.

He put on his coat, picked up the blue vase, and put it, still wearing the white cotton gloves, into his side pocket. He went out, closing the door behind him. He stopped in the hallway, unable to give a name to what he felt. Fear, but that was in its place. Something else. Edges, territories, a blind vastness? He went on, through the fire door and up the stairs. When he reached the sixth floor, he climbed a final flight to the roof.

Concrete covered with asphalt, gravel, secret traces of the World Trade Center. Alejandro had suggested that last, once, when he'd been up here. Tito remembered the pale dust, thick on the sill of his mother's bedroom window, below Canal. He remembered fire escapes, far from the fallen towers, filled with office papers. He remembered the ugliness of the Gowanus Expressway. The tiny front yard of the house where they'd stayed with Antulio. The N train from Union Square. His mother's wild eyes.

The clouds were like an engraving in some ancient book. A light that robbed the world of color.

The door to the roof faced south, opening out of the slant-backed structure that supported its frame. Against this structure's wedge-shaped, east-facing wall had been constructed shelving of unpainted timber, long gone gray, and on this had been arranged, or abandoned, a variety of objects. A corroded bucket on casters, with a foot-powered mop-squeezing unit. Mops themselves, heads gone bald and gray, the peeling paint on their wooden handles faded to delicate pastels. White plastic kegs that warned with a black skeleton hand in a black-and-white diamond, but were empty. Several rusted iron hand tools of so great an age as to be unidentifiable, at least by Tito. Rusted gallon paint cans whose paper labels had faded past reading.

He took the vase from his pocket and polished it between his cotton gloves. Ochun must have countless homes like this one, he thought, countless windows. He stood the vase on a shelf, shifted a can aside, put the vase against the wall, then moved the can back, leaving the vase concealed between two cans. In the way of these rooftops, it might be found tomorrow, or remain untouched for years.

She rules over the world's sweet waters. Youngest of

the female orishas, yet her title is Great Queen. Recognizing herself in the colors yellow and gold, in the number five. Peacocks are hers, and vultures.

Tia Juana's voice. He nodded to the shelf, the hidden altar, then turned and descended the stairs.

Letting himself back into his room, he found Vianca removing the drive from his PC tower. She looked up at him. "You copied what you wished to keep?"

"Yes," he said, touching the Nano around his neck. A charm. His music stored there.

He removed his coat, hung it on the rack, and put his hairnet back on. Settling himself opposite his cousin, he began again the ritual disassembly, this meticulous scrubbing out of traces, erasure. As Juana would say, the washing of the threshold of the new road.

26. GRAY'S PAPAYA

Sometimes, if Brown was hungry at the end of the day, and in a certain mood, they'd go to Gray's Papaya for the Recession Special. Milgrim always got the orange-ade with his, because it seemed more honestly a drink, less juice-like. You could get actual juices there, but not with the Recession Special, and juice didn't seem like part of the Gray's experience, which was about grilled beef franks, soft white buns, and watery, sugary drinks, consumed standing up, under brilliant, buzzing fluores-cent light.

When they were staying at the New Yorker, as it seemed they were again, tonight, Gray's was only two blocks up Eighth Avenue. Milgrim was comforted by Gray's Pa-paya. He remembered when the two franks and drink that were the Recession Special had been $1.95.

Milgrim doubted that Gray's comforted Brown, exactly, but he did know that Brown could become relatively talkative there. He'd have the nonalcoholic piña colada with his franks and lay out the origins of cultural Marxism in America. Cultural Marxism was what other people called political correctness, according to Brown, but it was really cultural Marxism, and had come to the United States from Germany, after World War II, in the cunning skulls of a clutch of youngish professors from Frankfurt. The Frankfurt School, as they'd called themselves, had wasted no time in plunging their intellectual ovipositors repeatedly into the unsuspecting body of old-school American academia. Milgrim always enjoyed this part; it had an appealing vintage sci-fi campiness to it, staccato and exciting, with grainy monochrome Eurocommie star-spawn in tweed jackets and knit ties, breeding like Starbucks. But he'd always be brought down, as the rant rolled to a close, by Brown's point that the Frankfurt School had been Jewish, all of them. "Every. Last. One." Dabbing mustard from the corners of his mouth with a precisely folded paper napkin. "Look it up."

Which was exactly what had happened, this time, after Milgrim's long day in the laundry. Brown had just said that, and Milgrim had nodded, and continued to chew the last of his second dog, glad of something in his mouth to preclude answering.

When they'd both finished their Specials, it was time to walk back down Eighth to the New Yorker. The traffic was moderate and there was something like a touch of spring in the air, a slight premonitory warmth that

Milgrim suspected of being hallucinatory, but welcomed nonetheless. When the yellow Hummer cruised past, in the nearest lane, as they were walking south, he noticed it. You would, he'd tell himself later. Not that it was a real Hummer, just one of those half-assed ones, and not just that it was yellow, but because it was a Hummer and it was yellow, and it had those goofy counterweighted hubcaps that didn't rotate with the hubs, just sort of rocked there. And these were yellow, matching yellow, and had a Happy Face on each one, or at least on the two on the sidewalk side, the two Milgrim could see.

But what really held Milgrim's attention, after the northbound yellow vehicle flicked past, was how closely its driver and passenger had resembled his two Moorish knights of the laundry, down on Lafayette. Black knit skullcaps snugged low over massy skulls, and sofa-like chest expanses of black, button-studded leather.

Gilbert and George, in the front seats of a Hummer.

27. THE INTERNATIONAL CURRENCY OF BAD SHIT

Held psychically together by the thick white Mondrian robe, her sunglasses, and a room-service breakfast of granola, yogurt, and a watermelon liquado, Hollis sat back in one wide white armchair, put her feet up on the shorter of the two marble-topped coffee tables, and regarded the vinyl Blue Ant figurine on the chair arm. It was eyeless; or rather its designer had chosen not to represent its eyes. It had a determined smirk, the expression of a cartoon underdog fully aware of its own secret status as superhero. Its posture conveyed that too, arms slightly bent at its sides, fists balled, feet in a martial artist's ready T-stance. Its stylized cartoon-Egyptian apron and sandals, she judged, were a nod to the hieroglyphic look of the company's logo.

Inchmale said that when you were presented with a

new idea, you should try to turn it over, to look at the bottom. She picked the figure up, expecting to find it copyrighted Blue Ant, but the bottoms of its feet were smooth and blank. Nicely finished. It wasn't a toy, not for kids anyway.

It reminded her of the time their soundman, Ritchie Nagel, had dragged a militantly disinterested Inchmale to see Bruce Springsteen at Madison Square Garden. Inchmale had returned with his shoulders hunched in thought, deeply impressed by what he'd witnessed but uncharacteristically unwilling to talk about it. Pressed, he would only say that Springsteen, onstage, had channeled a combination of Apollo and Bugs Bunny, a highly complex act of physical possession. Hollis had subsequently waited, uneasily, for Inchmale to manifest anything at all Boss-like onstage, but that had never happened. This Blue Ant's designer, she thought, as she stood the thing back on the chair arm, had aspired to something like that: Zeus and Bugs Bunny. Her cell rang.

"Morning." Inchmale, as if called forth by her having thought of him.

"You sent Heidi." Only neutrally accusatory.

"Did she walk on her hind legs?"

"Did you know about Jimmy's money?"

"Your money. I did, but I'd forgotten. He told me he had it, that he was going to give it to you. I told him to give it to Heidi, if he couldn't give it to you. Otherwise, it would vanish down that hole in his arm without a hiccup."

"You didn't tell me."

"I forgot. With major effort. Repressed the whole sorry episode, in the wake of his not-unexpected demise."

"When did you see him?"

"I didn't. He phoned me. About a week before they found him."

Hollis turned in the armchair, looking back over her shoulder at the sky above the Hollywood hills. Absolutely empty. When she turned back, she picked up the rest of her liquado. "It's not like I don't need it. I'm not sure what to do with it, though." She took a swallow of watermelon juice and put the glass down.

"Spend it. I wouldn't try to bank it."

"Why not?"

"You don't know where it's been."

"I don't even want to know what you're thinking of."

"The U.S hundred is the international currency of bad shit, Hollis, and by the same token the number-one target of counterfeiters. How long are you going to be in L.A.?"

"I don't know. Why?"

"Because I'm due in there day after the day after tomorrow. Found out about twenty minutes ago. I can vet those bills for you."

"You are? You can?"

"The Bollards."

"Excuse me?"

"Bollards. I may produce them."

"Do you really know how to check for counterfeit money?"

"I live in Argentina, don't I?"

"Are Angelina and the baby coming?"

"They may later, if the Bollards and I are go. And you?"

"I met Hubertus Bigend."

"What's that like?"

"Interesting."

"Oh dear."

"We had drinks. Then he drove me down to where they're building new offices. In a kind of Cartier tank."

"In a what?"

"Obscene car."

"What does he want?"

"I was about to say it's complicated, but actually it's vague. Extremely vague. If you have time off from the Pillocks, I'll tell you then."

"Please." He hung up.

The phone rang in her hand. "Yes?" Expecting an Inchmale afterthought.

"Allo? Ollis?"

"Odile?"

"You have experience the poppies?"

"Yes. Beautiful."

"The *Node* man calls, he says you have a new helmet?"

"I do, thanks."

"This is good. You know Silverlake?"

"Roughly."

"Rough—?"

"I know Silverlake."

"The artist Beth Barker is here, her apartment. You will come, you will experience the apartment, this environment. This is an annotated environment, do you know it?"

"Annotated how?"

"Each object is hyperspatially tagged with Beth Barker's description, with Beth Barker's narrative of this object. One simple water glass has twenty tags."

She looked at the white orchid blooming on the taller coffee table, imagined it layered with virtual file cards. "It sounds fascinating, Odile, but it will have to be another day. I need to make some notes. Absorb what I've seen so far."

"She will be desolate, Beth Barker."

"Tell her chin up."

"Chin—?"

"I'll see it another day. Really. And the poppies are wonderful. We must talk about them."

"Ah. Very well." Cheered. "I will tell Beth Barker. Goodbye."

"Goodbye. And Odile?"

"Yes?"

"Your message. You said you wanted to talk about Bobby Chombo."

"I do, yes."

"We will, then. 'Bye."

She stood up quickly, as if doing so would keep the phone, which she thrust into one of the robe's pockets, from ringing again.

*   *   *

"HOLLIS HENRY." The boy at the no-name rental lot a short walk down Sunset looked up from her license. "Have I seen you on TV?"

"No."

"Do you want full collision?"

"Yes."

He X'd the contract three times. "Signature, initials twice. Movies?"

"No."

"Singer. In that band. Bald guy with the big nose, guitar, English."

"No."

"Don't forget to fill it up before you bring it back," he said, staring up at her now with mild if unabashed interest. "That was you."

"No," she said, picking up the keys, "it wasn't." She went out to her rented black Passat, the carton from Blue Ant under her arm, and got in, putting it in the passenger seat beside her.

28. BROTHERMAN

Tito and Vianca packaged the contents of his room as ten parcels of varying sizes, each one double-wrapped in contractor-grade black trash bags and sealed with heavy black tape. This left Tito's mattress, the ironing board, the long-legged chair from Canal Street, and the old iron clothing rack. Vianca, it had been agreed, was taking the ironing board and the chair. The mattress, assumed to contain enough skin flakes and hair for a DNA match, would be on its way to landfill as soon as Tito left the building. Vianca had sealed it in two of the black plastic bags before she'd vacuumed the room. The black bags made a slithering sound, now, when you sat on the mattress, and Tito would have to sleep on it.

Tito touched the Nano again, on its cord around his neck, grateful to have his music.

"We've packed the tchainik," he said, "and the kettle. We can't make tea."

"I don't want to wipe them again."

"Carlito called Alejandro and I tchainiks," Tito told her. "It meant we were ignorant but willing to learn. Do you know that way of using 'tchainik'?"

"No," Vianca said, looking like a very pretty, very dangerous child, under her white paper hairnet. "I only know it to mean 'teapot.'"

"A hacker's word, in Russian."

"Do you ever think that you are forgetting Russian, Tito?" she asked in English.

Before he could answer, someone rapped lightly at the door, in protocol. Vianca came out of her crouch on the mattress with a peculiar grace, at once tight and serpentine, to rap a reply. "Brotherman," she said, and unlocked the door.

"*Hola, viejo,*" said Brotherman, nodding to Tito and pulling off a black knit headband that served him as earmuffs. He wore his hair in a vertical mass, touched a peculiar dark orange with peroxide. In Brotherman, Juana said, some African had surfaced in the Cuban, before mingling with the Chinese. Brotherman exaggerated this now, to his own advantage and that of the family. He was completely ambivalent, racially. A chameleon, his Spanish slid deftly between Cuban, Salvadoran, and Chilango, while his black American was often incomprehensible to Tito. He was taller than Tito, and thin, long-faced, the whites of his eyes shot with red. "*Llapepi,*" he greeted Vianca with a nod, backslanging *papilla*: teenager.

"*Hola*, Brotherman. *Qué se cuenta?*"

"Same old," said Brotherman, bending to catch and squeeze Tito's hand. "Man of the hour."

"I don't like waiting," Tito said, and stood, to shake unease from his back and arms. The bare bulb overhead seemed brighter than ever before; Vianca had wiped it clean.

"But I have seen your systema, cousin." Brotherman raised a white plastic shopping bag. "Carlito sends you shoes." He passed Tito the bag. The high-topped black shoes still had their white-and-blue Adidas logo tags. Tito sat on the edge of the bagged mattress and removed his boots. He laced the Adidas shoes and pulled them on over medium-weight cotton socks, removed the tags, and carefully tightened the laces before tying them. He stood up, shifting his weight, taking the measure of these new shoes. "GSG9 model," Brotherman said. "Special police in Germany."

Tito positioned his feet shoulder-width apart, dropped his Nano inside the neck of his T-shirt, took a breath, and backtucked, the new shoes missing the bare bulb in the ceiling fixture by less than a foot. He landed three feet behind his starting position.

He grinned at Vianca, but she didn't smile back. "I'll go out for some food now," she said. "What would you like?"

"Anything," said Tito.

"I'll start loading this," said Brotherman, toeing the pile of black packages. Vianca passed him a fresh pair of gloves from her jacket pocket.

"I'll help," said Tito.

"No," said Brotherman, pulling on the gloves and wiggling white fingers at Tito. "You twist your ankle, sprain anything, Carlito have our asses."

"He's right," said Vianca, firmly, removing her paper hairnet and replacing it with her baseball cap. "No more tricking. Give me your wallet."

Tito passed her his wallet.

She removed the two pieces of identification most recently provided by the family. Surname Herrera. *Adiós.* She left him his money and MetroCard.

He looked from one cousin to the other, then sat back down on the mattress.

29. INSULATION

There was something about Rize, Milgrim decided, re clining fully dressed across his New Yorker bedspread, that reminded him of one of the more esoteric effects of eating exceptionally hot Szechuan.

Not just hot, but correctly, expertly seasoned. Hot like when they brought you a plate of lemon slices, to suck on as needed, to partially neutralize the burn. It had been a long time since Milgrim had had food like that. It had been a long time since he'd eaten a meal that had provided any memorable pleasure at all. The Chinese he was most familiar with these days was along the lines of the stepped-on Cantonese they brought him at the laundry on Lafayette, but just now he was recalling that sensation, strangely delightful, of drinking cold water on top of serious pepper-burn—how the water filled your mouth entirely, but somehow without touching it, like a molecule-thick silver membrane of Chinese anti-matter, like a spell, some kind of magic insulation.

The Rize was like that, the cold water being the business of being Milgrim, or rather those aspects of being Milgrim, or simply of being, that he found most problematic. Where some less subtle formulation would seek to make the cold water go away, the Rize encouraged him to take it up, into his mouth, in order to savor that silver membrane.

Though his eyes were closed, he knew that Brown had just now come to the connecting door, which stood open.

"A nation," he heard himself say, "consists of its laws. A nation does not consist of its situation at a given time. If an individual's morals are situational, that individual is without morals. If a nation's laws are situational, that nation has no laws, and soon isn't a nation." He opened his eyes and confirmed Brown there, his partially disassembled pistol in his hand. The cleaning, lubrication, and examination of the gun's inner workings was ritual, conducted every few nights, though as far as Milgrim knew, Brown hadn't fired the gun since they'd been together.

"What did you say?"

"Are you really so scared of terrorists that you'll dismantle the structures that made America what it is?" Milgrim heard himself ask this with a sense of deep wonder. He was saying these things without consciously having thought them, or at least not in such succinct terms, and they seemed inarguable.

"The fuck—"

"If you are, you let the terrorist win. Because that is exactly, specifically, his goal, his only goal: to frighten you into surrendering the rule of law. That's why they call him 'terrorist.' He uses terrifying threats to induce you to degrade your own society."

Brown opened his mouth. Closed it.

"It's based on the same glitch in human psychology that allows people to believe they can win the lottery. Statistically, almost nobody ever wins the lottery. Statistically, terrorist attacks almost never happen."

There was a look on Brown's face that Milgrim hadn't seen there before. Now Brown tossed a fresh bubble-pack down on the bedspread.

"Good night," Milgrim heard himself say, still insulated by the silver membrane.

Brown turned, walking silently back into his own room in his stocking feet, the partial pistol in his hand.

Milgrim raised his right arm toward the ceiling, straight up, index finger extended and thumb cocked. He brought the thumb down, firing an imaginary shot, then lowered his arm, having no idea at all what to make of whatever it was that had just happened.

She drove to Malibu with the Blue Ant helmet in its carton beside her. It was sunny through Beverly Hills, but by the time she reached the sea something monochrome and saline had insinuated itself.

She went to Gladstone's, took the carton in with her, and stood it on the massive timber bench opposite her own, while she topped up her hyperhealthy hotel breakfast with a small chowder and a large Coke. The light on the beach was like a sinus headache.

Things were different today, she assured herself. She was working for *Node*, and her expenses would be covered. She had decided to look at it that way, and not think of herself as Bigend's employee, or Blue Ant's. There had, after all, been no real change in her formal situation; she was a freelancer, on assignment to *Node* to write seven thousand words on locative computing and the arts. That was the situation today and she could deal with it. The Bigend version, she was less certain of. Pirates, their boats, CIA maritime units, tramp freighters, the traffic in and hunt for weapons of mass destruction, a shipping container that spoke to Bobby Chombo—she wasn't certain of any of that.

As she was paying, she remembered Jimmy's money, back at the Mondrian, locked in the little keypad safe in her room, coded to open on "CARLYLE." She didn't know what else to do with it. Inchmale said he could tell her whether any of it was counterfeit. She'd take him up on that, she thought, then go on from there.

The thought of seeing him again woke an old ambivalence. While it had never been true, as the magazines had often had it, that she and Inchmale had been a couple, in any carnal or otherwise ordinary sense, they had nonetheless been married in some profound if sexless way; co-creatives, the live wires of the Curfew, held down and variously together by Jimmy and Heidi. She was grateful, ordinarily, to whatever fates might be, for Inchmale having found the excellent Angelina and Argentina, thereby to be translated, for the most part, out of her world. It was better that way for everyone, though she'd have had a hard time explaining that to anyone other than Inchmale. And Inchmale, never blind to the background radiation of his own singularity, would have been all too ready to agree.

When she got back to the car, she put the carton on the unopened trunk and got the helmet out, fumbling

with the unfamiliar controls. She put the thing on, curious as to whether anyone had been locatively creative in
the immediate vicinity.

A cartoonishly smooth Statue of Liberty hand, holding a torch a good three stories high, loomed above her,
blotting out the hurtful glow of the salt-metal sky. Its
wrist, emerging from the Malibu sand, would've had
roughly the footprint of a basketball court. It was far
bigger than the real thing, it was blatant copying to have
it emerging from the beach this way, and still it managed
to be more melancholy than ridiculous. Would it all be
like this, in Alberto's new world of the locative? Would it
mean that the untagged, unscripted world would gradually fill with virtual things, as beautiful or ugly or banal
as anything one encountered on the Web already? Was
there any reason to expect it to be any better than that,
any worse? The Liberty hand and its torch looked as
though they had been cast from the stuff they made beige
Tupperware out of. She remembered how Alberto had
described his labors in the creation of skins, textures. She
remembered the microskirted Aztec princesses on his
Volkswagen. She wondered where the wifi for this piece
was coming from.

She took the helmet off and put it back in its carton.

Driving back, as the sun gradually found its way out
again, she decided to try to find Bobby's factory, if only
to put him on her map in a different way. It shouldn't be
hard. Her body, she was finding, remembered Los Angeles much more thoroughly than her head did.

Eventually she found herself back on Romaine, looking for the turn Alberto had taken. For those white-painted walls. She found it, turned, and saw something big and bright and whiter still, just pulling away. She slowed, pulled over. Watched the long white truck turn, swinging right, out of sight at the far corner. She didn't know trucks, but she guessed this one was as long as they got without having the back end become a separate trailer. But big enough to move the contents of a two-bedroom house. Unmarked, shiny, white. And gone.

"Shit," she said, pulling up where Alberto had pulled up. She could see the green-painted metal door they'd entered through. She didn't like the diagonal of shadow across it now. The sun was high, and that diagonal meant the door was open, three inches or more. For the first time she saw the long, white-painted, horizontally corrugated doors of a loading bay. Back a truck up to that and take out anything you wanted.

She popped the trunk, getting out with her Power-Book over her shoulder and the carton in her arms. She put these in the trunk and closed it, retrieved her purse, clicked the transponder to lock the car, then squared her shoulders and walked over to the green door. As she'd assumed, it was standing open a few inches. On darkness, she decided, tipping her head to squint inside, over her sunglasses.

She dug through the smaller objects at the bottom of her purse, coming up with a flat little LED-light on a key ring whose only keys were for a commercial mailbox she no longer rented, and for a Club to secure a car she no longer owned. She squeezed the light between thumb and forefinger, expecting its battery to be dead, but no, it was working. Feeling stupid, she gave the green door a rap, hurting her knuckles. It was heavy, and didn't move when knocked on. "Bobby? Hello? It's Hollis Henry, Bobby . . ." She put her left hand flat on the door and pushed. It swung smoothly, but very slowly. With the LED in her right hand, she pulled off her sunglasses with the other and stepped into darkness.

The LED did little in terms of increased visibility. She turned it off and stood, waiting for her eyes to accommodate. She began to make out points and small, faint beams in the distance. Flaws in the painting of blacked-out windows, she guessed. "Bobby? It's Hollis. Where are you?"

She tried the LED again, this time pointing it at the floor. Surprisingly bright, it illuminated a length of one of Bobby's powdered white gridlines. Broken, she saw, with the partial print of one of his winkle-picker Keds clones. "Whoa," she said, "Nancy Drew. Bobby? Where are you?"

She brought the LED around in a slow arc, level with her waist, faintly making out a panel of switches. She crossed to them and tried one. Behind her, overhead, several of the big halogens came on.

She turned and saw, not unexpectedly now, the field-like floor, empty save for Bobby's GPS grid drawn in flour, churned and partially erased like chalk on a blackboard, where the table, chairs, and computers had been removed. She moved forward, stepping carefully, trying to avoid the white powder. There seemed to be a variety of prints, and quite a few of Bobby's—or someone else's, wearing those same ridiculous shoes, which seemed unlikely. There were beige filter tips, too, smoked down short and mashed flat against the concrete. Without picking one up, she knew that they'd be Marlboro.

She looked up at the lights, then back down at the prints and butts. "Bobby did a runner," she said, recalling an expression of Inchmale's.

Someone had removed the Safety Orange outline of Archie the squid.

She went out, avoiding touching the partially open green door. She got her computer out of its case in the trunk, woke it up, and while it booted, removed the Blue Ant helmet from its carton. With her right arm through the skeletal helmet and the PowerBook under her left, she closed the trunk and reentered the building. She opened the PowerBook and checked to see if that wireless network 72fofII00av, the one she'd accessed here before, had gone with Bobby. It had, but she'd expected that. She closed the laptop, tucking it under one arm as she fumbled to power up the helmet and put it on.

Archie was gone.

But the shipping container was still there, something glowing at its center, through wireframe.

She took a step forward and it vanished.

She heard a soft voice behind her, syllables not in English. She started to turn, then remembered to remove the helmet first.

A couple stood in the doorway, backlit by the sun.

They were small people. The male held a broad-headed push broom. *"Hola,"* he said.

"Hello?" Walking toward them. "I'm glad you're here. I'm just leaving. You can see they've left a mess." Gesturing behind her with the arm she'd again thrust through the helmet.

The man said something in Spanish, gently but questioning, as she stepped past them. "Goodbye," she said, not looking back.

A careworn silver-gray Econoline was parked beside the rented Passat. She used the transponder as she walked up to the car, quickly opening the door, getting in, helmet on the passenger seat, PowerBook on the floor, key in the ignition, pulling away, the dented rear doors of the Econoline in the mirror now, and then she was accelerating along Romaine.

31. PURO

Brotherman took the black packages down and loaded them into his truck, then the chair and ironing board, to be delivered to Vianca. She returned with Korean beef bowl. The three of them ate, silently for the most part, sitting in a row on Tito's black-wrapped mattress, and then Brotherman and Vianca left.

Tito was alone with the mattress, the Bulgarian's gun tucked beneath it, his toothbrush and toothpaste, the clothing he'd wear when he went to meet the old man, the old iron rack the clothing hung on, two wire hangers, his wallet, his telephone, the white cotton gloves he still wore, and three spare pairs of black socks he planned to tuck into the waistband of his loose black jeans.

His room had become larger, unfamiliar. The fossil imprints of plywood on the high ceiling were comfortingly unchanged. He brushed his teeth at the sink, decided to sleep in his jeans and long-sleeved T-shirt. When he turned off the light, the darkness was absolute and of no particular size. He got up and switched the light back on. He lay back down on the black-wrapped mattress, the plastic crinkling noisily, and placed one of the pairs of new black socks across his eyes. They smelled of fresh wool.

Then Alejandro rapped on his door in protocol, the rhythm utterly familiar. Removing the socks, Tito rolled off the mattress and rapped the response, waited for the answer, then opened the door. His cousin stood in the hallway, a set of keys in his hand, smelling faintly of alcohol, looking past Tito to the empty room. "It looks like a cell," Alejandro said.

"You always said it did."

"An empty one," Alejandro said, stepping in and closing the door behind him. "I've been to see the uncles. I'm to brief you on tomorrow, but I'm here to tell you more than I'm supposed to." He grinned, and Tito wondered how drunk he might be. "This way, you have no choice but to hear me."

"I always listen."

"Hearing is something else. Give me those socks." Tito passed him the pair of unworn socks and he separated them, pulling one over either hand. "I'll show you something." He grasped the bar of the rack with his sock-covered hands. Alejandro pulled the rack partially over, bracing the wheeled base with his shoe to prevent it rolling. "Look underneath."

Tito bent and peered under the ornately molded iron base. Something black, held there with tape. "What is it?"

"Mind your toes," Alejandro warned, as he raised the bar, lowering the base to the floor again.

"What is it?"

"It picks up incoming and outgoing cellular traffic. Messaging. The Volapuk. When you receive the message to deliver the iPod to your old man, regardless of your number, they'll have it." Alejandro smirked, an expression from their boyhood.

"Who? Who are they?"

"The old man's enemies."

Tito thought of their previous conversations. "He is from the government? The CIA?"

"He was a counterintelligence officer, once. Now he is a renegade, a rogue player, Carlito says. Mad."

"Mad?"

"It's beside the point. Carlito and the others have committed the family to his operation. Have committed you. But you know that. You didn't know about this bug," indicating the rack, "but the uncles did. Family were watching when it was placed here, and more recently when the battery was replaced."

"But do you know who put it here?"

"That's complicated." Alejandro crossed to the sink and propped himself against it. "Sometimes the closer to a truth one gets, the more complicated things become. The men in bars, who explain every dark secret of this world, Tito, have you noticed, no secret requires more than three drinks to explain. Who killed the Kennedys?

Three drinks. America's real motive in Iraq? Three drinks. The three-drink answers can never contain the truth. The truth is deep, cousin, and shifts, and runs away into the cracks, like the little balls of mercury we played with as children."

"Tell me."

Alejandro raised his hands, making puppets of the black socks. "'I am an old man who once kept secrets for the government here,'" he said for the sock on the left, "'but I detest certain policies, certain figures in the government whom I believe guilty of crimes. I am mad perhaps, obsessed, but clever. I have friends of a similar tendency, less mad perhaps and with more to lose. I find out secrets with their help, and plot to—'"

"Can it hear us?"

"No."

"How can you be sure?"

"Carlito had a friend look at it. No mere wire. Something only the government has, illegal to possess."

"Are they the government?"

"'Contractors,'" he said for the sock on the right, "'we are contractors. That is how things are done here now. We contractors, we work for the government, yes. Except,'" and the sock turned toward Tito and crumpled its mouth for emphasis, "'when we don't.'" Alejandro made the socks bow to one another, lowered them. "They are working for someone in the government, perhaps, but not on government business. But they don't necessarily know that. They wouldn't want to know that, would they? Sometimes these contractors find it most convenient to know nothing at all. Do you see?"

"No," Tito said.

"If I were more specific, I'd be inventing a story. Most of this, I infer from things Carlito and others have said. Here are some things that are definite, though. Tomorrow, you will meet a man in the basement of Prada, the men's shoe section. He will give you an iPod and certain instructions. You will already have received a message, here, in Volapuk, instructing you to deliver the iPod to the old man, at the farmers' market in Union Square, at one o'clock in the afternoon. You will leave here as soon as you receive the message. Once you have the iPod, you will be nowhere in particular, moving, until one. The family, of course, will be with you."

"The others had been left in drop boxes," Tito said.

"But not this time. You must be able to recognize this man later. You must do as he tells you. Exactly as he tells you. He is with the old man."

"Would these contractors attempt to take the iPod?"

"They will not try to apprehend you, on your way to the delivery. Above all, they want the old man. But they also want the iPod, and they will do whatever possible to capture you, once they have the old man in sight."

"But you know what I've been instructed to do?"

"Yes."

"Can you explain why I'm to do it?"

"It looks to me," Alejandro said, raising one sock-hand as if to peer into its nonexistent eyes, "as if the old man, or those who send him the iPods, wish to feed someone some puro."

Tito nodded. Puro, in his family, meant the most perfectly groundless of lies.

32. MR. SIPPEE

She ate a dollar-fifty-nine barbecue beef rib with broasted potatoes off a paper plate on the trunk of the Passat, waiting for Alberto to turn up at Mr. Sippee, a blessed oasis of peace and mutual respect situated in a twenty-four-hour convenience store at the Arco gas station at Blaine and Eleventh.

Nobody messed with you in Mr. Sippee. She knew that from her previous stay in Los Angeles, and that was what brought her here now. Close to the tents under the freeway, Mr. Sippee catered to an eclectic clientele of the more functionally homeless, sex workers of varied gender and presentation, pimps, police officers, drug dealers, office workers, artists, musicians, the map-lost as well as the life-lost, and anyone in serious search of the perfect broasted potatoes. You ate standing up, if you had a car to put your food on. If you didn't, you sat on the curb out front. She had often thought, while eating there, that the United Nations could do worse than investigate the pacific powers of broasted potatoes.

She felt safe here. Even if she'd been followed from Bobby Chombo's recently vacated space in the factory on Romaine. Which she didn't think she had, really, but it had definitely felt like she should have been. The feeling had made a knot between her shoulder blades, but now Mr. Sippee was taking that away.

The car nearest hers was an ivory-hued vehicle that aspired to mildly Maybachian proportions. The two young men who belonged to it, in capacious hoodies and elaborate sunglasses, weren't eating. Instead, they were soberly fiddling with their digital hubcaps. One sat behind the wheel, tapping patiently on a laptop, while the other stood staring at the left front hubcap, bisected by a sullenly pulsing line of colored LEDs. Were they, she wondered, the car's owners, or someone's technical support staff? Meals at Mr. Sippee could involve these questions of unfamiliar roles, of foreign economies of scale. Particularly when dining here in the small hours, as the Curfew had often done after an evening in the studio. Inchmale loved the place.

Now a classic Volks bug, frosted with doe-eyed Aztec princesses and quasi-phallic volcanoes, drew in past the magic hubcaps, Alberto at the wheel. He parked a few vehicles down and approached as she finished the last bite of her potatoes.

"He's gone," said Alberto, plaintively. "Is my car safe?" Looking around at their fellow diners.

"I know he's gone," she said. "I told you. And nobody messes with your car at Mr. Sippee."

"Are you sure?"

"Your car's safe. Where's Bobby?"

"Gone."

"Did you go there?"

"Not after what you said. But his e-mail addresses are all bouncing. And his work's gone. Not on the servers he uses."

"The squid?"

"Everything. Two pieces of mine, in progress. Sharon Tate—"

"I don't want to know."

He frowned at her.

"Sorry, Alberto. I'm on edge myself. It was creepy, turning up like that and finding the place cleaned out. Speaking of which, did Bobby have cleaners?"

"Cleaners?"

"A couple? Hispanic, oriental? Middle-aged, small?"

"By Bobby's standards, the place was clean when I took you there. He just let it pile up. He'd never trust anyone in to clean. The last place he had, he moved out because they kept asking him if he had a meth lab. He's that private, hardly ever goes out—"

"Where'd he sleep?"

"He slept there."

"Where?"

"On a pad, in a bag, in a fresh square of grid. Every night."

"Did he have a big white truck?"

"I've never even seen him drive."

"Did he always work alone?"

"No. He'd bring kids in, if he was in crunch mode."

"You get to know any?"

"No."

She studied the pattern of potato grease on her empty paper plate. If you knew enough Greek, she thought, you could assemble a word that meant divination via the pattern of grease left on a paper plate by broasted potatoes. But it would be a long word. She looked over at the LED-wheeled ivory car. "Is their display broken?"

"You can't see an image unless the wheels are turning. The system senses the wheel's position and fires the LEDs it needs, to invoke an image in persistence of vision."

"I wonder if they make them for a Maybach?"

"What's a Maybach?"

"A car. Did Bobby ever talk about shipping containers?"

"No. Why?"

"Somebody's piece, maybe?"

"He didn't talk about other artists' work. The commercial stuff, like that squid for Japan, sure."

"Do you know any reason he'd just blow, this way?"

Alberto looked at her. "Not unless something about you frightened him."

"Am I that scary?"

"Not to me. But Bobby's Bobby. What worries me about this, though, aside from losing my work, which is killing me, is that I can't imagine him getting it together to move out. Not that efficiently. The last time, getting out of the place where they thought he had a meth lab, and into the space on Romaine, took him three days. He hired some tweaker with a mail van. I finally had to come in to help him, to organize it."

"I don't know what it is that bothers me about it," she said, "but something sure does." The hoodie boys were still into their hubcaps, serious as NASA technicians, prelaunch. "Aren't you going to eat?"

He looked at the Arco station and the convenience store. "I'm not hungry."

"Then you're missing some jammin' potatoes."

33. COUNTERPANE

Brown, in a cloak and tight-fitting cowl fashioned from one of the New Yorker's foam-core blankets, gestured across the rolling beige plain with a sturdy wood-look staff, its length decorated in a traditional pattern of cigarette burns. "There," he said.

Milgrim squinted in the direction indicated, the direction in which they seemed to have been traveling for some time, but saw only the gibbet-like timber constructions interrupting the otherwise featureless expanse. "I can't see anything," Milgrim said, preparing to be struck for disagreement, but Brown only turned, still pointing forward with his staff, and put his other hand on Milgrim's shoulder. "That's because it's below the horizon," said Brown, reassuringly.

"What is?" asked Milgrim. The sky had a Turner-on-crack intensity, something volcanic aglow behind clouds that looked set to birth tornadoes. "The keep of great Baldwin," Brown declared, leaning closer to Milgrim's eyes, "count of Flanders, emperor of Constantinople, suzerain of every Crusader princeling in the Eastern Empire."

"Baldwin is dead," Milgrim protested, startling himself.

"Untrue," said Brown, but still gently, and still gesturing with the staff. "Yonder rises his keep. Can you not see?"

"Baldwin is dead," Milgrim protested, "but among the poor this myth of the Sleeping Emperor goes all about, and a pseudo-Baldwin, one so claiming, supposedly walks among them now."

"Here," said Brown, lowering his staff and gripping Milgrim's shoulder more firmly, "he is here, the one and true."

Milgrim saw that not only were Brown's hood and cloak made from the beige foam-core material, but so was the plain. Or rather covered with it, as it felt beneath his bare soles like a thin carpet spread over a dune.

"Here," Brown was saying, shaking him awake, "here it is." The BlackBerry thrust into his face.

"Pencil," Milgrim heard himself say, rolling upright on the edge of the bed. Cracks of daylight at the border of New Yorker drapes. "Paper. What time is it?"

"Ten-fifteen."

Milgrim had the BlackBerry now, squinting at its screen, scrolling unnecessarily. Whatever it was, it was brief. "Pencil. Paper."

Brown handed him a sheet of New Yorker stationery and a tooth-marked four-inch stub of yellow pencil, kept ready because Milgrim had insisted that he needed to be able to erase. "Leave me alone while I do this."

Brown made a strange little strangled sound, some deep combination of anxiety and frustration.

"I can do a better job if you go into your own room," Milgrim said, looking up at Brown. "I have to concentrate. This isn't like translating high school French. This is the very definition of idiomatic." He saw that Brown didn't know what that meant, and noticed his own satisfaction at the fact.

Brown turned and walked out of the room.

Milgrim scrolled the message again and started translating, printing in block capitals on the New Yorker stationery.

ONE TODAY IN

He stopped and considered.

UNION SQUARE AGRICULTURE

He used the eraser, which was nearly gone, the metal ferrule scratching the paper.

UNION SQUARE FARMERS MARKET

17TH STREET DELIVERY TO USUAL CLIENT

It seemed so simple.

He supposed it was, really, but Brown had been waiting for this, for the IF to receive one of these messages in his room, on one of the IF's steadily replaced cell

phones, where the fancy little bug under the coatrack
could also pick it up. Brown had been waiting for it since
he'd acquired Milgrim. Previous messages were assumed
to have been received elsewhere, when the IF was out
and about, drifting as he seemed to through lower Manhattan. Milgrim had no idea how Brown knew about
those previous deliveries, but he did, and it had become
evident to Milgrim that what Brown wanted most of all
wasn't the IF, or whatever it might be that he was delivering, but this "usual client," a second "he" in Brown's
phone conversations, sometimes also referred to as "Subject." Brown ate and slept Subject, Milgrim knew, and
the IF was merely some facilitator. Once Brown had
raced to Washington Square, his people converging in-
visibly with him, only to find Subject gone, and the IF
strolling back down Broadway like a small black crow,
narrow black legs moving over a broken cover of sooty
snow. Milgrim had seen this from the window of a gray
Ford Taurus that stank of cigars, over Brown's tactical
nylon shoulder.

Milgrim stood, massaging stiffness from his thighs,
discovered his fly unzipped, zipped it, rubbed his eyes,
and dry-swallowed the morning's Rize. It delighted
him, knowing Brown wouldn't interrupt him now. He
looked down at Brown's BlackBerry on the bedside table,
beside the translated Volapuk.

The dream came back. Those gallows things. They
were in Bosch, weren't they? Torture devices, props for
vast disembodied organs?

He picked up the BlackBerry and the sheet of stationery, and went to the connecting door, which as usual stood open. "Union Square," he said.

"When?"

Milgrim smiled. "One. Today."

Brown was in front of him, taking the BlackBerry and the paper. "This is it? This is all it says?"

"Yes," said Milgrim. "Will I be going back to the laundry?"

Brown looked at him, sharply. Milgrim didn't ask these questions. He'd learned not to. "You're coming with me," said Brown. "You might get to do some live translation."

"You think they speak Volapuk?"

"They speak Russian," Brown said. "Cuban-Chinese. The old man speaks it too." He turned away. Milgrim went into his bathroom and ran the cold. The Rize hadn't gone down smoothly. He looked at himself in the mirror and noted that he could use a haircut.

As he drank the glass of water he wondered when he'd quit looking at his own face in mirrors, other than for the most basic functions of grooming. He never saw himself there. At some point he'd decided not to.

He could hear Brown on the phone, energized and giving orders. He held his wrists under the cold stream from the tap, until it almost hurt. Then he turned it off and dried his hands on a towel. He pressed his face against the towel, imagining other people, strangers, whose faces had also touched it.

"I don't want more," he heard Brown say, "I want fewer and I want better. Get it through your head these aren't your sand monkeys. You're not over there now. These are operators, bred from the ground up. You lost him going into fucking Canal Street Station. You lose him in Union Square, you don't want to know. You hear me? You don't want to know."

Milgrim supposed he didn't want to know either, not in that sense, but this was all interesting. Cuban-Chinese, illegal facilitators who spoke Russian and messaged in Volapuk? Who lived in windowless mini-lofts on the fringes of Chinatown, wore APC and played keyboards? Who weren't sand monkeys, because this wasn't over there?

When in doubt, and when not compelled to simply enjoy his medication, Milgrim was in the habit of shaving, provided the necessities were at hand, as they were now. He began to run the hot.

Operators. Bred from the ground up.

Old man. That would be Subject.

He put the towel around his neck and tossed a washcloth into the hot water beginning to fill the sink.

34. SPOOK COUNTRY

Ezeiza," he said.

"What's that?"

"The airport. International Terminal B."

She'd gotten him on his cell in Buenos Aires, after getting hers activated for international calling. No idea what it was costing.

"And you're getting here day after tomorrow?"

"Day after that. It's a long flight up to New York but it's basically just flying north; odd to go that far without any time zones. I'm having lunch with a friend, dinner there with someone from the Bollards' label. Then I'm out to your end next morning."

"I think I've gotten myself into something, Reg, with this *Node* assignment."

"What did we tell you? The lady wife has your boy's

number. Been getting steadily harsher about him since you brought his name up. This morning she'd gotten it up to 'unclean.' Or is that down?"

"I haven't actually found him that personally repulsive, aside from his taste in cars, but I don't like the sense of enormous amounts of money at the service of, of, well, I don't know. He's like a monstrously intelligent giant baby. Or something."

"Angelina says he's utterly amoral in the service of his own curiosity."

"That probably covers it. But I don't like the sort of thing he's currently curious about, and I don't like the way it feels to me that things are starting to happen, around that."

"Sort of thing. Feels to you. You're being uncharacteristically oblique."

"I know," she said, and paused, lowering her phone in abrupt recognition of what was bothering her. She put it back to her ear. "But we're on the phone, aren't we?"

There was a silence, on his end. A true, absolute, and digital silence, devoid of that random background sizzle that she'd once taken as much for granted during an international call as she took the sky overhead when she was outside. "Ah," he said. "Well. There is always that. Increasingly more so, one imagines."

"Imagines more rapidly, around him."

"Ahem. I look forward to hearing more about this in person, then. But if my Spanish is at least semifunctional today, my flight's just being called."

"Good one, Reg."

"Call you from New York."

"Damn," she said, closing her phone. She'd wanted, needed, to tell him about Bigend's pirate story, about meeting Bobby, about seeing the white truck driving away and how that made her feel. He'd sort it out, she knew. Not make it make any more sense, necessarily, but just that his categories were so unlike hers. Unlike anyone's, maybe. But something else had happened; some recognition of a line crossed, some ambiguous territory entered.

Bigend and his James Bond villain's car, his half-built headquarters to match, his too much money, his big sharp curiosity, and his bland willingness to go poking it wherever he wanted. That was potentially dangerous. Had to be. In some way she'd never really imagined before. If he wasn't lying, he'd been paying people to tell him about secret government programs. The war on terror. Were they still calling it that? She'd caught some, she decided: terror. Right here in her hand, in Starbucks, afraid to trust her own phone and the net stretching out from it, strung through those creepy fake trees you saw from highways here, the cellular towers disguised with grotesque faux foliage, Cubist fronds, Art Deco conifers, a thin forest supporting an invisible grid, not unlike the one spread on Bobby's factory floor in flour, chalk, anthrax, baby laxative, whatever it was. The trees Bobby triangulated on. The net of telephony, all digitized, and all, she had to suppose, listened to. By whoever, whatever, made the sort of things Bigend was poking at its business. Somewhere, she had to believe, such things were all too real.

Maybe now, they already were. Listening to her.

She looked up and saw the other customers. Relatively minor functionaries in film, television, music, games. None of them, in that moment, looking particularly happy. But none of them, probably, touched in quite the same way by this new bad thing, this shadow, fallen across her.

35. GUERREROS

He left the black-wrapped mattress on the floor, with his keys at its exact center, the toothbrush and toothpaste on the edge of the sink, the wire hangers on the old rack that concealed the bug Alejandro had shown him. He closed the door behind him for the last time and left the building, stepping out into a startlingly fresh bright day, a new sun starting to warm the winter's residue of dog turds.

When he reached Broadway he bought a paper cup of coffee, black, and sipped from it as he walked, letting the rhythm of his stride find his systema. He let himself be focused by his progress, his road. There could be nothing but the road until he had completed his task, even if he were to turn back for some reason, or stand still.

The uncles who taught him systema had themselves

been taught by a Vietnamese, a former soldier, one who had come from Paris to end his days in the village of Las Tunas. Tito as a child had sometimes seen this man at rural family functions, but never in Havana, and had never spoken with him. The Vietnamese had always worn a loose black cotton shirt with no collar, untucked at the waist, and brown plastic shower sandals scuffed the color of dust in a village street. Tito had seen him, as the older men had sat drinking beer and smoking cigars, ascend a two-story wall of whitewashed concrete blocks, no more purchase afforded than the very shallow grooves of mortar between the courses. It was a strange memory, since even as a child Tito had taken what he saw there to be impossible, in the ordinary sense of the world. No applause from the watching uncles, no sound at all, the blue smoke rising as they puffed their cigars. And the Vietnamese rising like that smoke in the twilight, and as quickly, his limbs not so much moving as insinuating themselves into different and constantly changing relationships with the wall.

Tito himself, later, when it had come his time to learn from the uncles, had learned quickly, and well. When it was time for his family to leave Cuba, his systema had already been strong, and the uncles who taught him had been pleased.

And while he had learned the uncles' ways, Juana had taught him the ways of the Guerreros: Elleggua, Ogún, Oshosi, and Osun. As Elleggua opens every road, so Ogún clears each road with his machete. God of iron and wars, of labor; owner of every technology. The number seven, colors green and black, and Tito held these inwardly now, as he walked toward Prince Street, the Bulgarian's technology tucked within its handkerchief into the inside pocket of his black nylon jacket, from APC. At the very edge of perception rode Oshosi, the orishas' hunter and scout. These three, along with Osun, were received by an initiate of the Guerreros. Juana had taught him these things, she had said at first, as a means of more deeply embracing the systema of the Vietnamese from Paris, and he had seen in the eyes of his uncles the proof of this, but he had never told them. Juana had taught him that as well, how the holding of knowledge in dignified privacy helps ensure desired results.

He saw Vianca pass him on a small motorcycle, headed downtown, the brightly painted, mirrored helmet turning his way, glinting in the sunlight. Already Oshosi was allowing him a less specific way of seeing. The life of the street, its pedestrians and traffic, was becoming one animal, an organic whole. With half of his coffee gone, he removed the plastic lid, slid his phone in, and recapped the paper cup, depositing it in the first trash receptacle he passed.

By the time he reached the southwest corner of Prince and Broadway he was flowing with the Guerreros, an alert and interested marcher within some invisible procession. Oshosi showed him the black, black-clad store detective with the bead in his ear, as Elleggua hid him from this man's attention. Passing the thick frosted cylinder of the store's glass elevator, he descended the stairway built into the rolling slope of the floor. He had often come here to enjoy the strangeness of it, as of some carnival ride halted in mid-swing. The clothes had never appealed to him, though he liked the look of them displayed here. They spoke too much of money, to the street; they were clothes that Canal copied; anonymous in their way, but too easily described.

He saw another store detective, white, in a beige coat and black shirt and tie. They must be provided with allowances for clothing, he thought, as he rounded a white modular wall of cosmetics and arrived at the men's shoes.

The Guerreros recognized the stranger standing there, a three-eyelet black alligator oxford in his hand. The strength of their recognition startled.

Blunt and broad shouldered, dark hair cut very short, the other, perhaps thirty, turned. Replaced the shoe on its shelf. "Sixteen hundred," he said, his English warmly accented in some unfamiliar way. "Not today." He smiled, teeth white but crowded. "Know Union Square?"

"Yes."

"At the north end of the park, Seventeenth Street, the Greenmarket. One sharp, don't show before then. If you did, he wouldn't be there. If you get within ten paces, and nothing's happened, break and run. They'll think you've seen them. Some of them will try to take him. Others will try to take you. Get away, but lose this in the process." He dropped the white rectangle of the iPod, in its Ziploc bag, into Tito's jacket's side pocket. "Run for the W, the hotel on the corner of Park and Seventeenth. Know it?"

Tito nodded, remembering having wondered about the name as he'd passed the place.

"Main entrance on Park, up from the corner. Not the revolving door nearest the corner; that's the hotel's restaurant. But that's where you're actually headed, the restaurant. In past the doorman, but then right. Not up the steps to the lobby. Not into the lobby, understand?"

"Yes."

"Through the door, right, you've made a U-turn. You're headed south. When you get to the revolving door, at the corner of the building, left. Into the restaurant, straight through it, into the kitchen, exit onto Eighteenth. Green step-van with silver lettering, south side of Eighteenth. I'll be there." He turned his head, as if scanning the display of shoes, most of which, today, Tito found very ugly. "They have radios, the men who'll try to take you, and phones, but all of that will be jammed, as soon as you move."

Tito, pretending to look at a zip-sided black calf boot, touched its toe with his finger, nodding noncommittally, turning to go.

Oshosi knew that the white detective in the beige jacket had been watching them.

The door of the frosted-glass elevator slid aside. Brotherman emerged, tall hair streaked with copper, eyes glazed, gait unsteady. The white detective instantly forgot Tito, who crossed to the elevator, entered, and pushed the button for the twenty-foot ride to the ground floor. As the door closed, Tito saw the one the Guerreros had rec-

ognized, grinning at the detective's approach to Brotherman, who was about to become abruptly sober, dignified,
and firmly but courteously disinclined to be interfered
with by a store detective.

36. SPECTACLES, TESTICLES, WALLET, AND WATCH

By the time Milgrim had finished shaving and gotten dressed, Brown was holding a meeting in the adjoining room. Milgrim had never known Brown to have a visitor before, and now he was having three, three males. They had arrived within minutes of Brown having made his call, and Milgrim had gotten brief glimpses of them as they'd filed into Brown's room. From what little he'd managed to see, he knew that they were white and conventionally dressed, and that was it. He wondered if they too had been staying here, particularly as two of them were in shirtsleeves and carried no coats or jackets.

He could hear them talking now, conversing quickly, but couldn't make anything out. Brown was making various decisive sounds, yeas or nays, and periodically interrupting to reel off what Milgrim took to be revised strategic requirements.

Milgrim decided to treat this as opportunity to pack, and having considered the circumstances, to re-Rize. Packing consisted of putting his book in the pocket of his overcoat, and seeing to toiletries. He rinsed and dried the blades of his blue plastic razor. He used a piece of toilet paper to tidy up the threads and cap of his small tube of Crest toothpaste; replacing the cap, he carefully furled the tube to its shortest possible length, watching it plump out satisfyingly as he did so. He washed and rinsed his white toothbrush, dried its bristles with one piece of toilet paper, and then wrapped them loosely in another. He considered taking the small bar of New Yorker soap, which lathered up nicely, but then he wondered why it was that he assumed they wouldn't be coming back.

Something was up. Afoot. He remembered reading Sherlock Holmes, centuries before. Leaving the bar of wet soap on the edge of the soap-and-whisker-speckled sink, he tucked the rest of his possessions away in the various pockets of the overcoat. He assumed that Brown would still have the wallet and identification he'd confiscated on first picking Milgrim up (he'd pretended to be a cop, and Milgrim wouldn't have doubted it, not on that first meeting), but otherwise these grooming aids, and his book, plus the clothes he was wearing and the overcoat, comprised the whole of Milgrim's worldly possessions. Plus two 5 mg tablets of Rize. He thumbed the pack's penultimate dose into his palm and considered it. Was this a worldly possession, he wondered. Unworldly, he decided, swallowing it.

Hearing Brown's meeting conclude with what sounded like a determined slapping of palms, he walked to the window. No need to see them, really, or they him. If indeed they weren't already quite familiar with him. But still.

"Move it," said Brown, from the door.

"I'm all packed."

"You're what?"

"'Game is afoot.'"

"You want a broken rib?"

But Brown's heart wasn't in it, Milgrim saw. He was distracted, focused utterly on his impending operation, on whatever needed to be done now with regard to IF and Subject. He had his cased laptop in his hand, and his other black nylon bag slung across his shoulder. Milgrim watched him pat himself down with his free hand, locating pistol, handcuffs, flashlight, knife, whatever other empowerments he didn't leave home without. Spectacles, Milgrim recited to himself, testicles, wallet, watch. "Ready when you are," he said, and walked past Brown into the hallway.

As his benzo-boost kicked in, in the elevator, Milgrim became aware of a not unpleasurable excitement. Something really was afoot, and as long as it didn't mean another four hours in the laundry on Lafayette, it promised to be interesting.

Brown marched them across the lobby, to the main

entrance, and out into surprisingly bright sunlight. A bellman was holding open the driver's door of a recently washed silver Corolla and proffering the key, which Brown took, handing the man two dollars. Milgrim rounded the back of the Corolla and got in. Brown was placing his laptop and other bag on the floor behind the passenger seat. When they rode together in a car like this, Milgrim knew, he rode shotgun, probably because that made him easier to shoot. Was that why they called it that? He heard Brown power-lock the doors.

Brown headed east on Thirty-fourth. The weather was fine, bespeaking some genuine onset of spring, and Milgrim imagined himself a pedestrian, strolling pleasantly. No, he thought, a pedestrian strolling with a mere 5 mg of Rize on hand. He reframed the image, hanging Brown's black bag over his shoulder. Wherein, he assumed, was kept the brown paper bag with the Rize supply.

"Red Team One," Brown said, firmly, as they took a right on Broadway, "south on Broadway, for Seventeenth." He listened to some distant voice.

Milgrim looked over and saw the gray plug in Brown's ear, the gray wire vanishing into the collar of his jacket.

"I'm going to leave you in the car," Brown said, touching something at his collar, a mute control. "I've got Transit Authority tags that'll keep the traffic cops off it, but I'm thinking I'll cuff you."

Milgrim knew better than to offer an opinion on this.

"But this is New York," Brown said.

"Yes," Milgrim agreed, tentatively.

"You look like a junkie. Cop thinks you're doing a Transit Authority car, then sees you're cuffed to it, alone, not good."

"No," said Milgrim.

"So no cuffs."

Milgrim said nothing.

"I'm going to need these cuffs today," said Brown, and smiled. Milgrim couldn't remember having seen Brown smile. "You, on the other hand, are going to need the dope in this bag, aren't you?"

"Yes," Milgrim agreed, having already come to the same conclusion, a few minutes before.

"I get back to this car and your ass isn't in it, you're finished."

Milgrim wondered what Brown thought constituted deeper shit, for Milgrim, in his current situation, although having benzo-seizures while homeless and penniless on the streets of Manhattan actually did fully qualify, by Milgrim's own standards, and maybe Brown knew it. "I hear you," Milgrim said, trying for a tone that would match Brown's, but not antagonize him. He had a feeling, though, that Brown's "finished" meant dead, and that was a more peculiar feeling than he would have expected.

"Copy," Brown said, to the voices in his ear. "Copy."

37. FREERUNNERS

The Guerreros took him up Broadway, through the sunlight. He hadn't expected this, assuming he'd reach
Union Square by subway, then round and circle until
the time of his meeting. But no, and so he walked with
them, just as they led him. And soon he was simply a
man walking, the orishas spread through a seemingly
ordinary awareness, invisible as drops of ink in a volume
of water, his pulse steady, enjoying the look of the sun
on the floral ironwork that supported many of these old
buildings. This was, he knew, though he avoided directly
considering it, a still higher state of readiness.

A part of him felt dismay at the thought that he very
probably would leave this city soon, perhaps before sunset. It seemed impossible, somehow, but once it must
have seemed impossible that he would leave Havana. He

couldn't remember if it had, though he'd left Cuba on equally short notice, taking nothing but the clothes he'd been wearing when his mother had fetched him from a restaurant. He'd been eating a ham sandwich. He could still remember the taste of the bread, a type of square bun that had been a feature of his childhood. Where would he be, tomorrow?

He crossed Houston. Pigeons flew up from the crosswalk.

The summer before, he'd met two NYU students in Washington Square. They were freerunners, devotees of something loosely akin to systema, and also practitioners of what they called tricking. They were black, and had assumed him to be Dominican, though they'd called him "China." He wondered, now, continuing north, whether this sun would bring them to Washington Square today. He'd enjoyed their company, the demonstrations and exchanges of lesser techniques. He learned the backtucks and other tricks they practiced, incorporating them into his systema, but declined to join them in freerunning, for which they had already been charged with minor infractions of trespass or public safety. He had been looking forward to seeing them again.

He passed Bleecker, then Great Jones Street, the namesake of the latter always imagined as some giant, a creature from the age of iron-framed buildings, bowler-hatted, shoulders level with second-story windows. A figment of Alejandro's, from the days of his apprenticeship to Juana. He remembered Alejandro sending him into Strand Books, which he soon would be passing, for titles printed in particular years, in particular countries, on various specific types of stock. To be purchased for no content other than the blank endpapers, pages Tito had thought of as stories left unwritten, to be filled in by Alejandro with intricately constructed identities.

He walked on, never looking back, confident that he wasn't being followed by anyone who wasn't a relative; had it been otherwise, he would have been alerted by one or another family member from the team he knew was keeping pace with him, scattered along a constantly moving two-block stretch of either sidewalk, continually trading off positions according to a KGB protocol older than Juana.

Now he saw his cousin Marcos stepping off the curb, a half block ahead. Marcos the conjuror, the pickpocket, with his dark curls.

He walked on.

HAVING DISCARDED his phone, he began to check the time on clocks, through the windows of banks and dry cleaners, as he neared the southern end of Union Square. Clock time was not for the orishas. It would be up to him to coordinate his arrival.

Fifteen to one. On East Fourteenth, beneath the weird art numbers frantically telling a time nobody could read, he looked with Oshosi toward the distant canvas stalls of the market.

And then they passed him, laughing, his two freerunners from the summer and Washington Square. They hadn't seen him. He remembered, now, that they lived in NYU dorms, here in Union Square. He watched them go, wishing he could go with them, while around him the orishas briefly and very faintly rippled the air, like heat rising above August pavement.

38. TUBAL

She lay very still, on her back, the sheet forming a cool dark tunnel, and gave her body explicit permission to relax. This made her remember doing the same thing in an overhead berth on a tour bus, but with a sleeping bag instead of sheets, and foam earplugs instead of asking the desk to hold her calls, and setting the ring on her cell to silent.

Inchmale had called it womb-return, but she knew it was the opposite, really; not so much the calm of not yet having been born, but the stillness of already having died. She didn't want to feel like a fetus, but like the recumbent figure carved atop a sarcophagus, cool stone. When she'd explained that to Jimmy Carlyle, once, he'd cheerfully told her that was pretty much exactly what he was after with heroin. Something about that exchange had left her very glad she'd never been much attracted to drugs, other than garden-variety cigarettes.

But anything that shook her sufficiently, really hard, could get her into tube mode, preferably in a darkened room. The departures of serious boyfriends had done it, as had the end of the Curfew, her initial major losses when the dot-com bubble had popped (the fact of those holdings having been residue of a serious boyfriend, if you wanted to look at it that way) had done it, and her subsequent (and she supposed possibly final, the way things were headed) major financial loss had done it as well, when her friend Jardine's ambitious shot at an indie music emporium in Brooklyn had not so unexpectedly failed. Investment in that had initially seemed like a sort of hobby move, something fun and open-ended and potentially even profitable, that she could afford to take a chance on, given the dot-coms had briefly made her worth some single-digit number of millions, at least on paper. Inchmale, of course, had lobbied for her to dump the start-up stocks at what she now knew had been their white-hot and utterly evanescent peak. Inchmale, being Inchmale, had by then already dumped his own, which had driven acquaintances crazy, as they'd all believed he was throwing away the future. Inchmale had told them that some futures needed throwing away, badly. And Inchmale, of course, had never sunk a quarter of his net worth into founding a large, aggressively indie, bricks-and-mortar retail establishment. Selling music on the full variety of what were, after all, Inchmale had insisted, dead platforms.

Now, she knew, she'd been returned to the tunnel by that sudden stab of weird fear, in Starbucks; fear that Bigend had gotten her into something that might be at once hugely and esoterically dangerous. Or, she thought, if you looked at it as process, by the cumulative strangeness of what she'd encountered since she'd accepted the assignment from *Node*. If indeed *Node* existed. Bigend seemed to be saying that *Node* only existed to whatever extent he might ultimately need it to.

What she needed, she knew, however belatedly, was a second career. Helping Hubertus Bigend exercise his curiosity wasn't going to be it, and neither, she knew absolutely, was anything else Blue Ant might offer her. She had always, she'd reluctantly come to know, wanted to write. During the Curfew's heyday, she'd frequently suspected that she was one of very few singers who spent a certain part of every interview wishing she were on the other side of the microphone. Not that she wanted to be interviewing musicians. She was fascinated by how things worked in the world, and why people did them. When she wrote about things, her sense of them changed, and with it, her sense of herself. If she could do that and pay the grocery bills, the ASCAP check could pay the rent, and she'd see where that could go.

She had, during the Curfew days, written a few pieces for *Rolling Stone*, a few more for *Spin*. With Inchmale, she'd written the first in-depth history of the Mopars, their mutual favorite sixties garage band, though they hadn't been able to find anyone willing to pay them to publish it. In the end, though, it had run in Jardine's record store's in-house magazine, its publication one of the few things she'd gotten out of that particular invest-ment.

Inchmale, she guessed, was sitting up in business class, headed for New York, reading *The Economist*, a mag-azine he read exclusively on airplanes, swearing that on arrival he promptly and invariably forgot every word.

She sighed. Let go, she told herself, though she had no idea of what.

Alberto's virtual monument to Helmut Newton ap-peared, in her mind's eye. Silver-nitrate girls pointed into occult winds of porn and destiny.

"Let go," she said, aloud, and fell asleep.

NO BORDERS of glare edged the multiple layers of drapes, when she woke. Already evening. She lay there in her sheet-tube, no longer needing it in the same way. The edge of her anxiety had receded, not quite past the hori-zon but sufficient to have restored her curiosity.

Where was Bobby Chombo, now? Had he been hauled off, along with his equipment, by the Depart-ment of (as Inchmale called it) Homemade Security? Charged (or not) with dicking around with some scheme to smuggle weapons of mass destruction? Something about the quietly deep peculiarity of those two cleaners led her to think not. Rather, she thought, he'd done a runner, but with considerable help. Some crew had come in, loaded his gear into that white truck, and hauled him off, elsewhere. He might be no more than a few blocks from the first place, for all she knew. But if he'd cut himself off from Alberto, and the rest of that art scene, what were her chances of finding him again?

Somewhere, she thought, looking up at the almost invisible whiteness of the darkened room's ceiling, there was, supposedly, the container. A long, rectangular box of . . . were they made of steel? Yes, she decided, steel. She had had carnal knowledge of an Irish architect in one, on his rural property in Derry. He'd converted it into a studio. Oversized portholes cut with a torch, glass framed in with plywood. Definitely steel. His had been insulated originally for refrigeration, she remembered him telling her; the simpler ones too chilly, prone to condensation of human breath.

She'd never really thought about them, before. You glimpsed them from freeways, sometimes, stacked as tightly as Odile's robotic Lego. An aspect of contemporary reality so common as to remain unconsidered, unquestioned. Almost everything, she supposed, traveled in them now. Not raw materials, like coal or grain, but manufactured things. She remembered news items about them being lost at sea, in storms. Breaking open. Thousands of Chinese rubber duckies bobbing gaily along the great currents. Or sneakers. Something about hundreds of left sneakers washing up on the beach, the rights having been shipped separately to prevent pilferage. And someone else, on a yacht in the harbor at Cannes, telling scary transatlantic sailing stories; how they don't sink immediately, containers gone over the side, and the silent, invisible threat they then pose to sailors.

She seemed to have cycled through most of the fear she'd felt, before. Curiosity hadn't replaced it entirely, but she had to admit she was curious. One of the scary things about Bigend, she supposed, was that with him you stood an actual chance of finding some things out. And then where would you be? Were there things that were, in themselves, deeply problematic to learn? Definitely, though it would depend on who knew you knew them, she decided.

But then the small dry sound of an envelope being slid under the door, familiar from her life on tour, suddenly triggered, as it always had, the atavistic mammalian fear of nest invasion.

She turned on a light.

The envelope, when she retrieved it from the carpet, contained a color printout, on unexceptional paper, of a photograph of the white truck, parked beside the loading bay of Bobby Chombo's rented factory.

She turned it over, finding, inscribed in Bigend's vaguely cuneiform hand: "I'm in the lobby. Let's talk. H."

Curiosity. Time she satisfied some. And time, she knew, to decide whether or not she was willing to go on with this.

She went into the bathroom, to ready herself to meet Bigend again.

Milgrim remembered Union Square from twenty years before, when it had been a place of broken benches and litter, where a corpse might go unremarked amid the huddled and unmoving bodies of the homeless. It had been a flagrant drug bazaar, in those days, when Milgrim himself had had no need of such a place. But now it was Barnes & Noble, Circuit City, Whole Foods, Virgin, and he, Milgrim, had gone equally far, it sometimes seemed, in the opposite direction. Addicted, not to put too fine a point on it, to substances countering a tension at the core of his being; something wound too tightly, perpetually threatening to collapse his person; imploding, as though a Buckminster Fuller tensegrity structure contained one element that perpetually tightened itself counter to the balance of forces required to sustain it.

That was the experiential nature of the thing, though he was still capable, in the abstract, of considering the possibility that the core anxiety as he knew it today was in part an artifact of the substance.

Be that as it may, he decided, as Brown parked the silver Corolla on the south side of East Seventeenth, just short of Union Square West, the extra dose of Japanese pharmaceutical he'd treated himself to had certainly brightened things up, not to mention the unexpectedly fine weather.

Could Brown park here, Milgrim wondered. It didn't look like it, but after announcing to his throat-mike (or his inner demons perhaps) that "Red Team One" was on the scene, Brown hauled up his black bag from the floor behind Milgrim's seat, and drew out a pair of licenses, drably official-looking and encapsulated in long rectangular suction-mount envelopes of some transparent but slightly yellowed plastic. Transit Authority, in black sanserif caps. Milgrim watched as Brown licked a thumb, spreading spit on the concave faces of the two suction cups on one of these, and pressed it against the inside of the top of the windshield, directly above the steering wheel. He lowered the bag back down behind Milgrim's seat, on top of his laptop. He turned to Milgrim, producing his handcuffs, the two bracelets displayed in his palm as though he were about to suggest that Milgrim purchase them. They were as professionally lusterless as his other favorite things. Did they make handcuffs out of titanium, Milgrim wondered. If not, these had a sort of faux-titanium finish, like the faux Oakley sunglasses they sold on Canal Street. "I said I wasn't going to cuff you into the car," Brown said.

"No," Milgrim agreed, carefully neutral, "you said you were going to need them."

"You don't know what to say if a cop or a traffic warden shows up and asks what you're doing here." Brown snapped the cuffs back into their little formfitting plastic holster on his belt.

Help me, I've been kidnapped, Milgrim thought. Or, better: The trunk of this car is full of plastic explosives.

"You're going to sit on a bench, enjoy the sun," Brown said.

"Right," said Milgrim.

Brown unlocked the doors and they both got out. "Keep your hands on the roof of the car," Brown said. Milgrim did, while Brown opened the rear door on his side and bent in, to secure the second Transit Authority tag on the inside of the rear window. Milgrim stood with his palms flat on the clean, warm roof of the Corolla. Brown straightened up, closing the door. He clicked his key, locking the car. "This way," Brown said, then something else, something Milgrim didn't catch, probably in his role as Red Team One.

Brown's laptop, Milgrim thought. The bag.

Rounding the corner and finding the park spread before them, Milgrim squinted, unready for space, light, trees on the verge of leafage, the cheery canvas huddle of the Greenmarket.

Sticking close, he followed Brown across Union Square West and into the Greenmarket, passing young mothers with ATV-wheeled strollers and plastic bags of organic goodies. Then down past that WPA-era building he remembered, now apparently a restaurant, but closed. They came to the path that crossed the park at Sixteenth, with Lincoln atop his plinth at its center. Milgrim remembered trying to figure out what it was that Lincoln held at his side, in his left hand. A folded newspaper?

"Right here," said Brown, indicating the bench nearest Union Square West, on the south side of the path. "Not in the center. Here." He pointed to a spot directly beside the circular armrest, designed to be deliberately inhospitable to the back of any weary head. Milgrim sat, gripping the armrest to do so, as Brown pulled a skinny strip of shiny black plastic out of the waistband of his trousers, whipped it adroitly around the armrest and Milgrim's wrist, and fastened it, tightening it with a sharp, zipping sound. This left about a foot of excess plastic protruding from the cuff Brown had formed. He twisted this out of the way, making it less evident, and straightened up. "We'll collect you later. Keep your mouth shut."

"Okay," said Milgrim, craning his neck to watch Brown walk quickly south, his back to the Greenmarket. Milgrim blinked, processing, seeing the Corolla's curbside rear window shatter. That delicious instant, just before it fell into countless fragments. If you were careful, the alarm might not even sound. You could lean in, over the ragged edge of glass, and snag the strap on Brown's bag, wherein, Milgrim was certain, would be found the brown paper bag of Rize. And walk away.

Milgrim looked down at the narrow black band of unbreakable plastic around his wrist. He adjusted the cuff of the Paul Stuart coat, to make his situation less obvious to passersby. If Brown were using ordinary hardware department cable-ties, which this looked to be, Milgrim knew how to release it. The milky, translucent flexicuffs the NYPD used, he knew from experience, were not as easily unfastened. Had Brown not wanted to carry anything that wasn't black or titanium, he wondered.

Milgrim had briefly shared an apartment in the East Village with a woman who'd kept an emergency supply of Valium in an aluminum fishing-tackle box. The box's latch had a hole through which a small padlock could have been inserted, but she'd preferred to seal it with a plastic cable-tie, a slightly smaller version of the tie that now tethered Milgrim to this bench. When it was necessary to access the supply, Milgrim had determined, she'd snip the tie with pliers or nail-clippers, replacing it with a fresh one when she needed to reseal the box. This procedure made little sense, Milgrim had observed, but people did tend to be eccentric about their drugs. He'd supposed that the ties, like an embossed wax seal on a letter, provided proof that she was the last to have opened the box. Milgrim had looked for her supply of ties, the simplest way to bypass this, but hadn't been able to find it.

He had, however, determined that cable-ties are actually closed with a tiny molded internal ratchet. Once he'd learned to insert the flat tip of a jeweler's screwdriver, he'd been able to open and close her ties at will, even if she'd snipped them off short, as she tended to do.

The fact of his pilfering had quickly put that particular relationship behind him, but now he leaned forward, over his knees, to peer down at the unswept pavement between his feet. He'd already conducted a mental inventory of his pockets, and knew that he had nothing at all like a jeweler's screwdriver.

Uncomfortably aware that he could be taken for a tweaker looking for hallucinatory fragments of crack, he conducted a focused survey of the ground. He noticed, and as quickly rejected, an inch-long shard of brown bottle glass. Sawing through the tie was at least a theoretical possibility, but he had no idea how long it might take, or really if it would work at all, and he was also afraid of cutting himself. A paper clip, after what Brown might have called field-expedient modification, might do, but in his experience you didn't find paper clips or wire coat hangers when you needed them. But here, a few feet beyond the tip of his left shoe, was something slender, rectangular, apparently metallic. Glinting faintly. Getting a grip on the armrest with his captive hand, he swiveled awkwardly off the bench, extending his left leg as far as possible and scraping repeatedly over the object with his left heel as he attempted to bring it closer. The fifth or sixth scrape did it, and he was able to snatch up his gratifying rigid and narrow prize with his free hand, returning quickly to the bench and a more orthodox posture.

He held it between thumb and forefinger, like a seamstress her needle, and studied it carefully. It was the broken clip from a pen or pencil, stamped tin or brass, and rust flecked its cheap plated finish.

Very nearly perfect. He checked its tip against the small opening through which he intended to dislodge the invisible ratchet. Too wide, but not by much. He found a particularly rough section of cast iron on the side of the armrest and went to work.

It felt good to have something to do with his hands, or, anyway, hand, on a summer day. "Man the toolmaker," said Milgrim, filing away at his fairy Houdini shiv.

40. **DANCING**

Tito knelt and tightened the laces of his Adidas GSG9s, respectfully reminding the Guerreros that it was time. He stood, flexed his toes, crossed Fourteenth Street, and started up through the park, his hand on the iPod in its plastic bag in his jacket pocket.

Juana, once, in Havana, had taken him to a building of great and utterly decayed grandeur, though in those days he had had no idea that a structure of such age and intricacy might be found in any other condition. In the foyer, continents and oceans of distempered plaster were mapped on walls and ceiling. The elevator had shaken and screeched, carrying them to the top floor, and as Juana had heaved the cagelike metal door open, Tito had abruptly become aware of the drums he must have been hearing for some time, perhaps since they had first entered this street in Dragones. As they waited at the tall doors of the floor's single apartment, Tito had read and reread the handwritten message in Spanish on a grease-flecked slip of brown paper, fastened to the door with four thickly rusted carpet tacks: "Enter in the spirit of God and Jesus Christ, or do not enter." Tito had looked up at Juana, raising his eyebrows in some question he wasn't quite able to form. "It might as well say Marx and Lenin," Juana had told him. The door had been opened by a tall woman in a scarlet headscarf, a lit cigar in her hand, who smiled broadly to see them, and reached out to touch Tito's head.

Later, beneath a portrait of Our Lady of Guadalupe, and another of Che Guevara, the tall woman had begun the Dance of the Walking Dead, and Tito, pressed close to Juana, squinting through fumes of cigars and sweet aftershave, had watched as bare feet softly slapped the ruined parquet.

The Guerreros were around him now, talking among themselves in a language like weather, like high fast clouds. He shivered within his jacket, and walked on through the sunlight, toward the bare trees with their green buds. Oshosi showing him dead spots in the square's human matrix, figures that were no part of the unconscious dance formed here by this clearing amid the long city's buildings. He didn't look directly at these pretenders, watchers. He adjusted his path, avoiding them.

When he was closer to the canvas stalls of the market, he saw the old man, moving slowly along between displays of vegetables, his long tweed coat open to the warmth of the day. He walked now with a bright metal cane, and seemed to have some difficulty with his leg.

Oshosi rounded suddenly, sliding into Tito like a wind, dry and unexpectedly warm, showing him the convergence of the watchers. The nearest was a tall, broad-shouldered man with sunglasses and a blue base-ball cap, doing a poor job of pretending to stroll casually in the direction of the old man, an S of tension marking his brow between the glasses and the cap. Tito felt the two behind him as if Oshosi were pushing thumbs into his back. He adjusted his course, making it plain that he was headed for the old man. He slowed, and made a show of squaring his shoulders, hoping the men behind him would read and respond to this lie of the body. He saw the lips of the man with the sunglasses move, and remembered what the one in Prada had said about their radios.

Systema was in each fall of his black Adidas. Pulling the iPod from his pocket, held in the open plastic bag, not touching it with his fingers.

He was almost there, the Prada man's ten paces, but black glasses was a mere three from the old man when the old man pivoted, gracefully whipping the cane up and sideways, at arm's length, into the side of black glasses' neck. Tito saw the S of tension erased from the man's brow as the cane struck, and for what seemed far too long there was a face that consisted only of three holes, be-neath the visor of the blue baseball cap, the twin voids of the sunglasses and the equally round and seemingly toothless black hole of a mouth. Then the man struck the sidewalk like something deboned, the loaded cane clattering heavily beside him, and Tito felt their hands on his shoulders, and stopped moving forward.

"Thief!" cried the old man, with great force, his voice ringing out. "Thieves!"

Tito backtucked, as the followers' momentum carried them past him. As he came down, Oshosi showed him his elegant cousin Marcos, smiling urbanely between two handsome displays of produce, and straightening from having recovered something from between the wooden sawhorses of a farmer's stand. A length of wood, Marcos gripping it firmly at either end with gloved hands, his feet braced, as a trio of men running in the direction of the old man seemed to strike an invisible wall, and then to fly through it, becoming airborne. One landed on a farmer's display and women began to scream.

Marcos tossed the wooden handle of the tripwire down, as if discovering it fouled with filth, and strolled away.

The two men who had been following Tito, realizing he was behind them now, spun in unison, their shoulders colliding. The heavier of the two was slapping at something on his neck. Tito saw the wires of a radio. "Red team won," the man declared, furiously, with a savage and inexplicable emphasis on whatever victory that might be, then lunged for Tito, shoving his companion out of his way to do so.

Tito was having to feint, as if panicking, in various directions, in order to provide these two with the illusion of almost capturing him. Seeing the clumsiness of the one reaching for him, he decided that any more elaborate miming of fumbling and losing the iPod would be wasted. He dropped it, directly in the man's path, a square of white plastic separating as it struck the pavement. He pretended to lunge for it, in order to underline the fact that it was there. His would-be captor, seeing it, reflexively batted him aside. Rolling with the blow, Tito came up running, as the heavy man dove for the iPod. His companion tried to block Tito with a move he might have remembered from American football. Tito somersaulted between his legs and kicked off—on what must have been one of the man's Achilles tendons, to judge by his sharp yelp of pain.

Tito ran south, away from the intersection of Seventeenth and Park, his destination. Past the one from the Prada shoe department, in a tradesman's paint-splashed overalls, in one hand a yellow box with three short black antennas.

Around Tito ran the orishas, panting like vast dogs; scout and opener, opener and clearer. And Osun, whose role was mystery.

41. HOUDINI

With a click that he felt, rather than heard, the tiny ratchet at the heart of the cable-tie moved aside for Milgrim's modified ballpoint clip. He sighed, enjoying a moment of unaccustomed triumph. Then he loosened the tie, without removing it from the bench's armrest, and slid his wrist free. Keeping his wrist on the rest, he looked around the park as casually as possible. Brown was nowhere to be seen, but there was the matter of the other three he'd glimpsed in Brown's room at the New Yorker, plus whoever else comprised Brown's Red Team.

Why, he wondered, were such teams always red? Of tooth and claw, the teams of men like Brown. Seldom even blue. Never green, never black.

Past him moved a sunny afternoon's pedestrian traffic, across the width of the park. There were people here, he knew, who were playing at being here. Playing games. Brown's game, the game of the IF and those who worked with him. There were no police in evidence, he noted, and that struck him as odd, though in truth he hadn't passed this way for so long that he had no idea what sort of presence they currently chose to maintain.

"It must have been defective," he said aloud, of the cable-tie, rehearsing a line in the event of Brown's return before he could compose himself sufficiently to move away from this bench. "So I waited for you."

Very large hands found Milgrim's shoulders, pressed down. "Thank you for waiting," said a deep, measured voice, "but we aren't detectives." Milgrim looked over at the hand on his left shoulder. It was enormous, a black man's hand, with pink, glossily polished nails. Milgrim rolled his eyes, craning his neck gingerly, and saw, atop a vast bluff of button-studded black horsehide, a mighty black chin, perfectly shaven.

"We aren't detectives, Mr. Milgrim." The second black man, rounding the far end of the bench, had unbuttoned his heavy, cuirass-like coat, exposing a double-breasted black-on-black brocade vest and an elaborately collared satin shirt the color of arterial blood. "We aren't police at all."

Milgrim craned around a little further, to better see the one whose hands rested on his shoulders like two-pound bags of flour. They were both wearing the tight woolen skullcaps he remembered now from the laundry on Lafayette. "That's good," he said, wanting to say something, anything.

Horsehide creaked as the second man settled himself on the bench, his enormous leather-clad shoulder touching Milgrim's. "In your case, Mr. Milgrim, I wouldn't be so sure of that."

"No," said Milgrim.

"We've been looking for you," said the one with his hands on Milgrim's shoulders. "Not very actively, we'd be first to admit. But once you'd borrowed that young lady's telephone to contact your friend Fish, he had that number on call-display. Fish, being a friend of Mr. Birdwell, phoned him immediately. Mr. Birdwell phoned that number. He social engineered the lady, who anyway suspected you of having tried to steal her phone, you understand? Are you following me so far, Mr. Milgrim?"

"Yes," said Milgrim, feeling an irrational but very powerful urge to put the cable-tie back on, as though that would magically reverse the flow of events, taking him back to the uneventful park of a few moments before, seeming now a very paradise of security and light

"We happened to be nearby," said the one beside him, "and drove to Lafayette, where we found you. Since then, as a favor to Mr. Birdwell, we have been observing your movements, Mr. Milgrim, awaiting an opportunity to speak with you in private."

The hands on his shoulders grew abruptly heavier. "Where is that cop-looking motherfucker you always with, Mr. Milgrim? Drove you over here."

"He's not a cop," Milgrim said.

"He didn't ask you that," said the one beside him.

"Whoa," exclaimed the one behind, "old white man just deck that boy out the cuts!"

"Thief!?" shouted a man, from the direction of the Greenmarket. "Thieves!" Milgrim saw movement there.

"This place supposed to be gentrified," said the man beside Milgrim, as if offended by the disturbance. "Two million a unit, here."

"Shit," said the one behind, letting go of Milgrim's shoulders, "it's a bust."

"He's DEA!" shrieked Milgrim, lunging forward, his worn leather soles slipping nightmarishly, like feet in some ancient animation, one in which the gate of the projector is jumping. Or a very, very bad dream. And part of that dream, as he ran, was that he was still holding, before him, as if some tiny sword, his painfully honed Houdini key.

42. GOING AWAY

Systema avoids pursuit whenever possible, the uncles taught. Systema prefers not to flee; rather, it goes away. The distinction was difficult to express, but easily demonstrated through something as simple as the attempted grappling of wrists across a table. The wrist trained in systema went away.

But Tito, having been directed to a particular place, the mysteriously named W, could no longer fully practice going away, the art of which is dependent on a genuine lack of direction. To be pursued, as Oshosi assured him he now was, was to accept a certain disadvantage. But there was systema for this as well, and he chose to demonstrate it now, taking the back of a bench at speed, dropping, rolling, coming up with his momentum intact but headed in the direction opposite. A simple enough business, spending momentum in the roll, but he heard a child cheer to see it.

The nearest of his three pursuers was just rounding the bench as Tito vaulted back over it, past him, and hit the path, running east now. He looked back. The other two, untrained slaves to their own momentum, were carried past the first and very nearly ran into the bench. These were the ones he'd seen Marcos trip. One of them had a bloodied mouth.

With Oshosi at his shoulder, Tito ran toward Union Square East and Sixteenth Street. The orisha wanted him out of the park and its calculable geometries of pursuit. A cab slid in front of him as he reached the traffic on Union Square East; he went over its hood, meeting the eyes of its driver as he slid past the windshield, friction burning his thigh through his jeans. The driver slammed his horn and held it, and other horns woke reflexively, a sudden uneven blaring that mounted to crescendo as his three pursuers reached the stream of traffic. Tito looked back and saw the one with the bloody mouth maneuvering between crowded bumpers, holding something aloft like a token. A badge, Tito guessed.

Tito ran north, bent low, deliberately slowing, weaving through the crowd, some of whom were pausing to see what the horns were about. Faces peered from the windows of a restaurant. He looked back and saw the bloody-mouthed man spill a woman out of his way as he ran after Tito.

Tito sped up, Oshosi noting that his pursuer was still gaining. He ran across Seventeenth without slowing. Saw the entrance to the resturant, a revolving door. He ran on, to the hotel's entrance, an airy lip of glass protruding to shelter it. Under the startled doorman's black-shirted arm, past a woman just emerging. He saw Brotherman descending two broad marble steps, divided by a central railing. Brotherman wore a Federal Express uniform and cradled a flat red-white-and-blue carton upright in his arms. He'd never seen Brotherman in shorts before. As Tito threw right, his new shoes grabbing the white marble, he heard the bloody-mouthed man slam through the doors behind him.

He glimpsed a sinuous overhang of stairway, deeper in the lobby, and registered the distinctive sound of Brotherman, releasing, on his exit, thirty pounds of twelve-millimeter steel ball bearings, through the trick bottom of his FedEx carton and onto the white marble.

Tito sprinted south, Oshosi indicating that his pursuer, who must have missed the bearings, was only a few steps behind.

Into the restaurant, darting past the row of tables by the south-facing windows; past the unbelieving faces of diners, who an instant before had been lingering over desserts and coffees.

The man with the bloody mouth caught his left shoulder and he careened into a table, food and glassware flying, a woman screaming. In the instant of contact,

Elleggua, mounting Tito with nauseating speed, had reached back with Tito's right hand, slipped something from the man's belt, and now simultaneously drew and fired the Bulgarian's pneumatic gun with his left, from under Tito's right armpit.

An inhuman shriek unmounted the orisha as Tito saw the illuminated exit sign and slammed through the door beneath it, past the laden carts of busboys. Kitchen staff in white flung themselves out of his way. He slipped in something wet, nearly went down, ran on. Exit sign. Slamming out, into sudden sunlight, as an alarm triggered behind him.

A large green van, neatly lettered in silver, one of its twin rear doors open. Prada man, no longer wearing his painter's overalls, reaching down his hand.

Tito handed him the leather-cased badge Elleggua had taken from the pursuer's belt.

He flipped it open. "Ice," he said, and pocketed it. He boosted Tito into the truck. A dark, hollow, diesel-smelling space, with odd dim lights. "You've already met." He jumped out of the truck and slammed and locked the door.

"Be seated," said the old man, from a bench fastened lengthwise across the space with canvas strapping. "We wouldn't want you injured, in case of a sudden stop."

Tito climbed over the back of the padded bench. Discovering the two ends of a simple seat belt, he fastened them as the driver put the truck in gear, heading west, then swung north onto Park.

"I trust they took it from you?" the old man asked, in Russian.

"Yes, they did," Tito replied, in English.

"Very good," said the old man, in Russian. "Very good."

43. PONG

The lobby bar was full again.

She found him seated at the long alabaster table, snacking, from a rectangular plate, on what looked like sushi wrapped in raw meat. "Who took the picture?" she asked, when she was close enough to ask quietly and be heard.

"Pamela. She's an excellent photographer."

"Was she following me?"

"No. She was watching Chombo. Watching him pack up and move out."

"Are you sure he moved himself out? He wasn't arrested by the Department of Homeland Security?"

"I doubt the DHS would let him smoke cigarettes and get in the way, while they packed up the evidence."

"I wouldn't want a chance to find out, myself. Would you?"

"Of course not. Would you like a drink?"

"Not now, thanks. I'd like you to explain, if what you've told me so far is true, why you don't seem worried about that. I would be. In fact, I've discovered that I am. If you've been sniffing around covert American programs designed to intercept smuggled weapons, I'd imagine you're running some chance of getting yourself in trouble. If not, and what you've told me is true, why not?" Which was putting it more forcefully than she'd intended, but it felt right.

"Please," he said, "have a seat."

The stools here were deliberately mismatched. The one next to his reminded her of those elongated figurines of Masai warriors, carved from ironwood, but without the dangerously spiky bits. His was polished aluminum, sort of Henry Moore. "No, thanks."

"I don't know what might be in that one particular container, Hollis. Do you believe me?"

She thought about it. "I might. It depends."

"On what, exactly?"

"On what you might be about to tell me next."

He smiled. "Wherever we go with this, I'll never be able to tell you exactly how I came to be involved. Is that acceptable?"

She thought about it. "Yes." It really didn't sound like that negotiable a point.

"And I'm going to require a very sincere commitment to my undertaking, now, if this conversation is to continue. I need to know that you're with me, before I tell you more. But please, understand that I can't tell you more without taking you further into the thing itself. This is a matter in which possession of information amounts to involvement. Do you understand?" He took up a scarlet flesh-maki, regarded it seriously, then popped it into his mouth.

Whatever this was that Bigend was involved in, she decided, it was deep. Deep and possibly central. To something, she couldn't yet know what. She remembered seeing the white truck rounding the corner, going away, and realized that she really did want to know where it had gone, and why. If she imagined never knowing, for some reason, she saw Alberto's River Phoenix, prone on Viper Room concrete. Another ending.

Bigend touched his lips with a cocktail napkin, raising an interrogatory eyebrow.

"Yes," she said. "But if I ever find you lying to me, even by omission, it's over. Any obligation on my part. Over. Understood?"

"Perfectly," he said, cycling the smile and flagging down their server. "A drink."

"Double scotch," Hollis said. "One rock."

She looked down along the glowing alabaster. All the candles. Drinks. Women's wrists. What had she just done?

"Coincidentally," he said, watching the server's trim bottom recede with exactly the expression she'd seen when he'd considered his maki, "I learned something this morning. Something regarding Bobby."

"I wouldn't think that 'coincidentally' was ever a safe concept, around material like this." She decided to risk the Masai stool, finding it surprisingly comfortable.

"Even the clinically paranoid can have enemies, they say."

"What is it, then?"

"Bobby, I've known for some time, is charged with at least two tasks by his employers."

"Who are?"

"Don't know. The tasks of Bobby Chombo, though: One, as I've told you, consists of listening for the Flying Dutchman of shipping containers. When he took this job, he was given a set of parameters of some kind, and this task of fishing one particular signal out of a great many others. He did it. Does it still. The container sends a signal periodically, announcing its location, and probably that it hasn't been tampered with. It's an intermittent signal, encrypted, and it shifts frequencies, but if you're Bobby, evidently, you'll know when and where to listen for it."

"What's in it for whoever pays him?"

"Don't know. But I generally assume that it's not their container, not their signal. After all, they had to pay Bobby to find it for them. Probably after paying someone else for the information they gave him to help him find it. Quite roundabout, if it's theirs in the first place, though I don't rule it entirely out."

"Why not?"

"Never a good idea. I'm agnostic, basically. About everything."

"What's Bobby Chombo task two, then?"

"That's what I've just learned. When we were at Blue Ant, I told you that he ships iPods to Costa Rica."

"Right. Music, you said."

"What do you know about steganography?"

"I don't even know how to pronounce it."

"Bobby's other task consists of compiling elaborate logs of fictitious searches for the container's signal. These fictions of his, mathematical, enormous, recount his ongoing search for and utter failure to find the key he already has, but which he pretends not to have." He cocked his head. "Did you follow that?"

"He fakes evidence that he still hasn't found the signal?"

"Exactly. He's compiled three such epics, so far. He encrypts them steganographically on the drives of iPods—" Interrupted by the arrival of her drink.

"What was that word again?" she asked, when the server had withdrawn.

"'Steganographically.' He spreads his fictitious activity log very thinly, through a lot of music. If he's given you the key, or if you have sufficiently, hugely powerful decryption capacities, you can pull it out of the music."

"And the iPod's less likely to be checked than a laptop?"

He shrugged. "Depends who's doing the checking."

"And how did you learn this?"

"I can't tell you. Sorry, but it has a direct bearing on how I got involved, and we've agreed I can't discuss that."

"Fine." It wasn't, really, because she could imagine him using it whenever he found it convenient. But she'd deal with that as they went along.

"But I've told you that I know he sends them to a poste restante situation in Costa Rica."

"Right."

"Where so far I've lost track of them, but not before getting a whiff of retired U.S. intelligence officers. Which is a fairly distinctive pong. Never anything like a name attached, of course. But now I'm hearing that Bobby's iPods get reshipped, from San José."

"Where to?"

"New York. Unless I'm being played. But it looks as if the person Bobby sends them to, in San José, is lazy. Or nervous. The actual addressee never picks them up. But they employ the same functionary to ship them back out. By DHL. To an address on Canal Street. Chinese importer."

"Bobby keeps track of the wandering container," she said. "He generates false evidence that he hasn't found it yet. He sends that evidence to someone in Costa Rica, who then ships it back to New York . . ."

"You missed a step. He sends it to someone in Costa Rica whose job, apparently, according to Bobby's employers' wishes, is to sign for it, then hand it over to someone else, the intended recipient. The person Bobby ships to is just your average quasi-criminal postbox. But the intended recipient has never turned up for his end of things. Instead, he's cut a deal with the postbox, to simply turn it around. It's a gap, you see, a flaw in someone's architecture."

"Whose?"

"No idea."

"Can you tell me how you found this out, that they go to New York?"

"I sent someone down there with an armload of cash. Made the postbox a surprise offer. It's that kind of town."

"And that's all you got for your money?"

"That and the sense that Mr. Postbox finds the resident ex-CIA gerontocracy oppressive, and desires to retire farther south, away from them."

She went over it again, in her head, swirling the lone ice cube in her scotch. "So what do you think?"

"Someone's being scammed. Someone's being led to believe that someone else is aware of the container, but is unable to locate it. Why, do you think, would anyone do that?"

"To make the person who owns the container believe it's not being tracked. When in fact it is."

"It does look that way, doesn't it?"

"And?"

"We have a gap to exploit. We know that someone in San José is distancing themselves a little, not following through to the letter of the plan. Whoever's supposed to receive those iPods, and take them away for reshipping, isn't doing that. Instead, they're paying the postbox to simply turn the iPods around. I imagine they're frightened."

"Of whom?"

"Possibly of whoever owns the contents of that container. That's very interesting. And now we have another gap, as well."

"Which is?"

"Pamela put a GPS tracking device on that truck, about an hour before you arrived."

"Jesus," she said, "she did? What is she, James Bond?"

"Nothing like it. Likes a bit of a game, Pamela." He smiled.

"Where is it, the truck?"

He took a Treo from within his jacket and thumbed a sequence on the keypad. Squinted at it. "Just north of San Francisco, at the moment."

44. EXIT STRATEGY

Milgrim found himself heading for Brown's parked Corolla, or rather he found his body, cramping and gasping from its unaccustomed gallop, weaving unevenly in what he supposed to be that general direction. He'd had a general out-of-body experience, between lunging up from the bench and rediscovering himself this way, and he had no idea where those black gentlemen might be. He hoped they had taken his word for it, that Brown was a DEA agent. Since one of them had spontaneously concluded that a bust was in progress, possibly they had. Dennis Birdwell was unlikely to pay anyone enough to do otherwise; it was unlikely enough that he'd hired them in the first place. Milgrim found it rather shocking. His attempts to spot them, unsteady as he was, had yielded no very large leather-wrapped figures whatever.

Nor, indeed, anyone who looked like they were part of any Red Team. Nor even Brown himself.

The Greenmarket looked suddenly deserted, aside from those he took to be produce sellers, all of whom seemed to be trying to use cell phones, and some of whom were yelling at one another in a fairly hysterical fashion.

Now sirens were rising, ululating in the distance. Approaching. Many, it seemed.

In spite of the agonizing stitch in his side, which made him want to bend double, he forced himself to remain approximately upright, and to move as quickly as he could.

He was crossing Union Square West at Seventeenth, and had the Corolla in sight, when some of the sirens simultaneously arrived and ceased. He looked back, along Seventeenth, and saw a police car and an ambulance sitting at angles in the intersection at Park, their rooftop lights frenetically red and blue. Three identical black SUVs appeared, from the east, on Seventeenth, sirenless, to disgorge bulky, black-clad figures that appeared to Milgrim, at this distance, to be wearing spacesuits. These were the new post-9/11 superpolice, he guessed, though he couldn't remember what they were supposed to be called. Samson squads? Some of them entered the building through an entrance at the corner. Now the first of what sounded to be several fire engines.

No time to watch this, arresting as he found it. Brown's bag was still in the car.

But the streetscape, he now realized, with a sharp

pang of dismay, seemed utterly devoid of anything he could use to break a car window. His hand closed repeatedly on the nonexistent handle of the inexpensive Korean-made clawhammer he'd last used to access the interior of an automobile, but then someone else's hand closed viselike on his left shoulder, while his right wrist was twisted up behind his back with near dislocating force.

"They're gone," Brown was saying quietly. "They were jamming our radios and the cell frequencies. If we're talking, they're gone. Get out now. The others are already clear. They have him in custody? A Hercules team?" Brown sighed. "Shit," he said, with finality.

Hercules teams, Milgrim thought. That was it.

"Move," Brown ordered. "They'll be sealing off the area." He yanked open the Corolla's rear door and shoved Milgrim inside, face-first. "Floor," he commanded.

Milgrim managed to pull his feet in just as Brown slammed the door. He smelled relatively new automobile carpet. His knees were on Brown's black bag and laptop, but he knew that the moment, if there had ever been one, was past. He concentrated on breathing more regularly, and on preparing his excuse for having come uncuffed.

"Stay down," Brown said, getting in on the driver's side and starting the engine. He pulled away from the curb. Milgrim felt him turn right on Union Square West, then slow. The front passenger door opened, as someone scrambled in. They pulled away again, the door slamming.

"Give it to me," Brown said.

Milgrim heard something rustle.

"You used gloves?" The level calm in Brown's voice, Milgrim knew from experience, was a bad sign. Red Team One's day in the park must not have gone well.

"Yes," someone said. A man's voice, perhaps familiar from the meeting earlier, in the New Yorker. "That part came off when he dropped it."

Brown said nothing.

"What happened?" the other asked. "Were they expecting us?"

"Maybe they're always expecting someone. Maybe they've been trained to do that. Hell of a concept, isn't it?"

"How's Davis?"

"Looked like a broken neck, to me."

"You didn't say he was dangerous."

Milgrim closed his eyes.

"Blackwater dump your ass for dumbness?" Brown asked. "Is that what I'll find out when I ask them?"

The other said nothing.

Brown stopped the car. "Get out," he said. "Leave town. This afternoon."

Milgrim heard the door open, the man get out, the door close.

Brown drove on. "Get that Transit ticket off the rear window," Brown said.

Milgrim crawled up on the rear seat and pulled the suction cups off the glass. They were about to turn onto Fourteenth. He looked back up Union Square West and saw a black Hercules team vehicle blocking an intersection. He turned around, hoping Brown wouldn't order him back on the floor, and placed his feet, carefully, on either side of Brown's laptop and bag. "Are we going back to the New Yorker?"

"No," said Brown, "we are not going back to the New Yorker."

Brown drove instead to a rental drop-off in Tribeca.

They took a cab to Penn Station, where Brown bought two one-way tickets to Washington on the Metroliner.

45. BREAKBULK

Where do you think the truck's headed?" Hollis asked, poolside, from her cozy depression in the edge of the giant Starck futon.

"Not the Bay," said Bigend, sunken so deeply, beside her, that she couldn't see him. "Soon we'll know whether or not it's Portland. Or Seattle."

She settled farther back, watching a small plane's lights cross the empty center of the luminous sky. "You don't think they'd go inland?"

"No," he said, "I think this is about a port, one with a container facility."

She raised herself, as well as she could, on her right elbow, trying to see his face. "It's coming?"

"Perhaps that's what Bobby's sudden departure means, and not simply that you scared him off."

"But you think it's coming?"

"It's a possibility."

"Do you know where it is?"

"The Hook," he said. "Remember it? That large Russian helicopter? A helicopter capable of flying hundreds of miles, picking up our container from one vessel and transferring it to another?"

"Yes."

"There are some interesting possibilities for keeping track of commercial shipping, today. Of a specific vessel, I mean. But I doubt any of them would help us trace our mystery box, because I think it keeps changing vessels. At sea. We've heard about the use of that venerable Hook, early on, but you don't need to go that large to shift a single forty-foot container from one vessel to another. Provided you don't need to actually fly it too far, that is. Ours is a forty-footer, by the way. All either forty or twenty. Standardization. Containers full of merchandise. Packets full of information. No breakbulk."

"No what?"

"Breakbulk. Noncontainerized freight. Old-fashioned shipping. Crates, bundles. What shipping used to be. I've thought that in terms of information, the most interesting items, for me, usually amount to breakbulk. Traditional human intelligence. Someone knowing something. As opposed to data mining and the rest of it."

"I don't know anything about data mining," she said, "or the rest of it."

"We've been buying into data mining at Blue Ant."

"Shares in a company?"

"No. I suppose you could say we're subscribing. Or hoping to. No simple matter."

"To what?"

"The Swiss have a system known as Onyx, based on Echelon, the system originally developed by the British and the Americans. Onyx, like Echelon, uses software to filter the contents of satellite communication for specific search terms. There are Onyx listening posts at Zimmerwald and Heimenschwand, in Canton Bern, and at Leuk in Canton Valais. I spent a week in Heimenschwand, when I was thirteen. Dada."

"Excuse me?"

"Dada. My mother was researching a minor Dadaist."

"The Swiss? The Swiss have that kind of system?"

"Last month," he said, "the Sunday edition of *Blick* published a classified Swiss government report based on Onyx intercepts. It described a fax sent from the Egyptian government to their embassy in London, referencing covert CIA detention facilities in Eastern Europe. The Swiss government refused to confirm the existence of the report. They did, however, immediately initiate judiciary procedures against the publishers, for having leaked a secret document."

"You can 'subscribe' to something like that?"

"Bankers," said Bigend, "require good information."

"And?"

"Blue Ant requires good bankers. And they happen to be Swiss. But we don't quite have the work-around in place. New search terms have to be approved by an independent commission."

Her eyes were playing tricks on her. Vast translucent things seemed to be squirming, in the depth of the luminous sky. Tentacles the length of nebulae. She blinked and they were gone. "And?"

"Only two members of that commission, so far, would have reason to be favorably disposed to our bankers' suggestions. But we'll see." She felt him sit up. "Another drink?"

"Not for me."

"But you see," he said, "the sheer complication of that sort of intelligence, and of course the innate limitations. Not to mention that we'd have no idea who else might be keeping track of search terms. You, however, with your potential to get closer to Bobby Chombo . . ." He stood, stretched, adjusted his jacket, and turned, bending to offer her his hand. She took it, letting him help her to her feet. "You're breakbulk, Hollis." The smile flashed. "Do you see?"

"I keep trying to tell you. He didn't like it at all, that Alberto brought me there. It was an obvious deal-breaker, for Bobby. You may think he's blown town because his ship's coming in, but I know how little he liked it that I turned up."

"First impressions," he said. "Those can change."

"I hope you're not expecting me to just walk in on him again?"

"Leave all that to me. First I have to see where he's going. In the meantime, work with Philip. See what else Odile and her friends have to show you. It's no accident that Bobby Chombo overlaps two such apparently different spheres. The important thing is that we've had our conversation, reached our agreement. I'm delighted to know we'll be working together."

"Thank you," she said, automatically, then realized that that really was all she could say. "Good night," she said, then, before the pause had too much of a chance to lengthen.

She left him there, beside the ficus trees in their giant flowerpots.

46. VIP

You aren't carrying identification," the old man said, in English, turning off the small camera on which he'd been repeatedly observing a piece of video.

"No," said Tito. There were two cheap, battery-operated plastic dome lights stuck to the truck's ceiling, dimly illuminating the two of them on their uncomfortable bench. Tito had been counting the truck's turns, trying to keep track of their direction. He guessed they were northwest of Union Square now, heading west, but was growing less certain.

The old man took an envelope from his pocket and passed it to Tito. Tito tore it open and removed a New Jersey driver's license with his picture on it. Ramone Alcin. Tito examined the picture more closely. It seemed to be him, though he'd never posed for it, nor had he ever worn the shirt Ramone Alcin wore. He looked at the signature. He would first have to practice drawing it upside down, as Alejandro had taught him. It made him uncomfortable, having identification for which he hadn't yet learned the signature. Though for that matter, he reminded himself, he didn't know how to drive.

The old man took the envelope back, replacing it in his pocket. Tito took his wallet from within his jacket and slid the license behind the transparent window, noting as he did how someone had meticulously scratched the license's laminated surface by repeatedly removing it from and replacing it in another wallet. He thought of Alejandro.

"What else do you have?" the old man asked.

"One of the Bulgarian's guns," Tito said, forgetting that a stranger might not know them.

"Lechkov. Give it to me."

Tito produced the gun, in its handkerchief. A dusting of fine white salt spotted his black jeans as he passed it to the old man.

"It's been fired."

"I used it in the restaurant of the hotel," Tito said. "I was about to be taken. One of the men who came after me was a runner."

"Salt?" The old man sniffed delicately.

"Sea salt. Very fine."

"Lechkov liked to suggest that he made the umbrella used to assassinate Georgi Markov. He didn't. Like these,

his work seemed to belong to an earlier era. Likely he began as a village bicycle mechanic." He tucked handkerchief
and gun inside his coat. "You had to use it, did you?"

However familiar this man might be with his family's
history, Tito thought, he would not know about the orishas. Explaining that it had been Elleggua's choice to use
the Bulgarian's gun would not help. "Not in his face,"
Tito said. "Low. The cloud stung his eyes, but they would
not have been cut." This was probably the truth, as Tito
remembered, but the choice, if one had been made, had
been Elleggua's. "Water would relieve the blindness."

"White powder," said the old man, Tito deciding that
the extra lines in his hatchet cheeks constituted a smile.
"Not so long ago, that would've become very complicated. Now, I doubt it. In any case, you won't be carrying this through the metal detectors before boarding."

"Boarding," said Tito, his throat suddenly dry and
fear churning in the pit of his stomach.

"We'll leave it," said the old man, as if he sensed Tito's
panic, and wished to reassure him. "Any other metal?"

Crowded in the darkness of the tiny plane, curled
against warm metal, clutching his mother's legs, her hand
in his hair, the engine straining against their weight.
Moonless night. Barely clearing the trees. "No," Tito
managed.

The truck stopped. He became aware of a roaring, a
drumming, deep and terrible. Suddenly louder as one rear
door opened, sunlight slicing in. The one from Prada's
shoe department hauled himself quickly in. The old man
undid his seat belt and swung himself back over the bench.

Tito did the same, blank, terrified. "Union Square's locked down," the one from Prada said.

"Get rid of this," said the old man, passing the other the Bulgarian gun, in its handkerchief. He took his camera from his coat pocket and removed the coat, the Prada man helping him on with a pale raincoat. "Take your jacket off," the old man ordered Tito.

Tito obeyed. Prada man handed him a short green cloth jacket with something embroidered in yellow on the back. Tito pulled it on. He was handed a green cap with a yellow bill, JOHNSON BROS. TURF AND LAWN in yellow across the front. He put it on. "Sunglasses," said Prada man, handing Tito a pair. He bundled Tito's jacket into a small black nylon bag, zipped it shut, and handed it to him. "Glasses," he reminded Tito. Tito put them on.

They climbed out into the sunlight, into the terrible roaring. Tito saw the sign on the chain-link, a few feet from the truck.

AIR PEGASUS VIP HELIPORT

Beyond the chain-link, the roaring helicopters.

Then Vianca was there, on her motorcycle, face hidden by her mirrored visor. He saw the Prada man pass her the Bulgarian's gun, folded in its handkerchief. She shoved it into the front of her jacket, threw Tito a quick wave goodbye, and was gone, the whine of her engine lost beneath the thunder of helicopters.

Tito, his stomach full of cold heavy fear, followed the others into this VIP.

And when they had gone through the metal detector, and shown their identification, and had crouched, scuttling, under the whirling blades, and were belted in, and the roaring sharpened, until something seemed to pick the helicopter up as if on a cable, and bore it away, rising, out across the Hudson, Tito could only close his eyes. So that he did not see the city, as they rose, nor see it recede behind him.

Eventually, still without opening his eyes, he was able to pull his Nano from the front of his shirt, extract the earphones from the left front pocket of his jeans, and find the hymn he'd played on his Casio, to the goddess Ochun.

47. N STREET

There were ghosts in the Civil War trees, past Philadelphia.

Earlier the track had passed near streets of tiny row houses, in neighborhoods where poverty seemed to have been as efficient as the neutron bomb was said to be. Streets as denuded of population as their windows were of glass. The houses themselves seemed to belong less to another time than to another country; Belfast perhaps, after some sectarian biological attack. The shells of Japanese cars in the streets, belly down on bare rims.

But past Philadelphia, and after taking another tablet, Milgrim began to catch glimpses of spectral others, angels perhaps. The late-afternoon sun dressed the passing woods with Maxfield Parrish foxfire, and perhaps it was that epileptic flicker generated by the train's motion that called these beings forth. He found them neutral, if not actually benign. They belonged to this landscape, this hour and time of year, and not to his story.

Across the Metroliner's aisle, Brown tapped steadily on his armored laptop. An anxiety stole into Brown's face when he wrote, Milgrim knew, and he saw it again now. Perhaps Brown was uncertain of his writing abilities, or habitually prepared to have what he wrote rejected or criticized excessively, by whoever it was to whom he wrote. Or was it that he was simply uncomfortable with reporting a lack of success? As far as Milgrim knew, Brown had never been successful at what he had seemed to be trying to do, with the IF and the Subject. Capturing the subject seemed to have been a win position for Brown, and Brown had tried, but hadn't managed it. Seizing whatever it was the IF delivered to the Subject had seemed to be another, though secondary, win position, and possibly Brown had succeeded in that, today, in Union Square. Capturing the IF had never seemed like a win position. Had they captured the IF, Milgrim assumed, both the Subject and the IF's extended family would be alerted to Brown's game. The planting of the signal-grabber in the IF's room would have been negated. So, Milgrim, assumed, what Brown was doing now was drafting his report of what had happened in Union Square.

But he thought it unlikely that any such report would mention him, or Dennis's black associates, and that was probably a very good thing. He was concerned that Brown had not yet mentioned to him the fact of his having been discovered no longer cuffed to the bench, but he felt prepared; the cuff itself had failed, and Milgrim, sensing trouble in the park, had taken it upon himself to return to Brown's car, the better to facilitate their departure.

Tiring of the flicking of sun through the trees, he thought he might read his book. But putting his hand on the worn cover, in the side pocket of the Paul Stuart, was as far as he got. He fell asleep, then, with his cheek against the warm glass, and only woke as Brown was shaking him, as they pulled into Union Station in Washington.

He found he was horribly stiff now, no doubt from his uncharacteristic bout of exercise in the park, as well as from the burst of fear-driven adrenaline that had made it possible. His legs felt like stilts as he staggered upright, brushing at crumbs from the turkey sandwich he'd had before Philadelphia. "Move," Brown ordered, pushing him ahead. Brown had his laptop and his bag slung at his hips, packhorse-style, straps crossing his chest. Milgrim suspected Brown had been taught this at some point in a course on optimally securing one's hand luggage. He had the sense that Brown improvised relatively little, and never with much of a sense of ease; he was a man who believed there were ways to do things, and that those were the ways things should be done.

He was also, Milgrim thought, struggling to keep up with him along the platform, an authoritarian, but with what Milgrim assumed would be a fundamental need to obey orders.

The Beaux-Arts triumphalism of the station made Milgrim feel suddenly very small. His neck shrank into the collar of the Paul Stuart coat. He seemed to see himself, and Brown, from high up in those ornate arches, the two of them like beetles, far below, trundling across a vast expanse of marble. He forced himself to peer up, from between his shoulders, at inscribed stone, allegorical sculpture, gilt, all the pomp and gravitas of another young century's American Renaissance.

Outside, the air laced with a tonality of pollution not New York's, and faintly muggy, Brown got them quickly into a cab, driven by a Thai with yellow shooting-glasses, and out of there, into that street plan that Milgrim had never been able to grasp at all. Circles, radial avenues, Masonic complexities. But Brown had given the driver an address on N Street, and Milgrim did remember that, that other alphabet city, so different. He had spent three weeks here, once, in the salad days of the first Clinton administration, as part of a team translating Russian trade reports for a firm of lobbyists.

At some point they turned off a busy shopping street full of mall brands and into a suddenly quieter neighborhood, entirely residential, of smaller, older houses. In the Federal style, Milgrim remembered, and also that this must be Georgetown, recalled from a style seminar conducted in a townhouse. Not unlike these they were passing, but grander, with a walled rear garden in which Milgrim, having slipped out for a joint, had discovered an enormous tortoise and an even larger rabbit, the resident's pets he'd supposed, but remembered now as in some magical moment of childhood. Milgrim's actual childhood had been short on magical moments, he reflected, so perhaps he'd shifted this encounter back, along the subjective time line, to compensate for that. But definitely this was Georgetown, these narrow façades of mellow brick, black-painted wooden shutters, the sense that Martha Stewart and Ralph Lauren would have been hard at work on interiors, together at last, sheathing inherently superior surfaces under hand-rubbed coats of golden beeswax.

Their cab came to a sudden halt, the driver's acrid yellow glasses turning to Brown. "You here?" he asked.

Probably, Milgrim replied silently, as Brown passed the man a few folded bills and ordered Milgrim out.

Milgrim's shoes slipped on bricks worn cornerless with years. He followed Brown up three high granite steps cupped by centuries of feet. The black-painted door, beneath a simple fanlight, was decorated with a Federal eagle in recently polished brass, so old that it resembled no eagle Milgrim had ever seen, but some creature out of more ancient mythology, perhaps a phoenix. Cast, Milgrim guessed, by artisans who'd never seen an eagle, only some engraving of one. Brown's attention was entirely taken up, now, with a keypad of brushed stainless, set into the jamb, on which he was entering a code he copied from a slip of blue paper. Milgrim looked up the street and saw expensively old-fashioned streetlights wink on. Somewhere up the block a very large dog was barking.

As Brown completed his sequence, the door made a startling concise mechanical sound as it unlocked itself.

"In," Brown ordered.

Milgrim grasped the curved brass handle, depressed the thumbpiece, and pushed. The door swung silently open. He stepped in, knowing immediately that the house was empty. He saw a long brass plate set with reproduction antique light switches. He pressed the one nearest the door, his finger covering the round dot of mother-of-pearl. A bowl of creamy glass lit, above them, its rim held in flowered bronze. He looked down. Polished gray marble.

He heard Brown close the door behind him, its lock making that sound again.

Brown pressed more of the buttons on the brass plate, illuminating further reaches. He hadn't been too far off about Martha and Ralph, Milgrim saw, though the furniture wasn't real. It was like the furniture in the lobby of a more traditionally minded Four Seasons.

"Nice," Milgrim heard himself say.

Brown turned on the ball of one foot, staring.

"Sorry," Milgrim said.

48. MONTAUK

Tito sat, eyes resolutely closed, within his music.

Aside from vibration and the noise of the engine, there was nothing to suggest forward motion. He had no idea of their direction.

He stayed within the music, with Ochun, who held him above his fear. He saw her, eventually, as the waters of a stream, crossing pebbles, descending a hillside, through thick growth. He became aware of a bird overhead, above the stream, beyond treetops.

He felt the machine turning. The Prada man, seated beside him, touched his wrist. Tito opened his eyes. The man was pointing, saying something. Tito removed the Nano's earphones, but still he couldn't hear, only the sound of the engine. Through a curved plastic window he saw the sea below, low waves rolling in to a rocky beach. In a wide grassy clearing, shaven into low brown woods, white buildings were arranged around a squared loop of beige road.

The old man, in the seat in front of Tito, beside the pilot, had a large blue headset clamped over his ears. Tito had scarcely noticed the pilot, having closed his eyes as soon as he'd managed to fasten his seat belt. Now he saw the man's gloved hand on a bent steel stick, his thumb pressing buttons on a grip like the one on an arcade game.

The rounded, slightly irregular square of road, and the white buildings, grew steadily larger. The largest of the buildings, clearly a house, with lower wings extending from either side, stood beyond the loop, facing the sea, broad windows staring emptily. The other buildings, clustered as far away as possible on the loop, behind the house, seemed to be smaller houses and a wide garage. There were no trees or bushes, once the brown woods ended. There was a scoured quality to the buildings, which he now could see were made of white-painted wood. In this northern climate, he knew, wooden houses might stand for a very long time, as there seemed to be nothing to eat them. In Cuba, only the hardest woods from the Zapata swamp forests could withstand insects for so long.

He saw a long black car, stationary on one side of the beige loop, midway between the big house and the smaller ones.

They swung in over the beach, sand rushing past beneath them, low over the slanting gray roof of the big house. The machine halted, impossibly, in midair, then settled toward grass.

The old man removed his headset. The Prada man reached across, unfastening Tito's seat belt. He passed Tito the bag containing his APC jacket. Tito's stomach clenched, as the helicopter met solid ground. The tone of its roaring changed. The Prada man had opened a door, was gesturing Tito out.

Tito climbed out, and was almost knocked to the ground by the wind from the rotors. Crouching low, the wind tearing at his eyes, he grabbed the cap to keep it from being blown off. Prada man scrambled under the fuselage and helped the old man down from a door on the opposite side. Obeying the man's gestures, still crouching, he scrambled after the two, in the direction of the black car. The pitch of the roaring changed.

Tito turned to see the helicopter lifting, like some clumsy magic trick. It swung suddenly toward the sea, out over the big house, then rose higher, receding, against the cloudless sky.

In the sudden quiet, he heard the old man's voice, and simultaneously felt the stiff breeze, in off the sea: "Sorry about the uniform. We thought it would be better for you to make a specific impression at the heliport."

Prada man bent, retrieving keys from beneath the left front wheel of the black Lincoln Town Car. "Lovely spot, isn't it?" he said, looking toward the garage, the smaller houses.

"Underbuilt, by current standards," the old man said.

Tito took off the sunglasses, considered them, decided

against keeping them, and put them in one side pocket of the lawn-care jacket. He put the cap in the other and removed the jacket. He opened the black nylon bag, took out his APC jacket, shook it out, and put it on. He put the green jacket in the bag and zipped it shut.

"It was like this in the seventies, when it sold for a little under three hundred thousand," said the Prada man. "Now they're asking forty million."

"I'm sure they are," said the old man. "Nice of them to have allowed us to land."

"The Realtor suggested a lower offer, provided the terms are sufficiently simple. The caretakers, of course, have been instructed not to disturb us." He pressed a button on the keys in his hand, opened the driver's side door.

"Really? How wealthy am I, in this case?"

"Very."

"By virtue of what, exactly?"

"Internet pornography." Getting behind the wheel.

"Are you serious?"

"Hotels. A chain of boutique hotels. In Dubai." He started the car. "Ride up front with me, Tito."

The old man opened the rear door. He looked back at Tito. "Come along." He got in, closing the door.

Tito walked around the long, gleaming black hood, noting New Jersey plates, and got in.

"I'm Garreth," the man behind the wheel said, extending his hand. Tito shook his hand.

Tito pulled the door shut. Garreth put the Lincoln in

gear and they rolled forward, crushed shale crunching beneath its tires.

"Fruit and sandwiches," Garreth said, indicating a basket between them. "Water." He followed the loop toward the garage and the smaller houses, then swung right, taking a beige road into the brown woods.

"How long will this take?" asked the old man.

"Thirty minutes, this time of year," Garreth said, "through Amagansett and East Hampton, on Route 27."

"Is there a gatehouse?"

"No. A gate. But the Realtor's given us the exit code."

The car's tires, on the shale, were muffled by dark pads of crushed dead leaves.

"Tito," said Garreth, "I noticed you kept your eyes closed, on the way out. Don't like helicopters?"

"Tito," said the old man, "hasn't flown since he left Cuba. That may well have been his first helicopter."

"Yes," Tito said.

"Ah," said Garreth, and drove on. Tito stared into the brown depths of the woods. He hadn't been so far from a city since leaving Cuba.

Soon the one who called himself Garreth stopped the car, its hood a few feet from a low, heavy-looking gate of galvanized steel. "Give me a hand with this," Garreth said, opening his door. "It's motorized, but when I was here with the Realtor, the chain kept slipping."

Tito got out. There was two-lane blacktop, passing just beyond the gate. Garreth had opened a gray metal box, attached to a white wooden post, and was using the keypad mounted inside it. The smell of the forest was rich and strange. A small animal ran through branches overhead, but Tito couldn't see it, only a branch left swaying. An electric motor whined, and a chain like a very long bicycle chain, part of the gate, began to jump and rattle.

"Help it along," Garreth said. Tito took the gate in his hands and shoved to the right, toward the sound of the engine. The chain caught, the gate juddering sideways, following a raised track of the same metal. "In the car. There's a beam that closes it, when we're through."

Tito looked back, from the front seat, as the rear of the Lincoln cleared the gate. It closed smoothly enough, but Garreth stopped, got out, went back to check that it was fully closed. "That needs looking after," said the old man. "Gives a prospective buyer the impression the whole place is in poor repair."

Garreth got back in. They turned, onto the blacktop, and Garreth drove, picking up speed. "No more helicopters today, Tito," he said.

"Good," Tito said.

"Strictly fixed-wing, this next leg."

Tito, who had been looking at the bananas in the basket between them, thought better of it.

"Leg?" asked Tito.

"A Cessna Golden Eagle," said the old man, "1985. One of the last they manufactured. Very comfortable. Quiet. We'll be able to sleep."

Tito's body wanted to press itself farther back into the seat. He saw buildings ahead. "Where are we going?"

"Right now," said Garreth, "East Hampton Airport."

"A private plane," said the old man, "no security checks, no identification. We'll be getting you something more viable than a New Jersey driver's license, but you won't be needing anything today."

"Thank you," Tito said, unable to think of anything else to say. They passed a small building with a painted sign, LUNCH, cars parked in front of it. Tito looked down at the banana. He hadn't eaten since the night before, with Vianca and Brotherman, and the Guerreros were no longer with him. He picked up the banana and began resolutely to peel it. If I have to learn to fly, he told his stomach, I refuse to starve while doing it. His stomach seemed unconvinced, but he ate the banana anyway.

Garreth drove on, and the old man said nothing.

49. ROTCH

Odile sat in the white armchair with the white robot on its back in her lap, poking a white Mondrian pencil into its mechanism of plastic gears and black rubber bands. "They break, these thing."

"Who made it?" Hollis asked, from her own chair. Legs folded beneath her bathrobe. They were drinking room-service coffee. Nine in the morning, after what for Hollis had been a surprisingly undisturbed night.

"Sylvia Rotch," Odile said, levering with her pencil. Something clicked. "Bon," said Odile.

"Rotch? How do you spell that?" Hollis's own white pencil, poised.

"R-O-I-G," managed Odile, who struggled with the letters' English pronunciation.

"Are you sure?"

"Catalan," said Odile, bending to put the robot right side up on the carpet. "Is difficult."

Hollis wrote it down. Roig. "The poppies, are they characteristic of her work?"

"She only does the poppies," said Odile, eyes huge beneath her smooth, serious brow. "She fills the entire Mercat des Flores with the poppies. The old flower market."

"Yes," said Hollis, putting down her pencil and pouring herself fresh coffee. "When you left your message, you mentioned that you wanted to talk about Bobby Chombo."

"Fer-gus-son," said Odile, making it three distinct syllables.

"Ferguson?"

"His name is Robert Fer-gus-son. He is Canadian. Shombo, it is his art name."

Hollis took that in over a sip of coffee. "I didn't know that. Do you think Alberto knows that?"

Odile shrugged, in that complexly French way that seemed to require a slightly different skeletal structure. "I doubt it. I know because my boyfriend worked in a gallery in Vancouver. Do you know it?"

"The gallery?"

"Vancouver! It is beautiful."

"Yes," Hollis agreed, though actually the most she'd seen of the place had been their rooms at the Four Seasons and the inside of their rather too-small venue, a re-purposed second-story Deco taxi-dance hall on a weirdly traffic-free midtown artery full of theaters. Jimmy had been having a rough time. She'd stayed with him constantly. Not a good time.

"My boyfriend, he knew Bobby as a DJ."

"He's Canadian?"

"My boyfriend is French."

"I mean Bobby."

"Of course he is Canadian. Fer-gus-son."

"He knew him well? Your boyfriend, I mean?"

"He buy E from him," said Odile.

"Was that before he went to Oregon to work on GPSW projects?"

"I don't know. Yes, I think. Three years? In Paris, my boyfriend sees Bobby's photo, an opening in New York, Dale Cusak, his memories of Natalie, do you know it?"

"No," said Hollis.

"Bobby does the geohacking for Cusak. My boyfriend tells me this is Robert Fer-gus-son."

"Can you be sure, though?"

"Yes. Some other artists, here, they know he is Canadian. It is not so much of a secret, perhaps."

"But Alberto doesn't know?"

"Not everyone does. Everyone need Bobby. To work in this new medium. He is the best, for this. But a recluse. Those who know him before, they become very careful. They don't say what Bobby does not want."

"Odile, do you know anything about Bobby's having . . . moved, recently."

"Yes," said Odile, gravely. "His e-mail bounce. Servers aren't there. Artists cannot contact him for works in progress. They are concern."

"Alberto told me. Do you know where he might have gone?"

"He is Shombo." She picked up her coffee. "He may be anywhere. Ollis, will you come to Silverlake with me? To visit Beth Barker?"

Hollis considered it. Odile was an underutilized asset. Definitely, if her boyfriend (ex?) actually knew Bobby Chombo-Ferguson. "She's the one with the virtually annotated apartment?"

"Eeparespatial tagging," corrected Odile.

God help me, thought Hollis.

Her cell rang. "Yes?"

"Pamela. Mainwaring. Hubertus asked me to tell you that it looks as though they're going to Vancouver."

Hollis looked across at Odile. "Does he know that Bobby is Canadian?"

"Actually," said Pamela Mainwaring, "yes."

"I've only just learned."

"Had you discussed his background with Hubertus?"

Hollis thought about it. "No."

"There you are, then. He suggests you go. To Vancouver."

"When?"

"If you left immediately, you might make Air Canada's one o'clock."

"When's the latest?"

"Eight tonight."

"Book for two, then," she said. "Henry and Richard. I'll call you back."

"Done," said Pamela, and was gone.

"Ollis," said Odile, "what is that?"

"Can you come to Vancouver for a few days, Odile? Tonight. Entirely on *Node*'s ticket. Your flights, hotel, any expenses."

Odile's eyebrows went up. "Really?"

"Yes."

"You know, Ollis, *Node* pays to bring me here, pays for le Standard . . ."

"There you go, then. How about it?"

"Certainly," said Odile, "but why?"

"I want you to help me find Bobby."

"I will try, but . . ." Odile demonstrated her French shrugging anatomy.

"Excellent," said Hollis.

50. WHISPERING GALLERY

Milgrim woke in a narrow bed, beneath a single flannel sheet printed with trout flies, partial riverscapes, and the repeated image of an angler, casting. The pillowcase was made of matching material. On the wall opposite the foot of the bed was a large poster of an American eagle's head, depicted against the billowing folds of Old Glory. He seemed to have gotten undressed for bed, although he didn't remember doing it.

He looked at the poster, behind glass in a plain gold plastic frame. He'd never seen anything quite like it. It had a soft, worryingly pornographic quality, as though a Vaselined lens had been involved, though he supposed they no longer really did that, Vaselining lenses. Likely the whole thing had been executed on a monitor. The eagle's eye, though, was hyperrealist bright and beady, as if rendered to fix on the viewer's forehead. He thought a slogan would have helped, somehow, some nudge in a specific patriotic direction. Just these sinuous waves of stripes, though, a few stars up in one corner, and the raked and angular head of this really rather murderous-looking bird of prey, was too much, on its own, too purely iconic.

He thought of the peculiar, phoenix-like creature on the front door, downstairs.

But then he remembered eating pizza that Brown had ordered, in the kitchen, downstairs. Pepperoni and three cheeses. And the fridge, which had contained a six-pack of very cold Pepsi and nothing else. He remembered feeling the smooth white circles of the heating elements on the range, something he'd not seen before. Brown had taken his pizza into a sort of study, along with a glass and a bottle of whiskey. Milgrim had never seen Brown drink before. Then he'd heard Brown on the phone, through the closed door, but hadn't been able to make anything of it. And then, he guessed, he'd treated himself to another Rize.

Sometimes, he observed now, sitting on the edge of the bed in his underwear, a little too much had a way of clearing the air, the morning after. He looked up and encountered the eagle's gun-muzzle eye. Looking quickly away, he rose, surveyed the room, and began to search it, quietly and with an efficiency born of practice.

It had obviously been decorated to be a boy's room, and in the style of the rest of the house, though perhaps

with a bit less effort. Less Ralph Lauren than some dif-
fusion line. He hadn't yet seen a single actual antique,
aside from the Ur-eagle outside, which might even be
original to the house. The furnishings were faux-old,
and that rather halfhearted, more likely made in India or
China than North Carolina. For that matter, he thought,
noting the room's empty inbuilt bookcase, he hadn't
seen a single book.

He carefully, quietly opened each drawer in the small
bureau. All empty, aside from the bottom one, which
contained a wire coat hanger clad in tissue, printed with
the name and address of a dry cleaner in Bethesda, and
two pins. He knelt on the carpet and peered under the
bureau. Nothing.

The small, vaguely Colonial desk, finished, like the
bureau, in rather robotically distressed blue paint, offered nothing more, other than a dead fly and a black
ballpoint pen marked PROPERTY OF U.S. GOVERNMENT in
white. Milgrim tucked the pen into the elastic waistband
of his underwear, having at that point no pockets, and
carefully opened what he took, correctly, to be a closet
door. The hinges squeaked with disuse. Empty coat
hangers rattled on a hook. The closet proved to contain
nothing but more coat hangers, on one of which hung a
small navy blazer with an elaborately gold-embroidered
crest. Milgrim went through its pockets, finding a wad-
ded Kleenex and a stub of chalk.

The boy's jacket and the piece of chalk saddened him.
He didn't like thinking of this as a child's room. Perhaps
there had been other things here once, books and toys,

but somehow it didn't seem like it. The room suggested a difficult childhood, perhaps not too different from the one Milgrim himself had had. He left the closet, closing the door, and went to the blue ladder-backed chair on which his clothes had been draped. Forgetting the U.S. Government pen, he jabbed himself with it as he was putting on his pants.

Dressed, he approached the drawn striped drapes of the room's single window. Positioning himself so that he could move the outer edge of one drape as minimally as possible, he discovered what he took to be N Street, on what appeared to be an overcast day. But his angle down also revealed the right front fender of a parked car, black and highly polished. A large car, to judge by what he could see of its fender.

He put on the Paul Stuart coat, discovering his book in its pocket, clipped the government pen into the inside pocket, and tried the room's door, finding it unlocked.

A paneled, carpeted hallway, illuminated now by a skylight. He looked over a banister and down, two flights, to the softly gleaming gray marble of the hallway they'd entered yesterday evening. One of those central but minimal stairwell-shafts encountered in houses of this age, very long and narrow, running back to front. Beside his ear, a spoon rattled against china. He spun, starting violently. "I appreciate that," an invisible Brown said, with an uncharacteristic note of gratitude.

The hallway was empty.

"I understand what you have to work with," said a voice Milgrim had never heard before, the speaker equally close, equally invisible. "You're using the best men available to you, and finding them lacking. We see that all too often. I'm disappointed, of course, that you weren't able to apprehend him. In the light of your previous lack of success, I think it would have been wise to arrange to try to photograph him. Don't you? To be prepared to photograph him in any case, in the event he escaped again." The man had a lawyer's cadence, Milgrim thought. He spoke slowly and clearly, and as though he took it for granted that he'd be paid attention to.

"Yes, sir," said Brown.

"Then we might at least have a chance to learn who he is."

"Yes."

Eyes wide, gripping the banister rail as though it were the railing of a ship in a storm, Milgrim stared down at the distant, narrow slice of marble floor, tasting his own blood. He'd bitten the inside of his cheek, when that spoon had rattled against that coffee cup. Brown's breakfast conversation was being reflected off that marble floor, he guessed, or being sucked up this slit of Federal stairwell, or both. Had children stood here a hundred years ago, he wondered, suppressing giggles at some other conversation?

"You say the information intended for him indicates that he still has no tracking ability, hence no knowledge of whereabouts or ability to predict destination."

"Whoever he has working on it," Brown said, "doesn't seem to be getting the job done."

"And our friends," the other said, "are they able to

determine, when they go over this material, what it is, exactly, that's being so unsuccessfully searched for?"

"The assessment's handled by someone who has no knowledge of any of this. It's just information, to him, and he analyzes classified data constantly."

"Government?"

"Telco," Brown said. "You know who handles the decryption. They never look at the product. And our analyst has every reason to pay as little attention as possible to what this might actually be about. I've made sure of that."

"Good. That was my understanding."

Cutlery rattled loudly on a plate, so seemingly close that Milgrim winced. "So," the other man said, "are we in a position to bring things home?"

"I believe we are."

"So the shipment finally comes to port. After all this time."

"But not in conus," Brown said.

Conus? Milgrim blinked, terrified for an instant that this entire conversation might all be some unprecedented aural hallucination.

"No," agreed the other, "not yet on American soil."

CONUS, thought Milgrim, in Fourth of July capitals. Continental United States.

"And what are the current odds of it being opened for inspection?" the man asked.

"Extremely unlikely," Brown said. "Slightly more likely to have a gamma scan, but the contents and packing look fine, that way. We actually had it gamma'd ourselves, in a previous port of call, to see how it reads."

"Yes," said the other, "I saw those."

"You agree, then?" asked Brown.

"I do," said the other. "What steps are being taken in your absence, in New York?"

Brown took a moment to answer. "I sent a team to the IF's room, for fingerprints and to recover the surveillance device. They found the door open and everything under a coat of fresh latex paint. Even the lightbulb. No fingerprints. And there were none on the iPod, of course. The unit was where I left it, under a coatrack, but they'd dumped that outside."

"They didn't find it?"

"If they did find it, they might avoid doing anything to indicate that."

"Are you any closer to understanding who they are?"

"They're one of the smallest organized crime families operating in the United States. Maybe literally a family. Illegal facilitators, mainly smuggling. But a kind of boutique operation, very pricey. Mara Salvatrucha looks like UPS in comparison. They're Cuban-Chinese and they're probably all illegals."

"Can't you get ICE to roll them up for you?"

"You have to find them first. We found the kid and followed him home, in the course of trying to find the Subject. We found him, to the extent that we ever did, from what you told us about the Subject. The rest of them are like ghosts." Milgrim found that he knew Brown well enough, now, to hear the edge of a certain craziness in his voice. He wondered if the other man did.

"Ghosts?" The other man's tone was absolutely neutral.

"The problem," Brown said, "is that they've been trained. Really trained. Some kind of intelligence background, in Cuba. I'd need that professional a team, and it hasn't happened, has it?"

"No," said the other, "but as you yourself once said, they aren't really our problem. He is our problem. But if he knows what we're doing, we now know that he doesn't know when, or where. Perhaps, later, we can steer adequate professionalism in the direction of your facilitators. When it has nothing to do with us, of course. And we'll certainly have to find out who our man is, and do something about him."

China rattled on a table, as someone stood. Milgrim released the banister and made it back into his room in two long, agonized, exaggeratedly careful steps. He closed the door with utmost care, took off his coat, draped it over the chair, removed his shoes, and got under the angling-themed sheet, pulling it up beneath his chin. He closed his eyes and lay perfectly still. He heard the front door close. A moment later he heard an engine start, and a car pull away.

After an indeterminate period of time, he heard Brown open his door. "Wake up," Brown said. Milgrim opened his eyes. Brown stepped to the bed and tore the sheet away. "How the fuck can you sleep in your clothes that way?"

"I fell asleep," Milgrim said.

"Bathroom's down the hall. There's a robe there, and a garbage bag. Put everything you're wearing in the garbage bag. Shower, shave, put on the robe, and come down to the kitchen for a haircut."

"You give haircuts?" Milgrim asked, amazed.

"The housekeeper's here. He'll give you a haircut and measure you for some clothes. And if I catch you sleeping in them, you'll regret it." Brown turned on his heel and left the room.

Milgrim lay there, looking at the ceiling. Then he got up, got his toiletries out of his coat, and went to take his shower.

51. CESSNA

Tito discovered that he could sleep on an airplane.

This one had a couch and two chairs, behind the smaller, instrument-filled room where the fat, gray-haired pilot sat. Garreth and the old man sat in the two reclining swivel chairs. Tito lay on the couch, looking up at the curved ceiling, which was upholstered, like the couch, in gray leather. This was an American airplane, the old man had told Tito. It had been one of the last of its kind, made in 1985, he had said, as they'd climbed the little stairway on wheels on the runway at East Hampton Airport.

Tito had no idea why the old man would want such an old airplane. Perhaps it had been his, Tito thought, and he'd simply kept it. If it was that old, though, it was like the American cars in Havana, which were also very old, and shaped like whales made of pale ice cream, frosted greens and pinks, dressed with huge chrome teeth and fins, every inch rubbed to a perfect gloss. As they'd walked to it, from the Lincoln, Garreth and the old man each carrying luggage they'd taken from the trunk, Tito, for all his fear, had been taken with its lines, how it gleamed. It had a very long, very sharp nose, propellers built into its wings on either side, and a row of round windows.

The pilot, fat and smiling, had seemed very glad to see the old man, and had said that it had been a long time. The old man had said that it had indeed, and that he owed the pilot one. He didn't, the pilot had said, not by half, and had taken the two suitcases, and Tito's bag, and put them into a space built into the wing, behind one of the engines, hidden when he shut it.

Tito had closed his eyes, going up the stairway, and had kept them closed while Garreth had gone to park the car. "Cutting it close," the pilot had said, from the front of the plane, while Tito sat with his eyes closed on the couch, "Dawn-to-dusk operation, here." The old man had said nothing.

Taking off had been very nearly as bad for him as the helicopter, but he'd had his Nano ready, and had his eyes closed.

Eventually, he tried opening them. Sunset was filling the windows, dazzling him. The movement of the plane was smooth, and unlike the helicopter, it felt as though it was actually flying, not being carried along, suspended from something else. It was quieter than the helicopter, and the couch was comfortable.

Garreth and the old man turned on small lights, and put on headsets with microphones, and talked to each other. Tito listened to his music. Eventually the two men unfolded small desks. The old man opened a laptop and Garreth unfolded plans of some kind, studying them, marking them with a mechanical pencil.

It grew warm in the cabin, but not uncomfortable. Tito had taken off his jacket, folded it to use as a pillow, and fallen asleep on the gray couch.

When he woke, it was night, and the lights were off. Through the entrance to the room where the pilot sat, he could see many different lights, small screens with lines and symbols.

Were they leaving the United States? How far could an airplane like this fly? Could it fly to Cuba? To Mexico? He didn't think it likely they were flying to Cuba, but Vianca having said she thought that Eusebio was in Mexico City, in a neighborhood called Doctores, came back to him.

He looked at the old man, whose profile he could just make out against the glow of the instruments' lights, sleeping, chin down. Tito tried to imagine him with their grandfather, in Havana, a long time ago, when both the revolution and the whalelike cars had been new, but no images came.

He closed his own eyes, and flew through the night, somewhere above the country he hoped was still America.

52. SCHOOL CLOTHES

Milgrim found the housekeeper in the kitchen, where Brown had said he would be, rinsing breakfast dishes before putting them in the washer. He was a small man, in dark trousers and a crisp white jacket. Milgrim walked into the kitchen barefooted, wrapped in an oversized robe of thick burgundy terry cloth. The man looked at his feet.

"He said you'd give me a haircut," Milgrim said.

"Sit," the housekeeper said. Milgrim sat on a maple chair, by the matching table, and watched as the housekeeper tidied the last of the breakfast things into the washer, closed it, and turned it on.

"Any chance of some eggs?" Milgrim asked.

The housekeeper looked at him blankly, then brought

out electric clippers, a comb, and a pair of scissors from a black briefcase on the white counter. He covered Milgrim in what Milgrim assumed (jam spots) had been the breakfast tablecloth, ran the comb through Milgrim's damp hair, then began to cut it, as if he knew what he was doing. When he was done with the scissors, he used the clippers on the back and sides of Milgrim's neck. He stepped back, considering, then used comb and scissors for a few minor adjustments. He used a napkin to swipe Milgrim's hair clippings off the tablecloth, onto the floor. Milgrim sat there, waiting to be presented with the mirror. The man brought a broom and long-handled dustpan, and started sweeping up the hair. Milgrim stood up, thinking that there was always something sad about seeing one's own hair on the floor, removed the tablecloth, shook it out, and put it on the table. He turned to go.

"Wait," said the housekeeper, still sweeping. When the floor was clean again, he put his barber things back in the briefcase and brought out a yellow cloth measuring tape, a pen, and a notebook. "Take off robe," he said. Milgrim did, glad that he hadn't followed Brown's orders too literally, and was wearing his underpants. The housekeeper quickly and efficiently took his measurements. "Shoe size?"

"Nine," Milgrim told him.

"Narrow?"

"Medium."

The housekeeper made a note of this. "Go," he said

to Milgrim, making a shooing gesture with his note-book, "go, go."

"No breakfast?"

"Go."

Milgrim left the kitchen, wondering where Brown might be. He looked into the office-study, where Brown had taken his whiskey the night before. It was furnished like the rest of the house, but with more dark wood and more vertical stripes. And, he saw, it had books. He stepped to the door, peered around, swiftly crossed to what he'd taken for a bookcase. It was one of those pieces where the doors of a cabinet have been covered with the leather spines of antique books. He bent, taking a closer look at the remains of these skinned volumes. No, this was a single piece of leather, molded over a wooden form shaped like the spines of individual books. There were no actual titles, or authors' names, in the carefully faded gold stamping across these. It was a very elaborate arti-fact, mass-produced by artisans of one culture in vague imitation of what had once been the culture of another. He opened it. The shelf behind was empty. He quickly closed it.

In the hallway, he examined the housekeeper's handi-work in a mirror dotted with faux age spots. Tidy. Hyper-conventional. A lawyer's haircut, or a prisoner's.

He stood on the cool gray marble, at the foot of the slit of stairwell. He clicked his tongue quietly, imagining the sound sucked up the slit.

Where was Brown?

He went upstairs and collected the plastic garbage bag from the bathroom, along with his razor, toothbrush, and toothpaste. He went to the boy's bedroom, where he added his underpants to the contents of the bag. Naked under the oversized robe, he removed his book from the Paul Stuart coat draped over the ladder-backed chair. He'd helped himself to the coat from the rack in a deli, shortly before Brown had found him. It hadn't been new when he'd gotten it, already a season old, and it was past cleaning, now. He put the book on the blue desk, picked up the coat, and took it into the closet. He put it on the hanger closest to the boy's blue blazer. "I've brought you a friend," he whispered. "You don't have to be frightened anymore."

He closed the closet door behind him, and was picking up his book, when Brown opened the door from the hall. He looked at Milgrim's haircut. He handed him a crisp paper bag from McDonald's, marked by a few translucent spots of grease, picked up the garbage bag, tied a knot in its neck, and left with it.

Grease from the Egg McMuffin dripped on the robe, but Milgrim decided that that was not his problem.

In what he took to be little more than an hour, the housekeeper entered, carrying two paper shopping bags and a black vinyl hanger-bag, all marked JOS. A. BANK.

"That was quick," Milgrim said.

"McLean," said the housekeeper, as if that explained it. He dropped the two bags on the bed, and was turning to the closet door with the hanger-bag when Milgrim took it from him.

"Thanks," Milgrim said.

The man turned and left.

Milgrim opened the hanger-bag and found a black, three-button jacket, wool-poly blend. He laid it on the bed, atop the hanger-bag, and started unpacking one of the shopping bags. He found two pairs of navy-blue cotton briefs, two pairs of medium-weight gray socks, a white sleeveless undershirt, two blue oxford button-downs, and a pair of dark-gray wool trousers with no belt loops, tabs and buttons at either side of the waistband. He remembered Brown having taken his belt, the first day. The other contained a shoebox. In it was a pair of rather sad rubber-soled leather oxfords, generic office-wear. Also a black leather wallet and a plain black nylon carryall.

Milgrim dressed. The shoes, which he thought visibly cheap, actually helped. They made him feel less like he was heading back to boarding school, or joining the FBI.

Brown entered, a blue and black striped tie in his hand. He was wearing a dark-gray suit and white shirt. Milgrim had never seen him in a suit before, and assumed he'd just now removed the tie. "Put this on. We're taking your picture." He watched while Milgrim removed his jacket and knotted the tie. He assumed ties were like belts, as far as he was concerned.

"I need an overcoat," Milgrim said, pulling on his new jacket.

"You have one."

"You told me to put everything in the bag."

Brown frowned. "Where we're going," Brown said, "you'll want a raincoat. Downstairs. You're having your picture taken."

Milgrim went downstairs, Brown behind him.

53. TO GIVE THEM THE PLEASURE

Inchmale's cell wasn't answering. She tried the W, and was told he was no longer there. Was he on his way? Probably. She hated the idea of missing him, although she assumed he intended to be here for a while, if he was going to be producing an album. Vancouver wasn't that far away, and she didn't imagine she'd be there very long.

Odile called from the Standard to ask the name of the hotel in Vancouver. She said she wanted to tell her mother, in Paris. Hollis didn't know. She called Pamela Mainwaring.

"Where are we staying?"

"The flat. I've only seen pictures. All glass. Over the water."

"Hubertus has a flat?"

"The company. No one lives there. We haven't opened

in Canada. We're starting in Montreal, next year. Hubertus says we need to start there; he says Quebec is an imaginary country."

"What does that mean?"

"I only work here," said Pamela. "But we do have people in Vancouver. One of them will meet you and take you to the flat."

"May I speak with Hubertus?"

"Sorry," said Pamela, "he's in a meeting in Sacramento. He'll ring you when he can."

"Thanks," Hollis said.

She looked at the helmet Bigend had sent her. She supposed she'd better take it with her, in case there was locative art in Vancouver. It didn't seem like something you could safely check through, though, and it was going to be awkward for carry-on.

Before she started packing she called her own mother, in Puerto Vallarta. Her parents wintered there now, but they were a week from coming back to their place in Evanston. She tried to explain what she was doing in Los Angeles, but she wasn't sure her mother got it. Still very sharp, but increasingly less interested in things she wasn't already familiar with. She said that Hollis's father was fine, except for having contracted, in his late seventies, a fierce and uncharacteristic interest in politics. Which her mother didn't like, she said, because it only made him angry. "He says it's because it's never been this bad," her mother said, "but I tell him it's only because he never paid it this much attention before. And it's the Internet: People used to have to wait for the paper, or for the news on television. Now it's like a tap running. He sits down with that thing at any time of the day or night, and starts reading. I tell him it's not like there's anything he can do about any of it anyway."

"It gives him something to think about. You know it's good for people your age to have interests."

"You aren't the one who has to listen to him."

"Give him my love, and I'll check on you soon. Either from Canada or when I'm back."

"Was it Toronto?"

"Vancouver. I love you, Mom."

"I love you too, dear."

She went to the window, looked down at the traffic on Sunset. Her parents had never been very comfortable with her singing career. Her mother, in particular, had treated it as though it were some sort of nuisance disease, something nonfatal that nonetheless interfered with your life in serious ways, preventing you having a real job, and for which there was no particular cure, other than simply letting it run its course and hoping for the best. Her mother had seemed to regard any income from singing as a kind of disability pay, something you received for having to put up with the condition. Which hadn't really been that far off Hollis's own attitude to art and money, though unlike her mother she knew that you could have the condition yet never qualify for any compensation whatever. If being the kind of singer and writer she'd been had ever proven absolutely too difficult, she was fairly certain, she'd simply have stopped doing it. And perhaps that was really what had happened. The sudden arc of her career, the arc of the Curfew, had taken her completely by surprise. Inchmale had been one of those people who'd apparently known since birth exactly what he was supposed to do. It had been different for him, although maybe the plateau, after the arc up, hadn't been that different. Neither of them had really wanted to see what an arc down might look like, she thought. With Jimmy's addiction as a punctuation point, a blank, heroin-colored milestone driven into whatever that plateau had been made of, and with the band stalled creatively, they'd all opted to drop it. She and Inchmale had tried to go on to other things. As had Heidi-Laura, she supposed. Jimmy had just died. Inchmale seemed to have managed it best. She hadn't gotten that positive a feeling about Heidi's life, seeing her this time, but then Heidi was as difficult to read as any human Hollis had ever known.

The maids, she discovered, had actually saved and folded the Bubble Wrap that had come in the box from Blue Ant. It was on the shelf in the closet. Instant tip-upgrade. She put the wrapping, the box, and the helmet on the tall kitchenette table.

Doing this, she noticed the Blue Ant figurine that had come with it, standing on one of the coffee tables. She'd leave that, of course. She looked back at it, and knew she couldn't. This was some part of her that had never grown up, she felt. A grown-up would not be compelled to take this anthropomorphic piece of molded vinyl along when she left the room, but she knew she would. And she didn't even like things like that. She wouldn't leave it, though. She walked over and picked it up. She'd take it along and give it to someone, preferably a child. Less because she had any feeling for the thing, which was after all only a piece of marketing plastic, than because she herself wouldn't have wanted to be left behind in a hotel room.

But she decided not to take it carry-on. She didn't want the TSA people publicly hauling it out of the box with the helmet. She tossed it into the Barneys bag that held her dressier clothes.

ODILE WAS UNHAPPY that they weren't going to a hotel, in Vancouver. She liked North American hotels, she said. She liked the Mondrian more than the Standard. The idea of a borrowed flat disappointed her.

"I think it might be really something, from what they said," Hollis told her. "And nobody lives there."

They were in the back of a Town Car Hollis had arranged with the hotel, billed to her room. When she'd returned the Passat, the boy who'd almost recognized her hadn't been there. They were nearing LAX now, she knew; through smoked windows, she could see those weird bobbing oil-well things on a hillside. They'd been there since she'd first come here. As far as she knew, they never stopped moving. She checked the time on her phone. Almost six.

"I called my mother," Hollis said. "I did it because you mentioned yours."

"Where is she, your mother?"

"Puerto Vallarta. They go there in the winter."

"She is well?"

"She complains about my father. He's older. I think he's okay, but she thinks he's obsessed with American politics. She says it makes him too angry."

"If this were my country," Odile said, wrinkling her nose, "I would not be angry."

"No?" Hollis asked.

"I would drink all the time. Take pill. Anything."

"There's that," said Hollis, remembering dead Jimmy, "but I wouldn't think you'd want to give them the pleasure."

"Who?" asked Odile, sitting up, suddenly interested. "Who would I pleasure?"

54. ICE

Tito woke as the Cessna's wheels touched down. Sunlight through the windows. Grabbing the back of the couch. They sped along on the ground, the pitch of the engines changing. The plane slowed. Eventually, its propellers stopped. He sat up in the sudden silence, blinking out at flat fields, rows of low green.

"Here long enough for a stretch and a pee," said the pilot, getting out of his seat. He passed Tito on his way back through the cabin. He unfastened the door, and leaned out, swinging it open. "Hey, Carl," he called, grinning, to someone Tito couldn't see, "thanks for coming out." Someone propped the top of an ordinary aluminum ladder against the bottom of the door, and the pilot climbed down it, moving slowly, deliberately.

"Stretch your legs," Garreth said to Tito, getting out of his chair. Tito sat up, watching as Garreth started down the ladder. Tito rubbed his eyes and stood.

He climbed down to the packed earth of a straight road running in either direction through the flat green fields. The pilot and a man in blue coveralls and a straw cowboy hat were unrolling a black rubber hose from a reel on the back of a small tanker truck. He looked back and saw the old man descending the ladder.

Garreth produced a bottle of mineral water, a tooth-brush, and a tube of toothpaste. He began to brush his teeth, pausing to spit white foam on the ground. He rinsed his mouth from the bottle of water. "Got a tooth-brush?"

"No," said Tito.

Garreth brought out an unopened toothbrush and passed it to him, along with the bottle of water. While Tito brushed his teeth, he watched the old man walk a distance down the road, then stand, his back to them, urinating. Finishing with the toothbrush, Tito poured what was left of the water over its bristles, shook it dry, and tucked it into the inner pocket of his jacket. He wanted to ask where they were, but the protocol of deal-ing with clients prevented him.

"Western Illinois," Garreth said, as if reading his mind. "Belongs to a friend."

"Of yours?"

"The pilot's. The friend flies, keeps avgas here." The man with the cowboy hat yanked a cord on the back of the truck, starting up the engine of a pump. They moved away from a sudden billowing reek of fuel.

"How far can it fly?" Tito asked, looking at the plane.

"A little under twelve hundred miles on a full tank. Depending on weather and number of passengers."

"That seems not so far."

"Piston-engine prop. We have to keep hopping, this way, but it keeps us under all kinds of radar. We won't see any airport. All private runways."

Tito didn't think he meant actual radar.

"Gentlemen," said the old man, joining them, "good morning. You seemed to sleep quite well, finally," he said to Tito.

"Yes," Tito agreed.

"Why did you lift that Immigrations and Customs Enforcement badge, Tito?" the old man asked.

ICE. Tito remembered Garreth saying "ice," when he'd handed him the thing. Now he had no idea why he'd done that. And Elleggua, not he, had taken the badge case from the man's belt. He couldn't tell them that. "I felt it on his belt as he tried to hold me," he said. "I thought it might be a weapon."

"Then you thought to use the Bulgarian salt?"

"Yes," Tito said.

"I'm curious to learn what happened to him. I imagine, though, that he was taken briefly into custody, causing a jurisdictional pissing match. Until some entity, sufficiently high up in the DHS, ordered his release. You probably did your man a favor, Tito, taking that badge.

It's unlikely it was really his. You saved him having to refuse to explain it, until his fix came through."

Tito nodded, hoping the subject was now closed.

They stood, then, watching the fueling of the plane.

55. PHANTOM GUN SYNDROME

Miller," said Brown, from his enormous white leather recliner, across ten feet of off-white shag carpet. "Your name is David Miller. Same birthday, same age, same place of birth."

They were in a Gulfstream jet on a runway at Ronald Reagan. Milgrim had his own white leather recliner. He hadn't been to this airport since it had been National. Across a bridge from Georgetown. He knew this was a Gulfstream because there was an elaborately engraved brass plate that said "Gulfstream II" on the high-gloss wooden surround of the window beside his chair. Bird's-eye maple, he thought, but too shiny, like the trim in a limo that was really trying. There was a lot of that in this cabin. And a lot of white leather, polished brass, and off-white shag. "David Miller," he repeated.

"You live in New York. You're a translator. Russian."

"I'm Russian?"

"Your passport," said Brown, holding one up, navy blue with pale gold trim, "is American. David Miller. David Miller is not a junkie. David Miller, upon entering Canada, will neither be in possession of nor under the influence of drugs." He checked his watch. He was wearing the gray suit and a white shirt again. "How many of those pills are you holding?"

"One," said Milgrim. It was too serious a matter to lie about.

"Take it," said Brown. "I want you straight for customs."

"Canada?"

"Vancouver."

"Aren't there going to be more passengers?" Milgrim asked. The Gulfstream looked like it could sit twenty or so. Or serve as the set for a porn feature, as most of the seating consisted of very long white leather divans, plus a bedroom in the back that looked like a natural for your more formal money shots.

"No," said Brown, "there aren't." He slipped the passport back into his suit coat, then patted the place on his right hip where he kept his gun. Milgrim had seen him do this five times since they'd left N Street, and the micro-expression that always accompanied it convinced him that Brown had left his gun behind. Also his black nylon bag. Brown was suffering from phantom gun syndrome, Milgrim thought, like an amputee itching to scratch toes that were no longer there.

The Gulfstream's engines fired up, or started, or whatever you called it. Milgrim looked around the back of his white leather chair, to the front of the cabin, where a corrugated white leather curtain sealed off the cockpit. There was evidently a pilot up there, though Milgrim had yet to see him.

"When we land," said Brown, raising his voice against the engines, "customs officers drive out to the plane. They come aboard, say hello, I hand them the passports, they open them, hand them back, say goodbye. An aircraft like this, that's what happens. Our passport numbers, and the pilot's, went through when he filed our flight plan. Don't behave as though you're expecting them to ask you any questions." The plane began to taxi.

When it rushed forward, the roar of its engines deepening, and seemed to leap almost straight up into the air, Milgrim was completely unprepared. Nobody had even told them to fasten their seat belts, let alone about oxygen masks or life jackets. That seemed not only wrong, but deeply, almost physically, anomalous. As did the steepness of this climb, forcing Milgrim, who was facing backward, to cling desperately to the white, padded arms.

He looked out the window. And saw Ronald Reagan Washington National Airport recede, more quickly than he would have thought possible, and as smoothly as if someone had zoomed a lens in reverse.

When they leveled out, Brown removed his shoes, stood, and padded toward the back of the plane. Where, Milgrim assumed, there would be a toilet.

From behind, he saw Brown's hand touch the place where his gun wasn't.

56. HENRY AND RICHARD

A pale boy with a very thin beard was holding a rectangle of white cardboard inscribed with HENRY & RICHARD in green marker, as they left the customs hall. He wore a dusty-looking, no doubt expensively Dickensian chimney-sweep suit. "That's us," said Hollis, stopping their luggage cart beside him and offering him her hand. "Hollis Henry. This is Odile Richard."

"Oliver Sleight," he said, tucking his sign under his arm. "Like sleight of hand," offering his to shake, first with Hollis, then Odile. "Ollie. Blue Ant Vancouver."

"Pamela told me there was no office, up here," Hollis said, pushing the cart toward the exit. It was a few minutes after eleven.

"No office," he said, walking beside them, "but that

doesn't mean there's no work. This is a game design center, and we have clients through other offices, so there's still a need for hands-on. Let me push that for you."

"No need, thanks." They went out through an automatic door, and past a crowd of post-flight smokers working back up to functional blood-nicotine levels. Odile was evidently one of a new generation of non-smoking French, and had been delighted that Hollis no longer smoked, but Sleight, Ollie, as they followed him across a striped section of covered roadway, produced a yellow pack of cigarettes, lighting up.

Hollis started to remember something, but then the difference in the air struck her, after Los Angeles. It was like a sauna, but cool, almost chilly.

They went up a ramp, into a covered parking lot, where he used a credit card to pay for parking, then led them to his car, an oversized Volkswagen like the one Pamela had driven. It was pearlescent white, with a small stylized Blue Ant glyph to the left of the rear license plate. He helped them stow their bags and her cardboard carton in the trunk. He dropped his half-smoked cigarette and crushed it with an elongated, elaborately distressed shoe that she supposed went with his look.

Odile opted for shotgun, which seemed to please him, and soon they were on their way, something half remembered scratching fitfully in Hollis's head. They cruised past large, airport-related buildings, like toys on some giant's tidy, sparsely detailed hobby layout.

"You're going to be the fourth-ever residents in our flat," he said. "The Emir of Dubai's public relations team were there, last month. They had their own business here, but wanted to meet with Hubertus, so we put them up there, and Hubertus came up. Before that, twice, we had people in from our London office."

"It's not Hubertus's place, then?"

"I suppose it is," he said, changing lanes for the approach to a bridge, "but one of many. The view's extraordinary."

Hollis saw uncomfortably bright lights on tall poles, beyond the bridge's railings, overlooking a visual clutter of industry. Her cell rang. "Excuse me," she said. "Yes?"

"Where are you?" said Inchmale.

"In Vancouver."

"I, however, am in the lobby of your achingly pretentious hotel."

"I'm sorry. They sent me up here. I tried to reach you, but your cell wasn't answering, and your hotel said you were gone."

"Hotbed of locative art?"

"I don't know yet. Just got here."

"Where are you staying?"

"In a flat that Blue Ant has."

"You should insist on serious hotels."

"Well," she said, glancing at Ollie, who was listening to Odile, "I'm told we'll like it."

"Is that the royal 'we'?"

"A curator from Paris, who specializes in locative art. They brought her to Los Angeles for the piece. She'll be very helpful, up here. Has contacts."

"When are you back here?"

"I don't know. Shouldn't be long. How long are you there?"

"As long as it takes to produce the Bollards. Tomorrow we're having a first look at the studio."

"Which one?"

"Place on West Pico. After our time. Much is."

"Is what?"

"After our time. Why, for instance, are there these types with *Star Wars* helmets, standing at the foot of the Marmont's driveway, staring as if transfixed? I saw them earlier, when I checked in."

"They're viewing a monument to Helmut Newton. I know the artist, Alberto Corrales."

"But there's nothing there."

"You need the helmet," she explained.

"Dear God."

"You're at the Marmont?"

"I will be, when I've gotten back across Sunset."

"I'll call you, Reg. I should go."

"'Bye, then."

Long past the first bridge, and still on the wide street they'd turned onto, they drove through a stretch of carefully styled shops and restaurants. Jimmy Carlyle, who'd spent two years playing bass with a band in Toronto, before joining the Curfew, had told her that Canadian cities looked the way American cities did on television. But American cities didn't have this many galleries, she decided, after counting five in a few blocks, and then they were on another bridge.

Her phone rang again. "Sorry," she said. "Hello?"

"Hello," said Bigend. "Where are you?"

"In the car, with Ollie and Odile, going to your flat."

"Pamela told me you'd taken her along. Why?"

"She knows someone who knows our friend," she said. "Speaking of whom, why didn't you tell me he was Canadian?"

"It didn't seem important," said Bigend.

"But now I'm here. Is he here?"

"Not quite. Doing paperwork with a customs broker in Washington State, we're guessing. GPS matches up to a broker's address."

"Still. You know what I told you about being honest with me."

"Being Canadian," said Bigend, "even in today's fraught world, isn't always the first thing I'd mention about someone. When we were discussing him, initially, I had no idea he'd be headed that way. Later, I suppose it slipped my mind."

"Do you think he's bailing out?" She watched their driver.

"No. I think something's up, up there."

"What?"

"What the pirates saw," he said.

They came off the bridge into a sudden low canyon of much more downscale nightlife. She imagined Bobby's luminous wireframe cargo container suspended above the street, more enigmatic than any neon-skinned giant squid.

"But we'll find a better way to discuss it, shall we?"

He doesn't trust phones either, she thought. "Right."

"Do you have any piercings?" he asked.

They took a right.

"Excuse me?"

"Piercings. If you do, I must warn you about the bed in the master bedroom. The top floor."

"The bed."

"Yes. Apparently you don't want to crawl under it if you have any magnetic bits. Steel, iron. Or a pacemaker. Or a mechanical watch. The designers never mentioned that, when they showed me the plans. It's entirely about the space underneath, visually. Magnetic levitation. But now I have to warn each guest in turn. Sorry."

"I'm entirely as God made me, so far," she told him. "And I don't wear a watch."

"Not to worry, then," he said, cheerfully.

"I think we're here," she told them, as Ollie turned off a street where everything seemed to have been built the week before.

"Very good," he said, and hung up.

The Volkswagen rolled down a ramp as a gate rose. They entered a parking garage, brilliantly lit with sun-toned halogens above a pale, glassy concrete floor devoid of the least oil stain. The car's tires squeaked as Ollie pulled in beside another oversized Volkswagen in pearly white.

When she got out, she could smell the fresh concrete.

They got their things out of the truck and Ollie gave them each a pair of white unmarked magstrip cards. "This one's for the elevator," he said, taking Hollis's and swiping it beside doors of brushed stainless, "and access to the penthouse levels." Inside, he swiped it again, and they rose, swiftly and silently.

"I suppose I don't want to get this under the bed," Hollis said, visibly puzzling Odile, as he handed it back to her.

"No," he said, as the elevator stopped and its doors opened, "nor your credit cards."

They followed him along a short, carpeted hallway that a van could have been driven through. "Use the other card," he told her. She shifted the carton to her left arm and swiped the second card. He opened the very large ebony door, which she saw was a good four inches thick, and they stepped into a space that might have been the central concourse in the national airport of some tiny, hyperwealthy European nation, a pocket Liechtenstein founded on the manufacture of the most expensive minimalist light fixtures ever made.

"The flat," she said, looking up.

"Yes indeed," said Ollie Sleight.

Odile dropped her bag and started walking toward a curtain of glass wider than an old-fashioned theater screen. Uprights broke the view at intervals of fifteen feet or so. Beyond it, from where Hollis stood, there was only an undifferentiated gray-pink glow, with a few distant points of red light.

"Formidable," exclaimed Odile.

"Good, isn't it?" He turned to Hollis. "You're in the master bedroom. I'll show you." He took the carton, and led her up two flights of giddily suspended stairs, each tread a two-inch slab of frosted glass.

Bigend's bed was a perfect black square, ten feet on a side, floating three feet above the ebony floor. She walked over to it and saw that it was tethered, against whatever force supported it, with thin, braided cables of black metal.

"I think I might make something up on the floor," she said.

"Everyone says that," he said. "Then they try it."

She turned to say something, and in doing so saw him asking the girl at the counter, in the Standard's restaurant, for American Spirit cigarettes. Same yellow pack. Same beard. Like moss around a drain.

57. POPCORN

Commercial airliners were like buses, Milgrim decided, staring at the textured ceiling in his room in this Best Western. But a Gulfstream was like a taxi. Or like having a car. He wasn't ordinarily impressed by wealth, but his Gulfstream experience, Vegas decor aside, had left him struggling with issues of scale. Most people, he assumed, would never set foot on one. It was the sort of thing you knew existed, that you took for granted, however theoretically, as something some people owned. But most people, he now suspected, would never have to get their heads around the reality of the thing.

And he didn't know what going through ordinary Canadian customs was like, but everything had gone exactly as Brown had said it would, in the Gulfstream version. They'd landed at a large airport, then taxied to a dark place with nothing much at all outside. An SUV with lights on top had driven up, and two uniformed men had gotten out of it. When they'd come aboard, one in a jacket with gold buttons and the other in a tight, ribbed pullover with cloth patches over the shoulders and elbows, they'd accepted the three passports the pilot had handed them, opened each one, compared it to a printout, said thanks, and left. The one with the commando sweater was East Indian, and looked like he lifted weights. That was it. The pilot had pocketed his passport and gone back into the cockpit. Milgrim had never even heard him speak. He and Brown got their bags and left, walking down a long stairway that someone must have rolled up to the plane.

It had been cold, the air damp and full of the sound of planes. Brown had led them to a parked car, had felt under the front bumper, and come up with keys. He opened it and they got in. Brown had driven slowly away as Milgrim, beside him, had looked back at the lights of a tanker truck, rolling toward the Gulfstream.

They'd driven past an odd, pyramidal building and stopped at a chain-link gate. Brown had gotten out and punched numbers into a keypad. The gate had started rattling aside as Brown got back into the car.

The city had been very quiet, as they drove in. Deserted. Scarcely a pedestrian. Strangely clean, lacking in texture, like video games before they'd learned to dirty up the corners. Police cars that looked as though they had nowhere in particular to go.

"What about the plane?" Milgrim had asked, as Brown

drove fast across a long multilaned concrete bridge over what he took to be the second of two rivers.

"What about it?"

"Does it wait?"

"It goes back to Washington."

"That's quite a plane," Milgrim had said.

"That's what money will buy you, in America," Brown had said, firmly. "People say Americans are materialistic. But do you know why?"

"Why?" asked Milgrim, more concerned with this uncharacteristically expansive mode of expression on Brown's part.

"Because they have better stuff," Brown had replied. "No other reason."

Milgrim thought about that now as he lay looking up at the ceiling. It was textured with those crumbs of rigid foam, the size of the last few pieces left in an empty bag of popcorn. They were stuff, those texturizing bits, and so was a Gulfstream. But almost anybody got those bits, during the course of an ordinary life. He supposed you needed money just to get away from some kinds of stuff. A Gulfstream, though, was another kind of stuff. It bothered him, in some unaccustomed way, that Brown had access to such things. Brown belonged to the New Yorker, Milgrim felt, or to this Best Western. Low-pixel laminate. The Gulfstream, the Georgetown townhouse with the housekeeper who cut hair, that felt wrong, somehow.

But then he wondered if Brown might not actually have the DEA connections he'd imagined he might have.

Maybe he borrowed the plane from the people he got the Rize from? They seized things from serious dealers, didn't they? Boats. Planes. You read about that.

That would explain the shag carpeting, too.

58. ALPHABET TALK

The pilot followed highways.

Tito could see this now, sitting up in the front with him, the fear having somehow absented itself with the takeoff from Illinois and the pilot's offer of the seat beside his.

Like a stranger beside you on a bus, he thought now, fear, then unexpectedly getting up, getting off. Keep your mother and the flight from Cuba in its own separate drawer. This was much better.

Gratitude to Elleggua; may the ways be opened.

The flat country through which they followed the thin straight lines of highway was called Nebraska, the pilot had told him, pressing a button on his headset that allowed Tito to hear him with his own headset.

Tito ate one of the turkey sandwiches the man with the cowboy hat and refueling truck had given them in Illinois, careful with the crumbs, while he watched Nebraska unroll beneath them. When he finished the sandwich, he folded the brown paper bag it had come in, propped his elbow against the padded ledge at the top of the door, where the window started, rested his head on his cupped hand. His headset made a clicking sound. "Information Exploitation Office," he heard the old man say.

"It's a DARPA program, though," Garreth said.

"DARPA R and D, but always intended for IXO."

"And he's gotten into a beta version?"

"The Sixth Fleet has been using something called Fast-C2AP," the old man said. "Makes locating some ships as easy as checking an online stock price. But it's not PANDA, not by a long shot. Predictive analysis for naval deployment activities. If it doesn't get dumbed down, PANDA will comprehend behavioral patterns of commercial vessels, local to global; their routes, routine detours for fuel or paperwork. If a ship that always travels between Malaysia and Japan turns up in the Indian Ocean, PANDA notices. It's a remarkable system, not least because it actually would contribute to making the country safer. But, yes, he does seem to have accessed some sort of beta version, and cross-referenced a vessel on it with the box's most recent signal."

"Earning his wage in that case," said Garreth.

"But I ask myself," the old man said, "who is it we're dealing with, here? Is he a genius of some kind or, really, at the end of the day, just a talented and audacious burglar?"

"And the difference would be?" asked Garreth, after a pause.

"Predictability. Are we inadvertently creating a monster, assigning him these things, facilitating him?"

Tito looked over at the pilot, deciding he seemed most unlikely to be listening to this conversation. He was steering the plane with his knees, and filling in blanks on a white paper form, on a battered, boxlike aluminum clipboard, with a hinged lid. Tito wondered if there would be a telltale of some kind, a light perhaps, that could indicate to Garreth and the old man that his headset was on.

"Seems an abstract concern, to me," said Garreth.

"Not to me," said the old man, "although it certainly isn't that immediate. One immediate concern today is whether our positioning arrangement is reliable. If our box gets put down in the wrong spot, things will get complicated. Very complicated."

"I know," said Garreth, "but they're Teamsters, those two. Old hands. At one time they would've been 'losing' boxes like this. Driving them straight out of there. Now, with an upgraded security regime, they're not even thinking about that sort of thing. But good money for putting one down where we most need it, that's something else."

"For that matter," said the old man, "if that box isn't wearing the same owner code, product code, six-digit registration number, and check digit it was wearing when last seen, our Teamsters won't find it for us, will they?"

"It is," Garreth said. "The same ISO markings are encrypted in every transmission."

"Not necessarily. That piece of equipment was programmed when the box had those markings. We can't be certain that it still does. I just don't want you to forget that we have other options."

"I don't."

Tito removed the headset.

Without touching any of its buttons, he hung it from its hook above the door, put his head back, and pretended to be asleep.

Alphabet talk. He didn't like it.

59. BLACK ZODIAC

Brown rented a remarkably ugly and uncomfortable black boat called a Zodiac. A pair of huge inflated black rubber tubes, joined at the front in a crude point, a hard black floor down between these, four high-backed bucket seats mounted on posts, and the largest outboard motor, black, that Milgrim had ever seen. The rental operation, in the marina where the thing was docked, provided each of them with a semirigid flotation jacket, a red nylon garment apparently lined with sheets of only barely flexible foam. Milgrim's smelled of fish, and chafed his neck.

Milgrim couldn't remember the last time he'd been in a boat, and he certainly hadn't expected to find himself in one today, very nearly the first thing in the morning.

Brown had come in through the door that connected

their rooms, that now familiar arrangement, and shaken him awake, though not very forcefully. The gray boxes weren't on the doors, here, and Milgrim had to assume that Brown had left them in Washington, along with the gun, the large folding knife, and perhaps the flashlight and handcuffs as well. But Brown was wearing his black nylon jacket, today, over a black T-shirt, and Milgrim thought he looked much more at home in it than he did in his suit.

After a silent breakfast of coffee and eggs in the hotel's restaurant, they'd gone to the underground garage and retrieved the car, a Ford Taurus with a Budget sticker beside the rear license plate. Milgrim had come to prefer a Corolla.

Cities, in Milgrim's experience, had a way of revealing themselves in the faces of their inhabitants, and particularly on their way to work in the morning. There was a sort of basic fuckedness index to be read, then, in faces that hadn't yet encountered the reality of whatever they were on their way to do. By this standard, Milgrim thought, scanning faces and body language as Brown drove, this place had an oddly low fuckedness index. Closer to Costa Mesa than San Bernardino, say, at least in this part of town. It did remind him more of California than he would have expected it to, though maybe that was this sunshine, more San Francisco than Los Angeles.

Then he became aware of Brown whistling, under his breath, as he drove. Tunelessly, he thought, but with something akin to cheerfulness, or at any rate a degree of positive excitement. Was he picking up the vibe from this sunny but mildly overcast morning's crowds? Milgrim doubted that, but it was weird nonetheless.

Twenty minutes later, having had some difficulty finding the place, they were in a parking lot beside a marina. Water, distant mountains, greenish glass towers looking as though they'd been built the night before, boats with white masts, seagulls doing seagull things. Brown was feeding a ticketing machine with large silver-and-gold tokens of some kind.

"What are those?" Milgrim asked.

"Two-dollar coins," said Brown, whom Milgrim knew to avoid the use of credit cards whenever possible.

"Aren't twos unlucky?" Milgrim asked, remembering something about racetrack money.

"Lucky they aren't fucking threes," said Brown.

Now, the huge outboard roaring, marina and city were both behind them. The Zodiac went pancaking along over very cold-looking gray-green water, a glassy shade not unlike that of the towers overlooking the marina. The flotation jacket, stiff and odorous as it was, was agreeably windproof. The cuffs of Milgrim's Jos. A. Banks back-to-school trousers were flapping like pennants around his ankles. Brown drove the boat on his feet, leaning forward, only loosely strapped to his seat, the wind pressing unexpected angles into his face. Milgrim doubted Brown was still whistling, but he still seemed to be enjoying this too much. And he hadn't actually seemed all that familiar with the business of casting off, if that was what it was called. They'd needed help from the rental guy.

The salt wind of their passage stung Milgrim's eyes.

He looked back and saw an island or peninsula, nothing there but trees, out of which emerged a tall suspension bridge, like the Oakland Bay.

He zipped the floater coat higher, pulling his neck in. He wished that he could pull his arms and legs in. For that matter he wished there were a room in there, large enough for a cot, and that he could stretch out while Brown drove this boat. Like a tent, with semirigid red nylon walls. He could live with the fish smell, just to lie down, out of this wind.

Milgrim looked back at the city, a seaplane lifting out of the water. Ahead, he saw several large ships at varying distances, their hulls bisected with black and red paint, and beyond them what he guessed was a port, where giant orange arms craned in the distance, above a shoreline seemingly solid with the visual complexity of industry.

To their left, on some opposite, more distant shore, stood rows of dark tanks or silos, more cranes, more freighters.

People paid to have experiences like this, he thought, but it didn't cheer him. This wasn't the Staten Island Ferry. He was bouncing along at some insane speed on something that reminded him of a creepy folding rubber bathtub that he'd once seen Vladimir Nabokov proudly posing with in an old photograph. Nature, for Milgrim, had always had a way of being too big for comfort. Just too much of it. That whole vista thing. Particularly if there was relatively little within it, within sight, that was man-made.

They were gaining, he saw, on what he at first took to be some kind of floating Cubist sculpture in muted Kandinsky tones. But as they drew closer he saw that it was a ship, but one so burdened, pressed so far down in the water, that the red of its lower hull was submerged, only the black showing. Its black stern, though, stuck up shiplike enough, below the absurdist bulk of boxes, revealing it for what it was. The boxes were the colors of railroad freight cars, a dull brownish red predominating, though others were white, yellow, pale blue. He was almost close enough, now, to read the writing on this ship's stern, when he was distracted by his discovery of a smaller ship, draped with black tires as if for some eccentric designer's runway moment, pressing ardently against the tall black stern and churning out a huge V of foamy white water. Brown swung the Zodiac's wheel suddenly, sending them bouncing double-time across the white water. Milgrim saw the tug's name, *Lion Sun*, then looked up at the much taller letters on the back of the ship, their white paint streaked with rust. M/V *Jamaica Star*, and under that, in slightly smaller white capitals, PANAMA CITY.

Brown killed the engine. They bobbed there, in the sudden absence of the outboard's roar. Milgrim heard a bell ringing, far off, and what sounded like a train whistle.

Brown removed a fancily printed metal tube from his floater jacket, unscrewed the end, and drew out a cigar. He tossed the tube over the side, nipped the end of the cigar with a shiny little gadget, put the nipped end in his mouth, and lit it with one of those six-inch fake Bics, the kind Korean delis used to sell for lighting crack. He took a long ritual pull on the cigar, then blew out a great cloud of rich blue smoke. "Son of a bitch," he said, with what Milgrim, amazed at all of this, took to be immense and inexplicable satisfaction. "Look at that son of a bitch." Looking after the square, floating box-pile that was the freighter *Jamaica Star*, where Milgrim couldn't quite make out trademarks on the boxes, though he could see they were there. Slowly receding as the tug patiently shoved it on its way.

Milgrim, definitely not wanting to disturb this special moment, whatever it might be about, sat there, listening to little waves lap against the slick and swollen flank of the black Zodiac.

"Son of a bitch," said Brown, again, softly, and puffed on his cigar.

60. ROLLING THE CODES

Hollis woke on Bigend's maglev bed, feeling as though it was the altar atop some Aztec pyramid. Platform of sacrifice. And there actually was a pyramid of sorts above it, she saw, a glass-sided construct she suspected of being the pinnacle of this particular tower. She had to admit she'd slept well, however much magnetism she'd absorbed in the process. Perhaps it eased the joints, like those mail-order bracelets. Or perhaps it was actually the pyramid that did it, subtle energies sharpening her prana.

"Hello," called Ollie Sleight, from a level below. "Are you up?"

"Be right with you."

She slid off the Aztec altar, which moved slightly, and in a very strange way, and got into jeans and a top, blinking, as she did so, at the expensive emptiness of this bedroom, or sleeping-pinnacle. Like the lair of some design-conscious flying monster.

Ignore seà, she told herself, mountains. Don't look. Too much view. She found a bathroom, where nothing much resembled conventional amenities, figured out how to work the taps, and washed her face and brushed her teeth. Barefooted, she went down to meet Ollie, possibly to confront him.

"Odile's gone for a walk," he said, seated at a long glass table with an open FedEx carton and various bits of black plastic in front of him. "What kind of phone do you have?"

"Motorola."

"Straight two-point-five-millimeter jack," he said, selecting one from an assortment. "Hubertus sent this." Indicating the largest of the black bits. "It's a scrambler."

"What does it do?"

"You plug it into the headset jack on your phone. It uses a digital encryption algorithm. You program in a sixteen-digit code and the algorithm rolls the scrambling code up to about sixty thousand times. Gives you seventeen hours' scramble before the pattern repeats. Hubertus has already charged and programmed this one. He wants you to use it when the two of you talk."

"That's nice," she said.

"May I have your phone?"

She took it from her jeans pocket and handed it to him.

"Thanks." He connected it to the black rectangle, which reminded her of those snap-off automotive CD-player fronts. "It has its own charger, which won't work for your phone." He used the edge of his palm to sweep extra black bits and packaging back into the FedEx box. "I brought fruit and pastry. There's coffee on."

"Thank you."

He put a set of car keys on the table. She saw a blue-and-silver VW emblem. "These are for the extra Phaeton downstairs. Have you driven one?"

"No."

"You need to watch the width. It looks so much like a Passat that it's easy to forget how much wider it is. Look down at the painted lines, when you get in; that'll remind you."

"Thanks."

"I'm off, then," he said, getting up and tucking the carton under his arm. He was in a T-shirt and jeans this morning, both of which seemed to have been gone over with a Dremel tool for about as many hours as Bigend's gadget could roll its codes. He looked tired, she thought, but that might just be the beard.

When he was gone, she looked for the kitchen and coffee. It turned out to be across this very space, and disguised as a bar, but the coffeemaker and an Italian toaster gave it away. She took her cup back to the table. Her cell rang, various LED effects dancing excitedly on the black face of the scrambler.

"Hello?"

"Hubertus. Oliver told me you were up."

"I am. Are we 'scrambled'?"

"We are."

"You have one too?"

"That's how it works."

"It's too big to fit in a pocket."

"I know," he said, "but I'm increasingly concerned with privacy. All of which is relative, of course."

"This isn't really private?"

"It's more private than . . . not. Ollie has a box with a Linux machine in it that can sniff three hundred wireless networks at the same time."

"Why would he want to do that?"

He took a moment to think about it. "Because he can, I suppose."

"I want to talk to you about Ollie."

"Yes?"

"He came in the restaurant at the Standard while I was meeting with Odile and Alberto. Bought a pack of cigarettes."

"Yes?"

"Was he checking me out? For you?"

"Of course. What else do you think he would have been doing?"

"Just checking," she said. "I mean, I am. Just making sure."

"We needed a sense of how you were getting along with them. We were still making up our minds, at that point."

The Blue Ant "we," she thought. "More centrally, then, where's Bobby?"

"Up there," he said. "Somewhere."

"I thought you could keep track of him."

"Of the truck. The truck's in the yard of a leasing firm, in a satellite city called Burnaby. Bobby and his equipment were off-loaded beside a warehouse, just north of the border, early this morning. I've had Oliver up all night, on that. He went down to the GPS coordinates where they stopped."

"And?"

"Nothing, of course. We assume they switched trucks. How are things with Odile?"

"She's gone out for a walk. When she gets back, I'll try to work out what potential connections she might have here, to Bobby. I stayed away from that, on the flight up. Seemed too soon."

"Good," he said. "If you need me, use the ring-back for this call."

She watched the scrambler do its little LED-dance as the encrypted connection was broken.

61. THE PELICAN CASE

They took the black plastic Pelican case on in Montana. It wasn't another fueling stop, though Tito imagined they were due for one of those soon. The pilot landed on a deserted stretch of rural highway, at dawn. Tito saw a battered old station wagon pulling up beside them, two men standing on its roof, but then Garreth told him to stay away from the windows. "They don't want to see anyone they don't know."

Garreth opened the cabin door and a black case was handed in. It seemed to be very heavy. Garreth didn't try to lift it. He strained, dragging it in, while someone Tito couldn't see, outside, pushed. It looked to Tito like a Pelican case, plastic and waterproof, the kind Alejandro had sometimes used to bury documents and supplies. Then the door was closed, he heard the station wagon's engine, and the pilot began to taxi. As they took off, Tito imagined he could feel the additional weight.

When they'd leveled out, the old man held a yellow plastic instrument close to the black box, then showed Garreth the readout on its screen.

They landed again within an hour, at a rural strip where another avgas truck was waiting.

They drank paper cups of coffee from a thermos the avgas man had brought, while he and the pilot fueled the plane.

"That's really the ultimate handload he's put together, isn't it?" said Garreth to the old man.

"He told me he used JB Weld to seal the tips," said the old man.

"Is that all?" Garreth asked.

"When I was a boy, we fixed holes in engine blocks with JB Weld."

"They probably weren't quite so radioactive," said Garreth.

62. SISTER

This is Sarah," said Odile, when Hollis found her, on the crowded café patio of a municipal gallery. The Phaeton had a GPS-based guidance system, but it also had a map. She could have walked over here, she guessed, in the time it had taken her to get the car, find the place, and find parking. And Ollie had been right about it being wide. All of this in response to Odile having phoned and asked her to lunch with someone interesting.

"Hello," said Hollis, taking the girl's hand, "I'm Hollis Henry."

"Sarah Ferguson."

Hollis was pulling up a wrought-iron chair, wondering whether she'd missed her chance to have Odile put visiting the local locative artists on hold, when the French curator said, "Fer-gus-son."

"Oh," said Hollis.

"Sarah is Bobby's sister." Odile was wearing a narrow pair of black-framed sunglasses.

"Yes," said Sarah, with what Hollis took to be a possible lack of enthusiasm. "Odile tells me you met Bobby in Los Angeles."

"I did," said Hollis. "I'm doing a piece on locative art for *Node*, and your brother seems to be a key player."

"*Node*?"

"It's new," said Hollis. Could Bigend, or Rausch, have known that Odile knew Bobby's sister? "I didn't know he had a sister." She looked at Odile. "Are you an artist, Sarah?"

"No," said Sarah, "I work for a gallery. Not this one."

Hollis looked up at this retrofitted bank or government building. Saw public art, the statue of a ship, mounted where a roof started.

"We must go inside, for the food," said Odile.

Inside, an upscale cafeteria line that for some reason made Hollis feel they were in Copenhagen. The people ahead of them looked as though they could each identify a dozen classic modern chairs by the designer's name. They chose sandwiches, salads, and drinks; Hollis used her credit card, telling Sarah lunch was on *Node*. When she put her wallet back in her purse, she saw the envelope with Jimmy's five thousand dollars. She'd almost left it in the electronic safe in the room at the Mondrian.

Sarah resembled Bobby, Hollis thought, as they settled at their table, but it looked better on a girl. She had darker hair, nicely cut, and was dressed for work in a gallery that sold art to people who expected a certain seriousness of demeanor. Mixed grays and black, good shoes.

"I had no idea you knew Bobby's sister," Hollis said to Odile, picking up her sandwich.

"We've only just met," said Sarah, picking up her fork. "We have an ex in common, it turns out." She smiled.

"Claude," said Odile, "in Paris. I told you, Ollis, he knew Bobby."

"Yes, you did."

"I phone him," said Odile. "He gives me Sarah's number."

"Not the first call from a stranger I've had about Bobby, in the past twenty-four hours," said Sarah, "but at least there's the connection through Claude. And you weren't angry."

"Have the others been angry?" Hollis asked.

"Some of them, yes. Others simply impatient."

"Why? If you don't mind my asking."

"Because he's a fuckup," said Sarah.

"Artists in L.A.," said Odile. "They try to find Bobby. His geohacks are down. Their art is gone. E-mail bounces."

"I've had half a dozen calls. Someone down there must've known he has a sister here, and I'm in the book."

"I know one of the artists who works with him," Hollis said. "He was quite upset."

"Who?"

"Alberto Corrales."

"Did he cry?"

"No."

"He cried on the phone," said Sarah, spearing a slice of avocado. "Kept saying he'd lost his river."

"But you don't know where your brother is?"

"He's here," said Sarah. "My friend Alice saw him on Commercial Drive, this morning. She's known him since high school. She called me. As a matter of fact, she called me about twenty minutes before you did," she said to Odile. "She said hello. He couldn't dodge her; he knew she knew it was him. Of course she had no idea people in L.A. are looking for him. He told her he was in town to talk with a label, about releasing a CD. Of course that was the first I knew of him being here."

"Are you close?"

"Does it sound like it?"

"Sorry," said Hollis.

"No, I'm sorry," said Sarah. "It's just that he's so annoying, so irresponsible. He's as self-centered now as he was when he was fifteen. It isn't easy, having a monster of giftedness for a brother."

"Gifted how?" Hollis asked.

"Mathematically. Software. You know he named himself after a piece of software developed at Lawrence Berkeley National Labs? Chombo."

"What does Chombo . . . do?"

"It implements finite difference methods for the solution of partial differential equations, on block-structured, adaptively refined rectangular grids." Sarah made a brief and probably unconscious face.

"Could you explain that?"

"Not a word of it. But I work in a gallery of contemporary art. Chombo is Bobby's favorite thing. He says nobody else really appreciates Chombo, understands Chombo, the way he does. He talks about it like it's a dog, one he's been able to train to do things no one's ever thought of training a dog to do. Fetch things. Roll over." She shrugged. "You're looking for him too, aren't you?"

"I am," said Hollis, putting down her sandwich.

"Why?"

"Because I'm a journalist, and I'm writing about locative art. And he seems to be at the center of it, and certainly he's at the center of his sudden absence, and the upset it's caused."

"You used to be in that band," said Sarah. "I remember it. With that English guitarist."

"The Curfew," Hollis said.

"And you're a writer, now?"

"I'm trying to be. I thought I'd be in L.A. for a few weeks, researching this. Then Alberto Corrales introduced me to Bobby. Then Bobby vanished."

"'Vanished' is a little dramatic," said Sarah, "particularly if you know Bobby. 'Flaked off,' my father calls it. Would Bobby want to see you, do you think?"

Hollis considered. "No," she said. "He was unhappy with Alberto for bringing me to his place in L.A. His studio. I didn't think he'd want to see me again."

"He liked your records," said Sarah.

"That was what Alberto said," said Hollis, "but he really didn't like visitors."

"In that case," said Sarah, and paused, looking from Hollis to Odile, then back, "I'll tell you where he is."

"You know?"

"He has a place on the east side. Space in a building that used to be an upholstery factory. Someone lives there, when he's away, and I run into her occasionally, so I know he still has it. If he's here, and not there, I'd be very surprised. Off Clark Drive."

"Clark?"

"I'll give you the address," said Sarah.

Hollis got out her pen.

63. SURVIVAL, EVASION, RESISTANCE, AND ESCAPE

Tito watched the old man fold the copy of the *New York Times* he'd been reading. They were sitting in an open Jeep, its hood dotted with red rust through dull-gray paint that had been applied with a brush. Tito could see the Pacific, this new ocean. The pilot had flown them here from the mainland, and gone, having said a long, private goodbye to the old man. Tito had seen them clasp hands, the grip held hard.

He'd watched the Cessna become a dot, then vanish.

"I remember seeing proofs of a CIA interrogation manual, something we'd been sent unofficially, for comment," the old man said. "The first chapter laid out the ways in which torture is fundamentally counterproductive to intelligence. The argument had nothing to do with ethics, everything to do with quality of product, with not squandering potential assets." He removed his steel-rimmed glasses. "If the man who keeps returning to question you avoids behaving as if he were your enemy, you begin to lose your sense of who you are. Gradually, in the crisis of self that your captivity becomes, he guides you in your discovery of who you are becoming."

"Did you interrogate people?" asked Garreth, the black Pelican case under his feet.

"It's an intimate process," the old man said. "Entirely about intimacy." He spread his hand, held it, as if above an invisible flame. "An ordinary cigarette lighter will cause a man to tell you anything, whatever he thinks you want to hear." He lowered his hand. "And will prevent him ever trusting you again, even slightly. And will confirm him, in his sense of self, as few things will." He tapped the folded paper. "When I first saw what they were doing, I knew that they'd turned the SERE lessons inside out. That meant we were using techniques the Koreans had specifically developed in order to prepare prisoners for show trials." He fell silent.

Tito heard the lapping of waves.

This was still America, they said.

The Jeep, covered with a tarp and branches, had been waiting for them near the weathered concrete runway that Garreth said had once belonged to a weather station. There were push brooms in the back of the Jeep. Someone had used them to sweep the concrete, in preparation for their landing.

A boat was coming, Garreth had said, to take them to Canada. Tito wondered how large a boat it would be.

He imagined a Circle Line tour boat. Icebergs. But the sun here was warm, the breeze off the sea gentle. He felt as though he had come to the edge of the world. The edge of America, the land he had seen unrolling beneath the Cessna, almost entirely empty. The small towns of America, at night, had been like lost jewels, scattered across the floor of a vast dark room. He'd watched them pass, from the Cessna's window, imagining people sleeping there, perhaps distantly aware of the faint drone of their engines.

Garreth offered Tito an apple, and a knife to cut it with. It was a crude knife, like something you might see in Cuba, the handle covered in chipped yellow paint. Tito opened it, discovering DOUK-DOUK printed on the blade. It was very sharp. He cut the apple into quarters, wiped both sides of the blade on the leg of his jeans, passed it back to Garreth, then offered the slices of fruit. Garreth and the old man each took one.

The old man looked at his worn gold watch, then out across the water.

64. GLOCKING

Score some shit," said Brown, sounding like he'd re-
hearsed the line, as he handed Milgrim a fold of colorful
foreign bills. They were shiny and crisp, decked with metallic holograms and, it looked to Milgrim, printed cir-
cuitry.

Milgrim, in the passenger seat of the Taurus, looked
over at Brown. "Excuse me?"

"Shit," said Brown. "Dope."

"Dope?"

"Find me a dealer. Not some corner guy. Somebody
in the business."

Milgrim looked out at the street they were parked on.
Five-story brick Edwardian retail structures lacquered
with the unhappiness of crack or heroin. The fuckedness
quotient way up, down in this part of town.

"But what are you trying to buy?"

"Drugs," said Brown.

"Drugs," Milgrim repeated.

"You have three hundred and a wallet with no ID. If you get picked up, I don't know you. You get picked up, you forget the passport you came in on, how you got here, me, everything. Give them your real name. I'll get you out eventually, but if you try to screw me, you're in there for good. And if you can get the guy to do the deal in a parking garage, that's a major plus."

"I've never been here before," said Milgrim. "I don't even know if this is the right street."

"Are you kidding? Look at it."

"I know," Milgrim said, "but a local would know what's going on this week. Today. Is this where the biz is, or did the police just shift it three blocks south? Like that."

"You look," said Brown, "like a junkie. You'll do fine."

"I'm not known. I might be mistaken for an informant."

"Out," ordered Brown.

Milgrim got out, the foreign cash folded in his palm. He looked down the street. Every shop boarded up. Plywood papered with rain-wrinkled multiples of film and concert posters.

He decided it would be best to behave as though he were shopping for his own flavor of pharmaceuticals. This would up his authenticity immediately, he thought, as he knew what to ask for, and that the units would be pills. This way, if he actually managed to buy something, it might even turn out to be worth keeping.

The day suddenly seemed brighter, this foreign but oddly familiar street more interesting. Allowing himself to forget Brown almost entirely, he strolled along with a new energy.

An hour and forty minutes later, having been offered three different shades of heroin, cocaine, crack, meth, Percodan, and marijuana buds, he found himself closing a transaction for thirty Valium tens at five each. He had no idea whether these would prove genuine, or if they even existed, but he had an expert's conviction that he was being asked, as an obvious tourist, to pay at least twice the going rate. Having separated the hundred and fifty the seller required, he'd managed to slip the other half into the top of his left sock. He did things like this automatically, when buying drugs, and no longer recalled any particular event having led to the adaptation of a given strategy.

Skink, so called for the purpose of this transaction at least, was white, in his thirties perhaps, with vestigial skater fashion-notes and a high, intricately tattooed turtleneck Milgrim assumed disguised some early and likely unfortunate choices in iconography. A cover-up, perhaps of jail work. Visible neck or facial tattoos did serve, Milgrim thought, to suggest that one probably wasn't a cop, but the jail look rang other, less comfortable bells. As noms of convenience went, "Skink" wasn't particularly comforting either. Milgrim wasn't quite sure what one was; either reptilian or amphibian, he thought. Skink definitely wasn't the most reliable-looking retailer Milgrim had come across, in the course of his stroll along this diversely supplied thoroughfare, but he was the only one, so far, who'd responded positively to Milgrim's request for Valium. Though he didn't, he said, have it on him. They so seldom do, thought Milgrim, though he nodded understandingly, indicating that he was okay with whatever Skink's arrangements might be.

"Up the street here," Skink said, fiddling with the ring through the outer limit of his right eyebrow.

Milgrim always found these worrying. They seemed more prone to infection than things put through other, more central, more traditional parts of the face. Milgrim was a believer in evolution, and knew that evolution strongly favors bilateral symmetry. Asymmetrical individuals tended to be less competitive, in most species. Though he had no intention of mentioning it to Skink.

"In here," said Skink, portentously, stepping sideways into an entranceway. He opened an aluminum-framed door whose original glass had been replaced with plywood.

"It's dark," protested Milgrim, as Skink grabbed his shoulders, hauling him into a dense, ammoniac reek of urine. Skink shoved him, hard, and he fell back against what were all too obviously stairs, their painful impact complicated by a loud confusion of toppling bottles. "Chill," Milgrim quickly advised an abrupt darkness, Skink having shut the door behind him. "Money's yours. Here."

Then Brown was through the door, in a brief burst of

sunlight. Milgrim felt, rather than saw, Brown lift Skink bodily off his feet and drive him headfirst into the stairs, between Milgrim's legs.

A few more empties toppled from the stairs.

An uncomfortably bright beam, recalled from the IF's room off Lafayette, darted clinically across the crumpled Skink. Brown bent, ran one hand over Skink's lower back, then, with a grunt of effort, used both hands to flip him over. Milgrim saw Brown's spotlit hand unzipping the fly of Skink's saggy pants. "Glock," said Brown, thickly, plucking, like some gross-out conjuring trick, a large pistol from Skink's open pants.

Then they were back on the street, the sunlight surreal now. Getting back into the Taurus.

"Glock," Brown said again, pleased.

Milgrim remembered then, and to his relief, that this was a make of gun.

65. EAST VAN HALEN

She opened her PowerBook on the counter of Bigend's crypto-kitchen, taking wifi for granted. None of her trusted networks were available, she was advised, but did she want to join BAntVanc1?

The phrase "trusted networks" briefly made her feel like crying. She wasn't feeling as though she had any.

Bigend, she saw, pulling herself together, hadn't activated his WEP. No password required. But then he had Ollie, she supposed, who could eavesdrop on hundreds of other people's wifi at once, so maybe it all balanced out.

She joined BAntVanc1 and checked her e-mail. Nothing. No spam, even.

Her phone rang, in her purse. It was still attached to

the scrambler. How would that work if it were anyone other than Bigend? She answered. "Hello?"

"Just checking," said Bigend, and suddenly she didn't want to tell him about Sarah.

A reaction to her sudden sense of his ubiquity, if not yet actual then potential. Once he was established in your life, he'd be there, in some way no ordinary person, no ordinary boss, even, could be. Once she accepted him, past a certain point, there was always going to be the possibility of him ringing her up, to say "Just checking," before she could even ask who was calling. Did she want that? Could she afford not to?

"Nothing yet," she said, wondering if Ollie might not already have somehow transmitted their lunch conversation to Los Angeles. "I'm nosing around Odile's art circles here. She has a lot of them, though, and it can't be done too obviously. No telling who might let him know I'm here looking."

"I think he's there," said Bigend, "and I think you and Odile are currently our best chance of finding him."

She nodded silently. "This is a big country," she said. "Why wouldn't he head somewhere he'd be less likely to be found?"

"Vancouver is a port," said Bigend. "A foreign container port. Our pirates' chest. He's there to monitor the off-loading, though not for the shippers." There was an utterly silent digitized pause. "I want to set you up on a darknet we're having built for us."

"What's that?"

"In effect, a private Internet. Invisible to nonmembers. Scrambled phones, at this point, just serve as strings around our fingers to remind us of a fundamental lack of privacy. Ollie's working on it."

"Someone's here," she said. "Have to run." She hung up.

Leaving her PowerBook open on the counter, its sticker-encrusted lid the most colorful thing in sight, aside from the view, she went upstairs, undressed, and had a long shower. Odile had opted for a post-lunch nap.

She dried her hair and dressed, got back into jeans, sneakers. Finding the Blue Ant figurine in her clothes, she looked around for a perch for it. Selected a head-high ledge of talcum-smooth concrete and stood the ant on it, icon-style. It made the ledge look slightly ridiculous. Perfect.

She chanced on her passport, as she was folding things, and tossed it into the Barneys bag.

She put on a dark cotton jacket, took her purse, and went down to the crypto-kitchen, where she shut her PowerBook and wrote Odile a note on the back of a Visa charge slip, which she left on the counter: "Back later. Hollis."

She found the Phaeton where she'd left it, followed Ollie's advice to remind herself how wide it was, did some work with the map from the glove compartment, avoided activating the GPS screen (it spoke, if you let it), and drove out into late-afternoon sunlight, feeling reasonably confident she could find Bobby's place, and not confident at all that she'd know what to do when she did.

He didn't live that far from here, to judge by the map.

Rush hour. After a few moves designed to get her headed east, crosstown, she got with the flow, such as it was. Edging more or less steadily eastward, amid what she assumed to be commuters headed for eastern satellites, she saw that Bobby's place probably wasn't all that close, at least not psychogeographically. Bigend's stratatitle, atop one tower in a variegated hedge of greenglass, along what her map said was False Creek, was high end twenty-first-century. Here, she was driving into what remained of a light-industrial zone. The way they'd built on railway land, when land had been surplus. Not unlike the feel around Bobby's rental on Romaine, though studded now, here and there, with large pieces of brand-new metropolitan infrastructure, most of these apparently still under construction.

When she finally turned left, onto a wide, north-south street called Clark, she was past the fancy infra-bits and into a more low-down, more careworn architecture, a lot of it clapboard. Nonfranchise auto-repair shops. Small manufacturers of restaurant furniture. Chrome chairs recovered. At what she guessed was the foot of this wide street, suspended against distant mountains, some truly kick-ass Soviet Constructivist project appeared to have been erected, perhaps in belated honor of a designer who'd earned himself a one-way to the Gulag. Vast crazy arms of orange-painted steel, canted in every direction, at every angle.

What the hell was it, though?

Bigend's port, she guessed. And Bobby so close by.

She turned right when she spotted Bobby's street.

She'd lied to Bigend, she admitted to herself now, and it was bothering her. She'd told him she'd work with him as long as he didn't hold back information, or lie to her, and now she'd done exactly that, to him. She wasn't comfortable with that. The symmetry was a little too obvious. She sighed.

She drove to the end of the block, turned right again, and pulled over, behind a rust-streaked Dumpster with EAST VAN HALEN painted across its back in runny black spray-bomb.

She got her phone and Bigend's scrambler out of her purse, sighed, and rang him back.

He answered immediately. "Yes?"

"Odile's found his sister."

"Very good. Excellent. And?"

"I'm near a place he has here. His sister told us where it is. She thinks this is where he'll be." She didn't see any need to tell him she'd known this when she'd last spoken with him. She'd squared things.

"Is that why you're a block east of Clark Drive?" he asked.

"Shit," she said.

"This display only names the main streets," he said, apologetically.

"This car's telling you exactly where I am!"

"It's a factory option," he said. "A lot of Phaetons go to corporate fleets in the Middle East. Standard security feature, there. Why did she tell you, by the way? Do you know?"

"Because she's fed up with him, basically. Not an easy sibling. I just saw your port, a minute ago. It's down at the foot of the street."

"Yes," he said, "handy. What are you going to do?"

"I don't know," she said. "Look around a little."

"Would you like me to send Ollie?"

"No. I doubt I'll be long."

"If I don't see the car go back to the flat this evening, and I haven't heard from you, I'll send Ollie."

"Fair enough." She hung up.

She sat there, looking at East Van Halen's Dumpster. Beyond it, a few car lengths, was the opening into an alley. An alley that might lead, she supposed, to some rear entrance in whichever of these buildings was Bobby's.

She got out, activating the Phaeton's alarm system. "You take care of your crypto-luxurious ass," she told it. "I'll be back."

66. PING

Tito sat on a paint-spattered steel stool, looking up at a dirty skylight of wire-embedded glass. Pigeons kept landing on its peak, and taking off, with a flutter of wings he doubted the others were hearing. Garreth and the old man were talking with the man who'd been waiting for them here, in this dim third-story space, in a city and country Tito had scarcely even thought about before.

The boat that had come to pick them up was white; long, low, very fast. The boat's pilot had worn large sunglasses and a tight nylon hood, and had said nothing at all.

Tito had watched the island and its runway recede, and finally vanish, though it took a long time.

After changing directions several times, they'd approached another island. Cliffsides of soft, wind-eroded rock. A few small isolated houses, facing the sea. They'd followed the coastline to a wooden pier, jutting from a taller, more substantial-looking wharf. He'd helped Garreth swing the black plastic Pelican up out of the boat. It was too heavy to lift by its plastic handles, Garreth said; they might break, under the weight.

The pilot of the white boat, saying nothing, took it out fast, in a direction other than the one he'd come.

Tito listened to a dog barking. A man came to the railing of the high wharf and waved to them. Garreth waved back. The stranger turned away, was gone.

The old man looked at his watch, then at the sky.

Tito had heard the seaplane before he'd seen it, coming in only a few feet above the water. "Don't say anything," Garreth told him, as the plane's propeller stopped and it floated the last few yards to the pier.

"How are you gentlemen?" asked the pilot, a man with a mustache, climbing down onto the nearest pontoon as Garreth held the plane's wing.

"Very well," said the old man, "but I'm afraid we're overweight." He indicated the Pelican. "Mineral samples."

"Geologist?" the pilot asked.

"Retired," said the old man, smiling, "but it seems I'm still hauling rocks."

"Shouldn't be a problem." The pilot opened a hatch in the side of the plane, which looked nothing like the

Cessna. It had only one propeller, and looked built for work. Tito watched as Garreth and the pilot wrestled the Pelican case off the dock and up into the hatch.

He saw the old man blow air between his pursed lips, relieved, as they got it into the plane without dropping it.

"How long will we be?" the old man asked the pilot.

"All of twenty minutes," said the pilot. "Shall I call you a cab?"

"No, thank you," the old man said, climbing up into the plane. "We have our own transportation."

They landed on a river, near a very large airport, where Tito, still amazed at the mountains he'd seen in the distance, helped Garreth push the Pelican case and their other few pieces of luggage, on a cart, up a long ramp of steel mesh.

Tito sat on the edge of the cart, looking toward the river, where another seaplane was taxiing for takeoff in late-afternoon sunlight. Gravel crunched as Garreth and the old man drove up in a white van. Tito helped Garreth load the case and their other bags into it.

There were only two seats in the van, no side windows in the back. Tito settled himself, squatting, on the Pelican case. The old man looked back. "Don't sit on that," he said. "It wouldn't be good for your descendants." Tito moved away from the case, and used his own bag as a cushion instead.

After that, as they'd driven through a city, he'd seen almost nothing. Fragments of buildings, through the windshield and the rear windows. Until they'd arrived

here, Garreth opening the rear doors onto an only partially paved alley, strange green ferns growing between
broken asphalt and the peeling walls on either side. He'd
helped Garreth with the Pelican case, up two flights of
decrepit wooden stairs, and into this long, cluttered
room.

Where this strange man, the one they called Bobby,
had been waiting for them. Tito's mother's illness, which
had begun in Sunset Park, where they had gone to stay
with Antulio, after the attacks on the towers, had made
him very anxious around people who behaved in certain
ways.

He paced, this Bobby, and smoked, and spoke almost
constantly. Garreth and the old man listened, listened
and looked at one another.

Bobby said that it wasn't good for him, doing this
from home. It wasn't good for him to be here, in his
hometown, doing this, but it particularly wasn't good
for him to be here, in his own place, doing this, with the
box a few blocks away. Tito looked at the Pelican case.
Was this what Bobby meant by a box?

"But you knew that," the old man said, quietly. "You
knew that if it came here, it would be there."

"They've pinged it three times already," Bobby said.
"Not part of the pattern. I think they're here, and I think
they're pinging it from here, and I think they're pinging it
as they drive around, trying for a visual. I think they're
that close. Too close." He dropped his cigarette, ground
it under his shoe, and wiped the palms of his hands on
his dirty white jeans.

What did "pinged" mean, Tito wondered.

"But, Bobby," the old man said, softly, "you haven't told us where it is, exactly. Where is it? Has it been off-loaded? We do need to know that."

Bobby was lighting another cigarette. "It's where you wanted it. Exactly where you wanted it. I'll show you." He crossed to the long tables, the old man and Garreth following. Bobby tapped anxiously on a keyboard. "Right here."

"Which means they don't have anyone on the inside, otherwise they'd shuffle it deeper into the deck."

"But you do, right?" Bobby squinted through smoke.

"That doesn't concern you, Bobby," said the old man, more gently still. "You've done a long and very demanding job, but it's coming to an end now. Garreth has your last installment here, as we agreed." Tito watched the old man's hands, for some reason remembering him using the cane in Union Square.

Garreth took a pager from his belt, looked at it. "Delivery. I'll be five minutes." He looked at the old man. "You're okay?"

"Of course."

Bobby moaned.

Tito winced, remembering his mother.

"I'm not ready for this," Bobby said.

"Bobby," said the old man, "you don't have anything you have to be ready for. You really have nothing else to do, other than monitor the box for us. There's no need for you to leave here, tonight. Or for the next three months, for that matter. We'll be leaving soon, about our business, and you'll be staying here. With your final payment. In advance. As agreed. You're extremely talented, you've done an amazing job, and soon you'll realize that you can relax."

"I don't know who they are," Bobby said, "and I don't want to know. I don't want to know what they've got in that box."

"You don't. You don't know either."

"I'm afraid," Bobby said, and Tito heard his mother, after the attacks.

"They have no idea who you are," said the old man. "They have no idea who we are. I intend to keep it that way."

Tito heard Garreth, and someone else, coming back up the stairs. A woman appeared at the top of the stairs, Garreth behind her. In jeans and a dark jacket.

"What's she doing here?" Bobby shook his hair back from terrified eyes. "What is this?"

"Yes," said the old man, flatly. "Garreth, what is this?"

"I'm Hollis Henry," the woman said. "I met Bobby in Los Angeles."

"She was in the alley," Garreth said, and now Tito saw that he held a long gray rectangular case with a single handle.

"She's not supposed to be here," said Bobby, sounding as though he was about to cry.

"But you do know her, Bobby?" the old man asked. "From Los Angeles?"

"The strange thing," Garreth said, "is that I know her too. Not that we've met before. She's Hollis Henry, from the Curfew."

The old man raised his eyebrows. "The curfew?"

"Favorites of mine in college. A band." He shrugged apologetically, the weight of the long case keeping one shoulder down.

"And you found her, just now, in the alley?"

"Yes," said Garreth, and suddenly smiled.

"Am I missing something, Garreth?" the old man asked.

"At least it's not Morrissey," Garreth said.

The old man frowned, then peered at the woman over his glasses. "And you're here to visit Bobby?"

"I'm a journalist now," she said. "I write for *Node*."

The old man sighed. "I'm not familiar with it, I'm afraid."

"It's Belgian. But I can see I've upset Bobby. I'm sorry, Bobby. I'll go now."

"I don't think that would be a good idea at all," the old man said.

67. WARDRIVING

Milgrim sat beside Brown on one of the two benches in a very small park, under the bare branches of a row of young maples. In front of him was fifty feet of close-cropped grass, a six-foot green-painted chain-link fence, a short steep decline covered with brambles, a wide gravel roadbed stained rust-red by its four lines of track, a paved road, and a vast stack of those metal boxes he'd seen on the ship in the harbor. He watched a streamlined metallic-blue trailer-truck drive quickly past, along the road, pulling a long, rust-streaked gray box that evidently had wheels attached.

Beyond the box-pile were mountains. Beyond those, clouds. They made Milgrim uneasy, these mountains. They didn't look as though they could be real. Too big, too close. Snowcapped. Like the logo at the start of a film.

He looked to his right, focusing instead on a vast, almost featureless rectangular berg of concrete, windowless, probably five stories tall. On its front, in huge simple sanserif letters, reversed into the concrete between massive molded columns, he read

BC ICE & COLD STO RAGE LTD

RAGE. He glanced at Brown's busily shifting laptop screen, where satellite images of this port area zoomed in and out; were replaced, were overlaid with yellow grids.

They had been wardriving, Brown called it, ever since requisitioning Skink's Glock. This meant driving around with Brown's armored laptop open on Milgrim's lap, announcing wireless networks as they passed through them. The laptop did this in a flat, breathless, peculiarly asexual voice that Milgrim found distinctly distasteful. Milgrim had had no idea that people had these networks in their houses and apartments, the sheer number of them amazing, nor that they extended so far beyond the owner's actual property. Some people named them after themselves, others were simply called "default," or "network," and some were named things like "Dark-Harvester" and "Doomsmith." Milgrim's job was to watch a window on the screen that indicated whether or not a network was protected. If a network was unprotected, and had a strong signal, Brown could park and use his computer to get on the Internet. When he did this, color satellite images of the port would appear. Brown could zoom in on these, allowing Milgrim to see the tops of individual buildings, even the rectangles of individual boxes. Initially, Milgrim had found this mildly interesting, but now, after three hours of it, he was ready for Brown to find what he was looking for and take him back to the Best Western.

This bench had been an improvement on sitting in the car, though, and Brown seemed to have a solid connection from an apartment ("CyndiNet") in the three-story stucco complex behind them, its brown-painted steel balconies stacked with barbecues, plastic chairs, and bicycles. But now Milgrim's butt ached. He stood and rubbed it. Brown was engrossed in whatever he was doing. Milgrim walked forward, across the rough short grass, expecting to be stopped. No order came.

When he reached the green fencing, he looked through it, to his left, and found a rectangular orange diesel train engine, its blunt nose painted with crisp diagonals in black and white. It sat, inert, on the nearest set of tracks, beside a rectangular white sign, obviously intended to be read by trainmen, that said HEATLEY. On a yellow triangle a few feet before it, REDUCE SPEED. He read the names on individual boxes in their stacks: HANJIN, COSCO, TEX, "K" LINE, MAERSK SEALAND. Beyond them, farther inside the port, were tall buildings of unknown purpose, and the arms of those same orange cranes he'd seen from the black Zodiac.

He looked back at Brown, hunched over his little screen, lost to the world. "I could run away," Milgrim said, softly, to himself. Then he touched the green-painted steel horizontal that topped the fence, turned, and walked back to the bench.

He missed his overcoat.

68. SNAP

Hollis thought he looked a little like William Burroughs, minus the bohemian substrate (or perhaps the methadone). Like someone who'd be invited quail shooting with the vice-president, though too careful to get himself shot. Thin steel spectacle frames. His remaining hair neatly barbered. Seriously good dark overcoat.

They sat facing one another now in worn metal chairs that might once have done duty in a church hall. His legs were crossed. He wore shoes that made her think of old French priests, bicycling. Black toe-cap oxfords, polished to a dull glow, but thickly soled with black rubber.

"Miss Henry," he began, then paused, his voice reminding her of an American consular official she'd met in Gibraltar, when she'd been seventeen and had had her passport stolen. "Pardon me. You aren't married?"

"No."

"Miss Henry, we find ourselves in an awkward situation."

"Mr. . . . ?"

"I'm sorry," he said, "but I can't give you my name. My friend tells me that you're a musician. Is that correct?"

"Yes."

"And you tell me that you are also a journalist, on assignment from a British magazine." A gray eyebrow rose, above an arc of polished steel.

"*Node*. Based in London."

"And you'd approached Bobby in Los Angeles, regarding your article?"

"I did. Though I can't say he was pleased with my having done that." She glanced at Bobby, hunched on the dirty floor, gripping his knees, eyes hidden by his forelock. From another of these chairs, a dark-haired boy of interestingly indeterminate race watched Bobby with what she took to be a combination of fascination and unease.

The other man, the one who'd discovered her in the alley, and so politely but firmly invited her up here, had now opened the long gray case he'd been given by the man she'd surreptitiously watched him meet in the alley. Not quite surreptitiously enough. This lay with its lid up, now, on one of the long tables, but seated here she couldn't see what it contained.

"I'm sorry for coming here," she said. "He's in terrible shape."

"Bobby's under stress," the old man said. "His work."

"Locative art?"

"Bobby's been working for me, assisting with a project of mine. It's nearing closure. The stress Bobby is experiencing has to do with that. You've arrived at a most inopportune time, Miss Henry."

"Hollis."

"We can't let you go, Hollis, until we've completed what we've come here for."

She opened her mouth to speak, then closed it.

"We aren't criminals, Hollis."

"Excuse me, but if you aren't criminals, or the police, I don't see why I can't leave when I want to."

"Exactly right. The fact is, we are intent, here, on committing a number of criminal offenses, under both Canadian and American law."

"Then how aren't you criminals, exactly?"

"Not in your ordinary sense," he said. "Our motivation is decidedly nonstandard, and what we intend to do, as far as I know, has never been attempted before. I can assure you, though, that we do not anticipate killing anyone, and we hope to harm no one physically."

"'Anticipate,' in that context, isn't so reassuring. And I don't suppose you want to tell me what it is you're up to."

"We intend to damage a specific piece of property, and its contents. If we're entirely successful"—and here he smiled briefly—"the damage will go unnoticed. Initially."

"Do you have some optimal reason you'd prefer for

me to suppose you're telling me this? Maybe we could just cut to that. Save time. Otherwise, I see no reason for you to be telling me anything at all."

He frowned. Uncrossed his legs. With the black priest shoes flat on the floor, he rocked back an inch or so on the chair's rear legs. "If my associate weren't so absolutely convinced of your identity, Miss Henry, things would be very different."

"You didn't answer my question."

"Bear with me. There is public history, and there is secret history. I am proposing to make you privy to secret history. Not because you are a journalist, actually, but because you are, to whatever extent, a celebrity."

"You want to tell me your secrets because I used to be a singer in a band?"

"Yes," he said, "though not because you used to be a singer in a band, specifically. Because you are, by virtue of having been a popular singer—"

"Never that popular."

"You already constitute a part of the historical record, however small you might prefer to see it. I've just checked the number of your Google hits, and read your Wikipedia entry. By inviting you to witness what we intend to do, I will be using you, in effect, as a sort of time capsule. You will become the fireplace brick behind which I leave an account, though it will be your account, of what we do here."

She looked at him. "The scary thing is, I think you're serious."

"I am. But I want you to understand the price, before you agree."

"Who says I'm agreeing?"

"If you're to witness history, Hollis, you necessarily become a part of that which you witness."

"Am I free to write about what I might see?"

"Of course," he said, "although by freely agreeing to accompany us, in the eyes of the law you probably become an accessory. More seriously, though, the person we are about to interfere with is powerful, and has every reason to suppress knowledge of what you'd witness. But that will be your business. If you agree to go with us."

"And if I don't?"

"We will have someone take you to another location, and keep you there until we're gone. That will complicate things for us, as it means moving Bobby and his equipment, since you already know about this place, but that should be no concern of yours. Should you choose that option, you won't be harmed in any way. Blindfolded, but not harmed."

The man from the alley, she saw, had closed the long case, and had been joined, farther down the second long table, by the dark-haired boy. "I don't see why you have any reason to trust my end of that," she said. "Why would you trust me not to call the police, as soon as I'm free?"

"I was trained," he said, "by the government organization of which I was a member, to assess character very quickly. My work involved making crucial personnel decisions, often literal snap judgments, under extremely difficult conditions." He stood up.

"For that matter," she said, looking up at him, "why should I believe you?"

"You won't betray our agreement, should we reach one," he said, "because you simply aren't the type. By the same token, you'll trust us. Because, in fact, you already do."

He turned then, walked over to the man from the alley, and began a quiet conversation.

She heard the scratching of a cigarette lighter, as Bobby, on the floor, fired up a Marlboro.

Where would Bobby sleep, she wondered, without his gridlines? Then noticed, just in front of the old man's chair, a thin, dusty-blue, perfectly straight line, the kind produced with carpenter's chalk and a taut string.

Then saw another, crossing the first at right angles.

69. MAGNETS

Garreth took Tito to the far end of the second table, where ten disks, each no thicker than a small coin, and about three inches in diameter, were arranged on a half-sheet of fresh plywood.

Someone had sprayed these with turquoise-blue paint, then with a faint dusting of dark gray, then with a dull topcoat. Each one lay in its own blur of overspray. The three aerosol cans stood in a row at one end of the plywood. Putting on latex gloves, Garreth carefully picked one up, exposing the perfect round of unsprayed plywood beneath. He showed Tito its unpainted back, bright silver metal. "Rare-earth magnets," he said, "painted to match the box as closely as possible." He indicated two printouts, photographs of a shipping container, a dirty turquoise blue. "Once you place one on a flat steel surface,

it's difficult to remove, except with a knife or a thin
screwdriver blade. We have ten, but you'll have a maxi-
mum of nine holes to cover. The spare is in case you drop
one, but try not to."

"How do I carry them?"

"They either stick together, almost too firmly to separate, or they repel one another, depending on which
way they're facing. So you'll use this." He indicated a
rectangle of stiff black plastic, covered with silver tape. A
length of olive paracord was looped through two holes,
at one end. "Soft plastic envelopes under the tape, one
for each disk. You carry it in down the front of your
jeans, then hang it around your neck for climbing. Slip
them out one at a time as you cover the nine holes. They
should cover any spalling completely, as well as sealing
the hole."

"What is 'spalling'?"

"When the bullet pierces the painted steel," Garreth
said, "it bends the steel inward. The paint isn't flexible,
so it shatters. Some of it vaporizes. Result is bright,
shiny steel, visible around the hole. The hole itself is no
bigger than the tip of your finger. It's the spalling that
visually identifies a bullet hole, so we have to cover it.
And we want as tight a seal as possible, because we don't
want to be setting off sensors."

"And when they have been closed?"

"You have to find your own way out. The man who'll
take you in can't help us with that. We'll go over the
maps and the satellite images one more time. Don't climb
until the midnight buzzer stops. When you've sealed it,

get out. When you're out, call us. We'll pick you up. Otherwise, the phone's only for an emergency."

Tito nodded. "Do you know that woman?" he asked.

"I hadn't met her before," said Garreth, after a pause.

"I have seen posters of her, in shops on St. Marks Place. Why is she here?"

"She knows Bobby," Garreth said.

"He is unhappy to see her?"

"He's having a bit of a meltdown generally, isn't he? But you and I, we have to keep this central to mission, right?"

"Yes."

"Good. When you go up to the box, you'll be wearing this." He indicated a black filter-mask in a large Ziploc bag. "We don't want you inhaling anything. When you get down from the stack, stick it somewhere it won't be found for a while. And no prints, of course."

"Cameras?"

"Everywhere. But our box is in the top tier of a stack, and if everything's gone right, it's in a blind spot. The rest of the time, you hood up and we hope for the best."

"The woman," Tito asked, concerned by what seemed a serious breach of protocol, "if she isn't one of you, and you've never seen her before, how do you know she isn't wearing a wire?"

Garreth indicated the three black antennas of the yellow-cased jammer Tito had seen him use in Union Square, farther down the table. "Nothing here broadcasting," he said, softly, "is there?"

70. PHO

Brown took Milgrim to a dim, steamy Vietnamese restaurant, one with no English signage whatever. It felt like the anteroom of a sauna, which Milgrim found agreeable, but smelled of disinfectant, which he could have done without. It had the look of having been something else, long ago, but Milgrim found it impossible to say what that might have been. Perhaps a Scottish tearoom. Forties plywood with halfhearted Deco accents, long submerged under many coats of chipped white enamel. They ate pho, watching thin slices of pink beef graying in the shallow pool of hot, almost colorless broth, over sprouts and noodles. Milgrim had never seen Brown use chopsticks before. Brown definitely knew how to put away a bowl of pho, and tidily. When he was done, he opened his computer on their black Formica tabletop. Milgrim couldn't see what he was doing. He supposed there might be wifi here, leaking down from the single story above, or that Brown might be looking at files he'd downloaded earlier. The old lady brought them fresh plastic tumblers of tea that might have passed for hot water, except for a peculiarly acetic aftertaste. Seven in the evening and they were the only customers..

Milgrim was feeling better. He'd asked Brown for a Rize, in the little park, and Brown, engrossed in what ever he was doing on the laptop, had unzipped a pocket on its bag and handed Milgrim an entire unopened four-pack. Now, behind Brown's upright screen, Milgrim popped a second Rize from its bubble and washed it down with the tea water. He'd brought his book in from the car, thinking Brown would probably work on the laptop. Now he opened it.

He found a favorite chapter: "An Elite of Amoral Supermen (2)."

"What's that you keep reading?" asked Brown, unexpectedly, from the other side of the screen.

"'An elite of amoral supermen,'" Milgrim replied, surprised to hear his own voice repeat the chapter title he'd just read.

"That's what you all think," said Brown, his attention elsewhere. "Liberals."

Milgrim waited, but Brown said no more. Milgrim began again to read of the Beghards and the Beguines. He was well into the Quintinists, when Brown spoke again.

"Yes sir. I am."

Milgrim froze, then realized that Brown was using his cell.

"Yes sir, I am," Brown repeated. A pause. "It is." Another silence. "Tomorrow." Silence. "Yes sir."

Milgrim heard Brown close his phone. Heard the rattle of china up the narrow stairwell of the house on N Street. The same sir? The man with the black car?

Brown called for the bill.

Milgrim closed his book.

MOISTURE IN THE air threatened to fall but didn't. Larger drops fell from trees and wires. This had arrived while they were in the pho sauna, a different kind of moisture. The mountains had gone behind indeterminate scrims of cloud, shrinking the bowl of sky in a way Milgrim found comforting.

"Do you see it?" Brown asked. "Turquoise. Top one of three?"

Milgrim squinted through the Austrian monocular Brown had used in the surveillance van in SoHo. Superior optics, but he couldn't find the point of focus. Fog, lights, steel boxes stacked like bricks. Angular puzzle pieces of pipe, gantries of vast derricks, all of it jiggling, overlapping, like junk at the end of a kaleidoscope. And then it came together for him, one turquoise rectangle, topmost on its pile. "I see it," he said.

"What are the odds," Brown said, roughly taking the monocular, "of them stacking it where we can see it?"

Milgrim decided that the question was best treated as rhetorical, and kept silent.

"It's off the ground," Brown said, pressing the padded eyepiece into the orbit of his eye. "Up high. Less likelihood of tampering." Even with that bit of apparently better news, it seemed, Brown was still rattled by the sight.

They stood facing a length of new gray twelve-foot chain-link, beside a long, plain-looking tavern, beige brick, out of which grew, surprisingly, a small, brown, four-story Edwardian hotel, called the Princeton. Milgrim had noticed how bars here seemed to possess these vestigial hotels. This one also had a large satellite dish, one of so archaic a pattern that he could imagine a younger person thinking it original to the building.

Behind them was a T-intersection, a tree-lined street running down into the street the Princeton stood on. The port, Milgrim thought, was like the long but oddly narrow train layout that had hugged a friend's grandfather's rec-room walls. The Princeton's street bordered it, not far from CyndiNet's little park.

"Visible from the street," Brown said, the monocular like something growing out of his eye. "What are the odds against that?"

Milgrim didn't know, and if he had, he wouldn't necessarily have told Brown, who was obviously made very anxious and unhappy by this. But bolstered by the second Rize, he did attempt to change the subject: "The IF's family, in New York?"

"What about them?"

"They haven't been texting in Volapuk, have they? You haven't needed any translation."

"They aren't texting in anything, that we know of. They aren't phoning. They aren't sending e-mails. They haven't shown. Period."

Milgrim thought about the signal-grabber that Brown had used, to get around the IF's habit of constantly changing phones and numbers. He remembered his own suggestion, to Brown, to have the NSA do it, use that Echelon or something. What Brown had just said made him wonder, now, if someone might not already be doing that.

"Get in the car," Brown said, turning back to the parked Taurus. "I don't need you thinking, not tonight."

71. HARD TO BE ONE

What do you know about money laundering, Hollis?" the old man asked, passing her a round foil dish of peas and paneer. The four of them were having an Indian meal at the far end of the second long table. They'd ordered in, which Hollis supposed was what you did if you were plotting whatever these people were plotting, and didn't want to have to go out.

Bobby, who didn't like Indian, and didn't want to sit with them, was making do with a large plain cheese pizza that had required separate delivery.

"Drug dealers," she said, using her plastic fork to shovel peas onto a white paper plate, "wind up with piles of cash. Someone told me that the big guys throw the fives and ones away, too much trouble." Inchmale loved factoids relating to illicit behavior of all kinds. "But it's hard to buy anything very substantial with a truckload of cash, and the banks only let you deposit a certain amount, so the guy with bags of cash has to accept a steep discount, from someone who can get it back into circulation for him."

The old man helped himself to colorfully flecked rice and chunks of chicken in bright beige sauce. "A sufficiently large amount of cash comes to constitute a negative asset. What could you do with ten million, say, if you couldn't account for where it had come from?"

Why was he telling her this? "How big would that be, ten million?" She thought of Jimmy's five thousand, in her purse. "In hundreds."

"Hundreds, always," he said. "Smaller than you think. Two-point-four billion, in hundreds, only took up the same amount of space as seventy-four washing machines, although it was considerably heavier. A million in hundreds weighs about twenty-three pounds and fits in a small suitcase. Ten million in hundreds weighs a little over two hundred and thirty pounds."

"Did you see that two-point-four billion yourself?" She thought it was worth asking.

"June 2004," he said, ignoring the question, "the Federal Reserve Bank of New York opened its vault on a Sunday, to prepare that amount for shipment to Baghdad, aboard a couple of C-130 cargo planes."

"Baghdad?"

"We sent nearly twelve billion dollars in cash to Iraq, between March 2003 and June 2004. That June shipment was intended to cover the transition of power from the Coalition Provisional Authority to the interim Iraqi government. The largest one-time cash transfer in the history of the New York Fed."

"Whose was it?" It was the only question she could think of.

"Iraqi funds, generated mainly from oil revenues, and held in trust by the Federal Reserve, under the terms of a United Nations resolution. The Development Fund for Iraq. Under the best of circumstances, say in a country like this one, in peacetime, keeping track of the ultimate distribution of even one billion is practically impossible. Oversight of twelve billion, in a situation like the one in Iraq? It's literally impossible, today, to say with any authority exactly where the majority of that money went."

"But it was used to rebuild the country?"

"Does it look like it?"

"It kept the interim government afloat?"

"I suppose it did. Some of it." He began to eat, carefully and methodically and with evident enjoyment.

She met the eye of the Englishman who'd found her in the alley. He had dark hair, cut very short, probably in an effort to get the stylistic jump on early-onset male-pattern baldness. He looked bright, she thought. Bright and fit and probably funny. She could've fancied him, she thought, if he weren't some kind of international criminal, terrorist, pirate. Whatever these employers of Bobby's were. Or multicultural criminal, not to forget the dreamy-looking boy in black, indeterminately ethnic but somehow definitely not American. The old man was as American as it got, but in what she thought of as some very recently archaic way. Someone who would've been in charge of something, in America, when grownups still ran things.

"Join me," invited Mr. Bright Fit Criminal, from across the table, indicating the chair beside his. The old man gestured with his hand, mouth full, indicating that she should. She took her plate and went around the end of the table, noticing a yellow, rectangular plastic box, featureless except for three short black antennas, each of slightly different length, an on-off switch, and a red LED. It was on, whatever it was.

She put her plate on the table and took the seat beside him.

"I'm Garreth," he said.

"I didn't think you used names, here."

"Well," he said, "not surnames. But that's my actual given. One of them, anyway."

"What did you do, Garreth, before you started doing whatever this is that you're doing now?"

He considered. "Extreme sports. Some hospital, as a result. Fines and a little jail, likewise. Built props for films. Did stunts for them as well. And what did you do, between 'Hard to Be One' and what you're doing now?" He raised his eyebrows.

"Did badly in the stock market. Invested in a friend's music store. What do you consider 'extreme' sports?"

"BASE jumping, mainly."

" 'Base'?"

"Acronym. B building, A antenna, S span, as in bridge,

arch, or dome, E earth, a cliff or other natural formation. BASE jumping."

"What's the tallest thing you ever jumped from?"

"I can't tell you," he said, "you'd look it up."

"I can't just Google 'Garreth' and 'BASE jumping'?"

"I used my BASE-jumping name." He tore a long strip from a scorched-looking round of naan, rolled it, and used it to sop up his remaining tandoori and paneer.

"Sometimes I wish I'd used my indie rock singer name."

"Tito, there," indicating the boy in black, "he's seen your poster on St. Marks Place."

"'Tito' is his BASE-jumping name?"

"Maybe the only name he's got. He has a very large family, but I'm yet to hear a surname from any of them." He wiped his mouth with a paper towel. "Are you thinking of having children?" he asked her.

"Am I what?"

"Sorry," he said. "Are you pregnant?"

"No."

"How would you feel about being exposed to a certain amount of radiation? Make that an uncertain amount. Not really very much. Probably. Bit dicey, actually. But likely not too bad."

"You aren't kidding, are you?"

"No."

"But you don't know how much?"

"As much as a couple of serious X-rays. That's if things go optimally, which we expect them to. If there were a problem, though, it could go higher."

"What kind of problem?"

"A complicated one. And unlikely."

"Why are you asking me this?"

"Because he," indicating the old man, "wants you to go along and see me do what I'm here to do. There's a degree of risk in that, as described."

"Did it surprise you that he'd ask me?"

"Not really," he said. "He makes it up as we go along, and he's mostly been right so far. It's stranger who you are than that he'd invite you, if you see what I mean. Hollis Henry. Who'd believe that? But if he wants you there, you're welcome. You mustn't distract me, or go into hysterics, but he says you're not the type. I wouldn't think you were myself. But I had to ask you about the radiation risk. Wouldn't want that on my conscience if something goes wrong."

"I don't have to jump off of anything?" She remembered Inchmale describing Stockholm syndrome, the fondness and loyalty one could supposedly come to feel for even the most brutal captor. She wondered whether she might be experiencing something like that, here. Inchmale thought that America had developed Stockholm syndrome toward its own government, post 9/11. But then she thought that she really should have been more likely to develop it toward Bigend than toward these three. Bigend, her every gut instinct told her, was an infinitely spookier captor (ruling out Bobby, of course, though he scarcely seemed an actor in this now).

"Nothing at all," he said. "And neither will I."

She blinked. "When is it?"

"Tonight."

"That soon?"

"Stroke of midnight. Literally. But setup, on-site, requires some time." He checked his watch. "We'll be leaving here at ten. I have some last-minute preparations, then I'll do some yoga."

She looked at him. Never in her life, she thought, had she had less of an idea where she might be going, either in the short or the long term. She hoped the short term would allow for a long term, but somehow it was all so peculiar, since she'd entered this room, that she hadn't had time to be frightened.

"Tell him I'm in," she said. "Tell him I accept his terms. I'm going with you."

72. EVENT HORIZON

That jacket we put you in, in New York, for the helicopter," the old man said, walking around Tito, who had just put on a new black hooded sweatshirt that Garreth had given him.

"I have it," Tito said.

"Wear that, over the sweatshirt. Here's your hard hat." He handed Tito a yellow helmet. Tito tried it on, removed it, adjusted the white plastic headband, put it back on. "Lose the hat and jacket on your way out, of course. And give me that New Jersey license now. Remember your name?"

"Ramone Alcin," said Tito, taking the card from his wallet and handing it to the old man.

The old man handed him a transparent plastic bag containing a phone, two plastic cards, and a pair of latex gloves. "No prints on the container, of course, or the magnets. You're still Ramone Alcin. Alberta license and a citizenship card. These are only props, costume, not serious documents. Neither will stand up to a check. The phone will speed-dial either of two numbers of ours."

Tito nodded.

"The man you're meeting at the Princeton will have a neck tag, for Ramone Alcin, with your picture on it. It won't stand up to a check either, but you'll need to be seen wearing one."

"What is 'Alberta'?"

"A province. State. Of Canada. The man you're meeting, at the Princeton Hotel, will be parked on Powell, west of the hotel, in a large black pickup with a covered bed. He's a very large man, very heavy, with a full dark beard. He'll put you in the bed of the truck and drive it into the container terminal. He works there. If you're discovered in the truck, he'll claim not to know you, and you'll claim not to know him. We very much hope, of course, that that won't happen. Now we'll go over the maps again. Where he'll park the truck. Where the stack is. If you're apprehended after having positioned the magnets, lose the phone first, then the cards and neck tag. Be confused. Speak little English. It will be awkward for you, if that happens, but they'll have no way of knowing what you've just done. Claim you were looking for work. You'll be arrested for trespassing, then locked up on immigration charges. We'll do what we can. As will your family, of course." He passed Tito another bag, this with a fold of well-worn bills. "In case you get out, tonight, but for any reason can't contact us. Stay out of sight, in that case, and contact your family. You know how."

Tito nodded. The old man understood the protocol. "Excuse me," Tito said, in Russian. "But I must ask you about my father. About his death. I know very little other than that he was shot. I believe he may have been working for you."

The old man frowned. "Your father was shot," he said, in Spanish. "The man who shot him, an agent of Castro's DGI, was delusional, paranoid. He believed that your father was reporting directly to Castro. Actually he was reporting to me, but that had nothing to do with the suspicions of his killer, which were baseless." He looked at Tito. "If I'd valued your father's friendship less, I might lie to you now, and tell you that his death involved some high purpose. But he was a man who valued truth. The man who shot him died in a bar fight, not long after, and we assumed that that had been the work of the DGI, who by then had determined that he was both unstable and utterly untrustworthy."

Tito blinked.

"You haven't had an easy life, Tito. Your mother's illness, as well. Your uncles see that she receives excellent care. If they weren't able to, I would myself."

TITO HELPED GARRETH carry the Pelican case back down to the van. "All in the wrists," Garreth said. "Can't be straining them tonight, wrestling with this bastard."

"What's in it?" Tito asked, deliberately ignoring protocol as they slid the black case into the back of the van.

"Lead, mostly," Garreth said. "Almost a solid block
of lead, in there."

THE OLD MAN sat with Bobby, speaking to him quietly,
calming him. Tito listened. Bobby no longer reminded
him of his mother. Bobby's fear was on some other frequency. Tito guessed he chose to allow it to overwhelm
him, invited it, used it to make things the fault of others,
attempted to control them with it.

Tito's mother's fear, after the towers had fallen, had
been a deep and constant resonance, untouchable, gradually eroding the foundations of who she had been.

He looked up at the dark skylight and tried to feel
New York. Trucks were rattling over metal on Canal
Street, he told himself. Trains blowing past, beneath the
pavement, through a maze his family had mapped with
exquisite care. Had come to own, in a sense; every corner of every platform, every line of sight, many keys,
storage closets, lockers; a theater for appearances and
disappearances. He could have drawn maps, written out
schedules, but now he found himself starting to be unable to believe in it. Like the Russian voices on his Sony
plasma set, on the wall of the room that was no longer
his.

"I'm Hollis," the woman said, extending her hand.
"Garreth tells me you're called Tito."

She was handsome, this woman, in some simple way.

Looking at her now, he understood why they would make posters of her. "You are Bobby's friend?" he asked.

"I don't know him very well, really," she said. "Have you known Garreth long?"

Tito looked at Garreth, who'd swept himself a section of floor, stripped down to black underpants and T-shirt, and was doing asanas. "No," he said.

THE OLD MAN sat reading a news site on one of Bobby's computers.

Tito and Bobby had carried the other things down. The long gray case, a folding aluminum hand truck wrapped with bungees, a photographer's black tripod, a heavy canvas duffel.

"We're going now," Garreth said.

The old man shook hands with Tito, then Garreth. Then he offered his hand to the woman. "I'm pleased with our arrangement, Miss Henry," he said to her. She shook his hand, but said nothing.

Tito, wrapped from waist to armpits, beneath his jacket and sweatshirt, in sixty feet of black nylon climbing rope, with the rare-earth magnets down the front of his jeans, the black respirator bulging out of one side pocket of the green jacket, and the yellow hard hat under his arm, led the way downstairs.

73. SPECIAL FORCES

Going somewhere she'd never seen, at night, in a van with two men, with equipment, reminded her of the beginning of the Curfew, minus Heidi Hyde. Who had always insisted on driving, and could do all the loading alone, if she had to.

Garreth driving now. Perfect fifty kilometers per hour, along this downscale industrial strip. Smooth, considered stops. Even acceleration. Model driver. No excuse to pull him over.

Tito in back, sitting as far from the black plastic case as he could. White iPod plugs in his ears, nodding to some rhythm only he could hear. Looking tranced. Like a kid in a chill-out room. Why had they wrapped him in that black rope? It must be uncomfortable, but he didn't look uncomfortable. She'd watched him practice a trick with it, before Garreth and the old man had wrapped him in it. Tying one end of it quickly around a vertical pipe, pulling it tight, then standing back and flicking it. The knot tight and solid when he pulled on it, but letting go instantly when he flicked it. He did it three times. She couldn't follow his hands, when he knotted it. He was pretty enough, at rest, almost feminine, but when he moved with purpose, he became beautiful. Whatever it was, she knew she didn't have it herself. That had been her weakness, onstage. Inchmale had once sent her to a French movement teacher, in Hackney, in an effort to change that. The man had said he'd teach her to walk like a man, that that would make her very powerful onstage. She'd satisfied him, finally, but had never even considered trying it onstage. The one time she'd demonstrated it for Inchmale, though, after a few drinks, he said he'd paid good money to have her taught to walk like Heidi.

Garreth took a right onto a main street, heading east. One-story retail, car leasing, restaurant furniture. A few blocks later, he took a left. They headed downhill, into what once would have been a neighborhood of modest frame houses. A few were still there, but unlit, each one painted a single dark color, no trim. Placeholders in a real estate game, next to small factories, auto-body shops, a plastics fabricator. Patches of weedy grass that had once been lawns, gnarled ancient fruit trees. No pedestrians here, almost no traffic. He looked at his watch, pulled over, put out the lights, and shut off the engine.

"How did you get into this?" she asked, without looking at him.

"I heard that someone was looking for a really odd skill set," he said. "I had a friend who'd been in the SAS, another BASE enthusiast. We'd jumped together, in Hong Kong. He was approached first, actually, and didn't want it. He said he was too military, not unconventional enough. He recommended me, and I came down to London and he took me along to my meeting. I couldn't believe it, but he was wearing a tie. Bastard. Amazing. Turned out it was his club tie, the only one he owned. Special Forces Club. That's where we went. I'd no idea there was one."

"What did it look like? His tie."

"Black and gray, thin diagonal stripes." She felt him glance at her. "And himself waiting in an alcove off a sitting room."

She knew he meant the old man. She looked out the window, not really seeing anything.

"He introduced us and left me there. Pot of nasty coffee. Old-school British coffee. I had a list of questions I'd prepared, but I never asked them. Just answered his. It was like some weird inversion of a Kipling script. This old man, this American, in a Savile Row suit he'd probably bought in the sixties, asking me these questions. Pouring nasty coffee. Utterly at home in this club. Wee decoration on the lapel of his suit, the ribbon for some medal, no bigger than a windowpane of acid." He shook his head. "Hooked. I was hooked." Smiling.

"There must be things I shouldn't ask you," she said.

"Not really. Just things I mustn't answer."

"Why's he doing this, whatever it is?"

"He used to be in national security, American government. Career man. Retired a few years before 9/11. I think he went a bit feral, frankly, after the attacks. Frothing, really. Not a good idea to get him on the topic. He'd been hugely well connected, it seemed. Friends everywhere. And the lot of them pissed as well, at least to hear him tell it. Old spooks. Most retired, some not quite, some soon forced out because they wouldn't toe a party line."

"There's more than one of him, you mean?"

"Not really, no. I find it easiest to think of him as slightly off, really. I imagine they do too, though it doesn't stop them giving him help, and funding. Amazing what you can do with a little money, when you're given a free hand. He's as sharp as anyone I've met, sharper, but he has obsessions, topics he's queer about. One of them, a big one, is people profiting from the war in Iraq. He gets onto things, things he learns certain people have done. Through his various connections, he hears things, puts bits together."

"What for?"

"So that he can fuck with them, frankly. Fuck them up. Over. Sideways, if he can manage it. Loves it. Lives for it."

"Who are those people?"

"I don't know, myself. He says it's better that way. He also says that, so far, none of them have been anyone I'd ever ordinarily have heard of."

"He was telling me about money laundering, about huge shipments of cash, to Iraq."

"Yes indeed," he said, looking at his watch. He turned the key, starting the ignition. "We've been driving them wild, with this one. He plays this game of cat and mouse with them." He smiled. "Makes them think they're the cat."

"You enjoy it yourself, it seems to me."

"I do. I do indeed. I've a very diverse and peculiar skill set, and ordinarily no place to use the half of it. Soon enough, I'll be too old for most of it. Truth to tell, I probably already am. Main reason we've got our man Tito in the back here. Snake on ice, our Tito." He took a right, another left, and they were waiting at a light, turning left on a street with more traffic, more lights. He reached back and thumped the back of his seat. "Tito! Ready up!"

"Yes?" asked Tito, removing his iPod plugs.

"Hotel's in sight. Coming up. Climb over the lady, here, get out that side. He'll be parked just past the hotel, waiting for you."

"Okay," said Tito, as the van slowed, tucking his white plugs back into the hood of his sweatshirt.

He looked, just then, she thought, like a very serious fifteen-year-old.

AS DIRECTED

Milgrim had been thinking about offering Brown a Rize, when he spotted the IF walking along the sidewalk. They were headed east on the street where the Princeton Hotel was, coming up on it again, but bound, Milgrim guessed, for another wifi session, courtesy of CyndiNet.

They backed directly on the tracks, these places. Milgrim supposed you could see the floodlit stacks of boxes, from their rear windows. From some of them, even, the one particular turquoise box that had Brown so visibly stressed.

He knew that he wasn't really going to suggest that Brown try a Rize, but he did believe that, just now, it would probably be a good thing. Brown had been muttering, periodically, and when he wasn't doing that,

Milgrim could see the muscle in his jaw working. Milgrim had sometimes, though rarely, given tranquilizers to civilians, people who weren't habituated. Though only if they seemed to him to be in serious need, and if he himself was sufficiently well supplied. He always explained that he had a prescription (he often had several) and that these drugs were perfectly safe, if used as directed. He just didn't get into the matter of who or what might be doing the directing.

He had never seen Brown this tense, before.

Brown had come into his life a week before Christmas, on Madison, a solid figure zipped into the same black jacket he wore tonight. A hand around Milgrim's upper arm. Flashing something in a black badge case. "You're coming with me." And that had been it. Into a car that might as well have been this one, driven by an unsmiling younger man wearing a tie decorated with Goofy in a Santa Claus outfit.

Two weeks later, he'd been sitting with Brown at a table near the window of that magazine place on Broadway, eating sandwiches, when the IF had walked past in a black leather porkpie.

Now here he came again, the IF, but in a short, bright green jacket, with a construction worker's yellow helmet tucked under his arm. Sort of like a younger Johnny Depp, but ethnic, off to some nightshift job. It struck Milgrim as wonderful, somehow. A taste of home. "There's the IF," he said, pointing.

"What? Where?"

"There. Green jacket. That's him, right?"

Brown braked, peering, spun the wheel, and gunned the Taurus hard, left, into the path of oncoming traffic, aiming for the IF.

Milgrim had time to see that the furiously screaming girl in the passenger seat of the car braking violently in front of them was actually giving them the finger.

He had time to see the IF's face register the Taurus, the boy's eyes widening in amazement.

He had time to note the dullness of the beige brick of the Princeton Hotel.

He had time to see the IF do something patently impossible: shoot straight into the air, knees tucked, flipping over, the Taurus and Milgrim passing directly through the space he'd occupied an instant before. Then the Taurus clipped something that wasn't the IF, and a pale hard thing like a very large nursery toy, full of concrete, manifested from nowhere at all, somehow, between Milgrim and the dashboard.

The Taurus's alarm was sounding.

They weren't moving.

He looked down and saw something on his lap.

He picked it up. A rearview mirror.

The horrible, hard, pale thing that had hurt his face was deflating. He prodded it with the mirror. "Airbag," he said.

He looked to the left as he heard Brown's door open. Brown's airbag, undeflated, crowned the steering column like some nameless, ominous device in the window of an orthopedic supply house. Brown swatted it out of his way, feebly but viciously. Stood swaying, supporting himself on the open door.

Milgrim heard a siren.

He looked down at Brown's laptop, in its black nylon bag between the seats. He watched his hand unzip the side pocket, enter, and emerge with a number of bubble-packs. He looked out, over his detumescent airbag, and watched Brown, who seemed to have hurt his leg, hop awkwardly to a hooded trash receptacle, slip Skink's Glock from his jacket, and slide it quickly under the spring-loaded black flap. He hopped back to the car, more slowly now and taking greater care, and leaned against the mysteriously wrinkled hood. His eyes met Milgrim's. He gestured, urgently. Out.

Milgrim reminded his hand, bold but absentminded, to pocket the bubble-packs.

The door was stuck, but then it popped open, almost spilling him on the sidewalk. A crowd had emerged from the Princeton. Baseball caps and waterproof outerwear. Hair like a Dead concert.

"Get over here," Brown ordered, palms flat on the hood, trying to keep his weight off his injured leg.

Milgrim saw flashing lights approaching, homing fast, downhill, from the east. "No," he said, "sorry," and turned; walking west as quickly as he could. Expecting the hand, any hand, on his shoulder or upper arm.

He heard the siren shut off in mid-yelp. Saw the whirl of red lights from behind him, thrown across the sidewalk, animating his shadow.

His hand, in the pocket of the Jos. A. Banks jacket, decided to pop a Rize out of its bubble. He didn't entirely approve, but then had to dry-swallow it, as he didn't like loose tablets. He saw the painted lines of a pedestrian crossing, just as the light changed, and crossed with his gaze fixed on the jaunty little illuminated pictoglyph on the far side.

He walked uphill, then, into relative darkness, the hooting of the wounded Taurus fading behind him.

"Sorry," he said, walking, to tall dark houses looming amid low forties commercial, while his busy, clever hand patted down his own pockets as if he were some ambulatory drunk it had just encountered. Taking stock. The Rize. New wallet, empty. Toothbrush. Toothpaste. Plastic razor in a fold of toilet paper. He stopped, turned, looking back down the incline to the street where Brown had tried to kill the IF. He wished he were back in the Best Western, looking at the textured ceiling. Some old movie on the television, sound down low, just that little bit of movement out of the corner of your eye. Sort of like having a pet.

He walked on, feeling the dead fisheyes of the old houses. Oppressed by this darkness, silence, the specter of some long-vanished domesticity.

But then the upper stories of another street appeared, as if from nowhere, another, better world, with all the lurid gravity of major hallucination. As if glowing from within, the ornate gold-leaf sign of a tobacconist; beside it, a general store; more. The neighborhood of grim, dark houses reconstituting itself in its innocence, before him, in this most secret moment.

Then he saw a camera dip and smoothly turn, at the end of a craning metal arm, scooping up the bright vision, and knew that this was a set, constructed, he now understood, within the black and invisible ruin of some gutted foundry. "Sorry," he said, and walked on, past caterers' trucks and walkie-talkied girls, his ankle starting to itch.

He bent to scratch it, finding a hundred and fifty Canadian dollars tucked into the top of his sock, left over from the Glocking expedition.

But better still, in his other, his nonclever hand, he discovered his book.

Straightening, he pressed it against his cheek, swept with gratitude for still having it. Within it, beyond the worn paper cover, lived landscapes, figures. Bearded heresiarchs in brilliantly jeweled gowns, sewn from peasant rags. Trees like giant dead twigs.

He turned, and looked back at the precise, unearthly glow of the film set.

Brown, he was certain, would be gone now, explaining himself to the police. The Princeton Hotel would have a sandwich and a Coke, which would yield whatever change one needed for a bus, or even a cab. And then he would find his way west, to this city's downtown core, and shelter, and perhaps a plan.

"Quintin," he said, starting back down the hill, toward the Princeton. Quintin had been a tailor. God

incarnate of the Spiritual Libertines. Burned for seduc-
ing respected ladies of Tournai, in 1547.

History was queer, thought Milgrim. Deeply so.

Nodding, as he passed them, to the girls with their
saucily holstered walkie-talkies. Beauties from a realm
Quintin might have recognized.

75. HEY, BUDDY

Oshosi, scout and hunter, had entered Tito in mid-back-tuck. He heard the gray car strike the lamppost as his black Adidas found the sidewalk, confusing cause and effect. The orisha propelled him immediately forward, then, like a child walking a doll, making a puppet of its limbs. Oshosi was huge in his head, an expanding bubble forcing him against the gray interior of his skull. He wanted to scream, but Oshosi clamped fingers of cold damp wood around his throat. "Buddy," he heard some-one say. "Hey, buddy, you okay?" Oshosi walked him past the voice, his heart hammering within his rope-wrapped rib cage like a mad bird.

A bearlike, bearded man, in heavy dark clothing, hav-ing seen the crash, was climbing into the cab of an enor-mous pickup. Tito struck the flat black fiberglass cover of the pickup's bed with the palm of his hand. It boomed hollowly.

"What the fuck you doing?" the man shouted back at him, craning angrily back out of the open door.

"You're here for me," said Oshosi, and Tito saw the man's eyes widen above his black beard. "Open this."

The man ran back, his face strangely white, tearing at the fastening of the cover. It popped up, and Tito hauled himself in, dropping the hard hat as he collapsed on a large sheet of spotless brown cardboard. He heard a siren.

Something struck his hand. Yellow plastic, with a yellow cord attached. An identification badge. The fiberglass cover came booming down, and Oshosi was gone. Tito groaned, fighting the urge to vomit.

He heard the truck's door slam, its engine roar, and then they were accelerating.

The man who had followed him, in Union Square. One of the two behind him, there. That man was here, and had just tried to kill him.

His ribs ached, within the cruelly wound rope. He worked the phone from his jeans pocket and opened it, glad of the screen's light. He speed-dialed the first of the two numbers.

"Yes?" The old man.

"One of the men who were behind me, in Union Square."

"Here?"

"He tried to hit me, with his car, in front of the hotel. He struck a pole. Police are coming."

"Where is he?"

"I don't know."

"Where are you?"

"In your friend's truck."

"Are you injured?"

"I don't think so."

The signal fizzed, faded. Was gone.

Tito used the glow of the phone to look around the truck's bed, which proved empty, aside from the hard hat and the yellow-framed identification tag. Ramone Alcin. The photograph looked like anyone. He slipped the cord over his head, closed the phone, and rolled onto his back.

He lay there, slowing his breathing, then checked his body, methodically stretching, for sprains or other damage. How could the man from Union Square have followed him here? Terrible eyes, through the windshield of the gray car. He had seen his death coming, in another's eyes, for the first time. His father's death, at the hands of a madman, the old man had said.

The truck stopped, waiting at a light, then turned left.

Tito set the phone to vibrate. Put it back in the side pocket of his jeans.

The truck slowed, pulled over. He heard voices.

Then they drove on, over rattling metal grates.

76. LOCATION SHOOT

Having dropped Tito and driven on, not far at all along this strip of low-lying auto-body repairs and marine supplies, Garreth turned right, into the parking lot of what seemed to be a much taller building, one built on an entirely different scale. Behind it, they pulled in beside a pair of shiny new Dumpsters and a row of content-specific recycling bins. The Dumpsters, she saw, were covered in runny silk-screened multiples of photographic images. She smelled commercial art.

"We're location scouts," he said, taking an orange cardboard PRODUCTION placard from between the seats and putting it on the dash.

"What picture?"

"Untitled," he said, "but it actually doesn't have that

shabby a budget. Not even by Hollywood standards."
He got out, so she did the same.

And was stunned to discover the brilliantly floodlit
vastness of the port, right there, past twelve feet of
chain-link and some railroad tracks. The lights were like
the lights on a playing field, but taller. A grimly artificial
daylight. Towering rows of concrete cylinders, smoothly
conjoined, like abstract sculptures. Grain storage, she
guessed. Some other, much more high-tech sculptor,
had employed huge, strangely ephemeral-looking black
tanks, one of which was steaming, cauldron-like, in the
cool air. Beyond these, and far taller, were the titanic
Constructivist cranes she'd glimpsed on her drive over.
Between the tracks and these large-scale sculptures were
windowless geometrics in corrugated metal, and a great
many shipping containers, stacked like the blocks of some
unusually orderly child. She imagined Bobby's wireframe
container suspended above it all, invisible, like Alberto's
fallen River on the sidewalk below the Viper Room.

It generated white noise, this place, she guessed, on
some confusingly vast scale. Iron ambients, perceived in
the bone. A day here and you'd stop noticing it.

She turned, looking up at the building he'd parked
behind, and was again startled by scale. Eight tall stories,
its footprint broad and deep enough to allow its mass to
be read as a cube. The scale of an older Chicago industrial building, alien here.

"Live-work space," he said, opening the van's rear
doors. "Studio rental." He took out the bungee-wrapped

dolly, unhooking them, unfolding and extending it. Then the long gray case, which he lay carefully on the pavement beside the dolly. He wasn't moving too quickly, she thought, but he was moving just as quickly as he could without actually moving too quickly. "Would you mind carrying this tripod, and the bag?" He got a solid grip on the black case, grunting softly as he turned with it and lowered it onto the dolly. He put the gray case on top of it, angled against the extended handle, and began snapping it all together with bungees.

"What's in it?" she asked, meaning the canvas bag, as she pulled the folded tripod out and put it under her arm.

"A spotting scope. And an apron."

She picked it up by its canvas handles. "Heavy apron."

He closed and locked the van's rear doors, bent to grasp the dolly's handle.

She looked back at the container stacks, thinking of Bigend's pirate story. Some of them were close enough to read the names of companies. YANG MING. CONTSHIP.

He hauled the loaded dolly up an incline, to a double door that reminded her of Bobby's factory. She followed him, the heavy canvas bag bumping against her knee, as he used one of a ring of several keys to open one of the doors.

It swung shut behind her, locking, as she entered. Brown ceramic tile floor, crisp white walls, good light fixtures. He was turning another key, this one in a steel elevator panel. He pushed a button, which lit. Wide enameled doors jolted open, revealing a room-sized elevator walled with splintery, unpainted plywood. "Serious freight," he said, approvingly, wheeling the dolly in, the gray and the black cases bound with black bungees. She put the canvas bag down on the paint-spotted floor of the elevator, beside it. He pushed a button. The doors closed and they began to rise.

"I loved the Curfew, when I was in college," he said. "Still do, I mean, but you know what I mean."

"Thanks," she said.

"Why did you break up?"

"Bands are like marriages. Or maybe only good ones are. Who knows why a good one works, let alone why it stops working."

The elevator stopped, its doors opening to reveal more of the brown tile. She followed him along a white corridor.

"Have you been here before?" she asked.

"No." He parked the dolly beside a door and got out his keys. "I sent a friend to negotiate an evening's rental. She's in film production here, knows what to say. They think we're scouting it for a night shoot, checking angles." He turned the key. "But we really are checking angles, so keep your fingers crossed." He opened the door and pulled the dolly inside. She followed. He found a light switch.

A tall, partially lofted white space, lit by halogen fixtures strung like stainless-steel clothespins along taut high cables. Someone worked here in glass, she saw. Massive fist-thick slabs of green-edged glass, some of them the size of doors, were racked like CDs in raggedly padded

constructions of dull galvanized pipe. There were corrugated foil ducts, HEPA filters, exhaust fans. Live-work
didn't strike her as so attractive, if the work involved
ground glass. She put the heavy bag down on a workbench, propped the tripod beside it, and scratched her
ribs, under her jacket, thinking of ground glass.

"Excuse me," he said, picking up the tripod, "while I
play director of photography." He crossed to a wide,
steel-mullioned window and quickly set up the tripod.
"Could you open the bag, please, and bring the scope?"
She did, finding a sort of thickly truncated gray telescope
atop smooth thick folds of pale blue plastic. She brought
it to him, watched as he mounted it on the tripod, removed the black lens caps, and peered through it, making
adjustments. He whistled. "Oh. Dear. Fuck." He whistled. "Pardon me."

"What?"

"Very nearly buggered. By that roof peak there.
Look."

She squinted through the scope.

The turquoise container seemed to float, just above the
slanted metal roof of a windowless building. She assumed
it must be stacked atop others, the way they did that.

"Shit out of luck, if that roof were a foot taller," he
said. "We'd no idea." He was bending over the dolly,
unhooking the bungees now. He carried the long case
to the workbench and carefully put it down, beside the
canvas bag. He returned to the dolly, which lay on the
floor now, the black case on top of it. He knelt and took

something iPod-sized and yellow from his jacket pocket. He held it near the case, pressed something, then brought it closer, reading a screen.

"What's that?"

"Dosimeter. Russian. Surplus. Excellent value."

"What did you just do?"

"Radiation count. All good." He smiled at her, from where he knelt on the floor.

She was suddenly self-conscious, watching him. She glanced around, noting a zippered white tarp taped so that it sealed off the section under the loft. Pretending interest in this, she walked over and partially undid the white nylon zipper, a six-foot fly that curved to one side, near the bottom. She stuck her head through.

Into someone's life. A woman's. The contents of a small apartment had been shoehorned into this space. Bed, dresser, suitcases, bookcases, clothes sagging on a spring loaded rod. Someone's childhood staring out from a shelf, in stuffed acrylic fur. A lidded paper Starbucks cup forgotten on the corner of the Ikea dresser. The light, through the white tarp, was diffuse and milky. She felt suddenly guilty. Withdrew her head, zipped up.

He'd opened the long gray case.

It contained a rifle. Or some Surrealist's take on one. Its wooden stock, in deliriously grained tropical hardwood, was biomorphic, counterintuitive somehow, like something from a Max Ernst landscape. The barrel, which she assumed must be blue steel, like the other metal parts, was encased in a long tube of lustrous gray alloy that reminded her of expensive European kitchen-ware. Like a rolling pin by Cuisinart. But still, somehow, quite undeniably a rifle, one with a scope, and something else slung beneath its Cuisinart muzzle.

He was unfolding a small black cloth bag that seemed to have its own internal plastic framework.

"What's that?" she asked.

"Catches the shells, as they're ejected," he said.

"No," she said, "that," indicating the gun.

"Thirty-caliber. Ten-twist, four-groove barrel."

"He told me you weren't going to kill anybody." Behind him, through the window, she saw the glassy black tanks, so weirdly fragile-looking, with their ragged plumes of steam. What would happen if he shot them?

Her cell rang.

Backing away from him, she fumbled in her purse for it, pulling it out with the scrambler dangling from its stub of cable. "Hollis Henry."

"Ollie's outside," said Bigend.

Garreth was staring at her, still holding the black cartridge bag, like some esoteric piece of Victorian mourning equipment.

She opened her mouth to speak, but nothing came out.

"We lost you shortly after you left the car," Bigend said. "It's still where you left it. Then you came back on, headed north on Clark. Are you safe?"

Garreth tilted his head, raised his eyebrows.

She looked at the dangling scrambler, realizing that it must have another of Pamela's GPS units in it. Bastard.

"I'm fine," she said. "Ollie, though, is definitely not a plus."

"Shall I send him home?"

"Make sure you do. If you don't, it's a deal-breaker."

"Done," he said, and was gone.

She closed her phone. "Work," she said.

"They couldn't've reached you, before," he said. "I turned on a jammer, when I took you upstairs. You might've been wearing a wire. Left it on, until you were aboard. Should've told you earlier, but I've a one-track mind." Indicating the rifle, in its bed of gray foam.

"What are you planning on doing with that, Garreth? I think it's time you told me."

He picked it up. It seemed to flow around his hands, his thumb actually appearing through one fluidly carved hole. "Nine shots," he said. "Bolt action. One minute. Evenly spaced along forty feet of Cor-ten steel. A foot above the bottom of the container. That foot clears an interior frame, which we couldn't penetrate." He looked at his watch. "But look," he said, "you can watch me do it. I can't prepare and explain it to you at the same time, not in any detail. He told you the truth, you know. We aren't going to injure anyone." He was attaching the black bag to the rifle. He lay it back on its gray foam. "Time we get you into your apron," he said, reaching into the canvas bag and bringing out thick folds of pale blue plastic. It slid out to its full length.

"What's that?"

"Radiologist's apron," he said, putting a blue padded loop over her head and coming behind her, where she heard him unfasten, then fasten Velcro. She looked down at the blue and breastless tube her body had become, and understood why the bag had been so heavy.

"Aren't you going to wear one?"

"I," he said, taking something much smaller from the bag, "am making do with this butterfly." He fastened the thing behind his neck, the bulk of it beneath his chin. "Thyroid protection. By the way, would you mind turning the ring off, on your phone?"

She got it out and did so.

He was fitting a foot-long black nylon jacket around the rifle's fat tube. She looked at it more closely and saw loops of nylon webbing. He looked at his watch. Checked the dosimeter again, this time standing in the middle of the studio space. Went to the iron-framed window. It was divided into five sets of mullions, she saw, but only the ones on either end opened. He opened the one nearest the room's corner. She felt a cool breeze, laced with something that smelled like electricity. "Three minutes," he said. "Go."

He knelt beside the black plastic case and opened it. Removed a three-inch slab of dull gray lead and set this on the floor. There were nine holes drilled in the block of lead that filled the case. A row of five, another of four. Twists of something like Saran Wrap protruded from each hole. One after another, using his left hand, he plucked them out, nine film-wrapped, bottlenecked cartridges, placing each one on the palm of his right hand. He got up, cradling them carefully, and moved quickly to the workbench, where he put them down, with a muffled clink of brass, on the gray foam. He unwrapped them, placing each one in its black nylon loop, the way Mexican bandits wore bullets across their chests in cartoons. He looked at his watch. "Minute. To midnight." He picked up the rifle and pointed it at the wall. His thumb moved. An intense point of red light appeared on the wall, vanished.

"You're going to shoot the container."

An affirmative grunt.

"What's in it?"

He walked to the window, the rifle cradled at his waist. He looked back at her, the blue thyroid shield like a bad turtleneck. "One hundred million dollars. In a set of fake pallets, along the floor. About fourteen inches deep. Little over a ton of U.S. hundreds."

"But why," she said, "why are you shooting it?"

"Winchester Silvertips. Hollowed out." He opened the breech, extracted a cartridge from its nylon loop, and chambered it. "Inside each one, a brachytherapy capsule. Cancer therapy, localizes the effect on malignant tissue, spares the healthy." He looked at his watch. "They preplant tubes, insert the capsules. Highly radioactive isotopes." He raised the rifle to his shoulder, its barrel out the window now, his back to her. "Cesium, in these," she heard him say.

Then a buzzer or electric bell began to sound, from the port, and he was firing, ejecting, reloading, firing again, with a smooth machine-like rhythm, until the black loops were empty, and the buzzer, as if by some sympathetic magic, had ceased.

The Guerreros were not waiting for him, when he left the dark bed of the truck, blinking under artificial sunlight. Instead he discovered Ochun, calm and supple amid this noise and iron, hundreds of engines, the shifting of great weights.

She lent him a looseness he wouldn't have felt, otherwise, after meeting the madman in the gray car and, too suddenly, Oshosi.

Standing to one side of a crowded passage between stacked containers, he let the black rope snake off his ribs, swaying slightly to encourage it. When it lay at his feet, he picked up an end of it and coiled it, slinging it over his shoulder. Making sure his identification tag was visible, he picked up two sealed, almost empty cans of paint from a clutter of such things and walked on, mak-

ing certain he walked a little more quickly, more pur-
posefully, than the men around him. He stepped aside
for specialized vehicles, forklifts, a first-aid wagon.

When he judged that he'd gone as far as he should, he
circled a stack of containers and came back, still walking
as quickly, a man whose paint was needed, and who
knew exactly where he was going.

As indeed he did, as he was fifteen feet from the stack
topped with the old man's container when the bells and
buzzers signaling the start of the midnight shift all
sounded. Looking up, he thought he saw a disturbance in
the air, there, moving quickly down the length of the
turquoise container. He remembered the Guerreros twist-
ing the air in Union Square. But they were not here.

He set his paint cans aside, where they wouldn't be
tripped over, took latex gloves from his pocket, put them
on, and walked to the end of the stack of three containers. They were stacked with their doors at the same end,
as he'd been told they would be. He wiggled the black
respirator out of his jacket pocket and removed it from
its bag. Pocketing the bag, he removed his hard hat, put
the respirator on, adjusted it, put his hard hat back on.
Neither of these things were particularly good for slack
rope, he thought, but Ochun was accepting. He stepped
aside, nodding, as a forklift drove past.

The doors of the containers were locked with hinged,
vertical steel rods, sealed with tags of metal and colored
plastic. He drew the plastic rectangle from the front of
his jeans, pulled its paracord over his hard hat, and climbed
up the three door-rods, the soles of his Adidas GSG9

boots easily gripping the painted steel of the doors. He climbed, as Ochun suggested, as though he were delighted to do so, with no more purpose in mind than proving that he could.

His breath was loud, in the black respirator. He ignored it. Reaching the damp-slick top of the turquoise container, he climbed up and moved in, away from the edge.

He crouched there, suddenly aware of something he couldn't name. The goddess, the noise of the port, the old man, the ten painted disks slung around his neck like blank sigils. Something was about to change. In the world, in his life, he didn't know. He closed his eyes. Saw the blue vase glowing softly, where he'd hidden it, on the roof of his building.

Accept this.

I do, he told her.

Crouching, he moved to the far end of the container. At each corner, as Garreth had explained, there was a bracket, a sort of loop, with which these boxes could be fastened together. He threaded one end of his rope through the bracket on the side farthest from the ocean he could not see. He moved to the opposite end, playing out his rope, and knotted its other end. The black rope slid off the side of the container's roof, fastened at either end. He looked down at the slack rope, where it hung against the side of the blue container. He hoped he'd judged the give of the nylon correctly. It was good rope, climbing rope.

I do, he said to Ochun, and slid down the rope, slowing himself with the sides of his Adidas.

Slowly, gloved palms against the painted steel, he stood upright on the rope, knees slightly bent. Between the toes of his black shoes, concrete. Directly in front of his face was the first of Garreth's bullet holes. The steel around it was bare, edges bright. He pulled the first of his magnets from its plastic pocket and placed it over the hole. It bonded with the container with a sharp click, trapping a fold of his latex glove. He carefully tore his hand free, picking off the dangling bit. He moved his left foot, his left hand, his right foot, his right hand. He covered the second hole, careful this time not to catch his glove. A forklift rolled past, beneath him.

He remembered bringing the old man the first of the iPods, in Washington Square, by the chess tables. Snow. He saw now how that had changed things, had brought him here. He covered the third hole. Moved on. He remembered having soup with Alejandro. The fourth disk clicked in place. He moved. Five. Three men walked past, beneath him, their hard hats round buttons of plastic, two red, one blue. He stood with his palms flat against the cold steel. Six. He remembered running with the Guerreros through Union Square. Seven and eight were within a foot of one another. Click, and click. Nine.

He climbed back up, feet against the blue wall. He undid the knot at that end and let the rope go. He walked to the other end, where it hung straight, coiling on the concrete below, and slid down. He pulled down the hot respirator, gulped cool unfiltered air, and flicked the second knot free. The rope fell into his arms and he quickly coiled it, then walked away.

Out of sight of the old man's container, he tossed the rope, the respirator, and the bag it had come in into a Dumpster. He left his shredded gloves on the fender of a forklift. The green jacket went into an empty cement bag, and into another Dumpster.

He pulled the hood of his black sweatshirt up and put his hard hat on. Ochun was gone. Now he must get out of this place.

He saw a diesel train-engine rumble slowly past, a hundred yards in front of him, painted with black-and-white diagonals. It was pulling a train of flatcars, each one carrying a container.

He walked on.

HE WAS ALMOST OUT, when the helicopter came, out of nowhere, sweeping the tracks with its bubble of insanely bright light. He'd just taken ten minutes, trying to find a path through brambles, after jumping off his train. He'd thought he was well clear, that he had plenty of time. Now here he was, jeans caught on wire, on top of this six-foot fence, like a child, no systema at all. He saw the helicopter swing up, then out, toward where the sea must be. Still turning. Coming back. He threw himself off the fence, feeling his jeans tear.

"Dude," someone said, "you gotta know they got motion detectors in there."

"Coming back," another boy said, pointing.

Tito got to his feet, prepared to run. Suddenly the narrow park leapt into shivering, seemingly shadowless incandescence, the helicopter somewhere high above the new green leaves of the trees. Tito and three others, at the core of the beam. Two of them were resting a full-sized electric piano across the back of a bench, giving the helicopter the finger with their free hands. The other, grinning, had a white, wolf-shouldered dog on a red nylon lead. "I'm Igor, man."

"Ramone." As the light went out.

"You want to help us move, man? We got a new practice space. Beer."

"Sure," said Tito, knowing he needed to get off the street.

"You play anything?" asked Igor

"Keyboards."

The white dog licked Tito's hand.

"Awesome," said Igor.

78 . THEIR DIFFERENT DRUMMER

My purse," she said, as they drove back to Bobby's. "It's not in back." Craning around the seat.

"Sure you didn't give it to our dustmen?"

"No. It was right there, beside the tripod." Garreth wanted to give the tripod to the friend who'd arranged the studio for them. It was a good one, he'd said, and his friend was a photographer. Everything else had been passed to his "dustmen," who'd been waiting in the parking lot, two men in a concrete-spattered pickup, who were being paid to see that it became part of a warehouse foundation they were pouring that morning.

"I'm sorry," he said, "but we really can't go back."

She thought of Bigend's scrambler, which she didn't mind losing at all. But then she remembered the money from Jimmy. "Shit." But then, strangely, she found she was glad to be done with that as well. Something oppressive about it, wrong. Otherwise, aside from her phone, the scrambler, the keys to the Phaeton and the flat, her license and her single credit card, there was only some makeup, a flashlight, and some mints. Her passport, she remembered now, was back at Bigend's.

"They must've taken it by mistake," he said. "But that was strictly a one-way transaction. Sorry."

She considered telling him about the GPS tracker, but decided not to. "Don't worry about it."

"Were your car keys in your purse?" he asked, as they turned off Clark.

"Yes. It's parked up the street and around the corner, here, behind a Dumpster, just before you get to your . . . alley." She'd just seen a tall figure in black, getting out of a small blue car parked behind the opalescent bulk of the Blue Ant Phaeton.

"Who's that?"

"Heidi," she said. As he drove past the blue car and the Phaeton, she saw Inchmale straighten up on the other side, bearded and more balding than she remembered him. "And Inchmale."

"Reg Inchmale? Seriously?"

"Past the alley," she said, "pull over here."

He did. "What's going on?"

"I don't know, but I'd better get them out of here. I don't know what you still have to do, but I'll bet there's something. I'll get them to rescue me. I think that's probably what they're here for."

"Actually," he said, "that's a good idea."

"How do I get back in touch with you?"

He handed her a phone. "Don't use it to call anyone else. I'll call you when things are a bit more sorted, on our end."

"Okay," she said, and was out of the car, running back along the sidewalk, to intercept a biker-jacketed Heidi Hyde, striding toward her with some sort of three-foot paper-wrapped club in her hand. She heard the van pull away, behind her.

"What's going on?" demanded Heidi, tapping the palm of her hand with the gift-wrapped club.

"We're getting out of here," Hollis said, passing her. "How long have you been here?"

"Just got here," said Heidi, turning.

"What's that?" Indicating the club.

"An ax handle."

"Why?"

"Why not?"

"There she is," Inchmale said, around the stub of a small cigar, as they reached the blue car. "Where the hell have you been?"

"Get us out of here, Reg. Now."

"Isn't that your car?" Pointing at the Phaeton.

"I've lost the keys." Pulling at the rear door of the blue car. "Will you please unlock this?" It unlocked. "Take me somewhere," she said, getting in. "Now."

* * *

"YOUR PURSE," said Bigend, "is near the intersection of Main and Hastings. Heading south on Main, currently. On foot, apparently."

"It must have been stolen," she said. "Or found. How fast can you get Ollie over here with a spare set of keys?" She'd told him, at the start of the conversation, that she was in this particular bar. Otherwise, she realized, she'd have had to worry.

"Almost instantly. You're very near the flat. I know the place. They make a very decent piso mojado."

"Have him bring the keys. I'm not feeling like sitting around in a bar." She closed Inchmale's phone and handed it back to him. "He says you should try the piso mojado," she said.

Inchmale raised an eyebrow. "Do you know that that means 'wet floor'?"

"Hush a minute, Reg. I need to think." According to Bigend, he'd ordered Ollie away, when she'd told him to, shortly before midnight, from the live-work building on Powell Street. The GPS unit in the scrambler, Bigend had said, had remained there for about fifteen minutes, then had headed west. From its speed, obviously in a vehicle. A bus, Bigend guessed, because it had made a number of brief stops that weren't at intersections. She imagined him watching this on that huge screen in his office. The world as video game. He'd assumed, he'd said, that this had been her, headed back to the flat, but then the GPS telltale had gone walkabout, through what Ollie told him was the poorest-per-capita postal code in the country. She had already decided, she knew, for reasons as powerfully visceral as they were mysterious, that she wanted nothing more to do with either Jimmy Carlyle's fifty hundreds or Bigend's bugged scrambler.

"Phone," she said to Inchmale. "And a Visa card."

He put his phone on the table in front of her and dug out his wallet. "If you're making a purchase, I'd rather you use that AMEX. That's the one for business expenses."

"I need their eight-hundred number to report my card stolen," she said. Ollie arrived while she was dealing with Visa, which kept her from having to speak with him. Inchmale was good at getting rid of people like Ollie. Who left, quickly.

"Drink up," she said, indicating Inchmale's Belgian beer. "Where's Heidi?"

"Chatting up the bartender," he said.

Hollis leaned out of their white vinyl booth and spotted Heidi in conversation with the blonde behind the bar. Inchmale had insisted on her leaving the ax handle in their blue Honda rental.

"What are you doing here?" she asked him. "I mean, I appreciate that you've come to make sure I'm okay, but how did you get to where you found me?"

"The Bollards weren't ready to go into the studio, it turned out. Two of them had flu. I called Blue Ant. A number of times. They aren't really in the book. Then I had to get through to Bigend himself, which was like reverse-engineering every ordinary concept of corporate structure. When I got him, though, he was all over me."

"He was?"

"He wants 'Hard to Be One' for a Chinese car commercial. To run globally, I mean. Only the car is Chinese. He hadn't heard it for a while. Seeing you jogged his memory. Swiss director, fifteen-million-dollar budget."

"For a car commercial?"

"They need to make an impression."

"What did you say?"

"No. Of course. The foot you always start with, right? No. But then he segued into this really interestingly textured bullshit about how concerned he was about you, up here in Vancouver. James Bond shit in the company car, you weren't checking in, why didn't I take the Blue Ant Lear up in about fifteen minutes and check on you."

"So you did?"

"Not immediately. I don't like being gamed, and your man's all game."

Hollis nodded.

"I was having lunch with Heidi. I ran it by her. And of course she bit. Became worried about you. And I caught it, then. Even though I could see that it would be to his advantage to get us both up here, bit of harmless adventure, then he'd pitch it to the two of us."

"Pitch what?"

"The Chinese car commercial. He wants us to re-record 'Hard to Be One' with different lyrics. Chinese car lyrics. But I was getting this secondhand paranoia off our different drummer over there. So then she and I are in her car, headed for Burbank. I think it took us longer to drive to Burbank than it took the plane to get up here. I had my passport, she had her driver's license, and we both got here with what we were standing up in."

"And she bought an ax handle?"

"We got to that neighborhood where you'd left the car, and she didn't like it. I said she was misreading it completely, missing the cultural subtexts, and that it wasn't actually dangerous, not that way. But she stopped at a lumberyard and tooled up. Didn't offer me one."

"It wouldn't suit you." She reached under her jacket and scratched her ribs, hard. "Come on. I need a shower. I was where there was ground glass, earlier. And cesium."

"Cesium?"

She stood, picking up the two blank white cards that Ollie had left.

79. ARTIST AND REPERTOIRE

Where'd you say you're from?" asked the man from Igor's label, offering Tito an open bottle of beer.

"New Jersey," said Tito, who hadn't. When they'd reached the rehearsal space, he'd phoned Garreth and told him the job was done, but that he thought he should stay off the street tonight. He hadn't mentioned the helicopter, but he'd had a feeling that Garreth knew.

He accepted the beer, pressing the cold bottle against his forehead. He'd enjoyed playing. The Guerreros had come, briefly, at the end.

"Amazing," said the label man. "Is that where your family's from?"

"New York," said Tito.

"Right," said the A&R man, and sipped his own beer. "Amazing."

80. MONGOLIAN DEATH WORM

Business-class lounge for Air Asshole," declared Inch-male, enthusiastically, taking in the central area of the first floor of Bigend's flat.

"Has the bedroom to match, upstairs," Hollis told him. "I'll show you, after I've had a shower."

Heidi put her ax handle down, still wrapped, on the counter beside Hollis's laptop.

"Ollis!" Odile stood at the head of the floating glass stair-slabs, in what Hollis supposed might be a very large hockey jersey. "Bobby, you have found him?"

"Sort of. It's complicated. Come down and meet my friends."

Odile, in bare feet, descended the slabs.

"Reg Inchmale and Heidi Hyde. Odile Richard."

"*Ça va?* What is that?" Noticing the ax handle.

"A gift," said Hollis. "She hasn't found anyone to give it to, yet. I have to shower."

She went upstairs.

The Blue Ant figurine was where she'd left it, on the ledge, still poised for action.

She undressed, checked herself for the rash that fortunately didn't seem to be there, and took a long, very thorough shower.

What would Garreth and the old man be up to now, she wondered. Where had Tito gone, after they'd dropped him off? Why was her purse, or Bigend's scrambler at least, afoot on the street? What constituted the Mongolian Death Worm, in her current situation? She didn't know.

Had she just seen a hundred million dollars irradiated, with .30-caliber pellets of medical cesium? She had, if Garreth had been telling the truth. Why would you do that? She was soaping herself down, for the third time, when it came to her.

To make it impossible to launder. The cesium. It wouldn't come out in the wash.

She hadn't even thought to ask him, as he'd packed up to leave the studio. She hadn't asked him anything, really. She'd understood that he needed, absolutely, to be doing what he was doing, doing it rather than talking about it. He'd been so utterly focused, checking things with the dosimeter, making sure nothing was left behind.

She was certain she hadn't left her purse up there.

Someone must have taken it from the van, when she'd carried the duffel over to give it to the dustmen.

She toweled off, dressed, checked to see that her passport was where she'd left it, then dried her hair.

When she came back down, Inchmale was seated at one end of a twenty-foot couch, its leather very nearly the color of the seats in Bigend's Maybach, reading messages on his phone. Heidi and Odile were what felt like a half block of polished concrete away, taking in the view, darkness and lights, like figures inserted into an architectural drawing to illustrate scale.

"Your Bigend," he said, looking up from the phone.

"He's not my Bigend. He'll be your Bigend, though, if you sell him the rights to 'Hard to Be One' for a car commercial."

"I can't do that, of course."

"For reasons of artistic integrity?"

"Because the three of us would have to agree. You, me, Heidi. We own the rights jointly, remember?"

"I say it's up to you." Sitting beside him on the couch.

"And why is that?"

"Because you're still in the business. Still have a stake."

"He wants you to write it."

"Write what?"

"The changes to the lyrics."

"To turn it into a car jingle?"

"A theme. An anthem. Of postmodern branding."

"'Hard to Be One'? Seriously?"

"He's texting me every half-hour. Wants to pin it down.

He's the sort of man I could get sick to the back teeth of. Actually."

She looked at him. "Where's the Mongolian Death Worm?"

"What do you mean?"

"I don't know what I'm supposed to be most afraid of, now. Do you? You used to tell me about the Death Worm when we were touring. How it was so deadly that there were scarcely any descriptions of it."

"Yes," he said. "It might spit venom, or bolts of electricity." He smiled. "Or ichor," he said.

"And it hid in the dunes. Of Mongolia."

"Yes."

"So I adopted it. Made it a sort of mascot for my anxiety. I imagined it as being bright red . . ."

"They are bright red," said Inchmale. "Scarlet. Eyeless. Thick as a child's thigh."

"It became the shape I'd give to any major fear I couldn't quite get a handle on. In L.A., a day or two ago, the idea of Bigend and his magazine that doesn't quite exist, this level of weirdness he's nosed himself into, and taken me with him, that I can't even tell you about, that all felt like the Death Worm. Out there in the dunes."

He looked at her. "It's good to see you."

"Good to see you, Reg. But I'm still confused."

"If you weren't, these days," he said, "you'd probably be psychotic. The worst really are full of passionate intensity now, aren't they? But what strikes me is that you don't seem actually frightened now. Confused, but I don't feel the fear."

"I've just seen someone, some people," she told him, "tonight, do the single strangest thing I imagine I'll ever see."

"Really?" He was suddenly grave. "I envy you."

"I thought it was going to be terrorism, or crime in some more traditional sense, but it wasn't. I think that it was actually . . ."

"What?"

"A prank. A prank you'd have to be crazy to be able to afford."

"You know I'd love to know what that was," he said.

"I know. But I've given my word once too often in this thing. I gave it to Bigend, then gave it again to someone else. I'd tell you that I'll tell you eventually, but I can't. Except that I might be able to. Eventually. It depends. Understand?"

"Is that young Frenchwoman a lesbian?" asked Inchmale.

"Why?"

"She seems physically attracted to Heidi."

"I wouldn't say that that's any indication of lesbianism, particularly."

"No?"

"Heidi constitutes a sort of a gender preference unto herself. For some people. And lots of them are male."

He smiled. "That's true. I'd forgotten."

A chord sounded.

"The mothership," said Inchmale.

Hollis watched as Ollie Sleight wheeled a tinkling, cloth-covered cart in. He was back in his expensive chimney-sweep outfit, she saw, but now was clean-shaven. "We weren't sure you'd have eaten," he said. And then, to Hollis, "Hubertus would like you to call him."

"I'm still processing," she told him. "Tomorrow."

"You're serving breakfast," said Inchmale, hand coming down on Ollie's shoulder, cutting off any response to Hollis. "If you're going to make a go of this, and move up from being a Civil War reenactor"—he flipped the lapel of the chimney-sweep suit—"you're going to have to learn to stay on task."

"I'm exhausted," she said. "I have to sleep now. I'll call him tomorrow, Ollie."

She went upstairs. Dawn was well under way, lots of it, and there was nothing in sight that resembled a blind or drape. She got out of her jeans, climbed up on Bigend's maglev bed, pulled the covers over her head, and fell asleep.

IN BETWEEN EVERYTHING

"You can't give me a number? E-mail?" The man from Igor's label looked desperate.

"I'm moving," Tito said, watching for Garreth's van from the second-floor window of the rehearsal space. "I'm in between everything." He saw the white van.

"You have my card," the man said, as Tito ran for the door.

"Ramone!" whooped Igor, in farewell, crashing a chord on his guitar. The others cheered.

Downstairs and out the door, he ran across the wet sidewalk and opened the van's passenger door, climbing in.

"Party?" Garreth asked, pulling away from the curb.

"A band. Rehearsing."

"You're in a band already?"

"Sitting in."

"What do you play?"

"Keyboards. The man from Union Square, he tried to kill me. With a car."

"I know. We had to call in a local favor to make sure he got out of custody."

"Out?"

"They only had him for an hour or so. He won't be charged." They stopped for a light. Garreth turned to look at him. "His car's steering failed. An accident. Lucky nobody was hurt."

"There was another man, a passenger," Tito said, as the light changed.

"Did you recognize him?"

"No. I saw him walking away."

"The man who tried to run you over, the one who came after the iPod in the park, was in charge of trying to find us in New York."

"He put the bug in my room?"

Garreth glanced over at him. "Didn't know you knew about that."

"My cousin told me."

"You have a lot of cousins, don't you?" Garreth smiled.

"He wanted to kill me," Tito said.

"Not the steadiest tool in the drawer, our man. We imagine he got so frustrated, in New York, trying to grab you, or us, that when he saw you here, he lost it. Worked up about the box arriving, too. We've seen him lose it a few times, over the past year or so, and someone always gets hurt. Tonight it was him. The police report says not so badly, though. A few stitches. Big bruise on his ankle. He can drive."

"A helicopter came," Tito said. "I rode a train to where I could see streetlights, an apartment building, beyond a fence. I may have set off motion detectors."

"Your man called that helicopter in, we think. Some kind of general alert. He'd have done it as soon as he got out of custody. Had them raise security on the port. Because he'd seen you."

"My protocol was poor," said Tito.

"Your protocol, Tito," said Garreth, pulling over in the middle of a featureless block, behind a black car, "is fucking genius." He pointed at the black car. "Cousin for you."

"Here?"

"Nowhere else," said Garreth. "I'll collect you to-morrow. There's something himself wants you to see."

Tito nodded. He got out of the van and walked for-ward, finding Alejandro behind the wheel of the black Mercedes.

"Cousin," said Alejandro, as Tito got in.

"I wasn't expecting you," said Tito.

"Carlito wants to make certain you're settled," said Alejandro, starting the Mercedes and pulling away. "So do I."

"Settled?"

"Here," said Alejandro. "Unless you prefer Mexico City."

"No."

459

SPOOK COUNTRY   459

"It isn't because they think you'd be so hot in Manhattan," said Alejandro.

"Protocol," said Tito.

"Yes, but also real estate."

"How is that?"

"Carlito bought several apartments here, when it was less expensive. He wants you to live in one, while he explores possibilities here."

"Possibilities?"

"China," said Alejandro. "Carlito is interested in China. China, here, is very close."

"Close?"

"You'll see," said Alejandro, turning at an intersection.

"Where are we going?"

"The apartment. We'll need to furnish it. Something a little less basic than your last place."

"Okay," said Tito.

"Your things are there," said Alejandro. "Computer, television, that piano."

Tito looked over at him, smiled. *"Gracias."*

"De nada," said Alejandro.

82. BEENIE'S

The unfamiliar ringtone of Garreth's cell woke her. She lay on Bigend's mag-lev bed, wondering what was ringing. "Damn," she said, realizing what it must be. She scrambled off the strangeness, hearing one of the black cables thrum as it was depressed, then released. She found the phone in a front pocket of yesterday's jeans.

"Hello?"

"Good morning," said Garreth. "How are you?"

"Well," she said, surprised to note that it seemed literally true. "And you?"

"Very well, though I hope you've had more sleep. How do you feel about a traditional Canadian working-man's breakfast? You'd need to be here in an hour. There's something we'd like you to see, assuming everything's gone as planned."

"Has it?"

"A complication or two. We'll know soon enough. But signs are good, generally."

What would that mean, she wondered. Would the turquoise box be emitting money-colored clouds of radioactivity? But he didn't sound like a worried man. "Where is it? I'll get a cab. I don't know whether my car's been returned yet, and I don't feel like driving."

"It's called Beenie's," he said. "Three e's. Got a pen?"

She wrote down the address.

Downstairs, after she'd dressed, she found a Blue Ant envelope on top of her laptop. Across it, in a very beautiful cursive, in fountain pen, was written: "Your purse, or in any case the unit, are currently inside a Canada Post box at the corner of Gore and Keefer streets. Enclosed to cover incidentals in the meantime. Best, OS." It contained two hundred dollars, Canadian, in fives, tens, and twenties, fastened with a very nice paper clip.

Pocketing this, she went spelunking for Odile's room. When she found it, it was twice the size of her semi-suite at the Mondrian, though lacking in Aztec-temple pretensions. Odile, however, was snoring so loudly that she hadn't the heart to wake her. As she was leaving, she noticed the ax handle, still wrapped, on the floor beside the bed.

The street, when she'd found her way outside, was still very quiet. She looked up at Bigend's building, but it was too tall to show her anything of his flat. Its footprint was smaller than its full perimeter, its lower floors tapering outward as they rose. In one of these were the slanted greenish glass windows of a gym, where residents in trim outfits were exercising on uniformly white machines. Like a detail in a Hugh Ferris drawing of some idealized urban future, she thought, but one that Ferris might never have come up with. Gain the glass-walled gymnasia and the benign white ghosts of factory machinery, but lose the high curvilinear glass bridges connecting adjacent towers.

There seemed, however, to be no cabs at all. After ten minutes, though, she did spot one, yellow, and a Prius. It stopped for her, its driver an impeccably courteous Sikh.

Why, she wondered, as he followed a route she guessed was a more practiced and efficient version of the one she'd taken before, was Bigend's scrambler, and perhaps her purse, in a mailbox? Someone had put it there, she supposed, either the person who'd taken it, or someone who'd found it later.

Without the rush-hour traffic, it was a quick trip. They were heading down Clark already, and there, through the Prius's windshield, were the orange Constructivist arms of the port, differently arranged now, and, after last night, quite differently resonant.

They passed the corner leading to Bobby's. Was he still in there, she wondered. How was he? She felt a pang of sympathy for Alberto. She didn't like to see him lose his River.

They crossed a major intersection. Clark, opposite, split on either side of a fully elevated roadway topped with illuminated signs demanding picture ID. This must be the entrance to the port.

Her driver pulled over, in front of a strangely dis-placed-looking little white concrete-block diner. BEENIE'S CAFÉ BREAKFAST ALL DAY COFFEE, painted very simply, long ago, on lengths of peeling, white-painted plywood. It had a screen door with a red wooden frame, some-thing that made it look vaguely foreign here.

She paid and tipped her driver, walked over, and looked through the single plate-glass window. It was very small, two tables and a counter with stools. Garreth waved from his stool at the counter, nearest the window.

She went in.

Garreth, the old man, and Tito were seated at the counter. There were four stools, and the one between Garreth and the old man was empty. She took it.

"Hello," she said.

"Good morning, Miss Henry," said the old man, nod-ding in her direction.

Past him, Tito leaned forward, smiling shyly.

"Hello, Tito," she said.

"You'll want the poached," said Garreth. "Unless you don't like poached."

"Poached is fine."

"And the bacon," said the old man. "Incredible."

"Really?" Beenie's was as basic an eating establish-ment as she'd been in in a while. Unless you counted Mr. Sippee. But Beenie's was indoor sit-down, she reminded herself.

"Chef used to work on the *Queen Elizabeth*," said the old man. "The first one."

In the back of the room, a very old man, either

Chinese or Malaysian, was bent almost double beside a white-painted cast-iron range that must have been older than he was. The only thing in Beenie's that wasn't old seemed to be the steel fire hood suspended above the large square stove.

There was a pleasant smell of bacon.

A very quiet woman, behind the counter, without being asked, brought her a cup of coffee. "Poached eggs medium, please." The walls were hung with oddly framed bits of generic Orientalia. Hollis guessed the place would have been here when she was born, and would have looked pretty much the same, though without the massive stainless hood above the stove.

"Delighted you can be here this morning," said the old man. "It's been a long night, but it appears to have gone in our favor."

"Thank you," said Hollis, "but I still have only a very vague idea of what you're up to, in spite of what I saw Garreth do last night."

"Tell me your idea of what we're doing, then," he said.

Hollis added milk to her coffee, from a very cold stainless creamer. "Garreth told me that the"—she glanced at the woman, who was standing beside the ancient cook—"the box, contained a, a large sum?"

"Yes?"

"Garreth, were you exaggerating?"

"No," said Garreth. "One hundred."

"Million," said the old man, flatly.

"What Garreth did . . . You spoke of laundering. He . . . contaminated? Am I right?"

"Indeed," said the old man, "he did. As thoroughly as could be arranged, under the circumstances. The projectiles would be effectively atomized, as they entered. Of course they then encounter virtually solid blocks of extremely high-quality paper, edge-on. But our intent wasn't to destroy that paper, but rather to make it difficult to handle safely. And also to tag it, if you will, for certain kinds of detection. Though there hasn't been a remarkable lot of progress, in the past five years, with that sort of sensing. Another neglected area." He sipped black coffee.

"You've made laundering it difficult."

"Impossible, I would hope," he said. "But you must understand that for the people who first arranged to have that hundred put in that box, the fact that it's back here at all already borders on disaster. They did not originally intend for it to return to North America, or indeed to any part of the First World. Too unwieldy an amount. There are economies, however, in which that sort of money can be traded for one thing or another, without too punishing a discount, and it was to one or another of those economies that they intended it to go."

"What happened?" Hollis asked, thinking how very strange it was that she had at least a general idea of what the answer would be.

"It was discovered, in transit, by a team of American intelligence operators, assigned to look for a very different sort of cargo. They were ordered off the case immediately, but in a way that created a snag in the fabric of things, bureaucratically, and for that reason, and others, it eventually came to my attention."

Hollis nodded. Pirates.

"In terms of profiteering from the war, Miss Henry, this is a piddling amount. I found the sheer gall of it fascinating, though, or perhaps the sheer lack of imagination. Out the door of the New York Fed, onto the back of a truck in Baghdad, one thing and another, then sail it away."

She had been about to mention the Hook, she realized, the giant Russian helicopter, and bit her lip.

"In the course of determining who the parties involved were, I learned that this particular container had been equipped with a unit that monitored its whereabouts, and to an extent its integrity, and covertly broadcast the information to the parties involved. They had known, for instance, when it had been opened by the American intelligence team. And that put the wind up them."

"Pardon me?"

"They lost their nerve. They began looking for different venues, easier markets, steeper discounts perhaps but less risk. The box went on its own very peculiar journey, then, and nothing ever quite worked out for them, none of those various potential launderings." He looked at her.

As various friends of his saw to that, she guessed.

"And I imagine they were afraid, by then. It became a sort of permanent resident in the system, never quite arriving. Until it got here, of course."

"But why did it, finally?"

He sighed. "Things are winding down, for these people. So I sincerely hope. There's less to be made, and the wind begins to blow from a potentially cleaner direction. An amount of this sort, even quite stiffly discounted, begins to seem worthwhile. At least for the smaller fish. And make no mistake, these are the smaller fish. No faces you've seen on television. Functionaries. Bureaucrats. I knew their like once, in Moscow and Leningrad."

"So there's something here, in Canada, that they can do with it?"

"This country certainly isn't without resources of that kind, but no. Not here. It's headed south, across the border. Into Idaho, we think. Most likely a crossing called Porthill. Just south of Creston, British Columbia."

"But won't it be that much more difficult to launder, there? You told me last night that that much illicit cash constitutes a negative asset."

"I believe they've made themselves a deal."

"With whom?"

"A church," he said.

"A church?"

"The kind with its own television station. The kind with an adjacent gated attraction. In this case, with an adjacent gated community."

"Jesus," she said.

"I wouldn't go that far, myself," he said, and coughed. "Hundred-dollar bills in the collection plate are the norm, however, I'm told."

Now the woman appeared behind the counter, from the stove, and placed one plate of eggs and bacon in front of Hollis, a second in front of the old man.

"Look at that," he said. "Exquisite. If you were in the Imperial Hotel, Tokyo, and ordered poached eggs and bacon and toast, what you would be served would in no way differ from this. The presentation."

And he was right, she saw. The bacon was perfectly flat, rigid, weightless, grease-free, crisp. Pressed, somehow. The eggs poached with a whisk, equally perfect, on a small bed of potato. Two slices of tomato and a sprig of parsley. Arranged with a casual, accomplished elegance. The woman returned with smaller plates of buttered toast for each of them.

"You two eat," Garreth said. "I'll explain."

She broke the first of her eggs with her fork. Soft yellow yolk.

"Tito was in the container facility last night, at midnight, when the buzzer sounded."

She nodded, mouth full of bacon.

"I punched our nine holes through the box. Leaving nine small but painfully obvious bullet holes. When the box was craned down from that stack, today, and put on a flatbed trailer, those nine holes would have been glaringly obvious. Aside from which, with them open, there was the possibility that a sensor in the facility would register the cesium. Except that Tito climbed up and stuck custom-made magnetic plasters over each hole, both sealing and, we hope, concealing them."

She looked down the counter to where Tito was being served his plate of eggs. His eyes met hers, briefly, and then he began to eat.

"You said they put it on a truck today," she said.

"Yes."

"And they're taking it into the United States, through Idaho?"

"We think Idaho. The unit inside is still functioning, though, and Bobby is keeping track of that for us. We should be able to anticipate where they're going to cross."

"If we fail to do that," the old man said, "and they enter the country undetected, we do have other options."

"Though we prefer the radiation be detected at the crossing," Garreth said.

"And will it be?" she asked.

"It certainly will be if the border's told to expect it," said Garreth.

"The right combination of calls," said the old man, dabbing egg from his lips with a white paper napkin, "and careful timing, will take care of any collaborators our financiers may have at the crossing point."

The woman brought Garreth his eggs. He began to eat, smiling.

"And what will the result of that be?" Hollis asked.

"A world of trouble," the old man said, "for someone. A lot of that may depend on the driver, in the end. We really don't know. Although we'll certainly"—and he smiled more widely than she'd seen him do before—"enjoy finding out."

"Speak of the devil," said Garreth, taking a pager from his belt and reading something off its tiny screen. "Bobby. He says look up. It's rolling."

"Come here," said the old man, getting up, his napkin still in his hand. He moved closer to the window. She followed. Felt Garreth close behind her.

And then the turquoise container, on an almost invisible flatbed trailer, looking as though wheels had been glued to it, descended the ramp to the intersection, pulled by a spotless, shiny, red, white, and heavily chromed tractor-truck, its twin exhaust stacks reminding her of the Cuisinart casing around the barrel of Garreth's rifle. At its wheel was a dark-haired, square-jawed man she thought looked like a cop, or a soldier.

"That's him," she heard Tito say, very softly.

"Yes," said the old man, as the light changed and the truck and container crossed the intersection, up Clark and out of sight, "it is."

83. STRATHCONA

And you're writing your thesis on Baptists, Mr. Milgrim?" Mrs. Meisenhelter set a two-slice silver toast-rack on the table.

"Anabaptists," Milgrim corrected. "These are really delicious scrambled eggs."

"I use water, rather than butter," she said. "The pan is a little more trouble to clean, but I prefer them that way. Anabaptists?"

"They do come into it, yes," Milgrim said, breaking his first piece of toast, "though really I'm concentrating on revolutionary messianism."

"Georgetown, you say?"

"Yes."

"That's in Washington."

"It is."

"We're delighted to have a scholar with us," she said, though as far as he knew she managed this bed-and-breakfast on her own, and he seemed to be the only guest.

"I'm happy to have found such a quiet and pleasant place," he said. And he was. He'd wandered through a deserted Chinatown, into what Mrs. Meisenhelter told him was the city's oldest residential neighborhood. Not a very affluent one, that was evident, but it was also evident that that was starting to change. A place in the process of doing what Union Square had done, he guessed. Mrs. Meisenhelter's bed-and-breakfast was part of that transition. If she could get guests in to help her pay for it, she might do very well, later, when things had gone upscale.

"Do you have plans for the day, Mr. Milgrim?"

"I have to see to my lost luggage," he said. "If it hasn't turned up, I'll need to do a little shopping."

"I'm sure they'll find it, Mr. Milgrim. If you'll excuse me, I have to see to the laundry."

When she had gone, Milgrim finished his toast, carried his breakfast things to the sink, rinsed them, and went up to his room, the thick flat sheaf of hundreds like an oddly shaped paperback in the left side pocket of his Jos. A. Banks trousers. It was the only thing he'd kept from the purse, aside from the phone, a small LED flashlight, and a pair of Korean-made nail-clippers.

The rest, including whatever that was that the phone

had been plugged into, he'd deposited in a red mailbox. She hadn't had any Canadian cash, the handsome, vaguely familiar-looking woman on the New York State driver's license, and credit cards were more trouble than they were worth.

He needed to buy a loupe today, and a small ultraviolet light. A currency-testing pen, if he could find one. The bills looked good, but he needed to make sure. He'd already seen two signs declining American hundreds.

But first the secret flagellants of Thuringia, he decided, sitting on the edge of the candlewick bedspread and loosening the laces of his shoes.

His book was in the drawer of the bedside table, along with the phone, his U.S. Government pen, the flashlight, and nail-clippers. His place in the book was marked with the only scrap of the envelope he'd kept, the upper left-hand corner, marked "HH" in faint red ballpoint. It seemed part of something, somehow.

He remembered getting on the bus, the night before, with the purse under his arm, beneath his jacket. He'd already gotten change, at the Princeton, as planned earlier, had inquired about buses and fares, and had had exactly the right amount ready, in unfamiliar, oddly blank-looking coins.

He'd sat, almost the only passenger, midway back, by a window, while his hand, as stealthy as if expecting attack, had explored what at first had seemed the very ordinary and unpromising reaches of the purse.

Now, rather than picking up the book, he picked up

the phone. It had been on, when he'd found it, and he'd immediately turned it off. Now he turned it on. A New York number. Roaming. Almost a full charge. The phone book seemed to list mostly New York numbers as well, by first names only. The ring was set for silent. He set it on vibrate, to be sure that it was working. It was.

He was about to silence it again when it began to vibrate in his hand.

His hand opened it and put it to his ear.

"Hello?" he could hear someone, a man, saying, "Hello?"

"You have the wrong number," he said, in Russian.

"This is definitely the correct number," said the man on the other end, in accented but serviceable Russian.

"No," said Milgrim, still in Russian, "it is the wrong number."

"Where are you?"

"Thuringia." He closed the phone, immediately opening it again and turning it off.

His hand opted for the morning's second Rize, entirely reasonable under the circumstances.

He put the phone back in the drawer. It didn't seem a good thing to have kept, now. He'd dispose of it later.

He was opening his book, ready to pick up where he'd left off on the story of Margrave Frederick the Undaunted, when he suddenly saw St. Marks Place, that past October. He'd been talking with Fish, in front of a used-record store, the sort of place that actually sold records, the vinyl kind, and through the window, in black and white, a woman's face had regarded him from the wall. And for an instant, settling back on the pillows, he knew who that was, and that he also knew her in some different way.

But then he began to read.

84. THE MAN WHO SHOT WALT DISNEY

It's not bad," said Bobby, spilling a little of his second piso mojado as he leaned back in his chair to see the top of Bigend's building through Hollis's helmet. "The scale works."

Inchmale had really had an extraordinary effect on him, Hollis thought. She'd definitely been right about his being an Inchmale fan, but she wouldn't have expected quite this degree of cessation of anxiety. Although some of that might be his being five days off what she'd come to think of as the money shot, with Garreth and the old man, so she assumed, long gone.

Tito, she knew, though entirely by accident, was still here, or had been, just this afternoon. She'd seen him in the mall beneath the Four Seasons, where she'd moved when Bigend had arrived from L.A. He'd been with a man who might have been an older brother, with straight black center-parted hair to his shoulders. They'd been shopping, to judge by the bags. Tito had seen her, definitely, and had smiled, but then had turned away, down another concourse of heavily trademarked commerce.

"It's the lack of detail that I like," said Inchmale. "Early Disney."

Bobby removed the helmet, brushing his forelock aside. "That's not Alberto, though. That's because you wanted it yesterday. If you left Alberto on it, he'd skin it up like something out of a horror movie." He put the helmet on the table. They were outside the bar on Mainland, where she'd first gone with Inchmale and Heidi, the night she'd come back with them.

"These Bollards," Odile asked, stressing the second syllable, "they have seen it?"

"Just a frame-grab," Inchmale said. He had had the idea, when Hollis and Odile told him about Bobby Chombo deserting the locative artists of L.A., and about Alberto losing his River, of his going to Bobby with a video proposal from the Bollards. The song was called "I'm the Man Who Shot Walt Disney," Inchmale's favorite of the material he was to produce for them in L.A. Bobby would direct, and the video would jump a platform, introducing locative art to a wider audience while helmets like Hollis's were still in the beta-test stage. In order to make certain that Bobby picked up his abandoned obligations in L.A., Inchmale had pretended to be a particular fan of Alberto's. With Odile as go-between, things had come together very quickly, and they'd managed to make it necessary for Bobby to get everyone else's work back up on new servers, which he'd already done.

Heidi had gone back to the mysteries of her Beverly Hills marriage, leaving Odile initially disconsolate. Successfully sorting the geohacking issues of at least a dozen artists with Bobby seemed to have taken care of that, though. Hollis assumed that this had afforded the French curator some kind of major status-jump, something good to take home. Not that Odile showed any particular desire to do that. She was still living at Bigend's, sharing the place with him, while Hollis was at the Four Seasons in the room next to Inchmale's.

Bobby's video for the Bollards, with Philip Rausch's enthusiastic approval, had become part of her still-unwritten article for *Node*.

She'd decided, after her breakfast at Beenie's, to tell Bigend that she'd been held captive, albeit very gently and politely, between leaving Bobby's place and being returned there. It was a scenario that the old man had provided, without intending to; it was what he'd said they'd do if she were unable to accept his terms. Blindfolded, turned over to an unknown third party, and held at an unknown location until Garreth had returned to take her back to Bobby's. No idea what they had done, that night. Since Bobby didn't know exactly what they had done either, and since he hadn't been privy to her agreement with the old man, she didn't have to worry about him telling Bigend she was lying. And lying about this to Bigend was something she'd decided she just had to do.

And Bigend, for his part, was making that curiously easy. He seemed, with the advent of his zillion-dollar Chinese car commercial, to have put his foray into the secret world on the back burner. If indeed it was still on the stove. She assumed he'd take advantage of having met Bobby, sooner if not later, and extract whatever bits and pieces of the puzzle Bobby might have, but that was not her business. A part of her business, henceforth, she'd decided, would be to be that chimney brick behind which the old man had chosen to hide the secret of what he'd done.

Which apparently was still very much a secret, as nothing at all had appeared anywhere about a truck being seized as it entered Idaho from Canada. They had told her to expect that, though. The whole business had to play out initially in spook country, and might well remain there for a very long time, and that was why he'd entrusted her with it in the first place.

"Ollis," Odile was saying, behind her, "you must look at Eenchmale's willy."

"I don't think so," she said, turning, to discover a picture of the beautiful Angelina holding a drooling baby Willy Inchmale on a patio in Buenos Aires. "He's bald enough," she said, "but where's the beard?"

"He's mad for percussion," said Inchmale, tossing off the last of his own piso. "And tits."

Hollis reached across for the helmet. Soon, very soon, she'd have to give Inchmale her answer on the Chinese car commercial. That was why they were all up here, in this spring that became daily more ridiculously beautiful, rather than in Los Angeles, where Inchmale had his Bollards temporarily on hold. He wanted to do it. He was a father now, he said, a provider, and if it took "It's Hard to Be One" selling Chinese cars to do that, so be it.

For her part, she still couldn't say.

She put the helmet on, turned it on, and looked up, to where Alberto's giant cartoon rendition of the Mongolian Death Worm, its tail wound through the various windows of Bigend's pyramidal aerie like an eel through the skull of a cow, waved imperially, tall and scarlet, in the night.

THANKS TO:

Susan Allison
Norm Coakley
Anton Corbijn
Claire Gibson
Eileen Gunn
Johan Kugelberg
Paul McAuley
Robert McDonald
Martha Millard
R. Trilling
Jack Womack

THE *NEW YORK TIMES* BESTSELLER FROM
WILLIAM GIBSON
PATTERN RECOGNITION

Cayce Pollard is a "coolhunter" who predicts the hottest trends. While working in London, she's offered a different assignment: find the creator of the obscure, enigmatic video clips being uploaded online—footage that is generating massive underground buzz worldwide.

"A masterful performance." —*Chicago Tribune*

"*Pattern Recognition* races along like an expert thriller, but it rides on a strong current of melancholy, of elegy for the broken and the vanished." —*GQ*

"One of the first authentic and vital novels of the twenty-first century." *The Washington Post Book World*

Pattern Recognition **is William Gibson's best book since he rewrote all the rules in *Neuromancer*."**
—Neil Gaiman, author of *American Gods*

"So good it defies all the usual superlatives."
—*The Seattle Times*

"[An] eerie vision of our time." —*The New Yorker*

penguin.com

"A MIND-BENDER OF A READ."
—The Village Voice

FROM *NEW YORK TIMES* BESTSELLING AUTHOR
WILLIAM GIBSON

NEUROMANCER

The Matrix is a world within the world, a global-consensus hallucination, the representation of every byte of data in cyberspace…

Case was the sharpest data thief in the business, until a vengeful former employer crippled his nervous system. Now a new and very mysterious employer recruits him for a last-chance run. The target: an unthinkably powerful artificial intelligence orbiting Earth in service of the sinister Tessier-Ashpool business clan. With a dead man riding shotgun and a mirror-eyed street samurai named Molly hired to watch his back, Case embarks on an adventure that ups the ante on an entire genre of fiction.

"Freshly imagined, compellingly detailed, and chilling in its implications."
—The New York Times

penguin.com